TRAIN HOPPERS – TWO

THE LONG HAUL

PURSUIT OF HOPE

LENA GIBSON

Black Rose Writing | Texas

ISBN: 978-1-68513-423-5
LIBRARY OF CONGRESS CONTROL NUMBER: 2023952697
PUBLISHED BY BLACK ROSE WRITING
www.blackrosewriting.com

Printed in the United States of America
Suggested Retail Price (SRP) US $24.95 / CA $27.95

The Long Haul is printed in Minion Pro

For readers everywhere.

"Gibson lays the tracks into an exciting new post-apocalyptic world where corporate greed controls the necessities of life, one ancient society's trash is today's salvation, and the heart of one heroine can save a country's soul."
–D. Lambert, author of *Son of No Man* series

"What a ride! In a decimated 22nd-century America with one slim hope for the future, Lena Gibson's *The Long Haul* propels readers on an unrelenting journey of survival, love, and unwavering determination."
–Cam Torrens, award-winning author of *Stable* and *False Summit*

"Like all good dystopian stories, *The Long Haul* by Lena Gibson is a cautionary tale. It continues the story of Elsa and Walker in their quest to find the hidden seed bunkers that may be the answer to overthrowing the yoke of oppression by the GreenCorp monopoly. It's a well-crafted story on three layers, artfully blended into one engrossing saga. Like me, you will be looking forward to the next sequel!"
–Bill Schweitzer, author of *Doves in a Tempest: The Valley of Horror*

"Fans of dystopian fiction will stay up all night reading *The Long Haul*. It stays with you long after you read the last sentence, and you'll wonder what epic conclusion awaits Elsa's adventure as she kindles the spark of a revolution."
–Michele Amitrani, author of the *Omnilogos Singularity* series

"Another five-star read from Lena Gibson—a series you won't want to miss."
–A.J. McCarthy, bestselling author of the *Charlie & Simm* mystery series

"The saga of survival in what used to be America after The Collapse continues in Lena Gibson's latest installment, *The Long Haul*. It is a trek to grasp a last chance at survival and a great read. Highly recommended."
–Karen K. Brees, author of *Crosswind* and *Headwind: The WWII Adventures of MI6 Agent Katrin Nissen*

PURSUIT OF HOPE

CHAPTER 1: ELSA PLUS WALKER

There used to be a city here. Several in fact. They'd hugged the narrow edge before the mountains north and south of Salt Lake City, with a combined population of over two million. While Elsa could imagine brick buildings and shops, she couldn't fathom the idea of so many people. With seventy thousand inhabitants, Utah was one of the most populated areas remaining in what had once been America.

Elsa had once seen a map from the early twenty-first century, cities and towns bleeding together in continuous dots. Nothing like Salt Lake City and the outlying scattered farms of the present. For all the space in this sparse land, there were too many people on this particular farm.

At least one too many.

The five occupants tripped over each other daily; everyone was used to being solitary. Elsa glanced toward the house, relieved for the current peace outdoors. Walker and Hayden—brothers by choice who'd traveled together for eight years—weren't on the best of terms. Plus, Elsa would rather be on the road than stuck here impotent to move forward with her plans. She clenched her jaw. Everyone might get along better without so much time in a confined space, but it wasn't safe to wander off the Dawson farm.

Elsa scanned the landscape for the hundredth time today. The limitless sky seemed immense and made her skin crawl. The plains were exposed with nowhere to hide. She always worked with her back to the solid mountain range which stood like a fortress, guarding that approach, allowing her to focus westward. The idea that she might be taken by GreenCorps and sent south haunted her daylight hours. Without the view, she felt trapped so she always volunteered for outdoor chores.

She crunched a chunk of dry soil that turned to powder between her dusty hands and stood to stretch the cramped muscles in her back. Rotating her sore shoulder, she grimaced at the lingering pain from her fight with Jace. Taking a break from gardening, she stared at the empty countryside with a sigh. Dust motes floating in the air shimmered in the intense afternoon sun, making everywhere that wasn't irrigated parched, dry, and dull. Too much like SoCal, but brown instead of gray. She'd escaped the Heap, but she couldn't escape the heat. On the other hand, working with her hands and growing things instead of scavenging in old trash seemed worthwhile. She loved the idea of helping to grow their food.

Beyond Caitlyn's farmyard with its barn, corral, and pigpen, the neighboring farms spread out—too distant to see with the naked eye. Solitude might be an illusion, but so far nobody had reported their presence to the authorities. If discovered, they'd be back on the run, or worse, incarcerated. Even gardening, Elsa couldn't let her guard down.

Despite the sun's glare and baked land, it could be peaceful here if it wasn't for Hayden. She cast a quick look over her shoulder toward the house where he'd gone to find food two hours ago. What was taking him so long? At least she'd long since hidden her valuables, keeping the most important item on her person. Trying to put Hayden from her mind, she searched once more for signs of travelers. Other than the crowded farm, they seemed alone.

Swaths of building-sized mounds adorned the horizon. The earth's way of disguising the past to make way for the present. Remains of the previous civilization had been buried underground or repurposed as part of new structures.

Utah wasn't like SoCal, where Elsa had spent her youth in an endless garbage heap where women and children toiled to scavenge reusable items from trash to scrape out a living. Men worked the scrapyards, or if they were lucky, joined GreenCorps. Here there were options, possibilities. A chance to fight for a better life where everyone would have freedom to move and afford adequate food. She just needed to get back on the road and get on with her mission. She'd found a purpose, and waiting here until she withered wasn't it. Her gut told her she should leave soon. They'd been here almost two months; she was inclined to listen.

Maybe after her journey to the north, she should join the rebels in their canyon strongholds. She sighed. How much longer until she could travel? What if they got stuck here for the winter? She'd go stir-crazy trapped for months in such close quarters. She and Walker should go. The idea made her stand straighter. Heading out was the beginning of making a difference.

"Want help with the wheelbarrow?" Walker's voice interrupted her thoughts.

Elsa smiled, her heart fluttering as he approached; she never tired of his lopsided smile and warm gray eyes. She didn't need physical help with gardening anymore—he just liked to look after her. "It's almost full, but I can take it to the compost. My shoulder's better. Good as new." She lifted her arms above her head as proof. "It's healed. Really." It ached at times, the odd twinge while working the farm, but she kept that to herself.

Walker raised an eyebrow. "I got it."

For the first weeks after her knife wound, she'd needed Walker's help to get dressed, washing dishes, and pretty much everything. He'd coddled her, which had been a novel experience, considering she'd been the strongest in her old household for years. It hadn't been easy to learn to garden one-handed, but she'd insisted on doing her share from the first day. Caitlyn had taken them into her home, stitched Elsa's stab wound, and paid for the expensive antibiotics.

As soon as she was able, Elsa insisted she be put on the rotation for farm duties. She didn't like owing anyone.

"You push too hard." Walker's gray eyes twinkled as he ran a hand through his wavy brown hair, smudging his cheek with dirt from his leather work glove, which made her grin.

Squinting, she passed him her canteen and tugged her UVee goggles up. She'd taken them off when she'd been weeding in the shade. There wasn't a lot of shade, except where Caitlyn's late husband had planted and cared for a dozen trees near the house. Now the aspen grove had grown large enough to sit under. Perfect in the afternoon as a respite from the mid-August sun. Maybe a brief rest wouldn't hurt.

This part of Utah wasn't full desert, but dry enough that water was a limiting factor on this bench of farmland. The hot air sucked all the moisture and left her skin looking like one of the numerous small lizards that skittered among the rocks. Taking back the canteen, she took a long pull. Even warm, it was refreshing. It took getting used to, but Caitlyn's well was deep and Elsa could drink as much as she wanted. Best of all, the water was free.

"Caitlyn back yet from her rounds? She's been out all afternoon." Elsa didn't hide the worry in her voice. She didn't keep secrets from Walker.

"Not yet, but she's safe; this is her land. Want to walk the fences with me tomorrow with her repair list? Take a picnic lunch?" Walker quirked his eyebrow again.

She grinned in reply and shook her head in mock dismay. "The perimeter is a long walk. It might take all day." Warmth surged inside that she had someone who found time for just the two of them.

Walker winked and hoisted the overflowing wheelbarrow with ease. She kissed him, leaning into his muscular frame. He dropped the handles to return the kiss, one arm wrapped around her waist. Every touch, every kiss, left her wanting more.

It didn't hurt that he was tall and strong, and his touch sparked electricity between them. His strength made her feel safe, like he would share her burdens. He'd rescued her from being beaten to death and cared for her when she'd been sick. It hadn't been easy, learning to depend on someone else, to trust them, but he'd earned it.

"You two sicken me," Hayden sneered, his pinched features set in a scowl as he trudged past.

Elsa's hackles rose at his remarks. If Caitlyn or Tatsuda had made the same remark, it would've been teasing, but Hayden's hostility had worsened. Elsa had tried being nice. She'd tried ignoring him. Other times, she'd been confrontational, and she wasn't proud of those moments. She'd resolved to do better.

His left arm remained in a plaster cast and would for another week or two. The same night Elsa had been stabbed, Hayden had been beaten and left for dead. If she hadn't interrupted, he'd have been killed. Not that he seemed grateful. She grit her teeth but stepped back from his brother. Hayden's broken arm was his sole remaining visible wound, but his bitter tone made it clear he still struggled with other demons.

She clamped her lips tight to keep her mouth under control, though she'd rather speak her mind. It was difficult to pretend she'd forgiven him for attacking Walker and her Granny. It was equally difficult to forgive Hayden for stealing the tube with their best chance of making a better life for everyone. At least she'd saved the key. She remained vigilant about its safety—avoiding looking at it or touching it when he was nearby. He didn't know that it still existed.

"Did you collect the eggs and feed the scraps to the pigs?" Elsa bit her sharp tongue. That's all Caitlyn had asked him to complete before she'd gone to inspect the fences and make note of the necessary repairs.

"Nope." He didn't turn around.

She shouldn't bother, but his idleness got under her skin. Her whole life she'd worked herself to the bone to survive. Farm work and gardening seemed easy by comparison, especially with so many available hands.

Walker grimaced, lifting the wheelbarrow again. "I'll be back with this in a few. Try not to injure one another." He spoke in a subdued voice. "If you need me, just yell."

Retreat was a smart option. He didn't like it when she and his brother fought, but he'd have her back if the situation worsened.

Hayden opened the rope hammock where it swung between two of the larger trees at the farthest corner of the garden and climbed in. He stretched out in the shade with an exaggerated sigh. "I'm a prisoner. Prisoners don't work. Plus, I'm injured." He shut his eyelids and folded his hands across his chest. It was all she could do not to kick his ass. She pictured his fall to the hard-packed ground with satisfaction.

Elsa's jaw ached, and she turned away so she didn't have to deal with his indolence. Prisoners worked plenty. She'd been born a prisoner and had always worked. He was trying to bait her. Again. He insisted he wasn't here willingly because he'd been unconscious when Caitlyn had smuggled them out of the city. If they'd left him behind, he might have died of his injuries, or died of another overdose. He was free because they'd brought him. Hayden was in debt to Caitlyn as much as they were. He just didn't seem to notice—or care.

Elsa and Tatsuda had weeded the extensive vegetable garden this morning, picked raspberries, and fed the chickens. While they'd done this, Hayden slept in. They'd watered the goats, pigs, sheep, and the mule and herded all but the pigs out to pasture. Walker had organized the tools in the barn and repaired the pigpen. Earlier this week Walker had cut and gathered hay with Caitlyn and split firewood for the cookstove. Everyone worked hard all day, pitching in with whatever was needed. Except for Hayden, who lounged in the shade.

While Hayden had been sick from withdrawal, nobody had expected him to contribute. Now that he was clear-headed, he pouted and sulked, saying he wanted to leave. It was a shame he hadn't followed through. But he wanted Walker to leave with him, to return to their old life as vagabond train hoppers.

Walker wouldn't, not without Elsa and not knowing that there was something he could do to better the world. That battle was one Hayden always lost. One of these days, she and Walker expected to wake up and discover Hayden had given up and disappeared. She wished him good riddance.

Tatsuda, who'd been in the house, emerged with a basket; probably going to collect the eggs. He seemed happy to try his hand at something besides pick-pocketing. A few times they'd discovered any odds and ends that went missing were in his possession—spoons, spools of thread, or the set of folding scissors Caitlyn left on her table. He was like a crow, forever collecting shiny objects. He returned everything they asked him for with a shrug. Elsa smiled as the scamp came outside. He probably had a stash of items not yet missed that kept him satisfied. Maybe she should ask him to empty his pockets every evening before bed, as she felt responsible for his good behavior.

Walker returned with the now empty wheelbarrow, and they loaded another gigantic pile of weeds and garden trimmings. This batch could feed the goats. Elsa took another drink from her canteen and she choked as her breath caught when a figure came into view.

Her shoulders relaxed when it was only Caitlyn who strode into the farmyard, headed for the well. Caitlyn drew a bucket of water and drank with the communal cup left nearby and wiped the back of her hand across her mouth, sighing with satisfaction.

Their host's hair was blonder now than when they'd met—bleached by the summer sun—and wisps had escaped from her long braid. Despite her ever-present straw hat, her fair skin was covered in freckles. Caitlyn had the build and the kind of beauty that stopped men in their tracks. Elsa had become more confident in her own skin the past few months, but was still a little envious. Luckily, Walker appreciated her slim build, sharp tongue, and loved her how she was.

"Cloud of dust on the horizon. Rider headed this way." Caitlyn was red-cheeked as she joined the group beside the garden and she panted to catch her breath. "I ran to get back first."

Elsa nodded and then she, Tatsuda, and Walker hurried to the hidden room behind the feed locker in the barn. Despite her calm demeanour, her heart hammered—any rider was an unknown. Walker had built the hiding place the first week of their stay. It was shallow, but wide enough for all of them to stand or sit on the bench against the wall. They barred it from their side, remaining invisible from inside the barn.

Hayden stayed behind. He hated the enclosed space as well as being so close to Elsa.

His voice carried on the late afternoon breeze as he talked to Caitlyn.

"Let's see what they want," Hayden said. "Might be unrelated to me." He yawned. "I'm not a wanted criminal, unlike some." His cutting tone, once more, directed at Elsa—who had the staggering sum of ten gold on her head. Maybe more, as rumor had it that with Jace's murder, the reward had doubled.

Elsa kept her mouth shut. Caitlyn could decide how to handle Hayden. It was her farm, and the former rebel was in charge. More words were exchanged, but Elsa couldn't hear them.

They waited in their dusty hiding spot for a stifling hour, sweat pooling between Elsa's breasts and running down her back, making it itchy. She tried to distract herself from the discomfort, her mind wandering back over the recent months and how she'd gotten here, hiding in a sweltering secret room.

Back in the SoCal work camp where she'd been born, Elsa had found buried treasure in the Heap, treasure that had brought her here to Caitlyn's farm in a roundabout way. Last spring, scavenging the Heap for trash to trade for subsistence rations, she'd unearthed a metal tube. Inside had been two-hundred-year-old maps and a key.

After a vicious beating by Jace McCoy, the man she'd later killed, she'd left SoCal by hopping a train with Walker. They'd followed a map to a pre-Collapse bunker filled with seeds of edible plants and tree varieties long thought extinct—seeds that weren't sterile terminator seeds like those purchased from GreenCorps. She hoped to take the key north and find someone to help grow and distribute the seeds. With those future crops, they could supply food for the masses and break the GreenCorps monopoly and their stranglehold on the population.

Though the maps had been destroyed with Jace's body after his death, she remembered the bunker locations and was confident she could find them, as she would recognize the marker near the entrance. Her deepest secret was possession of the key.

She clutched the heavy metal, with its curves and jagged edges, around her neck. It was proof that a better life could exist. It just might take some work. No longer lost in thought, cooler air rushed in when Caitlyn knocked to retrieve them and Walker opened the door.

"Come on out. Just a messenger. There's a note from Grady for Elsa."

Elsa's heart quickened, and Walker squeezed her hand. She'd discovered she had long-lost family out here in the wide world, not just her great-grandmother, sister, and nieces in SoCal. Ryan Grady—the leader of the rebels that resisted GreenCorps, the corporation that controlled food, water, and the railroad—was her great-uncle. He wouldn't risk a message without sufficient reason. It couldn't be good news. Her stomach lurched as confirmation that something was about to change.

They returned to the house, passing Hayden still slouched in the hammock, his eyes closed. The farmyard was deserted, the horse and rider gone, but inside a brown envelope lay on the table. Elsa washed her hands at the kitchen sink with a small hand pump, dried them, and picked up the letter. She turned it over in her hands. There was no name. She raised an eyebrow in Caitlyn's direction.

"That's it. The rider referred to you as Grady's niece."

Elsa slid out the letter on thick homemade paper. Her hands trembled as she read the contents. The message was brief and she read it twice. The first time it was a struggle to comprehend the words. Her skin became clammy, and she shivered, breaking out in gooseflesh. One hand rose to cover her mouth, like she was pressing her emotions inward. The news wasn't unexpected, nevertheless; it left her shaken. Despite her chill, her face flushed, and the room spun. The dizziness passed. She got to the end the second time and her eyes swam with tears.

My dearest niece,

I hate to be the bearer of bad news, but find I must be. Earlier this summer, I sent a note to your great-grandmother to inform her that you are well. Your sister replied Granny passed soon after your departure. She urges you to continue your travels. It isn't necessary for you to return and she sends her love.

Her words cannot be a surprise, as travel is difficult and we live in dangerous times.

I'm sure this isn't easy to hear. Take care of yourself. If you need anything, don't hesitate to ask. I make no promises, but will do what is in my power to assist your endeavors.

Uncle Ryan

P.S. I also sent a letter to my friends in the north. They are interested in your project and will render assistance if you reach them in person and provide proof of your commitment.

In the letter, Grady used no names other than his own, but just his first name and not the name the world knew him by. He gave no specifics or details. Should the wrong eyes see this innocuous letter, it would raise few alarms. "Proof" meant the seed packets she carried from the bunker she and Walker had visited in Davis, California. They were still tucked safely in her backpack. Or would she need additional proof?

She passed the letter to Walker, her hands still shaking. He scanned it, giving her a look of concern. A tight band constricted her chest even when Walker pulled her into a hug. Her Granny had died while she was gone. Abandoned. It wasn't Elsa's fault; her great-grandmother had been over a hundred years old, but Elsa hadn't gotten to say goodbye to the woman who'd raised her and taught her how to survive. A lump of sorrow persisted, leaving her hollow. Safe in Walker's arms, her tears overflowed.

"That isn't all," said Caitlyn with a gentle voice from where she stood by the stove feeding chunks of wood to the fire. "Grady's sending someone here to stay. He should be here in a few days. Mason's coming from Texas and needs somewhere to lie low for a couple of months. He can sleep in the barn with the boys."

Something about her tone told Elsa that their host was unimpressed.

* * *

August 8th, 2195. Dawson's Farm, Utah.
Sunrise: 6:30 a.m. Sunset, 8:35 p.m.
Elsa, Tatsuda, and I have worked on Caitlyn's farm for almost two months while she's healed. Didn't know if I'd take to the settled life, but I've enjoyed staying in one place, even if it isn't the cabin. One day, I hope Elsa and I can have a place like this where we can work together, grow our own food, and live our lives free of GreenCorps. It's been easy to pretend they don't exist, but the messenger today was a reminder of the outside world.

Hayden is a lazy ass and a jealous, petty person. Don't know how I didn't see it before. Guess I blamed the drugs, not him. He's been clean six weeks since the overdose in Salt Lake. Thought he'd be better by now, more helpful; which is why I'm giving him one final chance to redeem himself, but he hasn't done his part. He needs to accept Elsa and that our lives have changed, but he's worse. Makes me want to shake some sense into him.

I don't trust him in the outside world because he's prone to relapse. I've seen it before. Despite his complaints and negative attitude, he's stayed. For now. But I'm afraid it's inevitable he will do something stupid. We watch him closely and I'm prepared to make him leave if he puts us in danger. That time is approaching.

We agreed to stay on the farm for our sakes, as well as Caitlyn's, but Hayden's been sneaking off at night. At least twice this week. Tatsuda came to me. Thought I should know. Hayden thinks I don't know about his late-night disappearances. Asked Tatsuda if he could follow next time without being seen. The kid looked at me with an expression that said it all. Next time Hayden disappears, he'll have a silent shadow. When we know what he's doing, we can determine if he'll bring trouble to the farm. That wouldn't be fair to Caitlyn. We already owe a debt to both Caitlyn and the rebels that we cannot repay.

Chapter 2: Elsa plus Caitlyn

The merciless yellow sun beat down on Elsa and Walker as they walked the extensive fence line, keeping a lookout. The other buildings were beyond the horizon, the flat land empty. Fat brown grasshoppers sprang from near Elsa's feet at every step through the thin golden grass as if they could escape. Her straw hat protected her face from the bright sun and the UVee light. She let out a breath of relief that so far, all was quiet. They turned onto the third edge, closest to the mountains, where they had the least chance of being seen.

It also had a long narrow patch of shade running along the cliff face.

Her shoulders loosened, feeling the solid mass of the mountain close at her back, while the prickling possibility of being watched faded. On the plains, her head had been on a swivel all day.

"This looks like a good place for lunch." Elsa pushed her goggles up after stepping out of the sun's glare. Walker dropped his pack from his back, leaning it against the orange-colored stone face of the mountain. Soon the sun would clear the mountains and there'd be no refuge until the sun dropped below the horizon and the land cooled—it would be midnight or later.

Sweat trickled down Elsa's back but evaporated before it dampened her clothes. SoCal had never been this hot. Most of her days had been underground in the scavenging tunnels, without the direct sunlight, so while she liked the fresh air, she hadn't gotten used to the open expanse.

A canyon mouth with tumbled broken stone, greenery, and a rushing creek ran east to west a few hundred yards beyond their position. The gurgle of the flowing water was soothing. One of these days, Elsa wanted to explore the canyon, though she hadn't yet found the time. Helping on the farm kept her days busy. Today was as good as a vacation, despite their assigned rounds and their vigilant watch for unexpected visitors.

Elsa slung off her daypack, removing a folded blanket and the picnic lunch Caitlyn had provided. It was still difficult for Elsa to believe the amount and quality of the food that she had access to now that she'd left home. On Caitlyn's farm, there were fresh greens and new vegetables from the garden, fresh berries, eggs, and milk. Her "wealth" was due to the proximity to Salt Lake City's black market—the only place a limited selection of non-GreenCorps seeds existed.

Caitlyn had taught her to bake biscuits and bread, though their supply of flour was low. Elsa had been raised on processed protein bars, oatmeal, and a smattering of dried fruit. All food in SoCal had to be purchased through the GreenCorps stores. Eating had been necessary, but monotonous. Now every meal was a feast.

Having choices and fresh food was one thing that felt almost unreal, like living in a dream. Spreading the blanket, she kicked off her boots, slid off her socks, and wiggled her toes. She relished the feel of bare feet.

"Food first?" Walker sat on the blanket next to her. Emulating her, he tossed his hat aside and removed his boots.

Elsa's answer was to pull off her shirt, slide closer to him, and tug his head down to hers so she could kiss him the way she wanted. While they had a private bedroom at Caitlyn's, the walls were thin and their host was close by. It didn't stop them from having sex, but they were aware of their surroundings and kept quiet. He responded by pressing her against the blanket, pinning her with his solid weight.

She gasped when his iron-like arms raised her arms over her head and held them with one hand. His intent look made her core tighten. He gazed at her, his gray eyes locked on her topaz ones, a crooked grin on his face. Reaching over his shoulder, he tugged his shirt over his head and threw it toward the packs.

"I like when you're eager." His mouth reclaimed hers.

When they were both breathless with tingling lips, they removed the rest of their clothes. Despite her eagerness, she didn't want to rush. Making love with Walker was worth being patient. He was a walking contradiction. He was fast and strong, but his caresses were as gentle as a kitten. His voice boomed in the world was loud, but his tender whispers were reserved for her ears alone. Other words of love, she interpreted from his breath and his touch against her skin.

The crazier for him she became, the slower and more patient he became. Before long, they were tangled and naked, taking turns controlling the pace. He took her apart and wrecked her with desire before she turned it about and did the same for him. When at last she shuddered to her climax, he came too. There was nothing about Walker she didn't appreciate. To her, he was love.

It was dangerous to lie naked and unprotected in the harsh sun, but she enjoyed the feeling of bliss and the breeze on her bare skin for as long as she dared. Walker traced circles on her back and touched the bones of her spine—as though counting. When he finished, he pressed a kiss to the nape of her neck. She sighed, turned over, and covered herself before her skin burned.

While they dressed, they talked about the farm.

"It isn't my home, like the cabin, but it feels like a home. I can see why Caitlyn loves it there." Walker leaned on his pack and drank from his canteen, his muscles glistening.

"I think she really only loves the animals," said Elsa. "Her face changes when she's caring for them. It's too bad she doesn't have children." She blushed, recalling Caitlyn's frank assessment that Elsa and Walker needed to take precautions if they didn't want to start a family right now. Caitlyn had given her an injection that would act as birth control for at least a year. Despite Elsa and Walker leaving the cabin at Lake Tahoe behind, in her stay it had felt like home, though she'd known it was temporary. Maybe someday they could go back. If they had children in the future, that would be the perfect place to raise them.

"Maybe someday," said Walker, his words echoing her thoughts. "She's only about thirty. Think she married young. She mentioned the other day that her Mathew's been dead almost exactly a year."

Elsa's throat tightened. Losing Walker would be more than she could bear.

"She cashed out from the rebels and left them early last fall. Used her back pay and her husband's death fee to buy stock and winter supplies on the black market in Salt Lake. Got some garden seeds that would regrow. Said she'd lost her heart for fighting and just wanted to go home." Walker was good at finding things out without being intrusive.

If Elsa was alone, where would she go? Even if she wanted to, she couldn't return to SoCal. With Granny dead, the reason for returning had diminished. Her sister and her nieces were there, but with Jaxon running their lives, Elsa couldn't return. Walker was her home. Without him, she wouldn't belong anywhere.

Not wanting to dwell on depressing what if's, she shoved the thought away, rolled over and grabbed the remains of their lunch. Wincing, she rotated her arm at a twinge as she hefted the pack closer. Her mouth watered as she unpacked ham sandwiches on homemade bread and baby carrots—ones she'd harvested yesterday. She dug deeper for the container of bright red tomato slices. It was still hard to get over the vibrant colors of food.

"How's your shoulder?" Walker sat up and kissed the top of it, smoothing her tousled hair from her face with a small smile.

"It still hurts sometimes," she said as he traced the puckered scar where Jace's knife had penetrated. "Not often. I try to be careful, but it must be almost better because I keep forgetting." She tried not to think about Jace McCoy or the fact that she'd killed him.

It had been self-defense, a kill-or-be-killed situation, and he'd been a despicable person, but she hadn't liked to do it. He'd been someone's brother, someone's son. There might be people out in the world who missed him, even if he'd been cruel and hard. She pushed the thoughts deep down again, not wanting the memories to taint the pleasant day. Jace was gone, and he couldn't hurt her anymore.

* * *

August 9th, 2195
Dearest Mathew,

I haven't written to you since the group came to the farm to stay. Maybe I've been embarrassed to write to my dead husband in their presence, but tonight I don't care. It's been nice to have companionship and to share the workload. Elsa and Walker have made themselves indispensable, and while Tatsuda is quiet, he's one of the most likable people I've met. I can't help but laugh at his sly humor. He reminds me of your younger brother, the one who joined the Saints, not the rebels.

Most of my guests have been helpful with the garden and the animals. Hayden's another story. That kid is trouble with a capital T, more like your other brother John than is good for him. I'd like to believe the best of him, but I don't think he's been clean long enough to walk away from temptation. One chance to get high, and he'll take it.

While Elsa and Walker have become friends and Tatsuda's a good kid, they don't belong here and will move on. It might not be this summer, and I'd welcome them over the winter, but at some point they're leaving. It will go back to being too quiet here. I've been thinking about what to do after they go.

As much as I enjoy caring for the animals, I'm not meant for a solitary life. I'm also not ready to rejoin the rebels and watch idealistic young men and women take too many risks and get hurt, then expect me to patch them up. But I might consider what Grady has for me in Salt Lake as part of his inner circle.

I can't take another winter here alone.
I miss you every day.
Your Caitlyn

CHAPTER 3: GINGER

Ginger found it challenging to contain her upwelling of giddiness as she dressed. Tomorrow she started her apprenticeship at GreenCorps publishing. She'd always been interested in books and reading, and now she'd have a chance to learn how they were made. It would also be a taste of freedom.

Twirling, she spun toward the enormous windows and the bright blue summer sky that surrounded her fourth-story corner room. There wasn't a cloud in sight. A perfect day for a walk by the lake. Her bubble of excitement popped, and she sighed. If only.

The sprawling estate below held extensive grounds with bountiful gardens and lush green lawns surrounded by walls to keep the peasants out. She'd explored every hidden nook on the grounds as a child, and a handful of times since, and there were never surprises. She'd smelled the flowers and tasted the fruit. Being supervised everywhere outside her rooms removed the flavor, and no matter how many times she sat on the velvety grass, the expansive walls always blocked her view of what lay beyond.

At least her room was sufficiently high that she could see beyond the massive walls, and her gaze wandered to the more distant view. The rugged mountains that lined Denver in the west were craggy and tipped with snow, even now in August. They protected the city like a fortress—

or like a prison. She sighed again. She'd been nowhere else. Even excursions into town or the lakeshore had been rare.

Footsteps on the stairs made her turn from the window. She tamped down her impatience, schooled her face into a pleasant mask, and sat. Being churlish was not the way out. She arranged her pale pink skirt and waited.

Though expected, the inevitable knock still made her jump.

"Come in." She faced the door. It wasn't exactly permission because even if she said nothing, they'd enter just the same.

The lock turned, and her father opened the door to her suite. His burly frame filled the door and sucked the oxygen in his direction, making it hard for her lungs to gather a full breath. His large personality didn't leave space for anyone else, least of all her, his inferior female offspring.

"I've got something for you." He strode into the room without making eye contact and dropped a stack of books onto the coffee table. Dark rings circled his haggard eyes as he snagged a cookie from her always-full cookie plate and popped a few green grapes into his mouth. He spoke between mouthfuls.

"Don't read them all at once. I'm going away soon and won't be here to replenish your supply." He paced across the hardwood floor, stopping once for more fruit. Why couldn't he just sit on the couch and relax? Maybe talk instead of giving orders.

"Maybe I could go to the library myself if I finish them?" Ginger's voice sounded tremulous, uncertain. She hated sounding that way. She wanted to be decisive, powerful and instead, she sounded like a little girl, despite her approaching eighteenth birthday. Her chest tightened as she pushed her agenda forward, even if it wouldn't be popular. "One of the guards could take me."

He gave a single hard shake of his head. "After what happened this spring, I'd prefer you stay here."

"Father, I finished the school's high school program two months ago. You promised when I was done that, as an adult, I could find a safe place to spend my days off the grounds." Her voice trailed off as the hard, brittle look entered his eyes. Her freedom. It was slipping from her grasp.

"After what happened with your brother, I've changed my mind."

"I'm sorry about Jace, but that shouldn't affect my future." Her voice shook. She'd loved her oldest brother, even if he'd become sarcastic and mocking once he'd started working for GreenCorps. He hadn't always been that way. That was what the world had done to him.

"It affects everything." His mouth twisted in anger as his blazing dark eyes met her hazel ones. "Show some respect." His lips turned white and his nostrils flared.

Ginger blanched, flinching away from his fury. She should have known mentioning her brother would set him off. That had been a miscalculation. Her palms grew sweaty, but she leaped to her feet, standing her ground though she itched to step back.

"What happened to Jace was far away and couldn't happen here in Denver, the GreenCorps stronghold. I won't take risks like he did. I'd just be here in town." She tried to infuse confidence into her tone, at the same time being reasonable. Anger would get her nowhere.

"Jaxon says the criminals remain at large. They could be hiding anywhere. I'm not risking your life for a few books." Her father narrowed his eyes. "That's not a good enough reason."

"Father, you're right. It isn't just the library books. You promised I could start my apprenticeship at the publishing company. I need to feel useful." She hated she ended with a whine, but she felt desperate to make her point. Had he forgotten?

"No."

It was like arguing with a stone.

Tears filled her eyes and her lip trembled. She took a deep breath. "The branch of the company is here in Denver. What could be safer?" A few hot tears escaped.

"No," he repeated, the ominous rumble in his voice rolled through the room. "You're my daughter, and it isn't safe out there." He clenched his fists at his sides, causing her to take a step backward, bumping into the couch.

He had that look in his eyes again, but her mouth wouldn't stop. She'd bottled her feelings up for too long for them to be contained.

"Father, I need more to do. You agreed that if I did well, I could get a job."

He cut her off with a sweep of his hand. "That's a very liberal interpretation of what I said. You don't know how lucky you are."

There was no turning back now. "I don't feel lucky. I feel trapped. I haven't even been off the grounds in almost two years."

"I refuse to listen to this rubbish." He spoke through clenched teeth and tugged at the base of his short iron-gray hair. Hair that was grayer than it had been before her brother's murder.

"Father, please," Ginger said, trying to reason with him. Futile or not, she had to try.

He took two steps toward the door, muttering, but the words were clear. "I bring you whatever you want, you ungrateful little bitch. You don't need to go anywhere. Just like your mother. Trying to leave when you have everything you could want. It's a familiar theme. Both spoiled."

Her heart twisted at the casual cruelty, and her tears overflowed. Her throat tightened, and she couldn't force herself to continue. She'd been trapped here forever, and he'd slammed shut the only door, her opportunity for something more than this room.

"Read the damn books and stop your complaining, or they'll be the last ones you see. I declined the apprenticeship months ago. Work isn't for my daughter, after all. Jaxon and I have figured out something different. Maybe marriage will give you something better to do than sit and whine."

"Marriage?" She couldn't help herself. Surprise drew more words, though. "To who? I've met no one outside the family, other than servants." Her father stared through her as she gulped for air. She might have crossed the line with the questions.

To her surprise, he answered. "An arrangement with someone in the Midwest could strengthen our alliance. Jace had ideas. Even Jaxon recommends following through. The cities out there might reconsider letting our trains through if they have the right incentive."

First canceling the apprenticeship, now this. He would send away her from everything familiar without being consulted, and it broke her heart that her opinion mattered so little. It brought her near her breaking point.

"Don't I have a say?" Ginger swiped at the tears on her burning cheeks.

"What in your life made you think that? You're here at my whim and pleasure. I didn't want you. You were your mother's idea, but I've raised you as she asked. I've done my duty. You sometimes forget that you're living a life of total luxury, with access to things most young women would kill to have." His words were no longer fire, but ice, and they stung.

He'd never said those heart-wrenching words before, but they weren't a surprise. He treated her like a disappointment. He'd probably wanted another son for his empire.

"Like what? What do I have that the others don't?" Her voice quavered and her chest heaved. "I didn't ask for this life. I want to see something beyond the windows."

"You've got a safe, clean house filled with servants. Beautiful flowers, your own rooms, and you always have food. You never go without. Not to mention the goddamn books." He shook a fist in her face and she braced for the blow. "I wish you'd never learned to read. Life was easier when you knew your place and sat there with your mouth shut."

"Others don't have food?" Ginger frowned, feeling her face tighten in confusion, stuck on his words about people going without. Food was a basic necessity. Like air or water.

Her father shook his head, his lip twisted in a sneer. "You're a naïve little fool. You know nothing."

A pang of guilt stabbed through her. Though this life of luxury wasn't her fault, she'd never missed a meal in her life. He wasn't wrong about that. She peered down at her rounded arms and comfortable shape.

Her father spun on his heels, heading for the door once more. "I've arranged visits for a potential suitor. A week from today. You're expected to come downstairs for dinner, look pretty, and speak only when spoken to. If you can't do that, I'll figure it out on my own."

"I won't marry someone just because you say so."

"That's where you're wrong," he said over his shoulder as he slammed the door, the windows rattling.

The lock clicked as the key turned. Stomping footsteps receded down the stairs and faded. He wouldn't be back for three or four days, time enough to cool his temper.

Ginger collapsed to the floor in tears. Once more, alone in her cell.

CHAPTER 4: MASON

Mason removed his battered cowboy hat, mopped his brow with his sodden handkerchief, and paused to catch his breath. He'd left Texas one step ahead of the law. He'd ridden his horse along the backways and trails, avoiding anywhere near the railroad tracks as he headed north. His bones ached, and he longed for a proper bed after many nights curled up on the rocky trail and his long ride at an exhausting pace. His tight shoulders ached with tension from worrying that he'd been followed.

It had been good timing that they'd bidden Mason home from Texas to discuss a secret mission. He needed to lie low and avoid the South. He wished he had time to relax or get cleaned up from the road before facing his little-known father.

"Fuck Grady. He can wait." Mason changed his mind about his first stop in town. The message had said to hurry, but he was going to wash and change. He didn't want to face his estranged father sweaty and covered in grime, especially when the man was the famous rebel leader. As a father, he'd been lacking, but as the leader, he deserved Mason's respect and had earned it a dozen times over.

Only four people shared the knowledge of his father's identity—and two of them were dead—unless Grady had told someone. Unlikely, because Grady had never been one to share more than strictly necessary. Mason worked his jaw back and forth as he rode. The leader didn't play favorites, even for kin. Nor had Mason asked.

This was a bad idea. Maybe he should turn around and leave, disappear into the canyons. He slowed his horse, considering. But it was at least worth listening to the man. He could always leave after he heard what Grady had to say. Despite Mason's allegiance to the rebels, he was his own man.

Shoving his hat back on, he reined his horse to a halt as they crested the rise to absorb the stunning view. They weren't far from Salt Lake City. Heatwaves rose before him, warping the view, but the place looked the same. Orange and red brick buildings and too many scurrying people. The city was hot, dusty, and filled with GreenCorps soldiers. He preferred the quiet and solitude of the mountains or the empty land between cities.

Passing the train station, the level of security surprised him. He kept moving to avoid attracting their interest. Three times more soldiers than usual manned the platforms—scattered across the grounds, pacing between the tracks, and inspecting each train. As a northbound train chugged into the station, a contingent of guards met it, each taking a section to search. What the hell had happened? Maybe this fuss related to Grady's cryptic message. He found it difficult not to reach for his pistols, but it would have drawn attention.

Mason shook his head. It must be impossible to be a hopper these days. He'd been interested in that kind of life in his youth. One filled with adventure and freedom to wander, but without the danger that the rebel life entailed. His hopping had lasted for one trip, then he'd come home. He might have tried again, had he not joined the rebels. It wasn't learning his father's identity that had convinced him to sign up, but Mathew Dawson, his closest childhood friend. They'd joined together and he'd never been sorry.

A wave of sadness cast a shadow over him at thoughts of his friend. Like most childhood friends, they'd drifted apart once they'd grown. They'd taken jobs for the rebellion, often separated by time and distance for more than a decade. A few months ago, he'd learned that the infamous rail yard ambush in Dallas last summer had been fatal for his friend. Mathew had left behind a widow; some medic he'd met in Colorado. He'd convinced her to join the rebellion, but she'd left it behind.

Mason scoffed at the idea of joining a cause for someone else and abandoning it when they died. He'd never met this woman, but she must be fickle. He chided himself for such uncharitable thoughts. Mathew had loved her and she must have reasons for leaving. Who was he to judge?

Clattering over the cobbled streets, Mason cursed as intense heat still radiated from the stone, even after the sun set. He found a clean stable for his horse for the night. Despite the rush, he took ten minutes to wash up and change his travel-worn clothes for a clean, but well-patched set he kept for good. Only then did he continue on foot, his saddlebags flung over his shoulder as he marched toward rebel headquarters where he'd find Grady.

Mason had been told he could stay there, which would save the cost of an inn. He crossed the already clear market square and sauntered into an alley, stopping at the green door with chipped paint. Glancing around, he determined he was alone; he'd been here three times and remembered the protocol. Shifting his feet, he ran through what he was doing one more time. Listen to the proposed mission and decide if he was interested. That's it.

Taking a breath, he pounded twice—the usual signal—and waited.

"Mason," said a familiar voice, as the door opened. Craggy, mountain-man-turned-rebel, Darren stood in the entrance. His father's oldest friend. If someone like Ryan Grady had friends. When Darren recognized him, the big man burst into a wide grin. Mason had never even seen his father crack a smile.

Steeling himself for the upcoming conversation, Mason gave a nod.

"Darren." Mason's mouth was parched from his dusty travels. At the very least, they owed him a drink.

"I see you're as chatty as usual. C'mon in. Boss is expecting you."

CHAPTER 5: ELSA PLUS CAITLYN

Elsa awoke with a start, her heart pounding, a gasp the only sound as she smothered her scream to avoid waking the other inhabitants. Despite it still being pitch black, Elsa grabbed her knife from the bedside table and clutched the hilt with sweaty hands. Walker rested his arm on hers as he sat up. Someone had pushed the bedroom window open, letting in the night breeze as the thin curtains fluttered.

A shadowy figure stood by the wall, only a silhouette in the pale glow of the silver moon. Her breath hitched once, but Walker didn't seem upset as he turned toward the intruder. Her muscles relaxed, and she lowered the knife, cradling it in her lap. It must be Tatsuda.

The boy stepped forward and whispered, "I didn't mean to wake you both."

Walker shook his head. "It's all right. I asked you to keep us posted. Hayden's gone again?"

"I pretended to sleep, and he snuck out right away."

Damn. That idiot was going to cause trouble. She didn't trust him as far as she could kick him. Walker had filled her in on Hayden's nighttime wandering. Having Tatsuda monitor him was a good idea.

Walker and the boy kept their voices pitched low enough that they wouldn't wake Caitlyn next door. Farmer's hours meant she wouldn't appreciate being awakened in the dead of night.

"He went toward town. Not quite two hours from here on foot, faster if you run. Not sure how Hayden found out about the place unless he talked to the neighbors." Tatsuda shot a look at Elsa.

She ground her molars together, fighting for control over her anger. Her gut had told her that Hayden was breaking the rules, but she had no proof. He had no business meeting with anyone. She waved her hand for Tatsuda to proceed.

"There's a man running a card game out of his barn a couple of nights a week. So far, it's a few farmers, a few miners, and now Hayden. One was talking about bringing in a group from the city. Better money."

"Anyone recognize him? Any soldiers around, or someone from GreenCorps?"

Tatsuda shook his head. "Not yet. But I think soldiers were there before if the rumors are true. Twenty gold for you and Elsa." He shrugged. "Nothing for me."

Elsa couldn't help grinning. "You're too sneaky to get your face on a Wanted sheet."

His chest puffed up and his eyes gleamed.

"Thanks for keeping us posted," said Walker. "Knew you could follow without him noticing. I'll talk to him later when it's just the two of us. He's an idiot."

Elsa looked at Walker while his jaw flared. She'd never seen him so angry. How much longer would he keep it bottled inside?

Tatsuda nodded and slipped silently out the window into the night.

* * *

Hayden's eyes were red-rimmed and blood-shot when he emerged from the barn just before noon the next morning. Tatsuda reported Hayden had returned at dawn—just before the farm stirred. He declined Caitlyn's offer of food and headed straight for the hammock.

He fell asleep while the rest of them continued their daily chores. Elsa reined in her temper. She longed for the day that Hayden would no longer be a thorn in her side.

That evening after dinner, Walker stomped in from the barn, his face closed. It must have been an unproductive talk with his brother. Holding his fist, he went straight to their room. Had he and Hayden come to blows? She trusted Walker knew what he was doing, but her instincts screamed Hayden would betray them again. Walker was in denial, but she sensed things coming to a head.

Two days later, it was the same. Hayden disappeared at dusk and returned in the small hours of the morning after a night away from the Dawson farm. It couldn't continue or they'd be discovered. Elsa was back to jumping at noises, her shoulders aching from the tension. Walker promised to talk to him again tonight.

Late that afternoon, Elsa sat on the porch snapping beans for dinner while Walker and Tatsuda stacked the wood Walker had split yesterday, and Caitlyn ventured into the barn to milk the cow. Elsa glanced up just as a single rider appeared in the farmyard. Her chest tightened, hoping she hadn't made a mistake by working on the porch. He'd only gotten so close because they'd all been occupied.

The rider was dressed from head to toe in gray, and coated in a layer of fine orange dust. A long hot day to travel. He paused in the middle of the farmyard and cleared his throat before speaking.

"Is Mrs. Dawson here?" His voice had a different twang, but the words were easy enough to understand. This must be the one who they'd been watching for—the someone Grady had sent.

"I'm Caitlyn Dawson." Caitlyn emerged from the barn lugging a pail of milk. She squinted in the bright sunlight after the dimness of the barn. The tall man tipped his hat and dismounted from his horse, turning the full regard of his steel-blue eyes on Caitlyn. As she came closer, a look of surprise crossed his face while hers went blank.

Could they have met before? Elsa watched their interaction with interest.

Caitlyn set her bucket down at her feet, wiped her hands, and shook the man's hand.

"Cait…" His voice was warm.

"Mrs. Dawson." Her tone gave no room for argument.

The man gave a sharp nod and flicked a glance at the others, his gaze stopping on Hayden's sleeping form in the hammock.

"I'm Mason. Grady sent me. I see you have other guests."

"A few friends are staying for a while," Caitlyn said without further elaboration.

"And a prisoner," called Hayden, without opening his eyes. "Not a friend."

Mason made a sound of disapproval in his throat and looked around again, this time his gaze lingering on the others. Perhaps he'd been told about them; he seemed to compare them to a list.

Elsa's guard remained up, even if he might not be a threat. She waited for her gut to let her know if Mason was to be trusted, but it remained silent. Her instinct was to like him, but Caitlyn's reaction had been confusing. She'd been friendly with the other rebels. Was something about this man different?

Walker strode forward to introduce himself, and setting the bowl of beans aside, Elsa followed.

Walker was taller and broader, but Mason's leathered face spoke of a few more years of experience. He was probably thirty or thirty-five, closer to Caitlyn's age. Mason held himself like a man used to fighting, like he was ready for anything—which made sense for a rebel who'd just returned from Texas. He might have seen a lot of action. He wore pistols on both hips and the way he stood reminded Elsa of Caitlyn's cat before she pounced.

Elsa stopped beside Walker, placing her hand on his broad shoulder as she leaned forward to shake Mason's hand with the other. His calloused hand met hers and his glance darted to her face.

"Grady mentioned you." He hesitated. "I've seen you on posters. You don't look like a thief and murderer." His neutral tone revealed nothing.

"Grady mention that I'm innocent?" Her uncle was careful with his words.

Mason shrugged. "Nope."

"False accusations and self-defense." Meeting his eyes, she kept her chin high and her voice calm. He quirked an eyebrow. He could raise his eyebrow all he liked; some things were too important to leave unsaid.

"I remember you." Caitlyn crossed her arms over her chest. "My late husband said you two joined up together." She stared past the man, toward the house.

"I was sorry to hear about Mat. He was a trusted friend. Grady sent me, but I'm not sure I'm staying." Mason shrugged. "If the messenger failed to mention that."

The tightness in Elsa's chest eased. Mason's connection to Mathew might mean he could be trusted. Was this why Grady had sent him here? His steel-blue eyes reminded her of Grady's—almost identical, in fact. She raised an eyebrow. Caitlyn and Grady had history. Maybe she'd heard about Mason from multiple sources. Elsa would ask later, as it didn't appear to be the right time, nor was it urgent.

Mason looked startled, then nodded almost imperceptibly to Caitlyn.

Elsa couldn't understand the odd expression in his eyes. Disappointment? In Caitlyn? That made little sense.

Caitlyn nodded and stepped back; her expression wary. She must have picked up something odd from his face, too.

"What's with Lazy Bones?" The newcomer jerked his head toward Hayden.

"My… brother," said Walker with a grimace.

A few months ago, he wouldn't have hesitated. Walker and Hayden weren't brothers by blood and Hayden had rendered it difficult to be close. Since the incident last year, Walker and Hayden were no longer tight. Drug addicts thought of themselves first. Always. She'd known no one to kick the habit long-term.

"You're talking about me again?" Hayden sprang to his feet, his face red and his eyes narrowed. "You can't even say the word brother anymore. Nice to know where I stand. She's poisoned you and I've had enough." The hammock swung behind him. "I don't have to put up with this shit. I'd rather be elsewhere." He stalked away emptied-handed and headed south.

"No one is making you stay," called Walker, his eyes blazing. "You've always been free to go. We were trying to help you." His temper got loose this once, though he normally kept it in check.

Without looking back, Hayden made a rude hand gesture and kept walking.

Tatsuda caught Elsa's eye, and she shook her head.

He might get caught if he followed in daylight.

Walker inhaled deeply before blowing the air out. He shrugged. "We can't let him just go. I'll talk to him. He's my responsibility." He ran after Hayden.

They stopped beyond Elsa's earshot for a quick conversation.

Walker jogged back, frustration still informing the set of his broad shoulders. "He says that his stuff is here. He just needs to cool off."

Elsa watched Hayden's figure recede. Her gut said that this was more than a cool-down break, though his backpack was still in the barn. Would he leave with nothing? Not the smartest move. She squeezed Walker's taut arm and he released a deep whoosh of air. This wasn't how he wanted things to be with Hayden.

One corner of Mason's mouth frowned, but he didn't say anything through the disturbance. He cleared his throat and kicked a pebble before his eyes flicked toward Tatsuda, who sat on the woodpile he and Walker had made.

"That's Tatsuda. That's all of us," said Elsa.

Walker's gaze followed his brother's angry form as he disappeared over the ridge and toward the fields below. Back toward the poker game and his new friends.

"Tatsuda can show you where to freshen up and where you'll sleep. In the barn," said Caitlyn, into the awkward lull. It sounded like a dismissal.

Mason nodded, one hard jerk. His eyes strayed to Hayden's distant form. He pursed his lips and turned toward the stacked wood.

Tatsuda jumped from his perch and walked toward the barn.

Mason tipped his hat again to Caitlyn. He stopped to tie his horse near the water trough in the barn's shade and followed Tatsuda while the others returned to their chores.

* * *

August 11th, 2195
Dear Mathew,

Your old friend Mason is here. On the farm. Grady sent a messenger a few days ago to say that someone important was coming to stay. Not too many people are important enough to rate those words from Grady. It shocked me that his son, your friend, and the young man I rescued in Denver a lifetime ago, are the same person.

All the stories of your childhood, about you and your best friend, you never mentioned that he was Grady's son. Your stories are full of Mace. It never occurred to me it might be short for Mason. I know you regretted not keeping in touch with him and you said he was lousy about writing, but I was unprepared for your Mace and Grady's Mason to be the same person.

I couldn't sleep tonight after Mason's arrival—for a couple of reasons. One being that I wanted to watch for Hayden to return. We interrupted his nap when he was high and mean. He was searching for an excuse to leave, and he stormed out of here this afternoon. He might sneak back for his stuff, and I didn't want him to think he could steal other things. He might also bring GreenCorps down on our heads. I need to be prepared.

The other reason is Mason himself. I can't reconcile the picture you created of your friend with the reality. You were always laughing and having fun. Not only is he quiet, but he hasn't smiled once. It couldn't have been easy to be such good friends with someone so close-mouthed. Unless you had the pleasant humor for both of you. He's not what I expected. I'm not sure he wants to be here or if he'll stay.

I was outside, thinking about you as a kid, when Mason surprised me in the farmyard. Guess he couldn't sleep either. I said something about his father and he said, "He might be my father, but I didn't know until I was sixteen. I came because my leader asked." I can see how a boy who grew up without a father around might feel that way. It might also make him overly serious.

I shouldn't have said anything, but I reminded him GreenCorps would forever seek Grady's son. Maybe staying away from him had been to protect him, to allow him to become his own man, not just Grady's son. Mason looked taken aback, like he'd never considered that possibility. I might be reading into it because he didn't actually speak. The only response I got was a stare from those steely blue eyes. Those eyes are the reason I'm convinced I'm right about Grady being his father, even if nobody told me. I'm sure Elsa picked up on them, too. She's sharp.

I wish you were here. You'd get him out of his funk and make him one of us. The rest of us have become a family of sorts. Still, Elsa said trouble is coming and I think she's right. I'll pack a bag. Just in case.

Love always,
Your Caitlyn

Chapter 6: Ginger plus Walker

Ginger had ignored the latest stack of books for three days, but taking out her frustration at her father by not reading wasn't punishing him. It was silly and juvenile. Besides, he wouldn't even notice. She flipped through each book, choosing one to read at random. She didn't recognize any of the titles, but they looked like twenty-first-century fiction. She wished there was someone with whom to share the romance and adventure stories.

In the past, she'd tried talking to the servants about what she'd read, but most of them couldn't read and showed little interest. When she'd tried talking to her father, he'd dismissed her; said he was too busy for her naïve questions and childish nonsense. She grimaced at that thought. She wasn't childish, she just wanted to talk and was lonely. She wanted to see the world.

That reminded her of her father's casual words about other people not having enough food. The idea persisted in her thoughts. Who would be without food today when there was plenty? She'd read books about people starving or not having money for food; could the stories be fact, not just fiction? Wasn't that a thing of the past, from the days before GreenCorps?

She'd paid extra attention to the servants as they'd come and gone from her suite the last several days, hoping they'd speak to her for the first time in ages, but they'd remained silent and focused on their jobs. Texas and SoCal were the poorest places and the most likely candidates to have hungry people. Was there a way to share the food better so they wouldn't starve? Surely GreenCorps was trying to help. They had wealth, massive farms, and the train system for distribution.

Taking all but one book to the bookcase, she stood on tiptoe and thumped them overhead into place on the top, her last remaining unused shelf. These books looked new, shiny and uncreased, but they didn't have GreenCorps logos on the spine. Perhaps her father had imported them from Canada or from back east, where they also had resources for printing. Restless, she didn't feel like reading right now, no matter how tempting the books were. If these were the last delivery for some time, she needed to make them last.

One book slipped and fell awkwardly. She got her footstool and stood on it to fix the books, replacing it in the row. It didn't sit right, so she ran her hand over the shelf, and found an irregular bump on the wood—a knot in the grain. She'd never looked at the top shelf before or she would have noticed the discoloration. She poked at it idly, wondering why wood grew that way sometimes, with swirls and holes.

The knot gave way beneath her finger. She pushed again, applying more pressure, then releasing. It moved like an elevator button. The third time, she pressed hard. With a clicking sound, the section of the bookcase closest to the window popped forward.

What the holy hell?

Stepping to the right, Ginger investigated the section that had moved. An inch-wide crack extended from the floor to the uppermost part of the bookcase several inches above her head. How had she never seen this before? Taking a deep breath, she slid her fingertips into the gap and tugged. The entire section of the wall swung open on invisible hinges. Cold, stale air from within assailed her face, and she sucked in her breath.

Behind her bookcase was a hidden room.

Her heartbeat stuttered at the possibilities. Was it for spying? Perhaps this was a way out. It wouldn't surprise her if there was an escape tunnel. Her ancestors had been paranoid about security. She looked around, but as usual, she was alone. There was nobody to share this excitement with. Curiosity tingled through her. Where did the secret door lead?

Swinging the bookcase as far as it moved, she revealed an opening two feet wide and about six feet in height. Though a full-grown man might have to duck or risk smashing their head—her burly father or brother, for instance—there was plenty of headroom for someone with her diminutive height. The hidden room was only two yards across in each direction. A few feet from the opening, a staircase wound into the shadowy depths.

She glanced back toward her door, the one that led to the majority of the house, hoping it wouldn't open. Despite the potential adventure that lay ahead, she hesitated, picking at the skin beside her thumb. Someone would arrive with her lunch tray soon. She needed to exercise patience. If she left before lunch, an alarm would be raised about her disappearance.

Retreating from the hidden room before anyone entered her suite, she closed the hidden passage and crossed to the intercom panel by the door. She glanced at the cobwebs on her arms and grimaced. She cleaned up before calling for lunch. Someone might wonder what she'd been doing to get so filthy.

Returning to the intercom, she buzzed the kitchen.

"Miss Ginger, what can we get for you?" said the cook's harried voice. "Your lunch is almost ready." Background noise with bangs and clangs filled the speaker.

Ginger winced before continuing. "Do you have candles or a flashlight I could have sent up? Father mentioned something about a power outage when they're working on the gatehouse. I saw the workers arrive." She'd seen them from her lofty window. Would it make her lie convincing? "I'm worried I won't be able to read if it's too dim this evening."

"Sure, Miss Ginger. I'll send up a handful of wax candles and a lighter." The cook shouted over the din, and Elsa pulled back from the speaker.

"Thank you. Would it be possible to send my lunch as soon as it's ready, rather than wait for noon? I'm starving today." She chewed at a hangnail by her thumb.

"Of course, Miss Ginger. I'll make it now and find Paul right away."

"With the candles?"

"Of course." In the background, the cook's voice said, "Miss High-and-Mighty wants her lunch now." She'd forgotten to thank the cook, but was frozen by the awful words that followed. "She's plenty well-fed already. Wouldn't hurt her to miss a meal or two. Now I've got to send it early and track down household supplies. Spoiled brat." The cook's voice faded, but was still clear as she said, "You, go find a bundle of candles and a lighter."

Tears filled Ginger's eyes. The intercom must not have turned off on the other end. Indistinct voices, grinding noises, then static continued while she listened, unable to say anything. At last, the intercom clicked and fell silent. Her cheeks burned, and she swiped the tears from her face. They didn't understand that she wasn't spoiled by choice. She was a captive.

It was better that the kitchen staff didn't know she'd overheard their names for her. Was that how they felt? Like she believed she was superior? She'd always felt the opposite, as if she didn't measure up. Wasn't that why she'd been locked away? Her chest ached to be mistaken. The only people she had contact with didn't like her. Not her father. Not the staff. No one wanted her here. The cook's words had been the final blow that shattered the illusion.

Ginger paced the length of her sitting room a dozen times before lunch arrived fifteen minutes later. The thought of food was like ashes in her mouth, and the hidden passage called to her. She was dying to have uninterrupted time to explore. Once lunch was delivered, she would be free until shortly before dinner. Her father's visits were much less frequent since Jace's death, and he'd already stopped by this week.

He was unlikely to return so soon, plus he seldom visited in the afternoon. Butterflies flitted about in her stomach. She'd have to take the risk.

Paul delivered her meal. He was one of several who rotated through the guard position at the foot of the stairs. Their interactions had been limited to him dropping off a tray and her thanks. Today was no different. turning away without acknowledging her presence. The door closed with the familiar locking sound. Alone again. This time, it was what she wanted.

Ripping into her ham and cheese sandwich, she devoured most of it, even if Cook had forgotten to slice off the bread crusts. Ginger ate around them and dropped the crusty edges back onto the white plate. Guilt set in, and she picked them up and ate them, her lunch sitting like a stone in her stomach. Snatching the lighter and one of the tall white candles from the tray, with clammy hands, she flicked the lighter. On the second attempt, a flame appeared. Holding the wick over the flame until it caught, she stuffed the base of the candle into a holder from an end table.

She examined the bookshelf against the interior wall and located the special knot. With a deep inhale, she pushed, hoping the mechanism still worked. When the bookcase clicked and opened again, blood rushed to her head, making the room spin. She flushed and her heart drummed so hard her ribs felt bruised.

Swinging the case open, she stepped into the hidden room, where the wooden floor seemed solid beneath her feet. She tugged the bookcase back, almost closed, but not quite. A sliver of light from her room remained, but the closet-sized landing glowed with the flickering yellow of the candle. The ceiling was festooned with low-hanging spiderwebs. She brushed some from her face and shuddered at the wispy contact, hoping the occupants stayed away. She returned to her room and grabbed something to help.

Armed with her butter knife to cut the dangling webs, Ginger descended the stairs, her skin crawling, still considering the lurking web spinners. Each tread wound lower and lower until she reached the lower level with a narrow hallway—only a foot wider than her shoulder span. It stretched beneath her rooms and toward the rest of the house in the distance.

Dusty light fixtures hung on the wall ten feet apart on alternate sides. She didn't know if the electricity worked here, but there was only one way to find out. Locating the switch on the wall, she waited with bated breath. Flipping it up, pale lights appeared, illuminating the long corridor. Draped in thick white cobwebs, it seemed spooky and was longer than expected.

Just like when she'd discovered the secret room, a thrill raced through her, tingling in her fingers and toes. This time, she was better prepared for adventure. Just in case, she tucked her lighter into her pocket, blew out her candle, and carried it with her. Plunging forward on quiet feet, she followed the secret hallway.

Dust motes filled the air near the lights and thick cobwebs draped across the expanse between sections of the low tunnel. Several times she suppressed the urge to sneeze, unwilling to make noise as she sliced her way forward. Next time, she'd bring a kerchief to cover her face and tie back her hair. It clearly had been a considerable amount of time since anyone had come this way. Perhaps she was the only one who knew of its existence.

A faint scratching caught her attention as a mouse scampered along beside the left-hand wall. She laughed, the sound echoing in the narrow corridor. The mouse flattened itself, disappearing through an impossibly small crack at the base. Correction, the only *human* who knew about the secret passageway between the walls. She smiled at her secret. Thirty yards in, she looked back.

The only footprints on the dusty floor were her own. She continued, the grittiness strange and crunchy under her sandalled feet. It reminded Ginger of the beach where she'd gone once with her big brothers when she was small. It made her sad to think of those days. Jace had paid no attention to her since she was young, but once he'd been her favorite brother. He'd let her ride on his shoulders, played with her in the sand, and taught her to read. She wished he hadn't died. Maybe she could have talked him into taking her on the road with him. With one last glance up toward the unseen windows in her room and the freedom beyond the walls, she forged ahead.

Ginger walked the length of the house inside the passage. Reaching the end, she discovered a pair of narrow staircases; one led up, and the other went down. Placing her hand on the end wall—it was warm. It must be an outer wall, baked warm in the August sunshine. She lost track of her whereabouts within the massive house because the halls twisted and turned. There were entire floors on which she'd never been allowed. She cleared her throat and wiped her sweaty palms as she looked down. What did the depths hold? She scraped her fingernail against the tender skin by her thumbnail, wincing because it was already raw.

The space below the floor was pitch black, so she looked around for another light switch. Spying one on her left hesitated; she didn't know which lights it was for, so holding her breath, she flicked it and was plunged into total darkness. She blinked and a faint glow came from upstairs as her eyes adjusted. After flicking the switch again with sweaty hands, she returned to the stairs and aimed for the dim source of light.

She shuddered to look downward, though that was the best chance to find a secret exit. That could wait for another day. Instead, she chose up.

The first stair creaked, and she froze mid-step. What if someone was nearby? She was clueless about where this staircase was located. Without windows, she had no frame of reference. Her ears strained at the silence, but nobody seemed to be alerted to her presence. She stifled a laugh. If she made small noises, they'd probably blame rats in the walls.

Ginger placed her foot tentatively near the wall on the second step and shifted her weight. It made no sound, and she proceeded, taking care to make sure the treads were solid.

At the top landing of the stairs, she discovered a small, closet-like room, much like the one where she'd started. She forgot to breathe as she sidled up the last few stairs to the faint rectangular outline of a door, similar in size and shape to the one hidden behind her bookcase.

"What do you mean you still haven't found her?"

She jumped at the angry voice and held her breath. Her father's voice was crystal clear. He was either on the phone or talking to someone. The room situated on the far side of the wall could be his office, where he spent most of his day. Or so she understood. She rubbed her damp palms on her pants one at a time. She turned to go. She shouldn't be here.

"When was the last time anyone saw her?" He paused and his words sank in.

Stopping mid-turn, she broke out in a cold sweat. His menacing tone scared her to death. What had made him so angry?

"Fuck. I hate Utah."

Ah. She released her breath. He was talking about Jace's killer. It always came back to that. It was all her father cared about. Justice for Jace.

Ginger positioned herself to listen. Her father didn't trust her to work like her brothers, but she settled in to listen and learn new information. Ignorance sucked, and this passage provided the perfect remedy. She'd finally learn about the world. Ginger twirled a lock of her red hair, sliding its length through her fingers before twisting it around her fingers.

"I'm frustrated with the damned Utah situation." Her father bit off each word. "I need more than a rumor. Let me know when you have something concrete."

What was happening there now? She'd gleaned clues in the past from conversations between her brothers. Rebels lived in Utah and made life difficult for GreenCorps. They sold illegal seeds and stole water shipments. They'd even broken people out of the designated work camps. Utah was where criminals roamed free on the streets—that was common knowledge. The rebels were little better than common thieves. Her father said they should all be rounded up and sent to SoCal or Texas like they had been in the past. He might plan such a move now.

She would love to surprise her father with how useful she could be—how knowledgeable. She might be able to ask intelligent questions about Utah and impress him. Maybe he would let her out of the house for a change.

Perhaps she wouldn't have been locked up if her mother had lived. Would she be part of her father's business plans? Instead, she'd been overlooked, almost forgotten.

Ginger had learned that she'd surprised everyone when she'd survived the difficult birth that had killed her mother. She'd been raised an isolated princess in a tower, not unlike the girl in her favorite childhood story, Rapunzel.

Being stuck here wasn't lucky, no matter what her father said. She needed to venture out beyond these restrictive walls and experience life. Maybe next time he traveled, she could stow away on board the train. She could make herself indispensable. Maybe he'd be glad she was along with her useful skills. She read and could type, plus she wanted an adventure. She just needed to figure out when he was leaving. He'd told her he would be away for a couple of weeks. She would devise a plan to go along. She was meant for more than this lonely existence.

* * *

Each day for the remainder of the week, Ginger used the time between lunch and dinner to explore the tunnels, each time venturing further, but she hadn't found a way out. Not yet, and she became more convinced that she would. Her favorite place was the tiny room behind her father's office. She couldn't get out that way because even when it was empty, she worried her father would return at any second. If she went beyond that room, she'd be in the house and surely spotted by the staff.

She sat cross-legged on the cushion she'd brought to her listening post. She'd learned he was in this room every afternoon. She would check in, explore, then stop by to listen again. She propped herself against the wall, waiting to see if he received phone calls. It had been quiet beyond the wall for almost an hour. His pacing footsteps were the only thing to indicate he was still in his office. She couldn't stay much longer if she expected to beat Paul and her dinner tray to her room. Another minute or two was all she could afford.

The loud ring of the phone startled her and set her heart racing.

"Jax, good news, I hope?"

She held her breath, willing this conversation to have interesting information. She'd learned nothing useful in days.

"The junkie's the first solid lead we've had. Good job, son. I'll head out in the morning and meet you in Salt Lake City. We can lead the raid from there." There was a pause. "Don't go yet. Wait for me."

If only she could hear Jaxon's side, too.

"Just a few loose ends. I'll let your sister know I'm leaving when I see her at dinner tonight. See you soon." He sighed. "Damn fool is going to rush and screw this up."

The phone clicked down on the desk like a wake-up call. She needed to find the way out today or she'd be left behind. Information would get her nowhere if she remained locked away like a songbird in a cage. She'd eliminated several possibilities and found a dozen dead ends in the halls below.

Scrambling to her feet, Ginger snatched the crushed pillow and retreated, her heart hammering. She didn't have much of time. There was a journey to plan and an exit to find. Her thoughts raced ahead. She had too much left to do in a limited time. She had to return to her rooms. Her father planned to stop by at dinner. Maybe he'd stay and eat. He hadn't done that in months.

She shuddered to think what might happen if he discovered her rooms empty. She'd learned which stairs creaked and which were safe, so she hurried.

Speeding through the dim corridor, she didn't bother to relight her candle from the place at the bottom of her stairs where she now left it. She grabbed it and scuttled upward, trusting her nimble steps on now familiar territory. She deposited the candle on the floor and slipped through the hidden door, swinging it closed. No light shone through the cracks from the lighted hallway below. She checked herself. As usual, when she emerged from the hidden passage, she was filthy. Had anyone wondered why she'd been rinsing out her own clothes?

Running into the bathroom, she jumped into the shower, glancing at the mirror on the way by. Black smudges streaked her arms and face. Grabbing the soap, she scrubbed away the evidence of her exploration, leaving her freckled skin milky white.

After an hour of winding through long passages and several flights of creaky stairs, she'd made it to the ground floor today. One staircase led deeper. There had been no lights, but a musty smell that had caused her to wrinkle her nose. She'd left that unpleasant place for last, but if it wasn't a way out, she'd be left behind. Again.

Keeping her shower short, she turned off the water and hopped out.

No sooner had she dried off, when the outer door opened into the suite.

"Ginger. Where are you?" Her father's voice boomed in the empty living room.

She cringed, but answered. "Just getting out of the shower. I'm coming."

"Good, you remembered," he said.

Remembered what? Oh, bother. The suitor. Her heart sank at his words. Her evening had just shrunken to minuscule proportions. Dinner downstairs was probably an elaborate affair that would take hours. Hours she couldn't afford. Her chest tightened and her throat became dry. It was a struggle to keep calm. She slipped into her blue silk robe and wound a towel around her damp hair as she headed out to face her waiting father.

He looked up from pacing across her living area, his fingers drumming on his thigh. He wore all black, as usual. That and a scowl at her state of unreadiness.

"While I'm glad you remembered your duty, I expected you to be further along in your preparations." He tapped his foot on the floor.

"Put on something pretty and feminine. I'll be back in fifteen minutes. Be ready."

He stomped out the door, slamming it on his way out.

She breathed a quiet sigh of relief and slumped against the wall. She hadn't been caught or her secret discovered. Should she leave now, or should she go to dinner and feign a headache so she could leave early? She had nothing prepared for a last-minute flight, and if they caught her, she was certain her father would never let her go anywhere, ever. Breathing deep, she calmed herself. She'd have the entire night to search for escape route and make her way to the train station. Hope swelled in her chest. She could go without sleep until she was on the train. That was the new plan.

* * *

August 12th, 2195. Dawson's Farm, Utah.
Sunrise: 6:30 a.m. Sunset: 8:34 p.m.
Mason is a quiet guy. Not sure he's spoken since his arrival yesterday. Keeps to himself. Not in a sinister way, but he watches everything. Maybe trying to figure us out. Not sure what Grady told him as he hasn't seen fit to share. Is he here because of the reason we were told? Or was he sent to help us when we go north? Perhaps both.

Elsa thinks he's related to Grady. Says they have the same eyes. She has good instincts, so I'm inclined to trust her. Mason didn't call Grady his father, but that might be something he doesn't want known. If my father was a wanted man, I'd keep the relationship quiet.

Utah's weather is hot. Late summer and stifling, but it feels like it could shift overnight. There was one serious storm the week after we got here with incredible wind. Caitlyn says the winters here are hard. Lots of deep snow. Can't decide if we should leave or wait for spring. Elsa's getting restless, but the stay has done her good.

We can't go back to Salt Lake to hop the train. We'll have to aim for somewhere else, which means a long overland hike. The nearest trains to the north are in Idaho territory. GreenCorps has a firm presence there too.

Tried to talk with Hayden again the other night. He called Elsa a whore and blames her for changing me, making me mean. Lost control of my anger and punched him. He pushes my buttons like no one else. Told him he needs to be civil until we leave, that he can go his own way then. He took off yesterday and hasn't been back. His stuff is still here, but there's nothing special. Just a change of clothes and that stupid green jacket. He sold everything of value in SoCal.

Think he found drugs at that card game. He wasn't just tired but sleeping off a high. If he comes back, I'll ask him to leave even if it risks him betraying us. We'll be ready and keep watch. I won't put up with that shit, not again.

CHAPTER 7: ELSA PLUS GINGER

Hayden hadn't returned in three days. Elsa fumed about what stupid thing he might do while unsupervised, especially if he was kiting. Had they taken him into custody? Her chest grew tight. For the right incentive, he might give them up to GreenCorps. It wouldn't be the first time he'd done things in the name of a fix. They would have to remain vigilant.

On the third night of his absence, before they went to bed, Walker sent Tatsuda to look for Hayden—toward the card games. Had Hayden stayed there, moved on, or was he in trouble?

Elsa tossed and turned, waiting for Tatsuda to return, alert to every noise in the night. The silence outside became deafening, but she must have drifted off at some point because she woke up gasping. She sat bolt upright in bed, her stomach twisted in knots, her legs tangled in the sweaty sheets. All her senses screamed it was time to depart. They were in danger.

She grabbed Walker's arm. His eyes flew open at her touch.

"We have to leave." Her heartbeat felt erratic, fluttering in her chest like a bird trapped indoors.

"It's just because Hayden isn't back." Walker's tired voice mumbled the words.

"It's more. My gut is telling me that someone has found us. We need to leave." Not waiting to convince him, she jumped out of bed and dressed. She grabbed the spare set of clothes she'd taken from the seed bunker from a drawer and crammed them into her backpack. She'd left everything else packed for just such an occasion. They all had. They hadn't known how long the farm would be safe. It was best to be prepared. Walker took a little longer to wake up, but he dressed in record time, running his hands through his long hair.

He retrieved his journal and slid it into the front pocket of his pack. "Toss me my boots." He kept his voice subdued.

Elsa threw Walker his boots, one after the other. She tip-toed to the window and lifted the hem of the curtain and peered into the darkness to the south. She couldn't spot anyone outside. But that meant nothing.

The noise of their preparations, even slight, must have alerted Caitlyn next door. Her feet thumped onto the floor, and her door creaked moments later as it opened. Elsa reached into her shirt and double-checked that the bunker key hung between her breasts. With her pack over her shoulder, she looked around the dim bedroom without turning on a lamp. She didn't want to reveal anything about when they'd left.

The moonlight streamed through the window as she made the bed. Better. She nodded with satisfaction. There wasn't anything in the room to show they'd slept here tonight. Caitlyn's farm had provided safe haven when they needed it most and had given her time to heal, but staying any longer put people in danger. Elsa trusted her instincts now. She'd learned that it didn't pay to ignore them. Walker laced his boots and followed, no longer worrying about being silent. They were all awake.

Caitlyn emerged from her room, dressed and rubbing her eyes. Her hair was braided, though she was barefoot.

"To what do I owe this pleasure?" She yawned. "It's three a.m." Her cat wound around her legs with a meow.

"We've got to leave," said Elsa. The words emerged of their own volition before she considered how they'd sound. "All evening it's been nagging at me. I can't sleep. I can feel it. Someone must have found us."

"We can't repay you by leading soldiers here," said Walker to Caitlyn.

"Let me decide how much risk is okay." Caitlyn leaned against her door frame, her arms crossed. "Can't this wait until morning? Do you have a plan?"

Elsa felt for her friend. This place had been Caitlyn's haven as well. She might not want to leave; this was where she'd lived with her late husband and was most connected to him. Plus, she had animals and responsibilities that hindered her ability to leave without notice. Still, Elsa needed to make Caitlyn understand the urgency.

"Come with us. You could get in trouble if you stay."

"You don't know anything for sure," Caitlyn said, indecision on her face. "This could be nothing. Just a bad dream."

"I don't want you arrested for harboring us. It's time for us to go." Elsa's words were harsh but she didn't have time for niceties. She turned to Walker. "Is Tatsuda back yet?"

"Shouldn't you wait to hear what he has to say before leaving?" Caitlyn yawned.

Walker shook his head. "It would take him a couple of hours to get to the other farm, check on Hayden, then double back." He checked Caitlyn's old-fashioned clock on the kitchen wall. "He should be back any time. We can wait for him past the main farmyard."

Before Elsa answered, Tatsuda slipped in the front door on cue. His almond-shaped eyes were wide as he gasped. "Good, you're up. We've got to run. All of us. They were drinking and disorganized, so I ran, but by now there must be thirty soldiers on their way."

"Hayden?" Walker's gray eyes looked sad as his gaze flicked past Tatsuda and back.

Tatsuda shook his head. "He's with them." He looked at Elsa. "Hayden told one soldier that he can identify you personally. He turned you in to get his brother off. He wants Walker back, and you locked up."

Her blood ran cold as Tatsuda continued.

"Another man watched from the shadows, giving the orders. He called Hayden by name. I couldn't get a good look at him. I didn't dare wait. I needed a head start."

Walker cursed under his breath and Elsa squeezed his arm.

"What do I do about Mason?" said Tatsuda as he turned to leave the kitchen.

"Get your stuff and meet us by the trees," said Elsa. "Tell Mason what's happening. Let him decide if he wants to come or leave on his own."

Tatsuda nodded and slipped away while Caitlyn ran into her room. She returned minutes later, her backpack on and her boots laced. She grabbed her hat and a long jacket from beside the door where it hung. She draped it over her shoulders and said, "Let's go."

"What about your animals?" said Elsa.

"If we turn everything loose, the neighbors will round most up or they'll learn to live free," said Caitlyn. "Mittens is coming with us."

Elsa looked for the cat. Caitlyn turned to show the tabby's head poking out from under a flap at the top of her backpack. She looked content enough.

"You're bringing your cat on the run?" said Walker, his eyebrows raised.

Caitlyn leveled a flat stare at him. "Yes." With that tone, it wasn't up for debate.

Cold, still air met them as they exited, slinking along the side of the house and around the back. Without cloud cover, the scorching heat of the day had dissipated. For all that desert days were hot, early morning hours could be bitterly cold without cloud cover to hold in the heat. Elsa shivered despite being dressed for the night, and Walker clasped her hand. They'd done this before, but at least this time she wasn't injured and they were no longer strangers.

He released her and helped Caitlyn prop the corral gates ajar for the stock. They'd leave things open enough for the animals to figure out they weren't trapped, but not obvious to a casual observer that they'd been freed tonight. The farm shouldn't look abandoned. Soldiers searching the premises should give them a few extra minutes to escape. Elsa's eyes strayed south, squinting toward Salt Lake City. Still no sign of GreenCorps, except for another lurch of her stomach. How much time was left until the soldiers arrived?

The shadowy figures of Mason and Tatsuda crept from the barn, Mason leading his horse.

"Hotter than Grady expected. I'll go with you." Mason swung into the saddle.

His impassive expression was difficult to read in the dark. At least they'd have more help.

Caitlyn strode from her farmyard without a backward glance and headed east, toward the mountains.

"Where are we going?" whispered Elsa.

They couldn't aim south for Salt Lake and the trains. Elsa and Walker had discussed traveling north when they left—a long trek overland to catch a northern rail loop. Hopping safely might be unrealistic, but Salt Lake City remained too dangerous for hopping trains, despite the months since they'd left.

"Up the canyon." Caitlyn didn't break her stride.

Walker whispered. "What's up there?"

He'd traveled all over the train routes, but overland would be new.

"Walk now, talk later," Caitlyn whispered. "Tatsuda couldn't have been much ahead of those on horseback."

They'd only crossed the first of three fences when the silence broke. A faint sound came from behind them. Elsa's chest tightened and everyone broke into a jog as the vibration of horses on the move traveled through their boots. Caitlyn vaulted the next fence, and the others followed more carefully as Walker held the strands of wire apart. The rumbling of their pursuers grew, thundering through the night up the hill and toward the farm. If they were within earshot of the riders, would the soldiers spot them before they fled the farm?

Elsa's heart drummed double-time, more thankful than ever for the gut instincts which had seldom led her astray. Tatsuda's warning might have been too late if they hadn't already been awake. They'd only just made it out in time. She broke into a cold sweat. At least now they had a head start. It was a matter of hiding their trail and remaining silent to escape undetected under the mask of darkness.

How long until their absence was discovered?

With the moon full, it illuminated their path through the sparse fields to the canyon mouth like a silver trail. Mason could have outstripped them on his horse, but he stayed at the rear, turning periodically to check for riders behind. Having him on horseback seemed like it could be a problem, because he'd be more easily seen than those on foot. Elsa strained, monitoring for sounds that meant their escape had been discovered.

After crossing through the third fence, they reached the gap in the cliff walls, where the stream emerged from the canyon. Shouts broke out behind them; the sound carrying in the still night air. Two gunshots rang out. Not close, but from this side of the farm. It wouldn't take the GreenCorps soldiers long to find their trail unless they changed direction.

Caitlyn flinched but pointed up the canyon where chunk-like broken rocks obscured the path. Passing over them, low, scrub-like leafy trees overhung the banks of a shallow creek like sentinels, making darker shadows in which to conceal their flight. The water's gurgle provided cover noise for their light footsteps. The canyon's steep cliffs hid all but the smallest part of the entrance where the moon's reflection caught the paler stone.

Mason diverted his horse further up the bank, away from the others, as they continued into the night. He became a darker shadow as his sure-footed mount carried him uphill. Now that the moon was hidden by the canyon walls, he blended into the night, becoming almost invisible.

The fleeing group faded into the hills, scrambling over the rocks, moving along the riverbank in the dark, scrambling for a hold on the bushes and smaller trees as they climbed. The canyon angled in a different direction and the moon's glow reappeared. On a dark night, this climb might have been impossible and far too dangerous.

As it was, the footing was precarious, with rocks rolling under her feet. Elsa extended her arms to catch branches, sometimes taking the brunt of whipping limbs on her forearms to protect her face. Soon, her shoulder ached and her arms stung. Twice she lost her balance when her sore arm gave way. Each time, Walker caught her when she stumbled. She wasn't quite back to a hundred percent strength, but she pushed onward.

* * *

Ginger's face smarted as she limped through the now-familiar tunnel from her bedroom, her belongings crammed into a pillowcase from her bed and thrown over her shoulder. She'd found nothing better for her essentials, as she didn't own a backpack or suitcase. Her footsteps' eerie echo put her on edge. She'd never been here at night. The house seemed almost alive, the staircase ahead a giant maw, waiting to swallow her in silence. She'd disappear and no one would ever know what had happened or where she'd gone. The hair on the back of her neck stood on end.

As a distraction, she poked her sore cheek where she wore her father's handprint. This time, he'd hit hard enough to cause a bruise.

This was the first time she'd gone behind the bookcase and latched the door, fastening it with a click. She wasn't coming back. The sound had reassured her she was on her way to freedom. Her heart rate quickened. She was leaving this place. She wasn't joining her father; she wanted to leave him behind forever.

Her disappearance would cause problems for the staff, as well as inconveniencing her father when he learned of it, but she was through caring—especially after tonight's occurrence. But it was too soon to think about this evening's debacle. She pushed thoughts of dinner and its aftermath away again. The first step was to exit the house and escape the grounds without getting caught. The train station wasn't far—her initial destination. After that, she didn't know where she was going, nor did she care.

Additional worries nagged at her. The fresh food she'd taken would spoil in just days, and she didn't have access to canned. None of her clothes were meant for traveling, and she didn't own a hat or a jacket. Tears pricked her eyes, and she blinked to clear them. She had to focus, because she wouldn't get another chance. Wiping her nose with a handkerchief, she kept going.

Ginger took a deep breath, and switched off the lights in the lower hall, which may be the basement level of the house. A wafting draft hit her candle, and it flickered out, plunging her into darkness. She shuddered at the pure black that enveloped her, stifling a scream. With shaking hands, she relit the candle, gulping in relief as the flame caught. Shadows lurked on the periphery of her vision and down the stairs, while the skittering sound of rodents moved just beyond her range. Turning her gaze back toward her room, a pair of beady red eyes gleamed from the dusty corridor; they were watching her leave, and that thought sent shivers up her spine.

Leaving the hall lights on had its appeal, wasting electricity for which her father would have to pay would reveal a hint about how she had escaped. She wanted to vanish. Her heart hammered as she placed her sandaled foot on the narrow tread of the stairs. She repeated this process until she arrived at the bottom. She'd made it this far yesterday, but she'd never been farther.

She pulled her sticky clothes away from her body; they dripped with sweat while her muscles shook from prolonged tension. Reaching up, she found cobwebs decorating her hair. Judging by the amount of candle left, she'd been on the move for about an hour. It seemed like she'd never escape and right now she wasn't certain which was worse, the fate planned by her father or the endless dark tunnels. She didn't have a backup plan if she was wrong. This had to be the route to freedom.

She located the stairs that descended below the house, into the basement, and hopefully beyond. Taking a tight breath to prepare, she eased one foot down at a time. Right away, this staircase was different. The treads weren't wood, but crumbly cement, and she had to be careful not to slip. The rank odor of something damp and rotten permeated the air as she descended into the cold ground. The temperature dropped, and she shivered, pulling her sweater tighter.

Ginger wrinkled her nose but continued. Stopping wasn't an option. She was supposed to leave Denver the day after tomorrow with her new fiancé, to whom her father had sold her in exchange for railroad rights to New Chicago. Until tonight, she'd never heard of New Chicago, but it was supposed to be her new home with that toad. Once more, she touched the tender place on her face. Her father had threatened violence in the past, but never followed through. Until tonight.

She'd hated their guest from the first moment she'd laid eyes on him at dinner. He'd dripped with sweat and had gray, rotten teeth. When they'd shaken hands, his had been clammy, and she'd wiped hers surreptitiously on her skirt once he'd turned away. Throughout dinner, he'd licked his thin lips whenever he'd looked in her direction. She'd had to glance down to be sure she was wearing clothes—or that he couldn't see through what she wore.

She couldn't believe her father would do business with someone so repellent. Not just do business, but arrange for her to marry the man? She was seventeen, while Mr. Kyle must be fifty. She gagged at the memory of their encounter. If she hadn't already been planning to run away, this was the catalyst. And she wasn't coming back.

The image of her father's ruddy, livid face floated before her in the darkness. She lifted her chin, determined to succeed.

She reached the bottom of the flight of stairs and the floor crunched beneath her feet. The candlelight flickered upon gray and white chunk-like sticks that littered the floor. A shudder ran through her as the brittle bones snapped beneath her feet and sent shivers down her spine. A desecrated rodent graveyard. Her breath hitched. Why were there so many dead rats? How had they been killed?

Ginger kept going, crushing skeletons with every step, setting her teeth on edge. For several long minutes, perhaps twenty or thirty, she walked, hot wax dripping from her candle as it shrank. Water dripped overhead and the air in the tunnel grew warmer and wetter. The odd wet splash startled her. She swallowed, hoping it was just water.

A musty smell took over as the most pervasive stench, stronger than the dank earth odor prevalent since the stairs. Rows of pipes lined the space overhead, bringing the ceiling lower; low enough that she could have touched it by reaching overhead, had she been inclined. The constricted sensation in her chest worsened as she panted to get a full breath in the close quarters with the humid, stinky air.

Twice the steady sound of dripping water made her pause to listen—not footsteps. Was she near the end? She couldn't take much more.

Just when she was about to turn back and search for another option, she spotted a round metal tank ahead—one large enough to heat and store hot water for dozens of people. A wooden staircase beyond led upward, its top lost in the dense shadow. It had to be the way out.

A valve on the near side of the tank hissed, leaking steam into the air—the source of the vapor. Clutching for the railing of the stairs, something brushed against the bare part of her sandaled foot, sliding over it. She flinched at the sound of another hiss. More steam, or something else? A silent scream choked her throat as she glanced down. A massive snake with dark patterned skin wound between her legs and over her right foot. Petrified, she froze while its length slid over, its head disappearing into the darkness.

Ginger forgot about being stealthy as a scream burst forth and she launched toward the staircase. She smashed her shin against the bottom stair as she misjudged the distance in the poor light. Her stub of a candle flew from her grasp and she followed its arc, her hand clamped to her mouth in horror. The candle landed out of reach, several feet away, and near the slithering snake. The light dimmed before the flame sputtered out, leaving her alone in the pitch dark.

She sobbed and scrambled upward, almost losing her grip on the pillowcase, too. She caught it as it hit the ground. Lifting it with trembling hands, she clutched it to her chest as she huddled on the stairs. Fumbling for the handrail, she pulled herself to her unsteady feet. In the dark, she felt unbalanced and a tight band cinched around her lungs. Her hands shook to the rhythm of her silent sobs as she inched upward in the dark. She tried to calm herself and catch her breath, but couldn't. She'd never imagined anything so terrifying. She refused to think about what else might lurk nearby. The waking nightmare of the snake was too much.

After what seemed an eternity of slow, hunched ascent, her cautious fingertips grazed a cool metal plate that blocked her way. She slid her hands up. The metal continued. She was tempted to pound and scream, on the verge of panic at being trapped in the dark, but logic kicked in. This could be the door.

Groping across the textured metal, Ginger found a round knob. Holding her breath and praying that it was unlocked, she grabbed the cool metal. Her hands trembled as it rotated and she shouldered the door open on screeching hinges. A faint light appeared, outlining the door and the way out. She shoved again and with her grip tight on her belongings, she burst free. Running for her life.

Chapter 8: Elsa

Elsa's calves burned from hurrying uphill through the canyon on their freezing cold flight from the GreenCorps soldiers. She rubbed her reddened hands and stuck them in her armpits to warm them. Living on the farm to heal, despite the chores, had made her soft. Two months ago, she could have walked all day and all night as long as she had food and water.

The sky paled as it neared dawn, and visibility improved. Hours later, she panted, hot and sweaty as they pushed on as the heat returned. The steep canyon wound back and forth, angling east along the creek bed carved into the bottom. The red rocks and the greenery contrasted with stark beauty.

If anyone lived here, their homes must camouflage well with the rugged landscape because it appeared uninhabited; the only sounds were their breath and the trickling water. When the canyon divided several hours into their trek, Caitlyn directed them to the left. Remnants of an ancient roadway made a recognizable trail.

In this desert region, vegetation was slower to reclaim the remains of the previous civilization, much like SoCal, and crumbled wreckage of brick and stone buildings dotted the countryside. In the canyon, there was limited erosion because the cliff walls provided protection from weathering by wind and sand, but broken rocks still littered the canyon floor. Caused by snow? Freezing temperatures? She'd ask Walker later, as just now she was saving her breath for hiking.

Their trail guided them to a still lake that was dark blue in the early morning light. The terrain leveled out; the path sandwiched along a narrow valley with steep sides. Above them, in both directions, rocky peaks capped with snow stood guard. The group stopped at the water's edge to catch their breath, drink, and refill their canteens. Elsa spun in a circle to take in the surrounding breathtaking mountains.

She scanned the trail ahead, but there was no sign of Mason or his horse.

"Was that a dam we passed?" Walker's head nodded back toward the split in the trail at the head of the lake.

Caitlyn nodded. "The reservoir extends up the valley. It's a big part of why GreenCorps never subdued the Mormons. Not only did the people have food supplies and their own stock of seeds, but they faded back into the canyons for water instead of relying on the tanker cars.

Elsa ground her teeth. The memory of the waiting water tankers abandoned beside of the train tracks near Sacramento back in May still made her blood boil. GreenCorps had withheld the vital supply of water from SoCal, forcing the price sky-high. Most people couldn't afford more than the bare minimum of food and water. They'd lived on the knife's edge of starvation.

She and Granny had worked themselves to the bone to afford water. No point in dwelling on GreenCorps and their wrongs, but she couldn't help worrying about her sister. Thanks to Jaxon's money and influence, Avery and her little girls should be safe.

"Do we have a plan?" she said. "Best guess. How soon are the soldiers going to find our trail and follow?"

Caitlyn shrugged. "No idea. I doubt they found our trail last night. It was too dark. It's been hot and dry for months, so we won't have left many tracks. Even in daylight, only an experienced tracker might find where we went. Still, they'll search this way before long."

"Hayden might have guessed our plan to trek north." Elsa shot a glance at Walker, who nodded but didn't speak. It must be tough to know that his brother had caused their current trouble. Nobody blamed Walker, but if they encountered Hayden, it wouldn't go well for him. "This might not have been what we planned, but now that we're on the road, we should head for Canada. Grady said the Canadians could help distribute seeds from the bunkers. Sooner rather than later."

She tried to maintain a reasonable tone but, despite their scare, exhilaration at the return to adventure was coursing through her veins. Walker caught her eye, and she grinned, sharing the undercurrent of excitement that raced through her.

Her mission to share the viable seeds in the seed bunkers was back on. This side journey was unplanned but could be included in the trek northward.

"All the more reason to do something unexpected," said Caitlyn. "Could Hayden have heard any specific plans? Even if you didn't share your goal?"

"Does he know anything important? No." Elsa had confided in Walker about the key from the beginning, and later Caitlyn and Tatsuda. Never Hayden. She'd been careful after Hayden's earlier betrayal.

"That's for the best. I'm hoping to walk for another hour. I want to get to the Saints Settlement. We can rest there for a few hours." Caitlyn nodded her head toward the path to show the direction.

Elsa raised her eyebrow, questioning Walker and Tatsuda. They shook their heads and remained quiet. "Who?"

"We call them the Mormons. They call themselves Saints. Mathew said they shortened it from Latter-Day Saints." Caitlyn seldom spoke about her husband, but he'd grown up in Utah.

At the drumming of hoofbeats on the hard-packed earth, Elsa looked up, eyes riveted on the trail, tension filling her muscles. There was nothing to see. Caitlyn's hand strayed to the small of her back where she must have a gun, but relaxed as Mason rode into sight.

He'd ridden ahead and now returned, trotting along the path. He waited until he was close before speaking. Elsa scrutinized the hillside;

they didn't need echoing voices or yelling to advertise their presence, but she couldn't see anyone.

"I laid several false trails last night before circling back. Signs of a settlement ahead on the left. About five miles." He nodded at Caitlyn. "But you knew that."

She nodded in return with a small smile. Interesting. Elsa had seen little to make Caitlyn smile in the two months they'd known her. She didn't seem sad, just self-contained. She maintained an even keel without being emotional. Perhaps Mason reminded her of Mathew, after all, they'd once been friends.

Despite their lack of sleep, the group kept up the pace on the more level trail beside the water. They scrambled over fallen rocks, ones that had cracked and tumbled onto the path, but it wasn't difficult. From behind, there was no sign of pursuit. Not yet.

The sun rose right before their eyes in a burst of color captured by the lake, stretching out before them until it was hard to tell what was sky and what was water. The snowy mountains reflected the sunrise with their rosy alpenglow.

They hiked on. Twice they startled small brown speckled rabbits that bounded into the bushes, while hawks soared overhead, searching for a meal. The air grew warm and Elsa's clothes stuck to her despite the aridity. She sipped from her canteen, automatically rationing her water, despite the lake on the right. Habit. The water looked more and more inviting.

At Lake Tahoe, Walker had been teaching her to swim, but Elsa had only had a couple of lessons before they'd been forced to leave the cabin. Her mind wandered to their time there. They'd been alone, newly in love, and those weeks had been the best in her life. The cabin had been Walker's favorite place for years, and now it was hers. Maybe one day she would be able to call it home. For now, it represented the reward at the conclusion of their task and freedom from GreenCorps. Her hope was one day to live a life free from their domination. The seeds and the bunkers were a step on that path.

* * *

Elsa's feet throbbed and her shoulder ached when they arrived at the settlement mid-morning. It resembled a smaller version of Salt Lake City, with buildings constructed of red and orange brick, perhaps repurposed from old buildings that had existed before the Collapse. Some could even be well-maintained original construction.

Caitlyn aimed their path toward an enormous church standing at the margin of the town square. Other than the one extensive building, the Saints' village consisted of rows of low brick walls and stores on all sides that faced the center. Everything looked closed and Elsa had long since lost track of the day of the week. Perhaps it was Sunday or a rest day. On the farm it hadn't mattered, all days were work days.

Three dozen small brick houses extended from the back of town, scattered across the rolling hillside to the north as the valley widened. Lush green fields spread out beyond the town center on one side and vast gardens filled with vegetables extended on another. Both the gardens and the fields held workers, distant figures of men, women, and children mixed together, some in groups, others working alone. Many wore bright colors, creating a peaceful and idyllic scene. This was the self-sufficiency she'd dreamed of when she discovered the bunkers. This was how she wanted everyone to live.

Caitlyn led them into the town square where a gnarled evergreen with thin green needles grew in front of the biggest building. Its twisted trunk wasn't much taller than Walker, perhaps six and a half feet tall, but its reaching limbs spanned twice that distance across. Elsa made for one of the benches placed underneath in the shade.

"If we wait here, someone will come to see what we want." Caitlyn's voice exuded confidence as she took a second bench, dropping her pack near her feet where Mittens stuck her head out to look around. The cat was a good traveler.

Mason dismounted and led his mare to a water trough across the square.

Walker joined Elsa on her bench while Tatsuda flopped onto the dusty ground near their feet like an overgrown puppy. He was taller than when Elsa had met him early last summer. Working on the farm and regular meals had been good for him—he'd filled out.

Tatsuda no longer looked like the street waif he'd been, one who looked young for his age and had worked that to his advantage. Elsa had always guessed he was older than he looked. Now she pegged his true age at about fifteen. His straight dark bangs had grown out fast, like weeds in a garden, and hung in his eyes. He was due for another haircut. Stretching out with his pack as a pillow, he closed his eyes. At once, his chest rose and fell with deep, even breaths of sleep. Both wrists and ankles stuck out beyond his clothes. He probably needed new shoes as well. Maybe they could get him something here, since she still had coin in her bag from SoCal.

She admired and envied Tatsuda's ability to sleep anywhere. It wasn't true restful sleep, more like power naps, but it would help. Weariness sat in her muscles and bones, and her eyes felt bleary. If they spoke to him or needed to leave, he would be up in a flash, but she let him rest. She wouldn't do that without cause. Besides, he needed rest as much as she did, if not more. He'd earned it racing across the desert at night to give warning.

Walker draped his arm across the rear of the bench behind her, and Elsa leaned into him—his presence reassuring and steady. No matter what came, she wouldn't be alone. She would rather sleep than sit and wait, but she wasn't comfortable letting others make the decisions, nor could she let down her guard in a strange place. She wanted to meet these Saints and take her own measure.

They didn't wait long.

A man dressed in dusty brown clothing exited one of the nearby buildings. He walked straight to the group on the benches and inclined his head with a gentle smile. "May you walk in peace and shade. If it is shelter that you seek, we provide a day and a night to weary travelers."

"We walk in peace and welcome the shade, though we fled those that have lost the way." Caitlyn's words sounded as if spoken by rote.

Elsa's eyebrows shot up. Caitlyn didn't seem the most peaceful of people, nor did Mason. This was a diplomatic side of her friend that exposed new talents. Elsa wouldn't have expected her to be friends with peace-loving Saints, and yet Caitlyn knew the right words. What other hidden talents would her friend show on the road?

The Saint may have agreed with Elsa's assessment. His gaze lingered on Walker and the knife at his belt that matched Elsa's and on the guns Mason wore at each hip.

"You will vouch for our guests, Sister?" he said to Caitlyn.

"Yes, Brother Campbell. I will provide surety for a day and a night. While we are under your shade, we will walk in peace."

"Good enough." The man broke into a smile that brought out the creases around his eyes in his sun-browned skin. He dropped the formal tone. "It's been a considerable time since you came this way, Sister Caitlyn. We were saddened to hear about Mathew."

She nodded. "It's been a year and I still miss him every day."

"Have you come to your senses and wish to join us?" His friendly smile took the sting from his words.

Caitlyn tugged at her long blond braid and shook her head. "I appreciate your offer, but we have business to the north. I was hoping for a map or a route through the mountains. We're headed to Idaho." She hesitated. "We left my farm, a step ahead of GreenCorps, but I had to leave my animals. Except for Mittens. I couldn't leave her." She looked down and swallowed, stroking the cat's head.

It was the man's turn to look surprised, and his smile disappeared. "Enough of our chatter," he said. "Perhaps you can introduce me to your friends. Then you can break your fast at my house. You must have walked most of the night to be here so early on this fine Sunday."

He turned to leave and Caitlyn said, "Brother, I understand it might be dangerous, but I would be in your debt if you could send someone to collect any of my sheep, goats, and the cow that might be wandering. I set the chickens loose and I suspect the mule and the pigs will have gone their own way. When we leave, I was hoping Mittens could find a temporary home with you."

"It will be done." Brother Campbell nodded.

The tension Caitlyn must have held in her shoulders lessened as they dropped away from her ears and she collected her pack. Elsa and Walker grabbed their belongings and got to their feet and Tatsuda unfolded himself from the ground. Mason didn't move.

"Your horse will be safe there," Brother Campbell said to Mason across the square. The Saint waved his hand to a post beside the trough in the shade of a building.

Mason looped his reins around the post and patted his horse's flank on the way past as they filed into the building with the open door. The temperature dropped when they stepped inside. The tile floor was clean and the respite from the heat was immediate. The Saint led them down a hall past a series of large meeting rooms filled with wooden benches and chairs that looked old, their dark wood contrasting with the paler brick. He stopped in a kitchen and motioned them to a table and chairs on one side.

Once the group was inside the room with the door closed, Caitlyn reached into her pack and pulled out her cat. Mittens wandered the kitchen, sniffing the floor and rubbing her face on the edge of cupboards and on the legs of Caitlyn's chair. Caitlyn removed a bowl from her bag and filled it with water from a hand pump at the sink and set it on the floor.

Brother Campbell said, "Excuse me for a moment." He returned minutes later. "I've sent a few of the young men to your farm on horseback. They'll pretend to be neighbors if necessary and they'll be careful. If they see anyone on the trail, either coming or going, they can let us know. They'll take your animals to the other settlement across the valley, so they aren't followed here. You can pack up and leave without anyone else knowing you were ever here."

"We aren't planning to unpack. Not for a day and a night." Elsa hadn't unpacked for two months. Maybe he meant it as an expression. Walker rested his large hand on her arm. "Not that we aren't grateful for the refuge." Walker's smile filled her chest with warmth and softened any edge her words may have held.

"Thank you," said Caitlyn. "Is Sister Hope here? I'd like a chance to speak with her before we leave."

Brother Campbell nodded. "I'll let her know you asked for her."

He served them toasted bread with crispy bacon and fluffy scrambled eggs, and then afterward showed them to a room to sleep. The bunkhouse attached to the rear of the kitchen had a separate entrance into a small courtyard out back. It held four sets of double bunks with space on the floor for a couple more people if needed. Mason moved his horse back here, where feed was provided. He carried his saddle inside, setting it beside his chosen bed without speaking.

Walker and Elsa chose a bunk together while Tatsuda scrambled up above them, while Caitlyn and Mason took lower bunks on opposite sides of the room. Mittens curled up beside Caitlyn's pillow after jumping on each bed.

When everyone was settled, Brother Campbell said, "I'll wake you before dinner."

After he left, Walker barred the door from inside with a heavy piece of steel that fit into brackets. They'd all sleep better when they felt safe.

CHAPTER 9: GINGER PLUS MASON

Ginger emerged from underground just outside the massive walls of the estate near the city laundry, a place she remembered as close to the train station—at least with her usual bird's-eye view. She used the cloak of darkness to run while those who slept near the trainyard in their small houses slept.

Her stomach rumbled, and she shivered in the cool air as she hid near a disconnected train car outside the trainyard. She dared to sneak closer, her heart pounding, but found the station was filled with patrolling guards. She waited with increasing frustration, trying to determine how to climb on without being caught. It had been fine to dream of fleeing while in her quiet rooms, but the reality made her stomach ache and her hands sweat. She didn't know how to jump on a moving train the way the vagabond hoppers did, so it had to be soon before it moved.

She'd watched the closest train from the shadows while it was unloaded and reloaded; busy railroad workers and security worked too close to allow her to make a move. It now sat unattended, ready to leave at a moment's notice. If she didn't get on soon, it would leave without her. Her chest tightened with worry. Two sets of tracks further over, another train waited for departure. Her gaze switched from one to another, and she hesitated, scraping her finger over the rough skin beside her thumb. Which to choose?

A man in a black and green GreenCorps uniform stood fifty yards away, his back toward her. Close enough that she feared he would hear her if she moved, but far enough that she could still run if discovered. Trainyard security guards were called bulls and were to be avoided. Jace used to be in charge of them, and they had promoted Jaxon to fill his brother's rather large shoes.

All hoppers and stowaways who were caught on GreenCorps Railroad property or the trains were locked up—at least overnight. She took a deep breath. She didn't want to be locked up in Denver. Once it was discovered that she was missing, her father would put off his travel and come looking. Sometimes prisoners were shipped south. She shuddered. That would be a worse fate than marrying a rich stranger. Wouldn't it?

Should she sneak aboard now? The train might sit for hours before departure. Maybe the bulls hadn't completed their final search. They might make another pass. If only she had more experience or had listened to Jaxon talk about his job. Her heart fluttered, her chest hurt from not breathing, and she'd scratched her arms on the bushes where she crouched. Boarding a train and leaving Denver wasn't as easy as she had expected.

As night disappeared, rain clouds moved in, ringing the mountains and blocking the colors of the sunrise. Cold droplets landed on her bare skin and she looked upward as the rain increased, becoming a cold gray drizzle that socked in the city. Soon, her clothes were soaked. She wore a long-sleeved shirt but didn't own a jacket. Her chin quivered, and she shivered, her teeth chattering. Water poured off her wet hair and face and pooled in her squishy sandals. She glanced down. Her shriveled, wet feet looked like she'd been in the bath for hours.

Should she go home? If she returned now, nobody would know she'd escaped and she could try again another time, in better weather. She shuddered, thinking of her future husband and the gigantic snake in the laundry cellar that he resembled. She couldn't go back. Maybe she could march to the front gates of the property and demand to speak to her father. She could try to convince him not to marry her off in haste. She touched her sore cheekbone where he'd hit her and struggled not to cry. Also not an option.

Ginger had to stick to the plan and run; the trains were the only way out of town unless she stole a horse. For a second, she allowed herself to consider that possibility. Fewer people were killed by horses than by trains. She sighed. Riding was unfamiliar and she had no idea what to feed a horse. If they caught her, she'd be charged with theft and returned to her father's house, anyway. Or face deportation for stealing.

She couldn't walk for days without supplies or maps. It had to be the trains.

Judging by the way the engines faced, the two trains were bound in opposite directions. She hadn't thought to look at a map was at a loss about what to do. She would have avoided the south at any cost. That much, she knew. South was Texas and SoCal—the workcamps. However, once the trains left Denver, the rails curved away from their current path. They might go anywhere.

Her stomach gurgled again. She'd have to gamble. She looked around before parting the bushes and pushing through the wet shrubbery into the open, expecting to be discovered. Scraping her nail near her raw thumb, she glanced back and forth and up at the light gray sky, trying to judge the time. It was still early, but no longer night. She took a deep breath and dashed to the nearest train car on the closest track. Keep it simple.

The metal ladder at the back looked too high, but she jumped and grabbed the slippery metal, gasping as the freezing cold bit into her hands. Her feet dangled until, straining her muscles while she whimpered, she pulled herself high enough to get a toehold on the rungs. Her red hands ached from the dampness and from contact with the chilly ladder. She didn't have a way to warm them, so, gritting her teeth, she managed to ignore the pain. Looking ahead, there was a flat spot at the back end of each train car that had a dry overhang. She'd sit there and get out of the rain.

Ginger climbed over the top rung, awkwardly swung over the railing, and stood on the grated metal flooring of the train car with its peeling yellow paint showing rusty sections beneath. She shook the long ropes of her hair, water spraying in all directions. She squeezed the excess water from her curls and wedged herself back into the dry spot. It was big enough, but the metal was cold beneath her backside. Wasn't summer supposed to be warm?

Setting her soggy pillowcase beside her, she removed a folded blanket she'd brought from her bed. Only one edge was damp. She wrapped herself, hugging her chilled legs inside its warmth. Pressing herself deep into the shadows, she hoped she wouldn't be discovered.

She didn't have long to wait.

Ginger looked up in alarm as metal scraped and crashed on metal ahead in the train yard. Covering her ears, the sound grew louder, coming nearer, and the train jerked forward, three times in succession before several more immediate crashes. The next deafening smash brought forward motion that continued. She glanced through the grating on which she sat. Her heart sped up and her stomach lurched. The train was moving. Ready or not, she was leaving.

The train's motion started slow, but soon picked up speed. She crouched low, pulling the gray blanket over her bag and head, hoping to blend into the shadows. The train accelerated past the busy buildings of the station where GreenCorps recruits stood guard with their guns.

She waited with bated breath, expecting an outcry. Though she was on the opposite side, she'd need luck to be missed. Perhaps the dim light helped her to blend into the gray and silver train. Her heart pounded in time to the train's wheels as they went around, faster and faster, the rails a blur underneath the wheels. The air whooshing past, creating an eerie whine. Leaving might have been an error, but it was too late to change her mind.

Curling into a small ball, she closed her eyes as the train sped up faster still. Her ears ached, and the vibration shook her jaw and lingered in her chest. Cold air rushed past, whipping the blanket and streaming through the covering that provided scant protection. Tears ran down her face as the train left Denver station, a distorted view seen in brief glimpses. So far, so good.

When the city of Denver had fallen behind, Ginger poked her head from beneath her flimsy layer of protection. Her eyes still streamed, but until now, she hadn't been aware that she was crying. She wiped her burning cheeks and released several shuddering breaths. There was no way to be comfortable, but she could rest. After her sleepless night, she needed it. With her make-shift bag as a pillow, she re-wrapped herself in the blanket and curled in on her side on her covered porch. Pressing her back against the frigid metal, she warmed it with her body heat. The rocking motion of the speeding train and her exhaustion lulled her to sleep.

* * *

When Ginger awoke, she didn't remember where she was. Somewhere cold and loud. She wiped the crust from her eyes and stretched. She lay on a metal grate with an unfamiliar pattern. Her memory came rushing back.

She'd hopped her first train.

Groggily, she took stock. Her clothes were still damp, although the rain had stopped. She blinked into the bright sunshine.

Fresh air streamed past the rushing train while the sun stood high in the cloudless blue sky that stretched into the distance. Two large birds circled far overhead. Her best guess was that it was afternoon, and she was traveling northwest. She ran her tongue over her cracked lips. The most important thing was that she was out of Denver, the rest she would figure out. This was an adventure now and she would make her own way. With the sunshine, things didn't feel as bleak as they had first thing this morning. She hadn't been discovered, and she'd gotten on the train with no help.

She unpacked her pillowcase to check her belongings. When she'd packed, she'd been in a panic and may not have brought everything she needed. She had an old cap with a brim that Jace had given her years ago, which she'd found stuffed in the back of a drawer. She smoothed her snarled hair with her hands and pulled on the hat, shading her eyes. She ran her tongue over her teeth, which felt grungy without water to brush them. She'd brought a toothbrush and Cook's homemade toothpaste, but not water. Not having water had been an oversight, but she'd had no way to carry it. Worst of all, her stomach ached in a manner that was impossible to ignore.

She hadn't brought much food, but she grabbed the two squashed buns she'd saved from lunch yesterday. She ripped them apart with shaking fingers, stuffing every crumb into her mouth. They were dry and difficult to chew or swallow, but she worked them down, trying to ease her knot of hunger. Her only other food was a handful of broken chocolate chip oatmeal cookies, wrapped in a clean handkerchief.

Ginger was tempted to gobble them too, but hesitated. She had no way of knowing when the train ride would end. Her insides lurched. What if it was an express and didn't stop for days? What would she do for water? She'd read that a person could only go two to three days without water. The train should stop before that. Right? Ginger blinked back threatening tears. Some brave adventurer. She'd been awake ten minutes and already she was crying. She needed to get tougher.

Re-wrapping the cookies, she collected her bathroom kit and cleaned up as best she could without a mirror or water. She removed the cap, combed out the worst of the tangles, and rebraided her hair. It took several attempts before she quit trying to make the braid perfect. It would have to do. It felt lopsided, but was out of her face.

She dry-brushed her teeth and spat over the edge. She moved to the far edge of the platform and around a flange, separating the overhang into two halves. She relieved her bladder, wrinkling her nose at the unsanitary bathroom situation. It was gross, but she became more comfortable with the pressure gone. She had a spare outfit, but she didn't change yet; she was saving her clean clothes for when she was off the train, or had some way to wash this set.

Ginger dried her damp clothes by moving into the sun. The warmth on her chilled flesh seemed like heaven though she needed to be cautious not to burn in the strong UVee light. She gave herself a few minutes, then with her hat on, she settled back to ride. It was almost comfortable—if she blocked her thirst, hunger, and the din of the steel wheels scraping along the railroad tracks.

While she'd been asleep, the train had left the familiar rocky mountains and now raced through brown rolling hills with no recognizable landmarks. The train continued for hours; the countryside empty except for the odd series of bumps that clustered together on either side of the tracks. What had caused them? Leaving a large section with dozens of mounds, the rusted remains of a gigantic machine sat tilted, one long wing stretching to the sky, the other dragging on the ground like a lame bird.

The train stopped once in a place called Rock Springs. The station was simply a brick shelter. The land itself empty and dry without a city or people. She huddled deeper into the darkest shadows and didn't move. If she got off here, she'd be remembered. She needed somewhere bigger, where she could disappear. Heavy-looking sacks of potatoes arrived by wagon and were loaded onto two boxcars in the center of the long train, about a dozen cars in front of her.

Only two GreenCorps men seemed to work security at the station instead of as labor.

"Just do a quick sweep before we send it on," the older man said to the younger before he turned back to the building and the shade inside the depot.

She prayed to remain unnoticed.

Her best estimate was that the train waited here three hours before continuing, the only inspection cursory. Her ears rang in the quiet, so much so that she welcomed the crashes as the train resumed its journey.

Ginger found her eyelids growing heavy as the sun set with a scarlet blaze amidst a swath of pink in front of the train and across the horizon. She hugged her knees, watching the sun slide below the plains—a band of pink lingered at the skyline. She swallowed and ignored her thirst and the persistent knot of hunger.

She fidgeted and squirmed that evening without finding a comfortable position, and she couldn't stay asleep for long. Once the blazing heat of the day disappeared, she shivered with cold, rubbing her arms to keep them warm.

She draped the blanket around herself for more warmth and sat, her arms still wrapped around herself, staring into the darkness. Ahead, a spark of light ignited and caught her eyes. As the train plunged toward it, the light expanded to be many lights. A small city lay ahead. Cars jolted and crashed with a metallic scream as the train decreased its speed. The moment had arrived to discover where this was.

* * *

Mason rested with one ear open, being attentive for sounds that didn't belong. Sounds that might be unusual or off in the blistering heat of the day in this sleepy settlement belonging to the Saints. He turned over. Why was he still here? He could tell Grady he'd decided not to help. Leaving the farm so soon hadn't been his intention. He'd expected time to assess before deciding. Instead, he was back on the run.

His eyes flicked open, and he stared across the room where Caitlyn lay snoring.

She hadn't been at all what he'd expected. He'd expected Mathew's widow to be small and pale, a waif-like piece of fluff who'd floated from one powerful man to another, clinging to them for protection. He'd seen that type plenty. The kind that could make compresses or change bedding, not real combat medics. The frail image in his head had vanished like a puff of smoke when he'd ridden into her farmyard.

Grady had said she was a tough nut, but Mason hadn't listened. If he'd paid attention, he might have connected the dots, figuring out that Mathew's widow and his long-lost angel were the same person. When they were younger, Mathew's type had always been someone who needed rescuing, not a tough-ass woman whose practical no-nonsense statements left Mason unable to speak.

Caitlyn had looked him straight in the eye, shaking his hand, her callouses and iron-like muscles proving she was strong and a hard worker—as did her orderly farm. She'd acted like they were complete strangers. Instead of what they were, two people who'd lost track of each other long before. His heart had broken a little at her chilly reception, but he couldn't blame her. He was the one who'd left her behind.

Caitlyn turned over on her creaky bunk situated at the furthest end of the room, flipping onto her side, and the snoring stopped. He almost missed the sound. The only window in the bunkhouse had been built high in the wall on his side, and a stray beam of light drifted across her face. She faced into the room, her full red lips open, her eyes closed, and escaped tendrils of blond hair fanned her pillow. She stole his breath.

Mason swallowed and flipped onto his back to block the sight, but instead, he tortured himself with images of her from their youth. He imagined her blue eyes twinkling with mirth instead of being sad and unfathomable, her warm strawberry mouth pressing kisses to his heated flesh. Dammit. He shifted as his body responded to the image, turning again, this time to face the brick wall. What was his next move? This was Mathew's widow, not some brothel wench he could pay and leave. Women like this had expectations—a wanderer like himself might not be enough.

Chapter 10: Elsa plus Walker

Elsa raised her hands and stepped back, expecting Jace's fists to pummel her again. Her face stung, and each breath stabbed her bruised ribs. Jace was dead. This had to be a dream, but she couldn't wake up. When she was exhausted, even Walker's presence couldn't keep the nightmares at bay. More often, it was the look of hatred on Jace's face as he plunged the knife into her shoulder that brought her awake, gasping for air.

"Anyone want dinner?" A soft voice issued the invitation, pulling Elsa from her usual dream before the expected ending. Her chest heaved and her heart slowed as she endeavored to regain her bearings.

It took several seconds for her sleep-addled brain to make sense of the words spoken outside the door. Sleeping during the day often left her disoriented. Walker's arm around her tightened for a second as another knock rapped against the wooden door and the words repeated. The others must be having trouble waking as well.

"Yep," Elsa answered. "Give us a sec." She stretched in place, reluctant to leave somewhere so cozy and enjoying the feel of Walker next to her. He made everything better and kept her from having to deal with her fears on her own. She opened her eyes and sat up, glancing up at the window above where Mason sat re-buttoning his long-sleeved gray shirt. The light outside was softer than earlier, so the sun must have passed overhead toward the west. They'd slept the majority of the day, but she'd needed that after the sleepless night and strenuous climb.

Behind her, Walker swung his feet to the floor, kissed the back of her neck where a patch of bare skin showed, and stood to stretch.

Across the room, Caitlyn straightened her hair and shoved her feet into her boots while Tatsuda jumped down from above. Elsa caught a silver gleam as his hand dipped into his pocket. She arched one eyebrow and offered her hand. With a sheepish grin and a shrug, he handed her a spoon. The handle had a different design than Caitlyn's silver. He must have lifted it at breakfast.

She gave it back. "Slip it in with the dishes at dinner. Try not to steal from our hosts." She held his mischievous gaze to make her point.

Tatsuda nodded. Elsa laced up her boots to find that she was the last ready. Walker lifted the bar locking the door and opened it. Brother Campbell stood outside with a woman dressed in brown and tan, her chestnut and gray-streaked hair twisted into a bun. She smiled at the group and nodded, perhaps in recognition of Caitlyn.

"I'm Sister Hope. Dinner's inside."

They trooped into the kitchen where platters of food heaped the table, including new potatoes, tomatoes, and a platter of fried trout. Grabbing plates from the counter, they sat and loaded up; when would they see such a feast again? They dug in with voracious appetites, and it was several minutes before anyone spoke.

"Thank you." Elsa served herself a second helping of potatoes, adding butter and salt. Until this spring, she'd never eaten a potato, and now she wasn't certain how she'd live without them. Walker caught her eye and smiled, perhaps also remembering that first meal, cooked over an open campfire. They'd evaded GreenCorps for three and a half months now—or perhaps a lifetime.

Brother Campbell returned from the hallway and spoke a few quiet words to Caitlyn before passing her a folded piece of paper. She read it, then slipped it into her pocket. He and Sister Hope left them to finish eating on their own.

"What's the plan?" Elsa said once their hosts were gone. They might be friends of Caitlyn's, as well as kind and helpful, but Elsa didn't know them. She took a calming breath. After the trouble last spring, she couldn't quite bring herself to trust new people without more information. She hated being snappish and mistrustful and despised owing strangers more.

"Brother Campbell drew a map and wrote instructions for a course through the mountains. Past a couple of large peaks before returning to the flatlands below. That should turn off our immediate pursuers. We can think about where we're going after." Caitlyn looked at Mason. "He says it's a goat track through the steepest mountains. Not possible on horseback. It'll discourage followers, but you have a decision to make. It's up to you whether you come with us or not. There're better places to hide out besides with a group of felons on the run."

Caitlyn raised her eyebrows, perhaps waiting for Mason to acknowledge her words.

His fish-covered fork stopped, and he set it down with a click. He refrained from making eye contact with her, and his tone gave nothing away. "You're coming back this way for your cat. I'll stop in for my horse."

Caitlyn's eyebrows shot skyward, her gaze meeting Elsa's.

Elsa shrugged. Mason may have decided before now and hadn't needed time to think. Maybe he believed in their cause. He was an impossible man to read.

Someone pounded at the rear entrance and Elsa leapt to her feet, her heart thumping.

It was too soon to be GreenCorps unless they'd found this trail through the canyon, despite Mason's diversionary tactics. She remembered the gunshots as they'd scrambled into the canyon. It was possible.

Despite promises of peace, Walker, Mason, and Caitlyn readied their weapons. Tatsuda slipped out of sight by hiding behind the door. In position, Caitlyn motioned Elsa to the door with her chin.

She controlled her breath as she cracked the door open, prepared to slam it shut if necessary. Her eyebrows rose after the first peek and she let out her held breath. A boy stood there, perhaps ten years old. She opened it a fraction wider.

He gasped for breath. "I need to speak to Brother Campbell. It's urgent. Riders in the canyon."

Elsa's throat closed. They couldn't even enjoy a pleasant meal without rushing away.

"Close?" said Mason, stepping forward to speak.

The boy shook his head. "But they'll be here within the hour. Brother Campbell said it was important that he be told if we saw anyone."

"That is important. I'll let him know right away," said Elsa, her voice returning.

The boy cocked his head and nodded before leaving. Elsa shut the door and examined everyone in the tense kitchen.

"Tatsuda, can you find our hosts?" Elsa had confidence in the boy to move through the building without anyone realizing he was there. The fewer people who saw them, the better their chances of escaping without endangering the folks who took them in. That would be her repayment.

He nodded.

"They went down the hallway to the right." Before her words finished, Tatsuda left.

Caitlyn returned to her half-full plate. "Eat up everyone. We have ten minutes before we leave. We need to be gone."

"You trust these Saints not to just give us up?" Elsa grimaced. "Brother Campbell seems honest. I just have a hard time with people I don't know." She needed to explain some of her snappishness because she valued Caitlyn's opinion.

"I do." Caitlyn's face remained calm. "They have no love of GreenCorps. The rebels in Texas freed a full half of their members or their parents. I brought Sister Hope here myself six years ago and treated her injuries. She wouldn't play me false."

"Caitlyn's right," said Mason.

Elsa turned her gaze on him.

He shrugged. "Those we free need a new life. Most join the rebels or the Saints."

"What about everyone else?" Elsa's hand swept to include the settlement.

"Brother Campbell will have kept our presence quiet," said Caitlyn. "I think that was his nephew at the door."

Elsa accepted the words, but the compressed feeling remained in her chest. She'd killed a man and might be a fugitive for the rest of her life. Maybe nowhere would feel safe.

Everyone finished the food on their plates, then Walker and Mason slipped out to the bunkhouse for their gear. When Mason returned, he'd converted his leather saddlebags to a backpack by rearranging the straps—both ingenious and awkward.

Tatsuda slipped back into the room to finish his food, nodding to Elsa to let her know he'd been successful.

Everyone drank their fill, topped up their canteens, and was ready in the prescribed amount of time. Elsa's brain had woken up now that she had food inside her. She stacked the used plates by the sink and counted the silverware, which seemed to all be there, plus an extra spoon. Caitlyn slipped out to say goodbye to Mittens on her own.

"Ready." Elsa said. They filed out the back exit where once more Brother Campbell and Sister Hope met them, and were rejoined by Caitlyn, who gave a last look into the bunkhouse before squaring her shoulders and standing straight.

"I'm sorry it has cut your stay short. I'd thought to provide a safe haven overnight." Brother Campbell handed Caitlyn a large brown bag. "Dried food. It should last at least three days."

"Thank you." She stuffed it into her pack. Turning to Sister Hope, she said. "My cat is named Mittens. I left her sleeping in the bunkhouse. I'll be back for her when I can." Her voice wavered on the last statement.

The other woman nodded.

Caitlyn's pack would be heavy, but it relieved one of Elsa's concerns about leaving the farm the way they had the night before. They'd brought no food.

"We'll take good care of your horse," Brother Campbell said to Mason, who nodded.

"Can you please send her to Grady?" Mason said. "She's an excellent trail horse."

"Someone can go that way in a few weeks. Brother Campbell affirmed with a nod, "We'll make it happen."

Taking Caitlyn aside, Brother Campbell spoke in tones too quiet for Elsa to make out.

Caitlyn nodded. "Thank you for the food and shade. We have kept your peace and wish you days of plenty." She clasped Brother Campbell's forearm and bowed her head. "Take care, old friend."

The others murmured their thanks to Brother Campbell and followed Caitlyn's lead. She strode north behind the buildings, into the smaller valley that extended toward the mountains.

The colorful glow of the evening sun shone behind them as they walked single file. The packed earth trail led past several of the homes on the hillside, but there was nobody about, though a few chickens roamed the hillside. Perhaps the people were all indoors, eating dinner. Behind, music swelled from within the church and dozens of voices joined in. At this time of day, the gardens and fields stood empty.

Nobody would see them leave. The fewer eyes who watched what direction they went, the better.

* * *

Rivers of sweat trickled down Elsa's back as the track wound through the thick shrubbery, following a meandering creek as the valley led to a mountain path. Less than an hour wasn't much of a head start when they were on foot and their pursuers rode horses, but it was preferable to being surprised. Maybe GreenCorps would be stalled by searching the settlement. She spared a thought for Brother Campbell and the Saints, hoping the soldiers wouldn't hurt anyone.

"If we can find the trail into the mountains before dark, we'll be fine tonight. We have a few hours," said Caitlyn.

Caitlyn was probably right. Their best chance of escape was to hide in the mountains. It chafed not to take a direct route north. Mason might have ideas. He seemed at ease in the outdoors. Walker had said that Vancouver was the best option, as the Western Canadian capital. Two 'safe' bunkers were inside the Canadian border, one in Pullman, Washington, the other in Corvallis, Oregon. That meant possibilities. How to choose?

Elsa visualized the maps from the tubes. GreenCorps may have accessed the Fort Collins close to Denver and their headquarters. That might explain how they'd known what the tube contained and Jace's interest. She and Walker had left another bunker behind in Riverside, part of SoCal, before she'd been brave enough to search with Walker's help in Davis.

That left one more, in Aberdeen, Idaho. From the map at Caitlyn's, that would be about 150 miles away, a little longer through the mountains, but between here and Canada. It should be outside Pocatello—a corporation town in southern Idaho.

There'd be Wanted posters in a town secured and controlled by GreenCorps. It wouldn't be safe, but Elsa needed to take a chance. She'd recognize the marker at the bunker entrance, similar to the rebel leaf, but with fewer veins. Her mind whirled. If they could access another bunker, they'd be able to gather more proof than the two varieties of seed packet she carried and perhaps additional information and survival gear.

"Found it," called Caitlyn.

Her voice chased Elsa's musing and returned her to the practicalities of evading capture today. They stood positioned at the bottom of a long-ago landslide from the cliff face on their left. Orange boulders and a thick layer of gravel littered the slope, but leafy bushes had grown over the lower portion. It should be stable.

Caitlyn held Brother Campbell's hand-drawn map out for the others and pointed. Following the directions between landmarks, it didn't seem like an actual trail, which was good. It would be more difficult to locate, provided they left minimal evidence. Elsa kept checking over her shoulder and startled at birds and scuttling rodents—always false alarms. Her nerves jangled from being on constant alert.

The sun disappeared behind the mountains and they hiked in its shade as the radiance dimmed. If it wasn't for the constant fear of pursuit and the tension between her shoulder blades, the alpine walk would have been gorgeous. Tangled red and purple flowers spread across the slopes in a riot of pale green and splashes of brilliant color.

Soon after turning onto the goat track, the path along the peak dwindled to a narrow width, perhaps enough for a pair of boots, but not much more. A steep cliff fell away on one side. She avoided looking down. The trail angled upward, requiring them to help each other where it was steepest. Except for Tatsuda, who was as nimble as the goats for whom the track was designed.

Elsa's lungs labored in the thin air and she developed an ache deep within her chest. When they stopped at dusk to discuss a campsite, everyone had bright red cheeks.

"Today and tomorrow should be the hardest," said Caitlyn. "Then we can cross down onto the plain again."

Elsa filled them in on her Aberdeen plan, hoping they'd agree. Walker's eyes shone, and he told the others about the riches in the previous bunker. They could get clothes and travel food and all kinds of equipment. A trip to the bunker would be useful since they'd had to leave the farm with so little preparation. Everyone was interested, and the vote was yes. It felt more concrete to have a destination. Better to run toward something than away.

* * *

August 15th, 2195. Ben Lomond Peak Trail, Utah.
Sunrise: 6:36 a.m. Sunset: 8:36 p.m.

On the move again. Spent almost half my life that way. Seems more normal to me than farming for all I didn't mind helping Caitlyn and learning something new. I'm in my element on the road, though it's weird without Hayden. Never thought he'd go so far as to turn us in. He was my best friend through childhood and for the eight years after the fire, we called each other brother. I bailed him out of more trouble than he understands. Breaks my heart that not only did he leave, he chose GreenCorps.

I gave him too much credit. Thought once he knew Elsa, he'd get over his jealousy. I care about both of them. Guess he couldn't see that. Hope GreenCorps doesn't hurt him. They aren't kind to traitors.

We're set up to sleep in a cave. I risked my candle lantern, away from the entrance so I could write. Caitlyn swept for rattlesnakes with a big stick before we sprawled for the night. No fire tonight. Can't afford even a hint of a blaze to be spotted. Back to cold food for a few days, at least. I can hide a cookfire in a sunken pit, but not here on the hard stone.

I like Elsa's plan to head for Aberdeen to explore another bunker. She's been kicking herself for not exploring further when we were in Davis. There could be so much down there, documents or tech that might be useful. I wanted to stay in the other one for longer, but it wasn't my place to decide. Back then, our friendship was new. I let her make the call.

CHAPTER 11: GINGER

Terrified of discovery at the station, Ginger retreated further into the shadows of the train car. She didn't move for a long time after the train stopped, waiting for an opportunity to run. Twice footsteps crunched in the gravel, but in the dark, she hadn't been seen. Her muscles cramped. Desperate for water, she poked out her head and scanned her surroundings.

Lights shone on the left, outside of the train station ahead of where her train car sat, which illuminated lettering over the door. This was Pocatello. She'd heard of the town, which could be busy. If she stayed here until morning, she'd be found and if she didn't find something to drink, she might not make it much longer. She hadn't had anything since last night at dinner, if not before, and had never experienced this kind of thirst.

She would've preferred to travel farther from Denver, but water had become more important than hiding. She shivered with fear and her head swam. If she waited too long, the train could leave again, traveling for another day or two. Another couple of days without supplies might have killed her. She needed to get off.

Gathering her belongings, she swung over the ladder to descend and stopped, listening for any noise that might give clues about what to expect. The silence pressed inward. Every sound magnified in the dark night, her breath, each step on the ladder, and the faint bustle of action inside the station. She climbed down until she stood on the bottom rung, but when she attempted to get off, her foot didn't reach the ground. She'd have to risk jumping and making noise.

Ginger grit her teeth and dropped, taking the force of the landing on bent knees, slipping to one side and wincing at the crunching sound of the gravel. She straightened and listened, her heart pounding. The station was left, so she went right. She tiptoed away, clutching her bag in sweaty hands. She followed the tracks back the way the train had come in the darkness until the station's lights had shrunk to the size of a candle's flame—a distant reference. There, she crossed the tracks and advanced toward the small cluster of lights that marked the town. Her stride became more confident as she left the train and the security guards behind.

To her family, she'd be a fugitive, but her chest filled with pride. She was now a hopper.

The town wasn't much more than a scruffy-looking market square with half a dozen shops marked with GreenCorps lettering, a hotel, and three bars. She'd never been in a bar, but she'd heard about them from the staff and her older brothers. She wrinkled her nose at the raucous noise, the smells of rancid body odor, and plumes of tobacco smoke emanating from the first of these. Nothing about it enticed her to go inside. It must not be too late if they were still open, though she had no idea what time they might close.

Ginger wandered into the space between the buildings, keeping to the shadows. Back here it was black as pitch, and she navigated with one hand trailing the rough brick wall at her side. She halted when she reached an alley.

To the left was the rear of the noisiest bar. Shouts and laughter interrupted the peace, even back here. She turned in the opposite direction. One shop's back door had a pale light, its charge not quite run down. It illuminated a row of garbage cans lined up against the wall behind the buildings, including a rusted dumpster at the far end. Nowhere she could get water. What had she hoped for? A town well with free water?

Maybe one of the doors farther down the alley would be unlocked. There could be something inside. She'd be risking being seen, but her thirst drove her to consider such actions. Her tight lips cracked and bled as she grimaced, and it hurt to swallow. Licking her lips no longer worked, it just made them dry out faster. She increased her pace and reached for the first door on her right. Wiggling it, the cool metal knob didn't move. Locked.

She let out a deep breath. One down, six to go. The second and third were the same. With each door, she breathed a sigh of relief not to be caught, but her spirits sank lower. She needed one to open, despite the fear of discovery gnawing at her insides. By now, her disappearance must have been discovered, and she hoped no one this far from Denver would recognize her. She practiced the lie she'd tell as her cover story if required; she was no longer Ginger, but Geri, an orphaned train hopper.

She listened at the fourth door, pressing her ear against the cool metal. She couldn't hear anything from inside. Inhaling, she went through the same motions of turning the knob, but this time, instead of catching, it turned until it gave a soft click. Heart racing, she cracked the door ajar a fraction, waiting for someone inside to protest. There was nothing.

She stepped further inside, leaving the door ajar in case she needed to make a quick exit. Inside the house, somewhere distant, soft voices stopped her in her tracks and she dripped with uncomfortable sweat. Someone might be awake. Ginger remained frozen with indecision. Should she retreat? Her eyes adjusted to the faint light emerging from deeper inside. The light source and the voices seemed distant and scratchy. Probably just the radio. At home, she'd had a radio that played music from up north at night; Denver had a radio station as well, but all the talk on it had been boring.

The sound of the radio might cover small noises she made. She'd be as stealthy as she could—like a mouse searching for crumbs. Swallowing, she took two more steps forward. Her chest ached as she eased herself far enough inside to see that the light came from a staircase beyond the small kitchen where she found herself.

In the gray light, the sink's faucet loomed like a black snake rearing up. She shook her head at her silliness. There wasn't a snake. She needed to focus, and she was finding it difficult to concentrate. Lack of basic food and water was bad for her brain. Not only did she need water, but she also needed something in which to carry it. Her first glance around the room showed nothing useful.

Once more tiptoeing, she made her way to the sink and slowly turned the tap on the right, allowing a bare trickle to escape. Not enough to make a sound. She stuck her mouth under the opening, letting it flow into her. It was like heaven to drink. She turned the tap farther, allowing a slow stream. She swallowed it all, not wasting a drop. Water was a precious commodity, and she'd never take it for granted again.

If she hadn't been so parched, Ginger might have cried in relief at the cooling sensation in her throat. She imagined her body soaking up the liquid like a dry sponge. She'd read that the human body was sixty percent water, but she felt like a dried-out husk. With her thirst quenched, she turned it off. Wiping her mouth with the back of her hand, she looked around, feeling braver.

She didn't dare to open the chiller, but half a loaf of bread sat on the counter and three apples lay in a shallow bowl on the counter. Her mouth watered. She needed food, too. Without thinking, she grabbed an apple, the slick peel cool in her hand. She stuck it in her bag, though guilt at stealing from someone who might need it filled her.

Opening several cupboard doors, she searched, being careful not to let them bang closed when she advanced to the next. Inside one, she discovered two boxes containing GreenCorps granola bars. With trembling hands, she stuffed a dozen foil-wrapped bars into her sack. The bars felt hard and didn't seem that appetizing, but they'd be better than going hungry.

Ginger scanned the dim room again. Taking the bread would be too obvious. Missing bread might cause a fuss or for the door to be locked next time. Even the apple might be too much, but she didn't want to return it. She left it in her bag, even though she might come back tomorrow or the next day. Unless she hopped another train.

Under the sink, at last, she located a glass jar with a lid. When she removed the metal lid, it slipped, falling with a clang on the hard floor. With a sound so out of place in the dark house, she held her breath, fighting tears, expecting footsteps from upstairs. When no one appeared, she snatched it from the floor, prepared to flee with her prize and try somewhere else, but the house remained quiet other than the faint radio sound.

She clutched the lid hard enough that her hand ached. She turned the tap and filled the jar, all the while listening for signs that people in the living quarters upstairs had awakened. Still nothing. So far, so good.

When Ginger finished, she glanced around the kitchen. Was there anything else that was edible and portable? She'd been here long enough. She retreated to the back door, slipped through it, and exited as quietly as she'd come. Once more in the alley, she debated what to do. Should she risk returning to the train tonight?

She'd taken only a few steps when the noise of another train arriving in town sent her scurrying for cover. This one came from the other direction. Crashing sounds echoed through the night air, covering the loud voices from the bars. The station might be busy with two trains to unload and reload. GreenCorps soldiers would be everywhere. She didn't dare go back right now. Perhaps it would be quieter later or tomorrow night. The most important thing was to stay free.

Checking over her shoulder, Ginger marked which door was the unlocked one. If it was the only source of water, it was the most important place in town. She continued up the alley to the dumpster. A large, rusted metal box sat near the dead-end—not quite shoved against the brick wall. There was room for someone her size to slide between the dumpster and the wall and be out of view of the street.

Turning sideways, she wedged herself in at the back and sat to eat her apple. The first crunchy bite almost made her swoon. She'd never had an apple that tasted so amazing. Tart juice ran down her chin with each bite. She wiped the excess with her hand, then licked her fingers. She devoured every scrap, the soft flesh, the stringy part near the core, and even the hard part surrounding the seeds.

To finish, she sucked the last of the juice from the thin core. When there was nothing left, she tossed the remaining strand with its woody stem under the dumpster and lay down. She curled up to keep her feet from sticking out where they might be seen.

Closing her eyes, her nerves jangling with every unfamiliar sound, Ginger couldn't rest. Twice she jerked awake at rodent noises and confirmed that her new store of food was secure. She couldn't afford to share with rats. Using her stuffed cloth bag as her pillow, she cinched the blanket around herself and closed her eyes again, determined to sleep. The tough new her was no longer scared of mice or rats.

* * *

Ginger's eyes were crusty and sore the next morning, as though they'd been filled with sand. Her stomach rumbled, feeling emptier than she could remember. She was lucky to have never known hunger until yesterday. Her back ached from sleeping on the hard ground and the granola bar packets had pressed on her face through the pillowcase, leaving a divot in her cheek that felt strange and numb.

Still, she was better off this morning than she'd been yesterday. Her thoughts flitted from one idea to the next as she considered the possibilities now that she was out in the world instead of locked away in the mansion.

She sipped a quarter of the mason jar's water before returning the lid, and ate one of her contraband granola bars, which tasted stale—like old sawdust—and bland without sugar. At least it filled her stomach and took away the hollow, shaky feeling. Her cookie bits wouldn't last much longer, so she ate them too, a few tiny crumbs at a time, savoring the rich chocolate and sweet bits. She hadn't considered a few old cookies as a luxury until now.

Ginger didn't dare be seen here in Pocatello and wasn't daring enough to walk back to the trainyard in the daylight. Her distinctive reddish-orange hair would be too easy to notice. Maybe she could tie it back and shove it under her hat, trying to look less like any description that might circulate. She'd have to stay here at least until dusk. She'd brought two books, ones she'd never read before, and pulled out one to read for the daylight hours.

CHAPTER 12: ELSA

Elsa woke from dreams of escaping Jace on the train, her heart thumping and her hands sweaty. Each time she'd hopped one, she'd been with Walker. In her dream, she'd been alone and in trouble. The train had gone faster and faster until it sped out of control and she was stuck onboard with Jace, too scared to jump. She lay staring at the stone ceiling, waiting for her racing thoughts to settle. She'd slept longer than usual, a good sign.

She and Walker had zipped their fancy bunker sleeping bags together to make a cozy bed for two in a secluded corner of the cave. She was reluctant to leave their comfy nest, but it was time to start hiking. Tatsuda must already be up, as his bedroll was flat. Caitlyn's soft snores came from the opposite end of the cavern. Mason sat by the entrance, leaning against a boulder. He and Caitlyn had split the watch last night. Elsa and Walker would watch tonight, while Tatsuda would rotate into a turn.

The sun hadn't risen in the pale gray sky, but mist rose from the valley, obscuring the path in a sea of white. The light increased as Elsa watched in the chilly dawn as they ate breakfast bars and tidied their camp. She took one more look down at the valley before they left. No indication of pursuers yet, but anyone could hide in the fog.

They would have to be careful again today, minimizing their noise and maximizing their distance traveled. The constant tension left her feeling drained. She didn't know how wide the search would expand from Caitlyn's farm. Perhaps the soldiers would leave the canyon and try to circle around and find them somewhere else.

They trekked past a seasonal waterfall with a bare trickle dripping down the smooth stone. Elsa's eyes lingered. To weather the stone like that, this had to have once been a torrent. What would it have been like in the spring? The first day, they hiked a mountain called Ben Lomond, scrambling toward the rocky summit in an arduous climb. Reaching the base of the peak, they veered toward the next mountain, Willard Peak, according to Caitlyn's map.

On the second day, they traversed a mountain ridge, descending after the second peak. Caitlyn guessed they would need to camp another night in the foothills before venturing onto the flatlands. Elsa looked forward to somewhere requiring less physical exertion and a chance to rest her shoulder from the constant motion.

Forty-eight hours after leaving the Saints, they hit a snag. After wading for hours through the underbrush, they came to a dead stop. Tatsuda and Elsa at the front stared down as bits of gravel fell into thin air. The mountain had fallen away, taking the trail with it. Elsa caught her breath, stuttering at the near-miss. One misstep and they'd fall to their deaths. She stepped back, where the footing was more stable, and gazed at the distant ground.

The group spread out to look, staying away from the sudden drop. Without warning, farther along, the cliff splintered off again. Right where Tatsuda stood. As though time slowed, the ground beneath his feet disappeared—the miss became an accident as he scrambled to catch hold.

Elsa's stomach plummeted with him as she stifled a scream, knowing it would carry in the mountains to potential followers. Right now, that was the least of her worries.

For a second, Tatsuda's hands clawed at the brink, but the bank crumbled again and he slipped out of sight. The sounds of falling rock and scraping continued. There was nothing anyone could do without joining him in the freefall. Elsa covered her mouth as silence descended, waiting for his body to hit far below.

The sound never came, instead, a scraping sound persisted. He must have caught something, or he'd have been long gone. From where she stood, she couldn't see the damage.

"Tatsuda," she called, her voice shaking.

Walker's hand clamped around her arm, locking her in position solid ground. She must have taken a step toward the broken ground, her feet moving of their own accord, terrified that he was gone. She glanced down to see that he'd planted his feet.

"Be careful," he said. "You can't go over too." His gray eyes were filled anguish.

"I'm here. I caught some roots," said Tatsuda's breathless voice. It didn't sound like he'd fallen too far. "But I don't dare move."

"I need to get him. I'll be careful," she said to Walker, who released her arm without speaking. He trusted her not to do something dangerous. She looked around. Caitlyn and Mason stood nearby, watching, probably afraid to risk a move closer. She unclipped her pack and dug out a coil of rope. Unwinding half, she handed the rest to Walker. She crouched down, the rope in hand. "I'll stay low."

She crawled to the brink of the cliff, imagining herself light, paying extra attention to each forward move, trying to sense any movement of the earth. Alright so far. Reaching the edge, she lay down and scooted forward until she saw Tatsuda and her heart caught. He'd slid six or seven yards down and was splayed out against the cliff, clinging like a lizard. With a bleeding gash on one cheek and scrapes on his arms, he looked otherwise unharmed. His filthy left hand clutched a minuscule ridge in the stone while his right gripped a handful of stringy roots. They didn't look strong enough to hold someone his size for long. He'd wedged one foot on something so small she couldn't see it.

"I can't climb from here." Tatsuda gazed upward, his dark eyes trusting her to help.

"No problem," she said, the words coming to help them both remain calm. "I'm lowering a rope." She slid it through her hands, and played it past the crumbling rocks and loose, crumbly soil. Tatsuda was farther to the right. She flipped the rope in his direction and continued to slide it.

"That's it. End of the rope," said Walker behind her.

She cast a quick glance over her shoulder to see Mason holding the rope between herself and Walker, who was braced at the back, his feet wide apart. Her anchor.

"I just need another couple of feet." Before anyone could stop her, she slid forward again, praying that the precarious bank held. She took a deep breath, willing herself to remain calm. "Just a bit more." She inched forward, positioning her chest, shoulders, and head over the edge. The rope still dangled several inches short of Tatsuda's grasp. Still too far away.

Caitlyn grabbed Elsa's feet, locking her in place. A fist-sized rock and a handful of pebbles dislodged and dropped, missing Tatsuda by a foot to the side as the chunk bounced, smashing off the cliff face, crashing until they lost its sound before it reached the bottom. This was it.

"I can't go any farther," she said to Tatsuda, marveling that her voice sounded steady.

He nodded; his eyes fixed on her gaze. "I'll let go and jump for it."

She swallowed. The rope behind her remained taut. They wouldn't let her fall or be pulled over. Nodding, she said, "Ready." Behind her, a chorus of, "Ready," came from the others. She took another breath and braced herself just as Tatsuda leaped upward. With his left hand, he caught the rope. The rope tightened as she took some of his weight.

"Got him," she said, her shoulder straining.

Tatsuda let go of the roots as he pushed upward and grabbed the rope higher up.

Suddenly, most of his weight hung from the rope and her recovering shoulder and arms. She wiggled backward, grateful for the hold on her legs and for her friends with the rope. Her shoulder burned and something stretched. A sharp stab turned her hand numb, but she didn't let go. Keeping her grip on the rope she slid backward. Once she was back on solid ground, Mason and Walker hauled the rope and she stood up, the rope sliding through her hands as they worked together. The burning sensation in her shoulder remained.

It felt like decades but could have been only a minute until Tatsuda came into sight, climbing in addition to being towed up the cliff. Reaching the edge, Tatsuda clambered over the edge and rolled away from the drop.

"Good thing you have quick reflexes," said Mason, pulling Tatsuda to a stand.

"And nine lives," said Caitlyn, examining his scrapes before wetting a cloth and cleaning them.

"I knew you'd get me," he said, his eyes on Elsa.

She rotated her arm. "We did it together." She gave the edge a respectful distance as she dusted herself off. Only her shoulder seemed worse after the incident. Ignoring it, she leaned over and hugged Tatsuda, squeezing tighter than ever before.

The stunning view of the Utah flatlands and the enormous lake opened up before them—a blue shimmer in the patchwork misty expanse of green farms and seared brown empty land. There was no way down the sheer cliff face unless they turned into one of the hairy white mountain goats or learned to fly like the soaring hawks. Her spirits plummeted. They wouldn't reach the lower level today after all, but it could have been worse.

They spent slow hours hiking without a trail, searching for a way down. The thick forest impeded their view of the path ahead—several attempts led to dead ends and steep cliffs and they had to backtrack. She ground her teeth at their lack of progress.

Eventually, they scrambled along a rocky creek bed in a ravine that ran west and sloped downward. In the spring, it may have been filled with run-off or meltwater as intermittent damp patches appeared in shady sections, but most of it was bone dry with large sharp-edged stones interspersed with smooth, rolling ones. They needed to be careful not to roll an ankle on the unsteady footing.

Elsa hadn't rationed her water much the first day, as the mountain was lush with vegetation, but by the second morning, she measured what remained in her canteen and cautioned the others to drink sparingly. There'd been nothing free-flowing, only patches of mud where it had been before the scorching summer. Since helping Tatsuda up the cliff, her shoulder ached all the time, and her arms and legs were scratched from fighting through bushes. Exhaustion weighed them all down, and even talking was more than any of them could bear.

When they came across a patch of red wild berries on brambles with thorns, Walker recognized them as wild raspberries and Caitlyn confirmed they were edible before they stripped the bushes of their fruit. They picked berries and lingered for half an hour, eating everything ripe.

Hunger and thirst sat heavy with Elsa. The sweet, juicy berries had been a treat, but not filling. Her hollow stomach reminded her of the old days in SoCal. But for all there was danger on the run, her life had improved. Here she had love, friends, and freedom.

Their packed food consisted of jerky and homemade oat bars with dried berries. She wasn't ungrateful, but they reminded Elsa of the processed food bars from the GreenCorps stores in SoCal, the ones she'd grown up eating. At least these had more fruit and were sweeter. With limited warm water to wash the food down, it brought back memories of the Heap, her sister Avery, and life with Granny. She couldn't think of Granny yet without a pang. She missed the old woman every day and it hurt knowing she'd never see her again.

Just then, loud rustling noises came from near where they walked, but out of sight. Not small bird noises, but something larger crashed through the underbrush. She jumped, grabbing Walker's arm.

"Could be bears searching for berries." Walker turned to look behind, probably for Elsa's benefit, adding, "This time of year they're not usually starving. If we meet one, back away. Give them space. They'll probably leave you alone." His voice remained calm and helped her fear to subside.

They'd been stumbling through the bushes, steadily making their way downhill near dusk, having left the creek bed when they turned a corner and came face-to-face with a large hump-backed creature. It had a huge, misshapen head and stood on four long spindly legs that didn't match the bulky body with short brown fur. What was this animal?

As they were about to retreat, more crashing noises came from behind, ones that stopped them dead in their tracks. Elsa's head swiveled and fear gripped her limbs. She wasn't sure where to turn, with something behind them and the enormous animal before them. Were there several? Something that size with those sharp-looking hooves could be dangerous.

The one in front huffed and lowered its massive head with a snort. It took a short charge at them, then stopped after two or three steps and pawed the ground. They'd all frozen in place, other than Walker, who stepped in front of her. Mason slipped one of his guns out of its holster. With an animal that size, he'd need a perfect shot to take it down.

In the underbrush behind them came a mournful moan with additional smashing and crackling sounds. Something broke through and almost bowled Elsa over in its haste. A smaller version of the brown creature stumbled past and ran to its mother. Despite no longer between the mother and its offspring, Elsa's body was taut as a bow, ready for flight. The two animals retreated, crackling through the leafy bushes. After a few dozen steps, their steps became muffled, then splashes. Elsa sighed with relief. She had to get better control of her nerves.

Elsa licked her dry lips and hefted the scant weight of her canteen. No more than a few swallows remained. She listened for the sound of running water, but the forest remained silent. There must be a pond or swamp hidden in the forest. It might be warm and stagnant, but it would be better than nothing. At least it would be wet.

"There's next to no water below on the plains," said Caitlyn, meeting Elsa's eyes. "Unless we rely on farms at night. Some abandoned ones may have wells, but we'll have to stop and check. It'll slow us down and leave us vulnerable to being reported. I'd rather make our way north without being seen."

"We should travel at night when we can. It won't be as hot." Elsa paused. "Should we wait for the animals to move so we can refill our canteens?" She tossed her chin toward the mystery animals.

"I'm out." Mason shook his empty canteen and kept his gaze fixed on the path through the bushes where the large animals had disappeared. "We should fill up."

Tatsuda licked his lips and Elsa swallowed.

"What exactly was that thing?" asked Tatsuda, swiping his long, sweaty bangs from his widened eyes.

Elsa shrugged.

"A moose," said Walker. "You should see the size of the males. With antlers out like this." He opened his arms wide. Elsa wouldn't want to meet one of the males.

One animal snorted again. They had only gone a short distance and the mother probably wouldn't like them coming close to its young again. Following them would be risky, but they couldn't go much farther without refilling the canteens. Maybe the mother would be protective of not just her young, but the water. Getting some might be dangerous, but leaving without it would be foolish.

"So that's a moose," said Caitlyn. "Mathew said they're unpredictable, but good eating. He shot one when he was younger." She looked at Mason. "I believe you were there."

Elsa looked at Walker. Mason and Mathew's history could be the reason for Caitlyn's strange reaction to Mason.

Mason didn't acknowledge the reference to Mathew or the moose, but focused on the current task. "Give me your canteens. I'll steer clear of mama moose."

Elsa shrugged the strap over her head and passed it to him. It was an appreciated offer. The others followed suit. Mason dropped the straps around his shoulders and neck; wearing all five canteens, he looked odd. Mason vanished into the bushes without making much noise. She hadn't noticed until now, but he moved quietly in the woods, especially for one so tall and gangly. He could have been awkward or clumsy, but he wasn't.

"Keep going downhill," he said from just out of sight, his voice low. "I'll join you in a few minutes."

Following the border of the treeline, they continued downhill toward an open field. A few minutes later, Mason joined them and passed around the canteens. Elsa took a swig. The water was brackish, but wet and smelled wholesome. It would have to last until the next time they found fresh water. Some of the tension eased in her shoulders with one less worry. At least today.

* * *

Elsa swallowed, once more down to rationing a mouthful at a time, never enough to slake her thirst, just enough to keep the thirst at bay for as long as possible. Her tongue seemed thick and her mouth a desert. It took discipline not to drink more, despite being something she'd been well-practiced at for most of her life. Walker and Tatsuda took their cue from her, not drinking unless she did.

The sun's merciless glare hurt her eyes, even with her UVee goggles and the scant shade from her hat. Walking during the day had become slow, more like a trudge, as no one had the energy to do more than plod, moving one step after another. The last few days they'd found abandoned buildings and once a derelict metal contraption that had once been a fragment of a long storage container or a transport vehicle where they rested in the mid-afternoon when it was hottest. How would it have felt to have lived through the Collapse? GreenCorps had existed, but it didn't seem like they'd been in control.

It didn't matter who used to own things; anywhere with shade was a relief, even with the scorching temperatures. Even the breeze was hot, wicking the moisture away from them. Nobody had much to say in the intense heat.

They resumed their journey after their quick dinner and continued until it was too dark to see before camping. After a few hours of sleep, they were up again, walking in the chill mornings before the sun came up. Elsa's exhaustion kept the bad dreams away.

The cool time before dawn had become Elsa's favorite time of day. It reminded her of the quiet mornings on the way to work the Heap with Granny. She allowed herself to think of the positive things about her childhood to distract her from their current predicament. By afternoon, she'd be counting steps and imagining water on the horizon as the heat waves created mirages.

The distance between abandoned farms stretched far between. Thin golden grass, seared parchment dry, and chunks of volcanic rock littered the otherwise barren land. Sagebrush clumps, scattered junipers, and long-gone house mounds broke up the flat monotony.

On the fourth day since returning to level ground, came the potato fields—vast expanses of tilled land, knee-deep in green leafy plants in mounded rows. They avoided any place with buildings that looked inhabited and skirted the edges of fields with workers, sometimes dropping to a crawl to retreat. They couldn't chance being seen.

Twice, they'd found abandoned farms with covered wells. One smelled strange. Despite their thirst, they'd turned away with shaking hands, not daring to fill their canteens. They'd get nowhere if they became sick from foul water. That day was the worst.

It was dusk when they stumbled into another farmyard with a collapsed cabin and a barn missing most of its silvered planks. It was the seventh day since they'd left Saints Settlement and eight days since they'd fled Caitlyn's farm. The light was giving out, and they needed to find somewhere to rest. This place would do, if it had water. They were all dead on their feet and parched.

A line of ragged trees ran behind the house, much like those at Caitlyn's, but more unkempt, with saplings jutting out from the surrounding ground. The others paused near the trees while Walker made a beeline for the well at the near side of the abandoned farmyard. He shoved aside the wooden cover and dropped a pebble into the darkness.

"There's water down there," he said. "Smells fine, but there's no bucket."

"I'll go down the well," said Tatsuda. "As long as you can pull me up after.'"

Good for him for offering. He was the lightest and, like her, he wasn't claustrophobic. If it wasn't for her shoulder, Elsa would have volunteered, but climbing back out with a bunch of heavy containers strapped to her would be too much of a strain. She resented her inability to contribute more.

Elsa dug through her pack for the length of coiled rope at the bottom. She'd taken it from the bunker near Sacramento, but hadn't needed it until this trip. She didn't know much about knots, so she handed the rope to Caitlyn, who looped it around Tatsuda's waist and wound it around a nearby fence pole.

Wearing all the canteens, he slid into the dark cylinder and walked down the wall of the well. Walker and Caitlyn held the other end, sliding out slack as needed. Mason and Elsa watched from the top until Tatsuda became a shadow, barely visible.

She lost him in the gloom, but followed his progress by the small sounds he made as he continued. When the water splashed, the rope stopped moving down, instead jerking back and forth. He must be filling the canteens. She waited, shuffling her feet and peering into the well every few seconds. She needed a proper drink, not just a few sips. If they stayed here, they could refill again in the morning. Their best guess was that they were another two days from Aberdeen. Until they passed Pocatello, occupied farms would be difficult to avoid.

The others said that Pocatello was another corporation town, like Long Beach. Here the farmers replaced heapsters, working from dawn to dusk to grow crops for GreenCorps to sell. The pittance the farmers made had to stretch to feed their families. The system was unfair. Elsa ground her teeth. This was another example of what was wrong.

There'd been seed packets in the Davis bunker for several varieties of potatoes, yellow, red, and purple ones, not just brown. Eyed potatoes that could regenerate on their own. Not radiated eyeless potatoes that needed new GreenCorps seed every year. The Aberdeen bunker was supposed to contain small grains. She wasn't sure what that included, but GreenCorps grew wheat as a grain. There should be other grains, though she hadn't heard of other kinds.

"Ready," Tatsuda called after a couple of minutes. Walker and Caitlyn strained at the rope and Mason ran to help.

Elsa joined them, but Walker said, "If you re-injure yourself, you're no good to us later." His words grated, though he said them without anger.

She hated that he was right. Her shoulder had healed outside but wasn't completely repaired on the inside. Jace's knife had gone deep.

They camped in the weathered and decrepit remains of the barn, taking separate empty stalls as bedrooms. She and Walker were desperate for privacy and took advantage of the dark to make love. Hot and sweaty, she fell asleep, half in and half out of their bedding as the night cooled.

She woke once on top of the bedding, covered in goosebumps. Out on the road, with days since signs of their pursuers, the nightmares had receded. She snuggled into Walker, who was always warm. He pulled her into him and draped an arm over her. With a relaxed sigh, she yawned and returned to a dreamless sleep.

The early morning was still cold when she woke. They still hadn't risked a fire for multiple reasons. They were hiding, and they had nothing to cook, but most of all because the land was as dry as tinder. She, Walker, and Tatsuda had been burnt out of their hideaway safehouse in Salt Lake City last June and barely escaped with their lives. A fire out here would burn unchecked. Tatsuda replenished their supply, and they filled up on water for breakfast before departure.

* * *

On the eighth day, with their food stores gone despite stretching it twice as far as Brother Campbell had predicted, they waited in a narrow valley outside Pocatello. This was a corporation town where GreenCorps sponsored farmers brought potatoes to ship them. Walker had disappeared an hour ago and now returned with a pack full of dusty potatoes. Elsa still didn't approve of theft, but their last meal had been early yesterday. Survival was more important than morals. In the end, they were stealing from GreenCorps.

Walker hadn't stolen from the farmers, but had waited to raid the GreenCorps supply depot. They needed somewhere to cook the potatoes, so tonight they'd make a fire and be careful. Her empty stomach clenched at the idea of food, and her dry mouth watered almost painfully. Food was one thing, but water was another. Their need had become critical.

In a small town, owned and operated by GreenCorps, water wouldn't be free, but Elsa had a few coins and Walker had more sewn into secret pockets inside his pack. Though everyone wished to avoid the town, someone would have to go into Pocatello. They'd decided that this morning and adjusted their course, crossing the railroad tracks and following them toward town.

"Who's going into town?" Walker said.

She again couldn't help. The smart play was to remain out of sight. Dead or alive, she was worth a fortune. The sooner GreenCorps forgot about her, the better.

Elsa couldn't trust regular citizens not to turn her in, not when it could change their lives. She caught Mason's eye and saw the keen interest in his eye. Despite his silent, taciturn nature, he'd been steady and dependable. Along the journey, he'd become part of their team. She hadn't found a time to talk to him about her suspicion that Grady was his father. If it was true, he was her kin. He might have been told, but he remained mute on the subject.

"I'll go," said Caitlyn. "No posters of me. Not that I know of. All I've done was harbor fugitives, and it's unlikely word has spread this far yet. They probably don't know about my previous connections to the rebels or I'd have had trouble on the farm earlier. Mason, you and Tatsuda could come." She shifted her attention to Walker and Elsa. "We'll be back in a couple of hours. Try not to miss us." She extended her hand for their canteens.

Elsa disagreed by shaking her head. "I'd be more comfortable if we have something, just in case." She sloshed her canteen. It was less than a quarter full, but some was better than none. If they needed to make a second trip once they'd filled the other canteens, that would work.

Caitlyn nodded and headed into town, trailed by Mason and Tatsuda.

Elsa and Walker leaned back to wait in the shade, hoping the others soon returned.

CHAPTER 13: MASON

Mason stretched out his stride as he followed Caitlyn and Tatsuda down the dusty path. It was fortunate Caitlyn had invited him on the trip. Getting a sense of the town and what had changed in the larger world over the past week had been something he needed to do. He would have gone on his own if not for the invite. This was better. He got to spend time with her without everyone overhearing their conversation.

He and Walker had shared a look before Mason left, tacit agreement to watch out for trouble. They'd spoken little, but they'd helped secure their campsite each night and looked after the others without being obvious. Neither Caitlyn nor Elsa would thank them if their protection was obvious, but they could keep it subtle and it was worth doing. Both women were tough and natural leaders, but they shouldn't have the entire burden of responsibility.

"Have you been here before?" Mason said as they left the camp. Tatsuda shook his head and smiled before dashing farther up the path on his own.

"I'm not really up for talking," said Caitlyn. "It's too hot."

She wasn't wrong about the heat, but it wouldn't kill her to be polite. Instead of being annoyed, he focused inward to assimilate all the new information he'd gleaned these past few days.

Walker loved Elsa. That was plain for anyone with eyes to see. The big man would throw himself in front of a train for her if it would help. Elsa was just as crazy about him, if you looked closely, and saw past her guarded exterior. Her eyes glowed and her face softened when she didn't know anyone else was watching. Walker and Elsa had become each other's family, and he'd bet it was permanent. He'd never thought that was something he wanted for himself, but, glancing at Caitlyn, now he wasn't so sure.

Grady had said Elsa was his kin, but Mason couldn't see any resemblance to himself or Grady. She was descended from his uncle's family, long thought lost to the Heap—dead by callous GreenCorps exile. Nobody'd expected the infant sent with Aki Lee to survive without her mother. A SoCal work camp was no place for a newborn. However, the tough old lady who'd been a rebel leader, had not just raised the baby on her own, but her granddaughters as well. This meant that besides Walker and Elsa, Mason had this Avery girl and her daughters as members of his family. He wasn't sure what to think of that. He'd been on his own a long time.

Growing up, his only family had been his mother. They'd been poor, like everyone, but better off than some. Mystery packages and coin showed up at regular intervals from an unknown source. Mason had never known his father as a child, but he'd never been forgotten or overlooked. As a child, he'd always resented the man who could send money for him but never show his face. Now, as an adult, he was content with having earned the man's respect these last twelve years.

Caitlyn had figured out his father's identity. As had Darren, Grady's right-hand man. Mason and Grady looked enough alike that, for those close to the rebel leader, it could be obvious. Caitlyn had suggested that it wasn't for lack of feeling, but Grady's sense of duty—to protect his son.

If GreenCorps had known Grady had a son, they'd have exploited him, used him to flush out his father long ago. If the price on Elsa's head was twenty gold, what was it on Grady's? A hundred? Some unknown fortune. Yet nobody turned him in. He had the loyalty of the people.

Not just those in Utah, but the downtrodden and rebels throughout the West. He and the rebels gave many a sense of hope.

Mason glanced at Caitlyn as they walked along the dusty trail beside the railroad tracks and peeled off toward town. Tatsuda still scampered ahead, continuing toward the train station, disappearing from sight into the distance. Soon, the boy would be out of earshot. He should worry about the kid and how he'd fare at the station with all the security, but if anyone was an accomplished sneak, it was Tatsuda.

He was so quiet that it was easy to forget that he was around. The rascal had light fingers, too. Mason checked his pocket. His coins were still there. Elsa had required Tatsuda to give them back twice this week, both times before Mason had realized they were missing. The boy might return from town with something useful, even without a stock of coin.

Mason and Caitlyn were alone together for the first time since the initial night on the farm. The silence stretched between them to the point of breaking.

"How did you and Mathew meet?" The words sprang from his dry mouth. He jammed his hands in his pockets, trying to look casual, but he'd been dying to find out how she'd come to be in Utah with the rebels. Dawson's farm was the last place he'd expected to see his onetime love. His jaw had hit the ground when she'd emerged from the barn the first day and he'd been reeling ever since.

"You may remember that my parents were miners in Denver." At his nod, she continued. "We weren't wealthy, but they had steady work and we ate. The mine collapsed when I was sixteen and they died." To his surprise, when speaking about an emotional subject, she kept her voice even. "Shortly before their accident, my parents shared their good news. They'd saved enough to buy me an apprenticeship with the mine's medic. What makes you ask now?" Her slanted look made his heart skip.

Maybe she wasn't indifferent. The blue of her eyes sent him daydreaming every time she looked at him.

"First chance I've had to ask without everyone listening. Maybe you don't want everyone knowing your business or about your past." He didn't intend to share his life story with everyone yet, even if he liked them. His childhood wasn't relevant, and his relationship with Grady was awkward and private.

"They're friends. Elsa wants to do something amazing for all of us. I'm proud I can help. If we can get into another of the seed bunkers and share them with the Western Canadians, it will benefit everyone. Well, everyone except GreenCorps and the wealthy." She paused so long he wondered if she would continue when she at last she spoke, her voice soft but passionate. "Living in Utah near the rebels and the Saints, you forget how much worse it is in places controlled by GreenCorps. Walker and Tatsuda would do anything for her, and I find I want to, too. We're caught up in something bigger than just us. I don't care if they hear my history. I have nothing to hide." Her last words were as sharp as a knife.

"I agree with their goal, but I didn't know what you'd consider private. I was trying to be polite." He snapped the head off a tall golden timothy weed and stuck the lower end in his mouth. Sometimes it helped with the thirst.

It was several seconds before he spoke again. "Will you please tell me how you and Mathew met? I never knew your full name. I called you Kate or my Angel, and you let me. I had no idea you were who Mathew had married." Mason's mouth twisted on the last word.

"I didn't know your last name either. You said it was safer for me not to know, but it meant when you left, that I had no way to find you. I didn't think I'd ever see you again. By the time I met Mathew, it had been so long. You didn't come back the way you'd promised." Her blue eyes slanted in his direction again, slaying him with their power.

A considerable amount of time had passed. She'd been fifteen, and he'd been sixteen. Too young to be serious. He'd just lost his mother and had hopped his first and only train. Mathew had refused to leave his parent's farm, so Mason had gone alone. He'd fallen in with some older hoppers who had roughed him up and stolen his supplies. They'd left him for dead, sprawled beside the tracks outside Denver. While he recovered, he'd seen so many people in the Denver slums who'd been unable to get ahead, even many with jobs, like Caitlyn's parents. Paying for her to be a medic was a rare accomplishment. Most despaired and turned to drink.

Caitlyn had found him, nursed him back to health in secret, then helped him join three families making a convoy to Salt Lake City, where he'd returned to Mathew and the Dawson's. The next spring, when they'd turned seventeen, they'd joined the rebels.

Her lack of inflection made him pause. He glanced at her profile. "You weren't a medic when I first met you." That topic should be safe.

"You're the reason I became a medic. You were my first patient." She raised her eyebrow.

Did she regret helping him? Or regret this conversation. His chest hurt and he lashed out.

"Medic or farmer?" He winced at his tone and shot her a rueful look of apology, wishing he could take back the question. He'd sounded ungrateful, bitter. He was happy she'd loved Mathew. He only wished her happiness and Mat had deserved a tough, beautiful woman— someone who would have been a real partner.

The tense silence stretched out, and they walked the next few moments in their own thoughts until the city loomed ahead.

Brick buildings lined the dusty streets of Pocatello. Not much to this isolated town. The train station and a small town courtyard with the usual GreenCorps stores and pleasure houses that kept the railroad men and soldiers occupied in their off-duty hours. They should be able to buy water, even if it cost too much. He stopped and touched Caitlyn's arm to get her attention. Electricity buzzed between them.

She shook off his hand. He might have overstepped.

He moved back to give her space as he glanced around. They were almost to the town, though at this time of the late afternoon, few people were about, and nobody was close enough to hear.

"You didn't answer my original question."

"I met Mathew when I was twenty. He came into the Med Center where I worked. His brother had been brought in because he'd collapsed on the job site." Her voice changed, becoming softer, like she was no longer angry.

"John," said Mason with a sharp nod. "Dumb junkie kid. We warned him not to play with drugs. I always guessed that would be what got him. He couldn't give up the high."

"Yeah. But he was Mathew's family, dumb or not. His brother wouldn't stay at the Center for long enough to get clean. Mathew brought him in twice more that summer to get treatment. Each time, Mathew and I talked a little more. Pretty soon, he was coming by a few times a week without his brother. Sometimes he'd bring lunch, or we'd go for walks in the evening. When John died from an overdose, I was there. We got close, and I didn't have anyone else. He proposed and brought me back to Utah to meet his folks, his youngest brother Clark, and Grady. We worked with the rebels until he died." She kept her voice low so they wouldn't be overheard. You couldn't be too careful mentioning Grady's name.

Mason's throat tightened. He should've gone back to Denver. He'd abandoned her. He hadn't believed she would wait for a nobody like him. With time and distance, he'd chalked up their feelings to teenage infatuation, the kind that wouldn't last. It had taken seeing Caitlyn in her farmyard for the thunderbolt to strike. He'd been searching for her his whole adult life without knowing. No one else had measured up. She'd stolen his heart when he was sixteen.

Seeing Caitlyn now a woman, one with curves he tried not to stare at, and the perfect sway to her walk. He could still imagine the willowy angel, his Kate, who'd saved him half his lifetime ago. His first love, who he'd promised to go back for when he was settled. He never had. One of the biggest regrets of his life. How did he say all that? He couldn't, so he did what he was good at, bottle it up inside. It had been fifteen years, but it seemed like yesterday.

Mason cleared his throat. "Mathew was good to you?" Of course, his friend had been decent. The Dawsons had been good people—his second family when he'd needed one. What had happened to the rest of the Dawsons? Caitlyn had returned to an empty farm.

She turned back, a single tear sliding down her cheek, but she seemed unaware. "He treated me like gold and promised he'd never leave. But just like everyone else, he did." She spoke half in a dream, her mind somewhere far away.

Mason kept his voice soft when he spoke. "I heard it happened in Dallas." It had been a gut punch when he'd learned of Mat's death, even though they'd no longer been close. The ambush had been fatal for a dozen rebels. If she didn't want to talk about it, she could say so. It surprised Mason when she answered.

With her voice still dreamy, she said. "We were in Texas, freeing sex workers from GreenCorps. Young women who'd been taken or sold south without their consent. They'd been forced to work the pleasure houses to survive. Like Sister Hope. We'd gotten good at those rescues. Efficient. Maybe too arrogant because of it. We'd hit a dozen transports and five workcamps that spring and gotten too casual. A third guard in the train car with the girls came as a surprise. He sounded an alarm and shot Mathew in the stomach. They killed a dozen other rebels outside. All of those we'd tried to save were gunned down like rabid animals. I hung back to stop Mathew's bleeding and somehow, they overlooked us as night fell. I'm still puzzled about how I got Mathew away and to the safehouse where I tried to patch him up."

Caitlyn shook her head. "I got the bullet out and bought antibiotics, but it was no use. His wound got infected. Some medic." Her voice was flat as she finished. "The most important person in my life and I had to watch him die."

"You left the rebellion. I'm surprised you didn't go back to Denver." He tried to keep the judgment from his voice, but her sharp glance said he'd been unsuccessful.

Her cornflower-blue eyes met his, her look piercing like an arrow. He didn't look away, though she might see his desire. Every word made him want her more. To earn back her respect, perhaps her love. She didn't have to be alone.

"I was on the front line for nine years straight," she said, heat infusing her words at last. She was a goddess with fire reddening her cheeks. "I patched up hundreds of kids who thought they were invincible, just to get careless and shot dead. I took care of dozens of battered women and found them better lives. Only a few of my friends lived to fight another day. I thought I'd lost everyone I'd ever cared about." She pulled on her long braid as she stopped to face him squarely.

"Turns out Grady and Darren are still there. They're my family now. Elsa, Walker, and Tatsuda are good kids, and I believe in their cause. I want to help someone be successful and take the fight to GreenCorps. They can't get away with bullying us forever."

Her brilliant eyes looked straight through him. "How about you? Why are you here?" She stepped closer, daring him to answer.

Mason looked down at the packed earth where they stood at the edge of town. It was still quiet, but the shift would change at the station and the railroad workers would soon flood toward the bars. "Grady told me about Elsa being our kin. And about the bunkers. He said he wanted to give me a chance to be a part of bringing a better future to Utah and the West. That Elsa was the real deal. I wanted to see for myself." He'd seen that and more. In little more than a week, he'd become part of a team, and he enjoyed being part of something important. As a rebel, that had long been his dream to do something that mattered.

"We've got stuff to do. We should quit talking. The others could use food and water and they're counting on us." Caitlyn's face shut down, closing off her emotions—keeping him at a distance.

The market square lay beyond them a hundred yards away, and music carried on the wind from an open door. He and Caitlyn had only a couple of hours before everything closed for the night, except the pleasure houses and bars. Once, those establishments would have been tempting, but no longer. He couldn't think of anyone except Caitlyn. She haunted his dreams and starred in his fantasies. He took a deep breath. They needed to find water, get supplies, and leave Pocatello. It wasn't safe to linger.

Despite being a small town, the GreenCorps accommodations were extensive. This was an important food production area and the train and farms would be guarded accordingly. With the wheat blight having destroyed most of that crop several times in the last fifty years, potatoes were an important source of carbohydrates and a major cash crop. GreenCorps guarded the seeds like gold, making them expensive on the black market in Salt Lake City. It had surprised him to see them growing on Caitlyn's farm. The potatoes these farmers bought wouldn't grow beyond one planting. They'd been modified by GreenCorps.

Mason wiped his brow and shoved his hat back on, glancing toward the rows of brick barracks sat by the station, reminding him about Tatsuda, who was on his own. "What about Tatsuda?"

"He'll meet us back with Walker and Elsa. He just came to give them time alone," she said, striding into town without looking to check if he followed.

"To the trainyard?" He didn't expect an answer and wasn't disappointed. They'd connected for a few moments and for that, he hoped they could at least be friends.

He headed toward the nearest shop. It didn't matter which one they used. The exorbitant prices would be the same.

Elsa's image and someone who could be Walker stared out from a Wanted poster on the front window. It was a reasonable likeness, especially the eyes. Elsa hadn't exaggerated. She needed to keep away from town or she'd be caught.

Caitlyn nodded. "Tatsuda will see if there's news, train schedules, and small shiny objects." Her soft laugh told him she'd moved past the intense conversation. "We might hop back on the train here after we've returned from the bunker in Aberdeen. Head for Canada. Have you given thought to coming all that way? Or do you have urgent rebel business elsewhere?" Her eyes dared him to answer.

He didn't want to discuss the future. "Let's find the water."

CHAPTER 14: GINGER

Ginger sniffed her sweaty armpits and grimaced. She'd only brought a couple of changes of clothes, and without access to water, she couldn't wash. Living rough had several disadvantages. She sat behind her usual dumpster, waiting for the sun to go down. She was giving up on Pocatello.

Hunger gnawed at her bones and stole her energy, making her listless. She didn't have the required energy for another door-to-door search tonight. She stared at her chipped nails and the raw patches at the ends of her fingers, the skin flaking and raw. A couple of places had cracked and bled, so she needed to be more careful not to worry at them. A bath would feel like heaven. Or even a quick shower with lotion afterward. She sighed and considered the upside of her shabby appearance. She was coated in a thin layer of grime and even the air tasted like dust. She didn't look like a pampered rich girl anymore. As far as disguises went, it wasn't half bad.

Tonight, she'd risk hopping back onto the train. She'd returned to the living quarters with the food and water three more times before someone had locked the door. She hadn't found another open door. Either they'd noticed the stolen water ration or the pilfered food.

Ginger had half a jar of water remaining but hadn't found other sources; everyone was too careful. There were no outdoor taps, hoses, or wells. She'd seen people in the alley plug tokens into water meters on the outside of the buildings, something their house in Denver hadn't needed. The water came in only for the day in these homes. She didn't have coins or tokens. If only she'd taken some from her father. He might not have noticed, but she hadn't dared. Now it was too late.

Her initial thought was to stay in this town and figure out her next move, but she'd need a job. She didn't grow potatoes and she didn't want to sell her body, and as far as she could tell those were her only options. Maybe there'd be something different she could do for work in a bigger city. Maybe Sacramento or New Vegas. She was literate. There had to be a decent job out there somewhere. She tried to stay positive.

Ginger had also run out of food, except two granola bars that she was saving for her journey. She wasn't brave enough to reveal herself or ask for help from anyone in Pocatello. The locals' lives looked little better than hers. Her fears of what she had learned proved to be true. It was shocking seeing the conditions for regular people in this small town.

Perhaps she should check the train station for information, but that might be too dangerous. It seemed busy there all day, every day. What had her father done about her absence? He might have disowned her. Had he put out a reward for her return? She felt like Denver was still too close. Finding out could wait until the next town.

Ginger's stomach rumbled, and she looked down. Most of the people she'd seen in town were thin and boney. With a week of limited food, she'd lost weight too. She wasn't slim like the others, but her clothes hung differently than a week ago. At this rate, it wouldn't be long until she fit in with the locals. She couldn't remember her last proper meal. Or she could, but didn't want to. A vision of her father's chosen suitor, her supposed betrothed, flashed before her eyes. That was one way to lose her appetite. There'd been ample food on the table that night, but she'd only picked at it—everything had tasted like ash.

The next place the train stopped might be better, but she couldn't imagine how most people made a living. Pocatello was a strange town, without many houses and not enough businesses. It wasn't what she was used to. Denver had neighborhoods filled with houses where people lived and stores for books, paper, soap and cosmetics, jewelry, and clothes. Not that she'd enjoyed the freedom to shop in Denver; she'd seen it from her window on the hillside. Most houses weren't as nice as her father's grand mansion, but the city had been filled with smaller homes for the shopkeepers, soldiers, tradespeople, and shacks for the miners.

Here, whores lived upstairs above the brothels; a few others, employed by GreenCorps, lived above the shops, but most folk worked the potato farms that surrounded the town. GreenCorps soldiers patrolled the farms in teams and lived in barracks behind the train station. She'd never noticed the plastic tokens that seemed vital in a GreenCorps town until all the farmers had bargained for them in trade for their crops at the station, counting and recounting before they left.

The house she'd snuck into a few times probably belonged to a GreenCorps railroad official who could afford daily water tokens as a matter of course and fresh food. Trust her to have been trespassing on dangerous territory.

Pushing to her feet, Ginger trudged along the dusty path to the railroad tracks at twilight, while the last of the sunset faded and the sky turned to purple velvet. This was another thing she liked about being away from the mountains and home. Here, the sky stretched on, almost without limit, making it feel like anything was possible.

Westbound trains came through every other day in the evening, or so she'd discovered during the last week. Hers had not been the only train. Tonight, scared or not, she'd be ready to sneak aboard at the first opportunity. The other unappealing choice was starving to death.

The train would be loaded with bulky burlap sacks of potatoes by dark. Her only worry was if the train would have some of the right kind of cars, like the one she'd arrived on. The day before yesterday, the train had looked impossible to sneak aboard. She wanted to get on without having to open a boxcar filled with potatoes. That looked too difficult, plus it would be harder to sneak if she had to deal with barred doors and sliding metal that scraped. The GreenCorps bulls wouldn't miss that much noise.

She didn't want to walk too close to the station until it was safer, so she settled into wait for the darkness of night to descend.

Ginger hadn't been settled long, behind a large stone and half in the bushes, when a pair of GreenCorps recruits in their black and green uniforms wandered up the tracks, their feet crunching in the gravel. They stopped near her hiding place. There was just enough light left to identify that they were soldiers. It was too dim to discern their faces, but not so dark that she felt secure. She ducked lower in the bushes and tried to calm her breathing.

One soldier pulled something from inside his shirt and leaned against the stone. Whatever he held flashed silver with reflected light. She couldn't see what he had, but he drank a huge gulp before coughing. In the distance, the glow of the station's porch light looked brighter as the shadows deepened. These young men probably had snuck away from their posts and thought they were alone. It was just back luck that they'd chosen her rock as their drinking spot.

"It's the good stuff," the soldier said before passing it to his companion.

The second recruit took a drink with a similar fit of coughing. They passed their illicit drink back and forth as they talked. At first, most of their words were too quiet to make out, but it must have been strong alcohol, because soon their voices grew louder, their words slurred. She couldn't concentrate on their conversation as her mind drifted to memories of her brother due to their foul language. Jaxon had been like that most nights after dinner, at least when drinking their father's alcohol. She focused.

"You hear what they did to that farmer that tried to hide some of his crop? He *claimed* bugs ate it. One of the field hands tipped us off." The soldier's voice sounded excited, pleased to share gossip.

Regardless of her apprehension about what she might hear, she leaned in.

"Nope, but I know what they shoulda done." The second voice was harder.

"They brought his family outside and held guns to his kids' heads. Threatened to kill them if he didn't find the missing potatoes. He suddenly remembered the new cellar below the barn. He'd built a false back inside the storm cellar, covering a whole second hidden area of cold storage. He brought back enough bagged potatoes to fill a wagon. Can you believe the greedy thief tried to steal from GreenCorps?"

"They teach him a lesson?" The second man's voice was disdainful.

"Took the potatoes, one of his daughters, and beat him bloody. He'll think twice before withholding crops from us again."

Bile rose in her throat. They'd taken the farmer's daughter? Taken her where? How could this man gloat? It was cruel.

His voice continued. "We made sure all the temp field workers saw him get what he deserved. Word will spread. We shouldn't have trouble for a couple of seasons. Not withholding crops trouble anyway."

Ginger covered her mouth in horror. It wasn't fair that the farmers should starve when they grew the food. Her father had complained about their greed before, but everyone was so thin. The actual conditions in Pocatello had opened her eyes. If the farmers were corrupt, shouldn't they be wealthy, even if their regular field hands or the temp harvest workers were poor? That didn't seem to be the case. She'd been lurking in town long enough to see that everyone looked half-starved and exhausted. Plus, even in the dark, these two men looked like her, lean but clearly well-fed. It was unfair.

"They should cut the water supply," said the second man. "That works like a dream at home in SoCal. We've tightened the screws there. I left as part of Jaxon McCoy's personal detail. We're out here hunting the bitch who stole from GreenCorps."

"The one worth twenty gold?"

"Yeah. I've known that bitch Elsa most of my life. I'd know her anywhere. If she comes through town, we'll get her. We've each been promised a cut of the reward if our patrol brings her to justice. Not just McCoy."

"You think she's likely to come this way?"

Ginger's thighs burned from crouching so long, and distracted at hearing her brother's name, she shifted her weight. Something snapped beneath her foot. She froze, willing the two men to be too drunk to notice.

"Who's there?" said one man, lurching closer to her hiding place, his feet crunching on the gravel.

She held her breath, hoping he'd give up if he heard nothing else. Time crawled.

Neither of the men spoke. She peeked but couldn't see them and she didn't know where they'd gone. Without their voices as a guide to their location, they could be anywhere. She crouched lower and slipped her hand over her mouth once more, afraid her breath or the hammering in her chest would give her away. Rivers of sweat ran down her back and her legs shook.

The night's silence became heavy. What were they doing? She shifted her weight, this time without a sound. They must not know where she was. A faint whisper came from her right, and the hair on her neck stood on end. Was it the wind or was she being watched?

She lifted her head and turned. Black trousers covering long legs stood beside her. She rose and stepped back, glancing at the hard eyes staring in her direction. His eyes caught a gleam of light from the station, shining orange and feral. Her breath caught, and she took another step back, intending to run. She bumped into the warmth of another person and before she could react, someone grabbed her arm from behind. He twisted it behind her back, wrenching her shoulder as he held it. Pain stabbed through her and she tried not to sob or give in to full-scale panic. Her breath came in gasps that seemed loud in the night.

His alcoholic breath whispered in her ear. "We've found us a playmate." The hard-voiced man with the dark beard stood before her, and her legs trembled.

Her stomach lurched from the strong fumes and bile choked her throat. "I wasn't doing anything." Her voice quavered and tears flowed as she stared at the man, only his eyes and teeth visible in the scant light.

He nodded and the second man twisted her arm and shoulder tighter. She cried out, and he clamped a dirty hand smelling of gunpowder and grease over her mouth. He dragged her backward, pulling her off her feet. Her toes dangled inches above the ground. She felt helpless, unable to regain her footing. He hauled her away from the exposed train tracks, deeper into the darkness. Away from both the town and train station, where they would be alone. She couldn't breathe.

Ginger struggled and flailed, but couldn't get away, her sounds no more than whimpers. She wanted to scream but couldn't, not with his hand pressing against her mouth and the tightness that spread across her chest. She tried to bite him so she could escape, but he was too strong. The small, muffled sounds she made wouldn't carry more than a few feet. No one would hear and no one would save her.

The man kept his hold as he dragged her further into the dark. The other man's crackling footsteps indicated that he'd followed. They stopped and someone yanked her pants to her ankles. The rush of cool air on her bare skin gave her goosebumps.

"Get her on all fours," the second man said to the one holding her. "If she fights, hit her hard enough and she'll stop."

She shivered at the words and the pain in her shoulder intensified until she couldn't stand it. He forced her to her knees, the hard ground painful and stony. She tried to fight again, but her arms were pinned and with her pants around her ankles, she couldn't kick. The second man crouched in front of her and stroked her cheek, his hand feeling icy cold on her warm flesh. He stood and unbuckled his belt. The sliding leather and buckle sound grated on her knife-edge nerves. This couldn't be happening. It couldn't be real.

The man stuck his hand down his pants and stroked himself. "Get ready to hold her down. If you can keep her quiet, you can have her next."

Ginger's eyes widened and scalding tears seared her cheeks as one of them punched her in the side, her breath knocked out of her. With her bare ass in the air, one man gripped her neck and throat while she gasped and the second fondled her from behind.

"What kind of whore are you? You need a bath," said the man holding her.

"Doesn't matter much, but I prefer them clean." He leaned over and spoke into her ear. "Back home at Ginny's, her girls bathe daily. You might want to consider that." Sliding a hand inside her shirt, he squeezed her breast. It hurt. "She's got great titties. This is a nice, well-fed whore for all that she stinks." He slapped her ass, the sharp sound and sting bringing her back to reality.

She had to get away.

Her strained breathing became loud in the night's silence, but she didn't have the breath to scream—not with the tight hands squeezing her throat. Her vision filled with spots as she fought to stay conscious, her limbs giving out. She collapsed to the ground. She hadn't imagined people could be so cruel.

Suddenly, something whizzed through the air and struck the man holding her throat.

He grabbed his head and yelled. "What the fuck. I'm bleeding."

He let go, and she rolled, but tangled in her dangling clothes, she couldn't move far. Still unable to scream, she gulped for air and fought her tears as she half scrambled, half crawled away.

Another stone struck the other man and bounced, landing beside her on the ground. Her chest heaved as she tried to stand. She grabbed the rock and pounded it against the first man's head like a hammer as he grabbed for her. He dropped to the ground while she stumbled and fell back to her knees. Several more stones flew toward her remaining attacker, who'd lurched toward the bushes, trying to find the thrower of stones. Ginger covered her head with her arms, hoping not to be hit.

At last, she got to her feet. Grabbing her pants, she pulled them up, intending to run. A hand grabbed her foot and yanked. She fell back to the ground, scraping her hands and banging her knees on the rough ground. Something hit the man's head and his neck snapped backward. He whirled around, once more looking for his attacker. His companion remained a motionless shadow by his feet. Another rock hit the bearded man in the cheek and he ran, headed for the station.

He spun once to shout, "Whoever you are, you'll be sorry."

She crawled back toward the tracks, using the sagebrush as cover. Maybe if they couldn't see her, she'd get away. She scrambled through the bushes, at last making it back to the railway. She was terrified to go much farther in case the man returned.

If he found her alone, he might finish what he'd started. She paused for breath by the boulder where she'd hidden. Shards of her water jar lay beside it, the wet ground a stain on the dry earth. She felt wrung out, and the loss of her precious water was almost her breaking point.

A hushed voice came from the darkness to her right. "Psst. Over here. Come with me."

Not knowing what else to do, she angled herself toward the voice and ran. Behind her, an alarm sounded at the station. She glanced back. Men poured from the barracks behind the trainyard. She needed to go. Now.

From the darkness, a warm hand touched her arm, and she flinched.

"Come with me. I know a safe place. This way." The quiet voice repeated the instructions, tugging to the left.

Ginger followed, running parallel to the tracks, away from the station, and leaving town. It didn't matter who he was or where they were going. It was better than staying here.

CHAPTER 15: ELSA

Elsa and Walker arranged their camp outside Pocatello in a ravine, making it secure for the night since they had time while they waited. Sweat trickled in rivulets down her back and soaked her shirt. Even after the sun set in a blaze of glory, it remained sweltering with radiating heat. As soon as they finished, she sat to conserve energy. The past few days had been draining.

They'd hidden in a shallow valley in the undulating hills. Walker felt it would be safe enough to dig out a fire pit to roast the potatoes. Elsa's mouth watered at the prospect of a proper meal. It had been three days since they'd had more than a few bites of jerky, and her stomach felt hollow. She passed the too-light canteen to Walker, who shook his head. He wouldn't drink either, not until the others returned with more.

What if the others didn't make it back? Walker would probably risk sneaking into town for supplies. They wouldn't survive another day without water. She refused to dwell on her worry about Caitlyn and Mason. Tatsuda would be back, though; she could count on that. There wasn't a reward for his capture, and he was adept at moving through towns. The only time they'd caught him was getting off a train in Salt Lake City, and that had been a deliberate move on his part to obtain information.

Elsa sighed. Unable to go to into town herself, she was useless. She felt ill depending on others for food and water. She'd rather get it herself. She picked up a palm-sized flat rock and threw it a couple of feet away; it clattered off another rock and bounced.

"They'll be back," said Walker, looking up from the firepit he was lining with flat rocks. "Mason and Caitlyn are capable and Tatsuda is… well, Tatsuda. He'll be fine." His gray eyes twinkled.

He already knew her so well. She hated people she cared about being in danger because of her.

"You're right. How long do you think they'll be?" She squinted at the fading light, a restless feeling inside. Something important was happening. While hoping it was something good, her gut said otherwise.

Walker stretched and climbed part-way up the bank, peering in the direction where the others had gone. He looked around and slid back down. "Mason and Caitlyn are almost here."

Elsa sprang up and ran to help with their burdens. They each carried a water jug and a bag that looked heavy. Hopefully filled with food. There was no sign of Tatsuda. He must have gone his own way.

"Any trouble?" asked Elsa, hurrying across the baked ground. The sun had set, but it was not yet dark. She peered up the path, still hoping to see Tatsuda. Like a mother hen, she couldn't help but fret, even if he was resourceful.

Mason answered with a quick shake of his head. "Lots of posters. It's smart that you didn't come. The new picture looks more like you than the old one I saw in Salt Lake."

Her heart sank. She'd never get to see a town or collect supplies if she had to watch her back at every turn. How long would it take GreenCorps to forget her face? Given what she'd done, it would be far longer than she hoped.

"Security is high here too," said Caitlyn. "There's a small reward for information about some runaway rich kid. The storekeeper also mentioned that a McCoy is in town. You said that Jace had a brother?" Her eyebrow raised with the question.

Elsa nodded. "Jaxon's here?" She took Caitlyn's water jug with her good arm and they headed back down the slope into their hidden ravine. It was a few degrees cooler below.

Caitlyn continued as they walked. "From what we heard, this McCoy takes it personally that you're still free. He's brought a special force out this way to search. Doubt you'll be surprised, but he led the group that missed us at the farm. His people have been bragging that they know where you're going. Supposedly, he came here to wait." She frowned and stopped. "We could have gone anywhere. How did he know to come here?"

Mason put his share of the supplies on the ground near Walker while the women talked.

"Do you think GreenCorps knows that there's a bunker in Aberdeen?" said Caitlyn.

Elsa chewed her dry lip as she considered the question. "I doubt they can get in, but they might know there's something there. They've had almost two hundred years to learn about the bunkers."

"How would Jaxon McCoy know where they are? Could Hayden have said something?" said Mason as he rejoined the group.

"I didn't tell him anything or show him the maps," Elsa said with a frown. "We're just going to be extra careful." She closed her hand around the key inside her shirt.

"Maybe this McCoy's just lucky," said Caitlyn. "And he wants you caught."

"Killing his brother, that's pretty personal," said Mason, his face as neutral as usual.

He might be unaware of the rest of the history between Elsa and Jaxon. "It goes back farther. Jaxon is married to my sister and doesn't treat her right." Elsa grabbed the water jug she'd set on the ground. "We've never liked each other, so the feeling's mutual."

Mason's impassive face gave away nothing at the information about how Elsa was connected to the McCoys. She hadn't meant to keep it from him, but she preferred not to talk about Jaxon. Thoughts of the McCoy brothers came too close to her nightmares about Jace.

"What about Tatsuda? Did he mention where he was going?" Elsa bit her lip, needing to change the subject. Walker joined their group, resting his hand on Elsa's hip.

"The train station," said Caitlyn. "We considered looking for him, but he'd be more inconspicuous without us around. Travelers like us just stopping for supplies is one thing. Hanging around the trains would be too noticeable. One stranger is easy to overlook, especially one young like him. Three is too many."

Mason picked up Elsa's canteen, filled it with a nod, and passed it to her. She tipped it back right away. The cool water slipped down her dry throat like nectar. Water had never been more delicious. After a second swallow, she passed it to Walker.

The light dimmed further while they spoke and Walker lit a small fire in the sunken fire pit. The ground would hide the flames and the darkness would hide the smoke. This afternoon, they had collected as much wood as they could from further up the gorge, most from the dead pine trees nearby. Walker had also carried back a few larger pieces of wood he'd found on his excursion to get the potatoes. With his set-up, the potatoes would roast on hot rocks heated by the fire's embers.

When the fire was burning on its own, crackling through the medium-sized branches of dry wood, Walker lined the potatoes around the perimeter of the pit. Mason passed around the filled canteens, while the others rested. Elsa listened for their other companion as dinner cooked, her ears straining at the tiniest sound. But the trail above remained empty, with no sign of Tatsuda. She wouldn't rest easy until he was back.

"I'll keep watch up top," Mason said after a while.

He didn't wait for an answer, but disappeared over the bank above them, not caring that it was steep. His soft footsteps didn't go far, and he settled nearby with a sigh. He must want them to know where he was or they wouldn't have heard a sound.

Elsa could hardly wait until the potatoes were ready, but she sipped her water and felt her energy revive while she stared at the dancing flames, listening to the hiss of the potatoes which steamed through the vents Walker had stabbed in their brown skins. While they sat, breathing in the aroma of cooking food, Walker turned the potatoes and repositioned them closer to the hot coals, their skins looking browned in the firelight. Her hands shook as she dug out the dishes for dinner.

From above, there were quiet voices and then Tatsuda scrambled down the bank, followed by Mason and a strange teenage girl with long hair and a dirty face. In the firelight, her hair glinted with hints of red. The girl met Elsa's stare with one of her own.

"Who's this?" Why would Tatsuda bring a stranger to camp? Maybe he had a reason, but now the scruffy girl knew where they camped. Would the girl turn them in?

"Jaxon McCoy is in town." Tatsuda looked around and, perhaps seeing no surprise on their faces, elaborated. "I didn't know who he was before, but he's the same GreenCorps officer I heard talking outside Hayden's card game. I recognized his voice."

The girl stood behind Tatsuda, shying away from both Walker and Mason, maintaining distance without trying to be obvious, casting uneasy looks in their direction. Perhaps men made her nervous. Her shirt was torn, and she had a scrape on her cheek, as well as streaks in the dirt like she'd been crying.

"Who's your friend?" Elsa kept her voice casual. The stranger didn't need to know how on edge she was.

"This is Geri," said Tatsuda, shooting a smile at the girl. "She was having trouble with a couple of GreenCorps recruits who'd dragged her off into the bushes alone in the dark."

Elsa's heart went out to the girl. Her nightmare flashed before her eyes. Jace's hands on her. His leering face. She shuddered.

"Are you okay, Honey?" said Caitlyn, standing up. "Did they hurt you?"

The girl's wide blue eyes turned to Caitlyn and filled with tears, sparkling in the firelight. Her lips quivered and she shook her head without speaking.

A near miss, then. Good thing Tatsuda had happened past.

"I heard the noises and threw rocks at them from the darkness." Tatsuda's eyes flashed with anger, and his tone indicated strong disapproval. "I made sure they couldn't see me and I kept moving so they didn't find me. I knocked one down and Geri knocked him unconscious. I chased the other one away. He ran back toward the station for reinforcements, but don't worry, I made sure we lost them long before we cut back here."

Their story dredged up her own terrible memories of that night months ago at Ginny's. The nightmare hovered; she wouldn't sleep tonight. Good thing Mason had volunteered for the first watch. She'd be all nerves and jumping at shadows. At least in bed, she'd have Walker.

"We're going to have to give Pocatello a wide berth," said Caitlyn, pulling her braid.

Mason narrowed his eyes at Ginger. "No way. What are the chances?"

"Chances of what?" said Elsa, returning her attention to the teenage girl for a more thorough look. She was older than Elsa guessed at first, perhaps sixteen or seventeen years old. Other than the filth and greasy hair, she looked young and healthy. Suddenly, Mason's words made sense.

"You're the runaway," Elsa sighed. They didn't need some spoiled rich girl slowing them down.

The girl flinched and balled her hands into fists.

Tatsuda put his hand on her wrist. "It's okay. That doesn't matter to them. Not like you'd think." With his dark eyes, he pleaded with Elsa not to make him a liar.

"Damn," said Caitlyn with one of the soft smiles she reserved for children and animals. "Grady was right. I seem to be a magnet for strays."

The corner of Mason's mouth twitched with as much expression as Elsa had seen from him. So, he had a sense of humor.

"No, I'm not," said the girl, shaking her head. "I'm not a runaway. I don't know what you mean. I live on the streets of Pocatello. I've been here all summer."

This girl was lying. Elsa narrowed her eyes, examining her from head to toe. "You aren't thin enough to have been homeless for long. Someone used to make sure you had square meals every day." For Tatsuda's sake, she kept the venom from her voice.

The girl hung her head.

Mason said, "Three gold for her safe return to Malcolm McCoy."

"Malcolm? Another McCoy?" How many McCoys were there? Elsa stepped back and studied the girl again. "Oh, my god." A breath of air whooshed out of her as she shook her head. "Who exactly are you?" Deep down, she knew. One of her nieces had ginger hair and the same fair skin and freckles. That explained why Malcolm McCoy cared about this runaway. She must be his daughter. "No way."

"You're right. No way," said Geri, stepping back toward the shadows, her hands held up as though to block Elsa's words. Tatsuda caught her arm, and she stopped moving.

"Elsa," he said. "Maybe you could listen."

She met Tatsuda's gaze. He'd seldom asked for anything. It was the least she could do. She nodded, but crossed her arms. "What's your story? The real one. I'm good at telling when someone lies."

Geri's eyes shifted down the valley, to an escape. Elsa softened her tone, so she didn't scare the girl. "We're not planning to hurt you or turn you in."

"You're safe with us. Tatsuda's right. We won't hurt you." Walker stepped closer to Elsa and put his hand around her shoulder.

Geri looked at Tatsuda again, who nodded. "My name is Ginger." She shrugged at Tatsuda and continued. "I hopped a train in Denver eight days ago." She spoke slowly, as if the words were being dragged from her. "I wasn't aware there was a reward, but I'm not surprised. I don't want to go back." She blinked, perhaps to keep back her tears.

"We aren't interested in the reward." Walker spoke like he would to someone much younger than this young woman, but she seemed to need soothing.

Elsa shot him a grateful look for knowing what to say.

The girl's shoulders slumped. "My father is rich and the president of GreenCorps. He decided I'm supposed to marry someone he does business with from far away. They're looking to expand. I'd never met the man before. He's old, older than my father. They locked me in my room, as usual, but I snuck out and hopped the train. I didn't really know what I was doing, but I got lucky and it worked. I would have gone farther, but I didn't have any water. I've been stuck here for just over a week."

"How'd you get water?" said Caitlyn, her voice soft.

"I found an unlocked door at night behind one of the shops and took water from their tap a few times. Last night the door was locked, and I haven't been able to find anywhere else to get any, so I decided to climb back on the train while I still had a supply. I wanted to travel farther away from Denver, anyway." She looked down. "I lost my water jug and my belongings when I was attacked."

Clever girl. Her story had the ring of truth. Finally.

"Would you like to share our dinner?" said Caitlyn, holding out her hand. "Come, sit and eat. You can tell us the rest of your story over dinner." Her soothing tone seemed to put the young woman at ease.

Ginger gave her a tremulous smile and nodded.

"Potatoes are done," said Walker. "Where are those plates?"

Elsa grabbed the plates, and he set a potato and a half, a knife, and a fork on each before passing the plates around. Caitlyn had a spare set for Ginger, who took her plate with shaking hands.

"I'll head back on watch," said Mason after he'd taken his share. He shifted his attention to Walker. "Fill me in later?"

Walker nodded, and Mason disappeared into the darkness again.

They sat blowing on the food until the food was cool enough to eat.

"If there's a reward," Ginger said, "Why don't you want it?" She sat between Caitlyn and Tatsuda, across from Elsa. "You don't look rich. You could use the money."

Her blue eyes looked at Elsa without guile. She cocked her head and tapped her finger against her lip as she spoke. "Why do you look so familiar?"

"Probably the Wanted posters," said Elsa, bringing the topic into the open. "You aren't the only person GreenCorps has an interest in capturing." There was no sense in beating around the bush. "GreenCorps wants me too, even if I'm innocent of the crime I'm accused of."

The girl burst into tears and launched herself at Elsa, fists swinging, almost stepping in the pit with the hot coals. Stunned, Elsa didn't move while Walker grabbed Ginger by the scruff of the neck like a kitten and held her off the ground, feet dangling while she flailed—not allowing her to strike Elsa.

"You killed my brother, you monster!" Ginger shrieked. "He's the only person who'd ever been nice to me."

"Jace?" said Elsa, shocked that someone might have considered Jace the best person in their life. Him, nice? What did that say about this poor girl's life? "Your brother might have been decent to you, but he was an asshole."

"It was you. You killed him." Ginger's eyes blazed with hatred, but she stopped struggling and her chest heaved as she fought to contain her sobs.

Elsa leapt to her feet, her chest tight with suppressed emotion. "He tried to rape me and when I fought back, he tried to kill me. We got away, and he sent someone to steal from us. If that wasn't enough, he double-crossed Walker's brother, beat him, and left him for dead. When he caught up to us, he set the house we were sleeping in on fire, and attacked me with a knife." Elsa's voice became louder and more heated as the list grew.

Ginger's eyes rounded, and her sobs slowed, though her tears continued.

"I defended myself and he ended up dead. It could have easily gone the other way." Elsa thrust her shoulder out of her shirt and traced the dark scar in the flickering light. "I almost bled to death." Her body trembled as she spoke.

"You finished?" said Walker to Ginger. His voice remained calm as his eyes flicked to Elsa. Perhaps to confirm that she was okay. She gave a small nod.

"Yes," Ginger muttered with a small voice as she spoke to the ground.

Walker released her.

After her initial outburst, Ginger's energy waned. She slumped back to the ground, her eyes awash in tears as she scrubbed at them, making a mess of her dusty face. "I'm sorry. He wasn't like that to me, but he got more like our father every year." She sounded resigned to the truth.

"Malcolm McCoy is your father?" Elsa wanted confirmation as she looked up at Mason, who'd come running at the disturbance. From the top of the ridge, she made out a motion like a shrug in the dim light. He said nothing. She glanced at Caitlyn, who nodded. Tatsuda smiled, lighting up his face. Elsa checked with Walker last.

He pulled her into an embrace and kissed her. "What's one more reason for them to hate you?"

"Okay," Elsa said as they all looked at her. "Ginger can come with us. At least until we've hopped another train and can leave her somewhere safer."

CHAPTER 16: ELSA

The next morning, they were up before the sun rose; all evidence of their camp gone with their fire pit filled in. For the first time in days, Elsa's stomach contained food, and she had an energetic spring in her stride. What a difference food and water made. No wonder GreenCorps kept people hungry; without food and water, they lacked the energy to fight.

The sky was cloudless and blue, promising to be another scorcher, but the early morning air temperature was bearable. They angled their trail to the northwest, avoiding farms and the town itself as they headed into country even more desolate than the last several days. It wasn't long before they left the farmland behind and came to an arid patch of uninhabited land that stretched for miles without trees or shade.

Very little grew here and the flat black and purple stone they walked on was the hottest Elsa had felt yet, and as the day progressed, the heat penetrated the soles of her boots. They seldom spoke as they hiked, conserving water and moisture. The harsh sunlight would have been devastating if not for her hat and UVee goggles. Caitlyn had lent Ginger a light, long-sleeved shirt for sun protection for her fair skin.

It was mid-day when they came over a rise and stopped, sliding to the ground before they were seen. Elsa's legs shook where they crouched. In the distance, a heavily guarded chain-link fence with loops of razor wire across the top stood tall and impenetrable, guarded by

GreenCorps soldiers spaced evenly every hundred yards. They couldn't go this way. Beyond them, and impossible to reach, lay a shimmering blue lake nestled into a bowl in the barren wasteland surrounding.

"Snake River Reservoir," said Mason in a whisper. "We'll have to swing further west. Come at Aberdeen that way."

Disappointed not to get near the tempting water, Elsa backed down the slope, and they followed Mason's path to the west, extending their trek. They wound their way across long stretches of molded, melted-looking black rock. The wasteland looked to be made of dried bubbles of stone. Nothing grew on them, even in the cracks. The heat emanating from the stone beneath was almost unbearable. The land rose and fell, or became pebbled and strewn with bright red rock crumbles on the surface. Its unique contrasting stone was stark and beautiful, but no less hot. The afternoon stretched on forever.

"What is this place?" said Elsa once when she took a mouthful of water.

"Hell," said Mason from where he led.

Caitlyn shot him a look, which he didn't see, and turned to Elsa. "It's called Craters of the Moon. We're just cutting across the southern corner. Long ago it was a massive park with ruins and caves that apparently enticed visitors from all over."

The sun was setting in a haze behind them when at last they approached the ruins of the old city of Aberdeen

They'd returned to flat land that had perhaps once been fields. Scattered mounds became more frequent, then thick and in rows. Elsa itched to excavate a few, to determine if there was treasure inside, but she couldn't afford to stop and give in to whimsy. They headed toward the center of the old town, looking for what might be the old university campus. They searched in vain for the university grounds until darkness descended and they had to give up the search for the night.

"The last one was out of town," said Walker. "We walked in from the south and west of town already. Tomorrow let's try the north."

Her shoulders slumped; but Elsa had to agree. Soon it would be too dark to see anything.

They set up camp, ate a quick dinner, and she took the first watch. Long after the others slept, Walker waited with her, his strong arm around her. She leaned into him and listened for anything out of place in the silence or signs of life. Most of the time, she stared at the blanket of white stars, enjoying their expanse in the night sky and the company.

* * *

They'd walked for only an hour the next morning, when voices carried to them on the breeze. Elsa dropped to the ground, her heart racing. Only steps behind, the others did the same, and Walker's big hand closed on her arm. Elsa froze. Walker motioned to Mason that they would check it out.

She and Walker slithered forward, leaving the others to wait while they investigated. Just behind the next long row of mounds, a camp was stirring in the morning. Close to two dozen GreenCorps recruits sat eating breakfast. Their horses were tethered together with ropes at the opposite end of the camp.

Smoke rose from a pair of cook fires and scent of roasting meat wafted through the air. She sniffed. Maybe bacon? She'd been looking forward to trying bacon on the farm if they'd stayed for the fall. Standing at the closer fire stood Jaxon, his back to her. He was clearly not expecting anyone else to overhear as his voice boomed across the camp.

"I want us headed north in under an hour," he said. "She could be here any day."

Elsa and Walker shared a glance and retreated, staying low. How did Jaxon know they'd be coming here? This encounter had been too close. Collecting the others, they crouched and ran northwest, giving Jaxon and his camp a wide berth before once more swinging north. When they could no longer hear the GreenCorps soldiers, or smell their extravagant breakfast, Elsa motioned them to halt.

She looked at Ginger, who shrugged, looking confused but defiant. "What?" The girl stepped back, perhaps nervous about Elsa's expression.

"Jaxon was there." Elsa wanted to be sure Ginger didn't plan to return with her brother. Her gut said the girl wanted to avoid the McCoys too, but she had to be certain.

"I want to be nowhere near him. He's crueler than Jace and tries to impress our father." Ginger's mouth twisted and her eyes narrowed. "He'll be just like him one day. Meaner than a junkyard dog."

Satisfied at her answer, Elsa set off at a pace slower than a run, but not by much. "If Jaxon's here already, he's waiting for me. Since they're out this way, that means we could be close to the bunker. The triangle on the old map should be near here."

North of town, they came to another set of ruins. Her pulse quickened; this could be it. The University of Idaho had once consisted of massive stone and brick buildings, but now many had crumbled and been overtaken by low-growing vegetation.

"You're looking for a small stone building with sturdy construction." Elsa pitched her voice low. "It should have a metal door with a carved leaf on the post beside the door frame."

"We should look in teams. We'll cover more ground," said Caitlyn. "Try to keep the next group in sight, or at least earshot."

"McCoy and his soldiers will be here soon." Mason glanced back in the direction where they expected Jaxon to come.

"Walker and I will search the center," said Elsa, making a quick decision. "You and Caitlyn, search the right where it's flatter so you can keep watch for the soldiers."

Mason nodded, already turning in that direction.

"Tatsuda, can you and Ginger take the left?"

He smiled and clasped Ginger's hand, leading her in the direction Elsa had asked. A fleeting smile touched her lips. The boy was obviously infatuated with his new friend.

Soon Tatsuda whistled—a quick bird-like whistle. Elsa and Walker trotted toward the sound and her heart accelerated. Coming around a row of mounds, Tatsuda stood in an old rock garden, the stone hut beside him, half-hidden behind a couple of smaller mounds and a crumbling brick wall. The glare of solar panels from the roof told her that this was probably the building for which they searched. The bunker needed power deep underground.

"We should get Caitlyn." She returned to the opposite side of the wall and waved to her friend, but Caitlyn and Mason weren't looking in her direction. They appeared to be having an intense conversation, standing close together and gesturing with large hand movements.

Tatsuda whistled again, a sharp piercing sound. At that, both Caitlyn and Mason turned. Instead of joining them, they pointed south and ran away from Elsa and the group. Jaxon must be close.

Caitlyn would buy them time. Elsa ran back and, with trembling hands, took the key dangling from her neck, and inserted it into the lock. It slid in with no trouble. She turned it and a round green light flashed before the lock clicked inside, releasing the catch. She grabbed the handle and pushed it down. It didn't move. Like before in Davis, the door must have shifted in centuries since they'd installed it and the hinges had bent. Move dammit. She shoved again, feeling a slight twinge in her shoulder.

It only opened a couple of inches.

"Trade with me," said Walker, stepping forward. "Shout if you see them."

Tatsuda's and Ginger's eyes widened as the sound of approaching riders shook the earth. Elsa glanced back. Fifteen riders headed their way.

"Soon." She chewed her lip as she moved out of the way.

Walker strained to lift the door while she threw her weight into pushing it open. The door groaned, and the frame shuddered while sweat drenched her clothing. Tatsuda braced himself against the door, pushing with all his wiry strength. They pried the door open a little more than a foot, creating a darkened opening. Enough that they could slip inside.

There was no obvious sign of Caitlyn and Mason, but several of the GreenCorps riders peeled off to the east, probably following them. Jaxon continued straight toward Elsa and the hut.

"Quick. Get inside," said Elsa, grabbing Ginger, who stared in fear at the advancing riders.

She trembled from head to toe. "That's Jax," she said, pointing to the lead rider. "He looks mad."

A gun shot rang out and the stone beside the door splintered with a bullet hit. Minute chips flew, one hitting Elsa on the leg. Her leg burned as if stung, but a glance confirmed that there was no blood.

"Ginger," roared Jaxon. He fired another shot, this one wild.

"Get in." Elsa pushed Ginger hard into the dark opening while the others followed. Once inside, she and Walker grabbed the door and pushed, scraping the door closed again, inch by inch.

"Tatsuda, can you make a light?" said Elsa, her voice strained with the effort of closing the door. Any second she expected Jaxon to thrust his hand in or drag it open from the other side.

Walker's muscles bulged and strained and Elsa's shoulder ached, but she threw every ounce of her weight into closing the door. They had only seconds. Continuing the grind against the concrete floor, the crack to the outside—and the light—diminished. Jaxon and his henchmen were almost upon them. Several shots rang off the thick door. With sweat running down her face, she gave a last heave.

The door ground closed and a red light flashed in the darkness beside the lock. Elsa breathed a deep sigh of relief. Moments later, from outside, came the muffled sound of someone pounding. They'd been just in time. She blotted the sweat from her forehead with the bandana that protected her neck from the sun. No light illuminated the space and the sounds of gasping breath echoed around the chamber.

Caitlyn and Mason remained outside, while everyone else was inside, trapped in the pitch dark. Hopefully, they found somewhere safe to hide. Jaxon would wait for some time. His need for revenge was clear. The hate in his eyes had been proof of that. They would need another way out, but for now, they were safe.

"I can't find matches," said Tatsuda, a catch in his voice.

Did the pitch-black make him nervous? Elsa's eyes were open, but she couldn't see anything now that the door was closed. Tight dark places seemed familiar after all those years working the Heap in garbage tunnels. She just needed a second to recover from the frantic action to close the door. Taking a calming breath, her heart slowed. Jaxon couldn't get in.

"Got it," said Walker. There were sounds as he rummaged in his pack and set something on the floor with a small clink. He struck a match and the quick flare of yellowish-orange glowed in the inky black room. Cupping his free hand around the flame, he lit his candle lantern.

Outside, the banging continued, both high and low, as if someone was pounding and kicking on the door.

"Elsa, open the fucking door," said Jaxon's muffled voice. "I just want to talk."

Like hell. No way did she believe him.

"Ginger, Father is worried sick."

"Does my brother know you beyond what happened to… Jace?" said Ginger, talking to Elsa instead of Jaxon.

"He's married to my older sister," said Elsa, slumping onto the wall.

"I didn't know he was married," said Ginger in a small voice. "Does that mean your sister is my sister now, too? There's another girl in my family?" In the subdued light, her face appeared softer and full of wonder.

"Plus her daughters. They're one and three," said Elsa. "The three-year-old has ginger hair too."

The girl shook her head. "Ginger is a princess, locked in a tower with no friends. I wish I had a new name. One my brother doesn't know." Her chin lifted, perhaps daring Elsa to deny her the right to change her name.

"I like your name," said Tatsuda. "Plus, you have friends now."

Elsa liked the girl's spunk. She hadn't thought of it before, but Ginger was her family, too. Elsa turned to Walker. "We'll have to trust

Caitlyn and Mason to look out for themselves." She didn't like that the group had been split up, but those two were tough.

Camped so near, Jaxon might have known roughly where to find the entrance. The thought was disturbing. "I think Jaxon's been in the area before," she said. "GreenCorps could have copies of the map or known about the bunker locations some other way. But they must not have keys, or they would have raided them years ago. We should head further in. I'd feel safer elsewhere."

"Go where?" said Tatsuda, looking around the small, enclosed space. Even by candlelight, it was dim inside and festooned in swaths of spider webs.

The gritty floor crunched underneath as Elsa walked toward a second door set in the back wall across from the first door, swatting cobwebs at every step.

"The seed bunker is downstairs." Excitement seeped into her voice now that the immediate danger was past.

"You've been in one of these before," said Tatsuda. "That's where your seed pouches came from, but I didn't picture it like this." He shivered.

She nodded. "So far, it's the same. Behind that door, there should be a flight of steep stairs and it'll be cold as it goes underground. At the bottom, there should be another door and an enormous room full of shelves and seeds."

"There were rations and rooms to sleep in, even if we didn't stay last time. There should be water too. We can hide out for a while if we need to." Walker's voice sounded excited.

Elsa met his sparkling eyes. Sharing this experience and its excitement was magical, like the first time. No one else had been here for almost two hundred years.

Behind them, the banging resumed. "Elsa, open up. Ginger, get out here. What did she promise to make you go with her?" He continued to yell.

Elsa ignored the shouts from outside, feeling confident that the door would hold.

"It'll just make him madder that you don't answer." Ginger stared at the door.

Elsa shrugged and inserted the key into the second lock. Once more, a vibrant green light flashed above the keyhole and the locking mechanism clicked.

This time, when she turned the handle, the door opened outward with a sucking sound and a blast of cold, dry air. After the intense heat of the day and their frantic run to get the door open, the coolness was welcome.

"You can lead this time," she said to Walker with a smile, thinking of their first descent into the Davis bunker when he'd given her the honor.

"Let's go," he said, holding the door open with a crooked grin.

Walker and Elsa went through the door and their motion triggered a pale strip of lights by their feet at the edges of the stairs.

Ginger hesitated and shook her head. "I don't like the dark."

"It'll be okay." Tatsuda took Ginger's hand, and they followed Walker as he descended, holding the light high.

Elsa shut the door and checked that it locked before she tromped down the metal stairway, lit only by the candle lantern and the pale glow by their feet. Now that they were safe, behind two sets of locked doors, she shivered at the near-miss. Right now, she was happy to be inside, away from Jaxon and GreenCorps, but she was unsure how they would get out.

CHAPTER 17: MASON

Mason sensed the GreenCorps riders before he saw them. Perhaps a vibration perceived through the soles of his boots, maybe something in the air. Whatever the cause, he heeded the feeling. It had kept him alive on more than one occasion. He pulled Caitlyn against him and ducked behind an earthen mound in the university ruins.

Her body softened and relaxed into him. Then she'd stiffened and pushed him away.

"What the hell? Don't touch me." Her eyes narrowed accusingly.

He put a finger to his lips before whispering, "McCoy's here. We either need to join the others right now or distract the soldiers. We might split their forces."

A sharp, bird-like whistle pierced the air. Another team had found something. He and Caitlyn glanced toward whoever had signaled to see that the group was gathering. Elsa waved for them to join, but Mason ignored the summons.

"We have to decide. If they found the bunker, Elsa and the others can enter. If we go with them, we're safe, but trapped." That was the dilemma. The notion of being stranded underground without an exit was unappealing.

"We can't just leave them." Caitlyn edged farther from his grasp.

His hand twitched to tug her back against him, but he wouldn't touch her and risk her anger again unless it was to keep her safe. "Just for now. I'm not leaving for good."

A second, shriller whistle rent the air. Time had run out. Now or never.

"Our best chance at helping them is to flee. Right now." He dashed away from Elsa and the group, hoping Caitlyn followed. She'd have to make her own decision. He sprinted from mound to mound, through the ruins—staying low at first. Shots rang out in the other direction. He glanced back, slowing just enough that Caitlyn sped past him, her arms pumping and her cheeks pink. If he hadn't been so busy running, he would have admired her for longer.

Another quick look showed that three of Jaxon's riders had peeled off toward them. He and Caitlyn could never outrun horses, but he kept running, leading the soldiers away as planned. He ducked behind the remnants of a brick wall and skidded to a halt, grabbing Caitlyn and pulling her aside. She hissed angrily, but he gestured to her to lie down and drew both of his pistols.

Understanding dawned in her eyes as she unholstered her own gun with a nod. If he missed, she'd take care of anyone else. Not that he had any intention of missing at this range.

Crouching until the three riders whizzed past, Mason squeezed the trigger several times. Four shots in quick succession rang out. The three riders tumbled to the hard-packed ground and lay still. All three had been chest shots, straight to the heart. The last man had turned at the last second, needing an extra bullet.

Perhaps Mason should feel remorse for shooting these men, but as a rebel, he'd been hunted, chased, and watched hundreds of decent men and women die. In turn, he'd shot his share of GreenCorps soldiers. In the majority of instances, it had been in defense of the rebel cause or to save his own life. He didn't like killing, but he no longer spared thoughts of feeling guilty when necessity required that he take a life.

Caitlyn kept her unfired gun at the ready, but there was no need for her to pull the trigger.

Two of the horses galloped away, riderless. Mason reloaded and grabbed the dangling reins of the remaining horse. "Check them," he tossed his chin toward the bodies. Caitlyn might be annoyed, but there was no time to explain. Her strength and experience were invaluable, and he trusted her to have his back.

"Dead." She straightened and holstered her pistol.

Mason crept back along the wall to assess the situation before they continued.

The rest of the soldiers surrounded the area where Elsa and the others had been. Muffled shouts, banging, and a variety of curses came from the remaining GreenCorps soldiers. He grinned, enjoying their frustration.

"The others must have made it underground." Satisfaction filled his voice.

He swung onto the horse and stuck out his hand. "Get their water. We've got to go. We won't do any good if we're caught."

Caitlyn glanced back the way they'd come. She would know that other soldiers would soon come to investigate and they couldn't stay. A horse was the best way to escape. She grabbed the dead men's canteens, slung the straps around her with the containers behind, near her pack. Smart. Water out here was better than gold.

She took Mason's hand, thrust her foot into the stirrup, and he swung her up behind him. They didn't both fit in the saddle, so she sat perched on the dead man's bedroll. It wouldn't be comfortable, but it would do for a brief ride. She grabbed onto his backpack to steady herself when he kicked the horse and they shot off at a gallop.

Mason kept the horse running on the uneven ground, watching for hollows and stones, racing through the old town of Aberdeen. He headed back toward the barren terrain they'd traveled yesterday. He looked behind several times but couldn't see anyone. Right now, GreenCorps cared more about Elsa and getting into the seed bunker. If Jaxon had recognized Ginger, that would add fuel to the fire. That didn't mean GreenCorps wouldn't chase Caitlyn and himself—pursuit would come—but he'd bought some time.

When the horse faltered, Mason slowed the pace, letting it drop to a fast walk for several minutes while Caitlyn watched the trail behind. When the horse had rested, he kicked it into a canter.

He repeated this three additional times before the horse was spent from the extended exertion in this heat. Its withers became lathered in white foam, its coat dark with sweat. He wouldn't get much more from it. Not without killing it, which he wouldn't do if he could help it. Making a rapid decision, he reined the horse to a stop and dismounted. Caitlyn swung down from behind the saddle. They'd ridden for a couple of hours. He searched the land for signs of soldiers. Still nothing.

He untied the bundle from behind the horse's saddle that Caitlyn had been sitting on and stuffed it into his pack. Extra gear wouldn't hurt. There was nothing else of value on the horse. He tugged the bridle loose and the bit from its mouth to make it easier on the horse, pointed the animal back the way they'd come, and slapped its rear. It bolted fifty yards but lacked the energy to run far. It slowed and wandered back toward Aberdeen, stopping to yank a mouthful of the sparse golden grass. It should continue back toward the others; horses liked company.

Caitlyn watched him, an inscrutable expression on her face. Damn that woman. Was she angry about being separated from her friends? Or was it the fact that he had taken charge of the situation? She was tough, and that thought left him mildly aroused.

"Let's go. I've got a plan." He wasn't leaving Elsa to GreenCorps for long. Grady would have his hide because his father had taken a strong liking to Elsa and Walker. Mason had gotten the impression that Grady truly regretted being unable to help more with the seed bunkers. The leader had sent him to be of assistance in his father's stead.

"Care to share?" Caitlyn said, crossing her arms. "What's the plan?"

"Not just yet. We need to get out of sight and into the hills. Trust me."

She cocked an eyebrow and nodded. "For now."

He'd take what he could get.

They veered right toward Craters of the Moon. Because of its desolation, it was the last place that GreenCorps should search. Who in their right mind would head into the furnace-like waste at the height of summer?

Right away the land changed, becoming more rolling than flat with a ring of distant hills in the west where it would be easier to hide. The temperature shot up several degrees as they left the former farmland behind, back onto the crumbled black volcanic rock. He'd met someone who'd hidden out here before and shared what he'd learned. He and Caitlyn wouldn't survive more than two days without finding water, but based on Darren's stories, Mason had a few ideas.

Mason kept a fast pace as they hiked across the hot stone, already baked by the mid-morning sun. He waited for shots to come from behind, his shoulder blades twitching. But nothing. Each time that he spun to check the horizon, the land remained empty. His chest clamped tight the whole time they stayed so exposed.

When they reached the first set of ridges, some of the tension left his chest and shoulders, even if it was too soon to relax. The folded, melted rows of black and purple rock would block them from sight and they could disappear. He aimed for the larger hills and volcanic formations in the distance.

As the day wore on, heat waves rose around them, warping their view of the barren landscape. He stopped several times to drink water. Sweat evaporated before clothes became damp when it was this hot, which was deceptive. He delved into his pack at mid-day and produced chunks of jerky and a pinch of salt for each of them. Caitlyn had lived through enough Utah and Texas summers to know that when it was this hot, your body needed salt.

Caitlyn had kept up all day without further explanation; few people would have trusted his day-long silence. Maybe it wasn't trust, but avoidance. She wouldn't stay that way for much longer. They hiked along the ridge of volcanic spires, where he watched for holes, caves, and hidden entrances.

The first two dark patches he'd tried had been filled with slick, black, glass-like rock, but the third, part-way up a stone spire looked like an entrance to a cave. His heart beat faster as he scrambled toward it over half a dozen rough boulders. Putting a hand back, he hauled Caitlyn up the last couple of yards where it was steep. She accepted his help but dropped his hand afterward as though burned.

He'd been zapped both times he'd taken her hand, but this was the first sign that she'd felt it too. Without the others' presence as a buffer, he might have to deal with his attraction sooner rather than later. He doubted his interest had gone unnoticed, but there'd been no sign that she reciprocated it. First and foremost, she remained Mathew's widow.

Mason crouched to crawl into the cave, but once past the first rocky outcropping, the cavern opened up, extending several yards on either side with ample headroom as he straightened up. It smelled damp, but not rank like animal or musty like snake, though it was wise to be cautious.

He dropped his make-shift pack, slung off both canteens, and looked around. Near the cave mouth, he found a ring of fire-cracked rock, ashes, and soot stained the cracked ceiling overhead. They didn't have fuel for a fire, but it was helpful to know that people had used this site. Light streamed in from a multitude of small holes in the spire's face, but soon they'd lose the light from outside as the sun went down. Best to explore now.

Several pillars of cracked stone were located at the rear of the cave, just like he'd been told to look for. The floor sloped downward at one end and he rested his hand against the stone of the floor. It wasn't just cool from being inside—it was damp. He was on the right track.

He lit a lantern and moved further inside, exploring the recesses in the split stone hidden by shadows at the back. There it was, a trickle of water, sliding down the wall and disappearing into a crack in the floor. He allowed himself a weary smile. This was what he'd been hoping for. A small amount of water pooled beside his feet.

Mason wedged himself deeper into the crevice and slid farther in, where the trickle was stronger. The cold stone contrasted with the heat from the day and relieved the burnt skin on the back of his neck. He immersed his mouth into the stream of water, enjoying the fresh, crispness of the water. It had a strong mineral taste and was icy cold.

Relieved that he'd found water, this was as far as they needed to go today.

After several swallows, each time savoring its chill, he slid out and motioned for Caitlyn to take a turn. She'd followed him to the rear of the cave and waited for him to emerge.

"How'd you know about this place?" she said, looking around.

"Darren's been here before, or somewhere like it. Many of the caves have water in them. He told stories about hiding out here for weeks."

"I've heard his stories," she said. "I just didn't know we were anywhere near where he comes from."

"We aren't, but Darren's often spent time out here. GreenCorps doesn't follow for long." Mason motioned her toward the water. "The water's cold. Take a turn. It feels great." He'd rubbed some on the back of his neck and face.

She sidled into the crack and slaked her thirst. She came out, wiping water from her chin.

"Grady's out here somewhere too," Mason said. "He mentioned a hideout here that they would occupy in late summer, moving into fall, as a gathering place to train. If he isn't here yet, he will be soon. My plan is for us to find Grady. I think he would help distract GreenCorps, at least enough that we might spring Elsa from that bunker. They want him even more than they want Elsa. If he shows himself, they'll follow."

"Except Jaxon," she said with a tightening of her forehead, which was her precursor to a frown. "He won't leave that bunker door unless he's forced." She hesitated before continuing. "What makes you think you can find Grady? There's a lot of territory out here and nobody's been able to catch up to him when he wants to stay hidden."

Mason swung around to look at her. In the softer light in the cave, she was even more beautiful and the light coming in from outside above her head gave her a halo effect—once more his angel. He swallowed.

His thoughts must have shown on his face because she said, "How do you do that?"

Others said he was difficult to read, but to Caitlyn, he always seemed to be an open book.

How did he do what? It was on his tongue to ask, but he couldn't speak. She took his breath away sometimes and left him speechless.

"Why do you look at me that way?" Her tone gave nothing away.

Was she angry? He tried to gauge what she felt, but he couldn't decide. Blood drained from his face and he became almost light-headed. He couldn't seem to breathe properly. She'd always had that effect on him.

"I can't help myself," he said at last. He took three steps toward her and stopped. He expected her to tell him to try harder, or to get over it, or to smack his face as he stepped into her personal space. He was close enough that he'd touch her if he reached. Her shirt was damp and clinging to her where it had gotten wet. She wasn't much shorter than he was and he stared into her blue eyes, drowning.

Caitlyn rested her hands on his chest as if to shove him away, but the push never came. Could she feel his heart pounding like a hammer?

Mason was playing with fire, but no risk, no reward, and there was so much to gain. He wrapped one arm around her and nudged her an inch closer. Bracing for the smack, he pulled off his hat, tilted down, and kissed her.

Her lips were as soft as he remembered, and she tasted like ripe strawberries—sweet and tart. He'd never been able to eat the fruit without thinking of his first love. At first, she didn't respond and stood stiff as a plank in his arms. The only surprise was that she didn't pull away following his bold move. He deepened their kiss.

He wouldn't blame her if she punched him in the gut or kneed him.

When his lips left hers, a deep whimper burst from her throat and his heart stuttered. If he wasn't wanted, he would stop, but was that sound pain or encouragement? His skin was on fire and he yearned for her, but he needed her to feel it too, or there was no point. His balance shifted as he stepped back.

To his shock, with her eyes open wide, she threw her arms around his neck and pulled his mouth back to hers with a fierce sound of longing. Her kiss set fire to him everywhere as her lips captured his and didn't let go. When she stopped, he couldn't move and could barely breathe. He waited for her to speak because he didn't dare.

"Make me feel again. I want you, despite everything." Her voice shook and though he wanted to pounce and kiss her senseless, he paused, weighing her words. He wanted more than something physical, he wanted a genuine connection. "I'm sick of being alone and feeling nothing."

Her eyes begged for him to care, and it shot through him like lightning.

He took her face between his hands. His thumbs traced her strong jawline, and he kissed her again, slow and deep. Time slowed. The moment was almost unreal. One hand dropped to her lower back, and he tugged her slim body against him. He wanted her to feel how hard he was. How much he wanted her.

Caitlyn rubbed against him and moaned into his mouth as she nibbled at his lips. Her tongue slipped into his mouth, meeting his with every flick, becoming more urgent with each passing second. He'd dreamed about her for so long, he couldn't believe this was real and not one of his fantasies.

Mason unzipped her pants and slid his hand inside, all the while braced for the blow that would tell him he'd gone too far. But this was a woman who knew her own mind. She was wet and slippery and wriggled on his fingers, guiding him to the most sensitive places. Stroking her more surely, he kept kissing, devouring her mouth, her lips, her tongue. He was on fire and the blaze became almost uncontrollable when she thrust him back against the cold stone wall.

"Get undressed." She stepped back, unbuttoning her shirt, her eyes smoldering.

He swallowed and tried to follow her orders, fumbling at his belt but unable to look away as she exposed her creamy skin. Her face and forearms were tanned and freckled from the sun, but the rest of her was like milk. The sight of her bare breasts almost made his heart stop. God, he wanted her. He wanted to touch every inch of her and make her his angel in truth. He remained frozen, unable to move.

Caitlyn smiled a predatory smile. "Now."

Mason kicked off his boots and slipped off his pants. His hands shook as he unbuttoned his shirt. He looked up, afraid she might have changed her mind.

He met her eyes and she licked her lips. His cock jumped.

She stepped forward again, pale and naked. He almost didn't know where to start. She was a goddess. He ran his hand up her side, feeling her smooth skin and glorious curves. It seemed as though sparks jumped from his hands and they tingled. She grabbed his cock and slid her hand along its length. He groaned and shuddered all over. She repeated the motion and he gasped. Hefting one of her breasts in his hands, he felt how it had changed. It was fuller and more rounded than long ago, but fit his hand perfectly. He'd never wanted anyone like this. It was fierce, almost painful, yet still, he let her dictate the pace.

"Kiss me," her voice was little more than a whisper, and her eyes smoldered.

He tipped his head and kissed her again, inhaling her sweet fruity smell. It didn't matter that they'd been on the run, hiked all day, and until a few minutes ago, been hot and sweaty. Her skin's salt tasted delicious and her natural scent intoxicated him more than whiskey. The hard rock wall dug into his back, but it didn't matter—he was wild for her every touch.

When she dropped to her knees, landing on the pile of clothes at their feet, he gasped and glanced at the rough ceiling before watching her every move. She licked his shaft and took him in her mouth. He couldn't hold still and thrust into her mouth while she sucked. The world faded and he couldn't see or hear anything but every move of her red lips. He was a second from coming in her mouth when she stopped with a knowing look. He ached as she stood up.

Mason couldn't look away from her swollen lips. If she'd wanted him to be desperate, mission accomplished, but if she was having second thoughts, he wouldn't push.

"My turn," she said, as she touched herself, her fingers swirling between her legs. She lifted a single finger to his lips. When he sucked her taste from her finger, she smiled.

"You sure?" He didn't want her to regret this. To regret being with him.

Caitlyn pressed her breasts against his chest as she stepped closer. "It's been too long. Don't make me beg."

He wanted her to beg, but that wasn't fair. Asking was more than enough. His back stung from his stone scrapes and he couldn't do the same to her unmarked skin. Instead, he grasped her by the hips and whispered, "Brace yourself on the wall, Love."

She smiled and tossed her braid over her shoulder as she turned and bent at the waist, spreading her hands open on the wall beside him. "Do it now. I need you."

He couldn't wait another second. His cock still glistened from her mouth and when he touched her from behind, she wiggled and rubbed her wetness against him. He stood behind her and grasped her hips and sheathed himself inside her in a single move. The sound he made couldn't be described as anything except primal.

"Mason. Fuck," she cried, bucking beneath him. "Again." As he moved, she threw her head back and narrowly missed colliding with his. He pulled out and thrust again, sinking into her exquisite heat, barely maintaining control. He braced one hand on the rock above her hands, the other on her lower back as he thrust again, rocking with a natural rhythm he could no more control than stop. Part of him worried that he'd hurt her, but she called out and squeezed, pulsing around him. Stars swam in his vision and nothing existed except the places their skin touched. He wasn't just on fire; he was being consumed.

Caitlyn cried out as she shuddered beneath him, orgasms rolling through her. He paused as deep as he could and let her ride each one before thrusting again. His balls ached, and his vision faded as he neared his climax. When he spasmed, the world went black as he gave her everything.

Mason collapsed on her back as he shivered, spent. He allowed himself a few seconds to bask in the feeling before he stood up, afraid to find she might already regret what they'd done.

Instead, she turned and slid into his arms, tilting her head up for a deep kiss. He savored her taste on his lips and the sensation of her pliant body against his. Her skin was so soft. He hadn't thought this would ever happen. It had been far different from their desperate and awkward fumbling fifteen years ago. That hadn't gone this far—except in his dreams.

"I needed that," Caitlyn said when they stopped kissing. She would no longer meet his eyes as she patted his shoulder and stepped away. The bottom dropped out of his stomach. He'd been dismissed. "Apparently so did you." Her eyebrow lifted as she left him speechless while she collected her clothing off the cave floor and dressed.

What the hell was he going to do now?

CHAPTER 18: ELSA

The cold descent and the clanging metal stairs winding deeper and deeper seemed the same as the first time she and Walker had found a bunker. Elsa's fingers tingled like they had in her Heap days whenever she found treasure. Whatever they found down here would be significant. The farther they descended, the more she shivered and goosebumps rose on her arms. They'd been dressed for the heat outside, not for the cold below ground in a concrete stairwell.

Would this bunker have the same survival gear? If so, they could outfit those that needed equipment, like Ginny and Tatsuda, and they could grab a real backpack for Mason. Would the bunker have similar seeds? With the doors closed and the possibility of days or weeks underground, would there be enough oxygen? She couldn't watch her friends suffocate.

A faint background whir and the freshness of the air suggested that air must circulate somehow or it would have been stale or musty. She took a deep breath and thrust her worries away.

At the bottom of the stairs, Walker, Ginny, and Tatsuda gathered by the metal door waiting for her. She'd fallen behind with her thoughts. With a quick inhale, Elsa removed the key from inside her shirt and slipped it into the keyhole. The familiar green light flashed, and the door unlocked with a satisfying click. The sound of possibility.

Elsa pushed the handle and opened the door, which triggered a snapping sound that she'd forgotten. Inside, banks of lights flicked on in waves, the sound cascading farther and farther away until they stood at the entrance to an enormous underground bunker lit by dozens of rows of overhead lights.

Taking another deep breath, she stepped over the threshold and the others followed. Walker blew out his candle lantern but clutched it tight, perhaps not wanting to be without a light if the others went out. Like the previous bunker last spring, the walls of the first room inside the door were covered in racks of gear. Sleeping bags, backpacks, hand-crank appliances, rope, dehydrated rations and so much more. She'd spend more time looking at these supplies later. There was more food than the four of them could eat in months or even years—as long as there was water. She frowned. Not that she wanted to be stuck underground for long.

Elsa shut the door to the stairs, checked that it was locked. "There are a million things I wished I'd looked at before. Let's explore." Her breath plumed white as she spoke in a breathless tone. Her mouth was dry as she dug a long-sleeved shirt out of her pack, almost unable to contain her excitement about being in a bunker again at last. She grabbed a jacket off the closest shelf, held it up with a frown, then rifled through the pile for one that looked smaller, which she tossed to Ginger. Ginger's eyes opened wide with surprise as she caught the jacket.

"Thank you," Ginger said, unwinding her arms from her body and putting on the jacket. Tatsuda grabbed the first one Elsa had held up, which was more his size.

"We might adjust the heat in the living quarters, but this part stays cool. The next room is even colder to keep the seeds viable." Elsa looked around again, checking for anything she might have missed before moving on.

The near wall was made of glass so they could see inside the seed vault that made up the majority of the bunker. Racks of foil-wrapped packets stored in boxes lined the shelves. Above the entrance to the massive room, a sign read, *Small Seeds and Grain Collection*.

Instead of entering the door to the seed storage room, Elsa strode down the corridor that ran parallel to the elongated room. Moving down the long hall, she opened doors to four bedrooms, each with a series of bunk beds attached to three of the walls. They'd designed this place to hold a lot more than their group of four. There was space for a couple of dozen people to sleep comfortably. Had anyone ever stayed here? If so, what had happened to them?

"This room work for you?" She asked Walker.

Walker's gray eyes twinkled as he put down his pack. "I'll stay wherever you are. You know that."

She smiled at his easy-going nature and unclipped her backpack, setting it down with a sigh. She rolled her shoulders and loosened her neck. It was a relief not to carry weight on her back. "You two could find rooms, too."

"I don't want my own room," said Ginger. "I've spent enough time alone." Her wide blue eyes looked fearful, and she continued to clutch Tatsuda's hand.

"We can share," he said with a shy smile. "Lots to choose from. Let's pick one."

Elsa smothered a grin and turned to Walker with a cough. Tatsuda and Ginger were cute. He was street smart and tough, but naïve in other ways. She didn't get the feeling that either of them had a case of raging hormones, more like they could use a friend their own age. Before he'd joined her and Walker, Tatsuda had been on his own for years, which would have been lonely.

While Tatsuda and Ginger chose the room across the hall, Elsa explored further down the corridor and Walker headed in the other direction, back toward the entrance.

"You can share your discoveries. I'll share mine." His voice echoed in the long corridor.

The next two rooms were spacious washrooms. While she'd bathed at the cabin and Caitlyn's, she hadn't had a shower since her sister's house in SoCal and hoped there would be hot water. She loved feeling the dirt wash away. There must be towels somewhere, she'd watch for them.

A fine coating of dust covered everything. Much less than she would have expected, but there was no indication that anyone had been inside in a very long time. Despite that, the fresh air must have originated from outside somehow.

Elsa turned a tap at one of the sinks. At first, nothing happened. Disappointed, she reached to turn it off again when the spout spat out a quick burst of water. It hissed and spit again before running smoothly. Running water. She dipped her mouth into the stream and quenched her thirst of cool water for the first time since they'd left the farm a week and a half earlier. She tried the tap for hot water and was gratified to find that it worked. She sighed with relief. Food, water, and fresh air. Even if they were stuck for a while, they could survive.

The next room appeared to be storage, with hundreds more boxes of dried rations lining the walls. The labels had interesting names: beef teriyaki, chicken tetrazzini, and lasagna. She and Walker had sampled others from the previous bunker, but these were things she'd never heard of, let alone tried. Another room had floor to ceiling shelves with books, many labeled by place and date. Granny had said she'd been to libraries when she was younger, before her imprisonment at SoCal. This looked like how she'd described one.

Excitement raced through Elsa at the prospect of learning more about the world's history. She'd love to stay and investigate the library in depth, but there'd be more time for that. She wanted to inventory everything she found first, but before leaving, she snagged a volume titled, "Twenty-first Century North America" and took a moment to flip through the pages.

The map on the inside cover matched the maps of America and Canada from Caitlyn's, with slightly larger land masses. SoCal was just called California, and part of something much larger that extended up an unfamiliar coastline. She ran her finger over the smooth, glossy paper, finding Sacramento. She traced the route to Reno and then Salt Lake City. The path she and Walker had taken on the trains last spring.

Aberdeen wasn't on the map, but she found Pocatello. The landscape had changed little, except the small towns between the cities were gone. She wasn't familiar with Ogden and Harrisville, but they looked close to where Caitlyn's farm had been. She couldn't wait to read the book. Tucking it under her arm, she continued her exploration.

When Elsa opened the last door situated at the end of the hall, at first she didn't know what to make of the contents. The room was small, with a large desk that wrapped around two of the walls and glaring overhead lights and a lamp on the desk. Two unusual padded chairs sat positioned in front of the desk and sitting on it was a black box with several knobs and dials and two strange, flat black screens. A booklet had been left on the desk surface, as though it was the first thing someone was supposed to find and read.

Satellite Relay Instructions.

She flipped it open. Inside was a series of instructions for *System Reboot*, *Connectivity*, *Operation*, and others, with a series of pictures that matched the screens and equipment. Mostly gibberish, but Walker would love to decipher a puzzle like this.

Stopping by a storage room, she found towels and sheets wrapped in a clinging film of thin plastic that she removed and set aside. In her old life, she would have tried to find a use for it. Collecting a stack, she returned to the others to share what she'd found so far. She passed Ginger and Tatsuda in their room and placed the stack of sheets and towels inside on one of the unclaimed bunks.

She continued down the hall to where Walker had opened a door on the other side of the entryway. There was a kitchen and eating area with long tables and benches. He'd arranged four bowls and several pouches of food near an electric kettle and the sink. Turning to her, he set a handful of forks on the counter.

"I'm going to take a shower," Elsa said, walking over to Walker and kissing him, enjoying the way their lips fit together, even though he hadn't shaved in over a week and was prickly.

Touching her lower back, Walker said, "I'll join you," sending jolts of electricity through her. "I'm not hungry yet. I was just seeing what there was to eat."

She glanced up as Tatsuda appeared in the doorway. "Showering can wait if you need us," she said to the boy.

Tatsuda winked. "Don't worry, Elsa, we can entertain ourselves." The joking note left his voice as he lowered his voice. "Anything I take down here, I can keep, right?"

She laughed. That was his burning question? "Within reason. When we leave, we have to carry anything new in our backpacks. So, if you decide to take everything that isn't fastened in place, your pack will weigh you down."

For a second, his shoulders slumped, crestfallen.

"Why don't you and Ginger pick out sleeping bags, backpacks, and new boots to start? Maybe clothes too. You've outgrown most of yours and Ginger lost everything except what she's wearing. You can shower in the bathroom on your side of the hall. I left you towels." She looked up to see Tatsuda's face flaming tomato red. It took her a second to catch up.

"Shower separately, of course." Elsa hadn't meant to embarrass him.

He gave a quick nod and left.

Grimacing at Walker, she left to gather soap, a comb, and clean clothes.

* * *

"I've wanted to get you alone," said Walker, once he'd shaved and joined her under the running water, letting the heavenly spray wash away the dirt of their long overland journey. Some of her tension had seeped down the drain with the muddy water.

"I like when we have time alone too." Elsa slid her arms around his neck to pull him closer. She looked into his eyes, expecting a good-natured reply, but found that he was in a more serious mood. She left her hands where they were and bit her lip. "What did you want to talk to me about?"

His gray eyes flashed with acknowledgement, and he tugged her against his hard body. They found contact helped with the serious discussions. "Your nightmares."

She stiffened and tried not to cringe. Of course, he'd noticed.

She looked down, watching the soapy water swirl down the drain. She avoided giving an explanation. He might think less of her.

"Jace can't hurt you anymore," he said, his voice soft. "He's dead."

Her head jerked up. "That's the problem. I killed a man. Now his ghost follows me in my dreams. It's like he's haunting me." Her voice sounded shrill, but the tight feeling in her chest became less as she admitted her fear. "I never wanted to be a murderer." Her voice caught and her vision blurred.

The word hung between them for a moment in the shower's steam. Walker tipped her chin upward. His eyes looked as dark and fierce as she'd ever seen them. Usually she was the intense one, not him. "I'll tell you as many times as you need to hear it until you believe it. You may have killed that asshole, but if you hadn't, I would have. He deserved everything he got. You aren't a murderer."

"You would have killed him?" Her legs felt weak. Walker's arms around her tightened.

"I'd do anything to keep you safe. As much as you'll let me. You insisted on fighting him with me. You're my fierce hawk for a reason, but I wish you'd been spared this pain, this guilt. He wasn't worth it alive and he sure as hell isn't worth it dead."

Walker's words washed over her as she tipped her hair back into the stronger stream to rinse out the shampoo. He was right. Jace had deserved what had happened. A weight fell from her chest, allowing her to breathe freely for the first time in months.

Elsa stood on tiptoe to kiss Walker, excitement coursing through her, the stronger for unburdening herself. She'd been going about this wrong. Walker would help her just like she could help him deal with his brother's absence. They were a team.

Afterward, safe in his arms, she basked in the feeling of bliss and vowed to release her guilt. It wasn't her fault that Jace was dead. He'd brought it on himself with his own actions. Walker was right. It was time to forgive herself.

* * *

Four days later, Elsa put down the third book she'd finished. Her mind had been blown by what she'd learned about North American society in the twenty-first century. There'd been billions of people in the world on several continents, which was so much larger than she imagined. Whatever catastrophe had happened to this continent must have affected other places as well, or why hadn't people with so much wealth and technology helped? It had decimated the people here. It might have been something to do with climate change or disease that would have affected people everywhere. There was a reason it was known as the Collapse.

Perhaps somewhere else there would be a clue about the final events that culminated in the world's current state, or perhaps she could find something about GreenCorps and how they'd thrived for another two centuries. The corporation had been mentioned by name in the letter she'd found in the tube from a hundred and seventy years ago. It hadn't sounded like GreenCorps had always been the far-reaching power that they were now, but perhaps there would be something about their origin that could help bring about their destruction.

Elsa shook her head. Unable to chase the thought that this fight was bigger than even the seed bunkers and food supply. She sounded like a rebel.

Chapter 19: Mason plus Walker

In the days following their overnight stay in the first cave, Mason led Caitlyn further west and deeper into Craters of the Moon. Each night, they sought refuge in the caves that pocketed the volcanic wasteland. Once, they found free-flowing water underground, where they bathed in the icy stream as well as drank their fill. Mason imprinted the location in his mind so they could return if necessary. The hot black and dark purple rocks remained sweltering at mid-day, but they used the early morning and late evening to traverse most of the distance between caves and shaded overhangs. Whenever possible, they holed up during the most extreme heat.

Mason glanced at Caitlyn many times as they walked. Her confident stride never faltered, despite the sweat dripping down her face. There was a lot of ground to cover and he couldn't expect to find the rebels in a day or even four. He stuck near the ridges and the caves. That was the best bet. He'd find them in time. His chest tightened. He hadn't found signs that Grady or the rebels were out here yet, but that wasn't what left him frustrated.

He studied Caitlyn again, admiring her self-possessed walk. That damn woman. His body ached for her. Their lone encounter hadn't left him satisfied, instead it had whetted his appetite and left him craving physical contact. But it was more than that, because if that's all it had meant, he wouldn't have had any scruples about trying for a repeat performance. His heart yearned for the connection.

He'd never been close to anyone except her, long ago, and until he'd seen her emerge from her barn two weeks ago, he hadn't felt the lack. But now, a gaping hole existed inside him and he was tired of being alone.

After they'd had sex, she'd shut him out. Oh, she'd been polite and civil, but frosty and unapproachable—like she'd erected a brick wall between them. Perhaps she sensed his thoughts, half turning to look at him with a sideways glance.

There was no warmth in her regard. He clenched his jaw. The woman was aggravating. She acted like their sex had been only physical, but he'd been there. There'd been a moment of vulnerability in her eyes. He'd see it plain as day before she'd locked herself away again behind her practicality.

Mason could be patient. Hell, he would be somehow. What was a week, or a month, compared to all these years? She'd waited five years before moving on. Even if she hadn't been consciously waiting for him, it had been years before she'd opened up and trusted Mathew. The thought was staggering. He owed her time to adjust, but he had to convince her see him as more than a convenience, more than just a way to relieve their mutual needs. If not now, then eventually. This time on their own may be his best chance to demonstrate his genuine feelings and allow her to see the real him.

The bright sun burned his eyes, forcing him to squint as they walked toward the sunset; orange light spreading along the horizon, the edges lost in the haze. He turned his head to scan the nearby formation for caves when the sound of human voices carried on an errant breeze. Heart pounding, he sank to the ground and hissed at Caitlyn to follow his example. She crouched beside him and lifted an eyebrow in inquiry, looking more curious than worried.

Mason raised his hand, entreating her to wait, to trust his instinct. The voices could be Grady and his men. Or not.

The sound came again, louder and more distinctive. This time, her face lit up with a wide smile and his heart skipped a beat. He wished he could make her look like that. He hadn't realized how much she guarded her expressions until moments like this. She glowed. She sprinted toward the sound without looking back. Was she in love with whoever was out there not too far away?

He'd never been one for envy until this moment. He'd never had a use for jealousy or patience for those in its grip. He wasn't jealous of Mathew—the man was dead. No point in being envious of a corpse, but he wanted to hate whoever was over that rise. He kicked a rock and watched it bounce before he followed her path.

At the summit of the ridge, he looked down. Caitlyn was fifty yards away, in the arms of a familiar man. The joy on her face had been for Darren, his father's right-hand man. The same smile remained on her face as she turned to the slim, unassuming man in denim. Grady.

Like a thunderbolt, it struck Mason as he strode to meet them. He'd been a fool for even that brief burst of jealousy, and felt like a petulant child. With Mathew and her parents dead, these men were her family.

Grady looked up, peering at him through his tinted glasses, the dark, ax-shaped birthmark on his forehead prominent in the sun. The man could never be mistaken for anyone else, though he often wore a hat or bandana to cover his identifying mark. Grady didn't look like anyone important, but to GreenCorps, he was public enemy number one.

Grady's gaze met Mason's and the older man nodded. "Mason. We didn't expect to see you out here." He hugged Caitlyn from the side, a quick one-armed squeeze.

Her eyebrows shot up. Grady wasn't a demonstrative man. Perhaps surprising them both, she kissed his father's cheek.

"You two lose my niece and her boyfriend?" said Grady, looking around in case more travelers appeared from over the stony ridge at their backs.

The man didn't look angry, more curious than anything. That was a positive sign.

Caitlyn shook her head. "We found another seed bunker, but they're inside, with Jaxon McCoy camped on the doorstep. He was waiting nearby, like he knew she'd be coming. GreenCorps may have their own maps."

"But no key. Excellent." Grady said, satisfaction in his voice. "That girl is too tough for her own good." His admiration was obvious. "How'd her shoulder heal? That was a nasty stab wound."

"Full range of motion. Twinges of pain, but she's fine," said Caitlyn. "In another month or two, she won't feel a thing."

Turning to Mason, Grady said. "You decided about going to Canada?"

Apparently, Mason had to answer now. In front of Darren and Caitlyn. He hated to be put on the spot, but he'd already made his decision. He swallowed, his father's direct gaze making him nervous. Buying a moment to collect his thoughts, he watched a dozen leathered, hard-looking men gathered at the base of the slope a hundred yards away. They were sparring on the plain, crumbly black stone with an equal number of young recruits, bashing away with wooden staves. The young men looked younger every time Mason saw the newest volunteers. Had he and Mathew looked that green to Darren and the men who'd trained them?

"I'm in for the long haul." His glance flicked to Caitlyn, who was chatting with Darren. As the words left his mouth, he wasn't sure if he was talking about her or the mission. Grady clapped him on the shoulder and nodded, his glance also straying to Caitlyn with a nod.

Grady's tone turned to business. "Tell me what that feisty Elsa's gotten herself into this time. How can we help?"

For a second time, an uncharacteristic spike of jealousy stabbed Mason. What was a niece when you had an unacknowledged son? Shouldn't his father be more concerned with why he was here? Pushing the thought away, he followed Grady and Caitlyn to the shade of a three-sided tent that had been set up where they could sit and have a drink.

"How can I help with GreenCorps?" said Grady. The patch of shade did nothing to lessen the temperature, but it helped to be out of the direct glare of the blazing sun.

Mason wiped his face with a handkerchief and shoved his battered hat back into position, once more shading his eyes.

"GreenCorps wants you more than they want her," said Mason, one corner of his mouth turning up.

"You're thinking to dangle me as bait? Create a diversion," said Grady, pursing his lips. "I'm not ready to risk the new kids, but we could arrange something. How will Elsa know when to run? Does her bunker have windows?"

Mason signalled the negative. He didn't think so, though he hadn't inspected the small surface building.

"It's been four days," said Caitlyn, leaning back in her chair. "Doubt she's been waiting by the door all day, but she, Walker, Tatsuda, and the new girl won't stay inside forever."

Picking up on what she was saying, Mason said, "The younger McCoy might have split loyalties right now. GreenCorps and family duties."

"How so?" said Grady, his hands steepled before him.

"Jaxon's little sister has run away and McCoy Sr. wants her back. Tatsuda collected the girl in Pocatello when some soldiers were about to rough her up. She's in the bunker, though I don't think McCoy considered her his number one priority. He's likely been given orders to find his sister and send her home."

"Find Ginger." Caitlyn shrugged when Mason turned his gaze on her. "She has a name."

"Another stray," laughed Grady, perhaps noticing the protective note in Caitlyn's voice.

It surprised Mason how different his father acted around Caitlyn— more relaxed than he'd ever seen the man. Admittedly, he'd only met with his father a few times. Each conversation had been awkward and stilted, for which Mason was also to blame. It was heartening to see this other side of Grady. For the first time, he seemed approachable, not just a legend.

"We'll have to think about this," said Mason. Getting Elsa's attention would be the hardest part.

"Easy," said Caitlyn, grasping her long blonde braid. "Grady pulls Jaxon and GreenCorps away and I bang on the bunker door. Elsa trusts me. If she can hear, she'll come out and we'll split. Run hell-bent to the north and hop a train at Idaho Falls."

"Not Pocatello?" The words left Mason's tongue before he thought.

"Too many guards around that lake," she said. "We could go north. Eliminate that immediate threat of reinforcements McCoy could call on."

Mason liked her plan so far. "Once on the train, then what?" he said, getting caught up in their discussion. This was the most she'd spoken in days.

"Head for Western Canada. Oregon maybe, like Elsa wants."

"GreenCorps will be watching the trains," said Mason, noticing that Grady's calm gaze never wavered as he let them talk this out on their own. "I've never seen such high security as Salt Lake City. Not even in Texas."

"Walker can get us on," said Caitlyn with a wave that dismissed his concerns. "I'm not sure there's anything he doesn't know about trains and hopping, based on his account of the last eight years. Though he didn't brag, I can tell that the man's got skills."

Mason nodded. It could work.

"Is the brother still with them?" said Grady into the lull.

A look of disappointment crossed Caitlyn's face. She shook her head. "He couldn't stay clean and offered to trade Elsa for Walker's pardon. He brought soldiers to the farm in the dead of the night. We fled into the mountains, stopping to get supplies from the Saints and then came north."

"That young man was trouble," said Darren as he joined them in the shade, taking the fourth chair. "Junkies are selfish and weak."

Mason agreed. They seldom stayed clean for long.

"Walker was never leaving Elsa," said Grady. "I saw that the first minute I met the man."

Mason agreed with that assessment, though he hadn't gotten much of a read on the younger brother before he'd stormed off. Mason had been reeling at the discovery of Caitlyn's identity; he'd seen little else.

* * *

Walker followed the instructions for the strange control room. There were lots of unfamiliar words and the going was slow. Even after several reads of the manual, satellites and what they did, remained a mystery. From what he understood, they sounded like technology that the people long ago had shot into space where they orbited the earth and… then he shook his head. He wasn't sure. What was the point of sending chunks of metal into space? Still, his interest was piqued, and it kept his mind occupied.

Elsa had given him this puzzle to solve, a way to spend his time while they remained trapped underground. After years of hopping and the freedom of wandering, being underground for so long became stifling. He missed the fresh air and the open sky.

The lights were on a cycle and shut off at the end of what they were calling a day, but it was difficult to gauge the passage of time without the sun. Each 'morning' he trekked up the long flights of stairs to listen and determine if he could hear noise from outside. They felt no sense of urgency yet, but they couldn't stay here forever. Each time he pressed his ear to the inner door, the indistinct sounds of horses and men remained. Jaxon hadn't given up. Walker had to give the man credit for his persistence.

Hard to believe that a man like that was married to Elsa's sister. Avery must be Elsa's opposite in temperament if she put up with a jackass like Jaxon. It preyed on Elsa, the power this man had over her sister and young nieces, but there was nothing to be done. At least if Jaxon was out here chasing Elsa, he wasn't at home abusing his wife.

Walker twisted his body on the swivel chair, from one side to the other, his long legs under the desk, his feet planted on the concrete floor. He examined the switches, dials, and console again. He'd studied the manual for days and was confident that he understood the first part. He held his breath and pressed a series of buttons on the black box and another at the base of the screen in front of him. He reached and did the same to the second screen.

A faint hum of static filled the small room as the screens came to life, changing from flat black to grainy gray and white. Flipping up a red switch on the console, he pushed the green button, and a message appeared on the right-hand screen, *Searching*.

A few seconds later, the writing changed and read, *Enter coordinates*.

This had stumped him yesterday, and though he still didn't know coordinates for other places, though another manual was referenced, the numbers for here were clear. He'd use the ones for the Aberdeen bunker, listed as the University of Idaho site.

Latitude: 46° 43' 19.79" N
Longitude: -117° 00' 22.80" W

Paying close attention to the numbers and symbols, he entered them on the letter board he'd found yesterday, tucked into a thin pull-out drawer of the desk. He checked the manual for the next step. *Hit Enter*.

Walker held his breath as he clicked the Enter button. The screen on his left changed almost right away. The image sharpened. He gasped.

The picture on the screen was a bird's-eye-view of the bunker entrance and the surrounding land. He couldn't believe the detail on the screen. Though the image was black and white with shades of gray, he recognized Jaxon McCoy surrounded by more than a dozen milling GreenCorps soldiers. He watched the screen as the men moved. Some cooked, another tended the horses. Was this happening outside right now?

Walker could see outside the bunker.

Good. He wouldn't have to climb those bloody stairs anymore to check if GreenCorps had moved on.

On the screen, the burly man with a beard who was speaking to Jaxon caught his attention. Walker clenched his jaw. It was the nasty recruit from Elsa's hometown, the one who'd sold his sister south. Figures that someone with his character rode with McCoy.

Elsa would love this discovery. It could help them escape. Tearing his gaze from the screen, Walker went to find her.

Elsa's reaction was as expected. She dropped everything to stare at the screens. Her eyes went wide when she realized the implications.

"At least we'll know when we can leave now. I hated feeling as blind as a bat." She put her hand on his shoulder. "We need to pack and be ready. I'll gather the seed packets I want to take. All those different grains and several varieties of potatoes. Tatsuda and Ginger have their gear chosen."

Walker couldn't take his eyes from the screen. "If we haul our stuff to the top of the stairs and leave it by the inner door, we can leave a lot faster when the time comes. Wouldn't want to miss an opportunity because our backpacks are heavy." In his head, Walker ran through what he had to pack besides the new socks and his journal. Not much. He'd learned to keep his pack manageable after all these years on the road.

"Good idea," Elsa said. "While the supplies down here would last our small group for years, we can't help anyone if we're stuck here. Mason and Caitlyn will figure out a way to get us out of here. All we have to do is wait for our opportunity."

* * *

Interdepartmental Memo
Western Canada
August 28, 2195

Observations:
Unexplained satellite activity observed from one of our inactive satellites. The satellite was owned by the former United States of America. Last known activity May 2025.
The satellite is listed as last used by the Department of Agriculture.
Satellite position changed to track something at the following coordinates:
Latitude: 46° 43' 19.79" N
Longitude: -117° 00' 22.80" W
The coordinates indicate a position in the ruins of the Idaho University Research facility outside Aberdeen, Idaho.
Conclusion: Someone has accessed the seed vault and bunker at this location and manually changed the satellite position.
Recommendation: Further monitoring of other seed bunker locations within GreenCorps territory—they may have gained access.

Chapter 20: Caitlyn plus Ginger

Perched inside the mouth of the cavern where they'd bunked down, Caitlyn looked up from the letter she was trying to compose and took in her surroundings. She endeavored to write using the remaining natural light before turning in for the night.

The rebels had situated their camp in an extensive system of interconnected caves, accessed through one main entrance. Grady had given Caitlyn a cavern of her own. She could have slept with the group but liked that he'd been considerate of her needing privacy.

Below, rebels moved around, training. As always these days, her gaze was drawn like a magnet to Mason, his lean strength holding her attention. No matter where she went, he seemed to be in her line of sight. She wasn't sure which of them was responsible for this, but it was unlikely to be by chance. She frowned. She hadn't meant to put herself where she could watch him drilling with some of the younger men and women, and this wasn't the first time today.

She ended up watching more and writing less.

The plan to distract Jaxon and GreenCorps had come together over dinner. They were leaving early tomorrow for the long, hot walk back toward Aberdeen and the bunker. She sighed. At least their route would be more direct than on the way here, because they were no longer searching for Grady. They would arrive south of Aberdeen and the reservoir after two days of trekking instead of four. Mid-morning on day three, they'd strike. Once Elsa emerged, they would hike overland to Idaho Falls, another three grueling days.

In Idaho Falls, they'd hide until the train came through and then on to the next stop in either Boise or the coast. Caitlyn turned off the milling thoughts in her brain; that part of the plan would have to wait. They still had to collect Elsa's group first.

Grady had made arrangements for Darren and two other people to stay at the training ground, while he and most of his experienced rebels planned an operation where they would be sure to be seen heading toward Pocatello at the time they expected Caitlyn and Mason to be in position. They'd move closer to the Snake River Reservoir so that the soldiers stationed there would send a messenger to Jaxon. Of course, Grady and his men would fade into the desert and circle back when the bait had been taken.

The bunker would still be guarded—from what she'd heard Jaxon was like a dog with a bone when it came to Elsa—but the diversion should pull sufficient personnel that she and Mason could deal with whoever was left. She and Mason would attempt to alert Elsa when they were outside. If it didn't work, they'd try again in a couple of days.

Caitlyn forced herself to look away from the tall, handsome man and focused on her notebook filled with letters. She'd written less since Elsa and Walker had come to the farm; she hadn't been as lonely. She flipped back, scanning the dates. She'd only written once since Mason's arrival, and nothing since what had happened a few days ago in the cave. Telling Mathew about her attraction to Mason and their history seemed thoughtless. Though illogical, part of her felt like she'd cheated on Mathew.

Her husband was dead, and hadn't been harmed by what she'd done. He'd likely even be happy that she'd gone on living and found someone to care for. Her guilt was misplaced, and she needed to let that go. Having sex with Mason had just been to break the sexual tension, to get it out of their systems—or that's what she'd pretended to herself afterward.

Instead, she craved more. She'd missed sex, missed being loved and in love, but she most of all she'd missed feeling anything. Too much of her life was going through the motions. She needed more than that.

Mason made her feel like no one else. It was as true now as it was long ago. Did that make her disloyal? Or just human?

Caitlyn couldn't believe she'd given in to it once and found herself considering ways to get Mason alone again. Something about the way his cool, steely blue eyes saw through her was a turn-on. It might be unfair. She'd seen the hurt in his eyes when she'd pretended to be indifferent. Others found him inscrutable, but she'd always seen the emotion at his heart.

She hadn't fooled him, though. He'd seen through her as well.

This time when she glanced up—still without having written a word—he tipped his hat. The setting sun framed his figure.

Mason had caught her.

Her cheeks flamed as she stared back, unwilling now to be the first to drop her eyes. Heat spread downward until she flushed all over. Beads of sweat gathered on her brow and her stomach fluttered. Mason's lips twitched with a fleeting smirk.

Darren walked between them, unknowingly breaking the spell.

Caitlyn used that to bolt back toward her small cave to the left, where none of the men would bother her. Everyone else would sleep in the passage off to the right. Or so she'd been assured. With her heart racing, she guzzled a long drink of water. What the hell was she doing? Her hand shook as she fumbled to refasten the lid.

"You want me to do that?" Mason's presence filled the cavern.

She hadn't heard him approach, his steps as quiet as a cat.

She'd tried ignoring him for four days, but it had taken its toll. She'd tried not to see him, not to notice the way sparks flew between them. Back in that first cave, she'd told him she wanted to feel. This is what she got for playing with fire. Her resistance had lowered. If she turned around now, she wasn't sure she'd be able to shut him out the next time. She wasn't certain she wanted to. Her heart thumped against her ribs, its rhythm increasing.

"What are you scared of?" he asked, his voice pitched low.

Mason hadn't touched her, but now that he was here, she couldn't concentrate on anything else. Thoughts of him crowded out everything.

"I don't think I could handle losing another person," she said, trying to keep her voice steady. His scent of sweat and dried grass enveloped her as he moved closer. He stood right behind her, his warmth close enough to feel.

His outstretched hand took her canteen. He tipped it back and drank. "You want me."

His voice was flat, but that just meant that he was suppressing his emotions. Somehow, she just knew. The less intonation, the more it mattered.

"I want you too." His voice seemed to reach for her like drifting smoke. "I never should have left you in Denver. I was a stupid kid and I've regretted it every day since. Will you give us another chance?"

Her shoulders ached with tension, but she answered before she could stop herself. "You won't leave? Everyone says that, but they do." She grimaced at her biting tone. This bitterness was a slow poison that had almost destroyed who she used to be. Even her bones were sick of loss.

"I won't if I can help it." His voice was steady but soft.

Caitlyn turned, searching his face. He was dead serious, and she wanted to believe him. Trembling like an aspen leaf, she touched his stubbled jaw. He pulled her close, and she didn't resist as he wrapped his arms around her and clasped his hands behind her back.

"Caitlyn, be my angel," Mason whispered, resting his forehead on hers.

Pulse racing, unable to speak, she kissed him as a tear rolled down her cheek.

* * *

Ginger wrapped a fluffy white towel around herself after her long shower and returned to the room she shared with Tatsuda. It was so nice to have access to running water again. She wasn't sure when that would happen next. She double-checked that she was alone before grabbing new clothes. Tatsuda wasn't there because it was his turn to monitor the screens Walker had discovered. In half an hour, she would take her first shift watching the bunker door next. It was unbelievable to think that they could watch outside with old technology that allowed them to see what was happening without Jaxon and his henchmen ever knowing.

She dressed in her new clothes, durable blue pants and a plain yellow t-shirt. She'd been drawn to its lovely color, like that of the pale roses she'd admired from her window, and it was softer than anything she'd ever owned. The clothes choices had been limited, but she'd loved a chance to choose things herself rather than accept what had been chosen for her by whoever her father had tasked with the job.

She grimaced at thoughts of her father. Jaxon had seen her outside and would report her whereabouts at the first opportunity. There might be a phone in Pocatello, or if not, Idaho Falls. When Jaxon had screamed her name outside the bunker, she'd frozen, scared that he would take her home no matter what she wanted. Elsa had broken the spell by shoving her through the door. It had surprised Ginger that Elsa hadn't left her outside. Tatsuda said she never would have done that, but Ginger still wasn't sure how she felt about Elsa.

On one hand, the other woman was tough while still being understanding. She'd allowed the others to convince her that Ginger could travel with them, but she'd also killed Jace. If Ginger believed the story Elsa told, which had the ring of truth, then Jace had deserved to be stabbed. It was one thing to accept that, it was another to be friendly with his killer. Ginger couldn't do it. For Tatsuda, she tried to be polite, but she did her best to avoid Elsa, who spent most of her days reading old books. She was researching what life was like a couple of hundred years ago, before the Collapse.

Ginger had made use of the library too, but mostly for novels, and had packed four battered paperbacks in her new backpack—which now sat at the top of that huge flight of metal stairs. If she became separated from the others or left behind in town, she could always sell her excess supplies. She was determined not to starve or sell her body.

She'd also read a little about the collapse of the previous civilization from yellowed newspapers left in the library. The world had been overpopulated and a mess, heading toward shortages and something called climate change, caused by human activity. The final blow had been an asteroid that had been broken into pieces before it struck the coast of what had once been America. The main impact and several smaller ones had triggered earthquakes and volcanoes worldwide and sent climate change into a spiral that had led to massive food shortages.

Even now, GreenCorps claimed to be the heroes, leading the return of food production and spearheading environmental clean-up efforts. She'd seen firsthand in Pocatello how GreenCorps spun lies to sound like facts, and to make good people seem like villains—she wasn't sure GreenCorps history was the authentic version.

It still blew her mind how much more there was to learn about life beyond Denver. She hadn't asked Elsa for details, but Tatsuda had gleaned information about Elsa's past in the months they'd been together. She'd grown up in a SoCal workcamp, scavenging from trash to survive. Ginger couldn't imagine surviving that way. Elsa had been born there. An infant couldn't have done anything wrong to deserve to live in a political workcamp. Through no fault of her own, Elsa had grown up with nothing. In contrast, Ginger had had the advantage of wealth and unlimited food and water, even if they hadn't led to happiness.

Ginger laced up her new hiking shoes while she considered Jaxon's mysterious wife, and Elsa's sister Avery. What had drawn Jaxon to marry her? He hadn't told the family about his wife and children, though perhaps only she hadn't known. Perhaps he'd been ashamed of a wife from the Heap. If he'd had sons, would he have told their father? Probably. Boys seemed worth more than girls to Malcolm McCoy. Her father wouldn't have considered granddaughters of consequence or value. Meeting tough and independent women like Elsa and Caitlyn made Ginger more confident that changing to become more like them was the right path. Was there a way she could help her nieces? She liked the idea of being Aunt Ginger, world traveler.

With Jaxon chasing first Elsa, and now herself, was he still providing for his family? He'd always had a tendency to obsess about one thing and forget about everything else. She couldn't help but worry. Were Avery and the little girls getting enough to eat? Was that something she could ask Elsa? The idea was terrifying. Ginger had overheard the soldier say they'd cut water supplies to SoCal. That might affect the hundreds, perhaps thousands of children, which was wrong.

It seemed like living isolated and away from everyone else in SoCal, was much like how she'd grown up. Just dirtier. Maybe her nieces would end up being bargaining chips the way she almost had. Ginger shook her head. Life differed from what she'd thought. She felt compelled to do something, if not only for herself, but for all the children who lived, wanting for basic necessities.

CHAPTER 21: MASON

Mason and Caitlyn woke at dawn, still entangled in her bedding after a night with little sleep—the best kind of sleepless. His skin thrummed with energy and Mason couldn't help but smile at her, disheveled and lovely as he rose and dressed. He stamped his feet into his boots, he looked down and found her watching him. He'd prefer to linger, but the others would expect departure soon.

"You regret last night?" He had to know if he'd be chasing her again tonight.

Pink stained Caitlyn's cheeks as she got ready and packed her bedroll. Looking up, she shook her head, her smile lighting up the cave more than the lantern on the gritty floor. They were headed out this morning, and he was glad that something had settled between them before they rejoined the others.

Mason settled his hat and gave Caitlyn one last kiss, once more marveling at the softness of her lips. It would have to last the day. Maybe two. She might need time to figure out where she stood. Moving on from Mathew physically was one thing, emotionally would be harder.

Grady gave him a nod when they rejoined the primary group in front of the cave. Despite the privacy of Caitlyn's alcove, it wouldn't have gone unnoticed that Mason had chased her inside last night and not returned until now. While he didn't need Grady's approval, it might be easier this way for Caitlyn. She trusted Grady and valued his opinion.

Hats on and gear packed, ten rebels joined them, hiking single file back toward Aberdeen. Darren accompanied them for the first hour to set them on the correct path and point the way to the next landmark. The temperature was pleasant throughout the pale morning, but it would soon be scorching hot. Darren told jokes and fooled around with everyone.

Mason watched him, moving throughout the troop. It was hard not to like someone who was always in a pleasant mood. Mason could understand why Grady trusted Darren. He had a solid relationship with each of their comrades. He even teased Caitlyn like an older brother. Darren hugged Caitlyn, slapped Mason on the back, and spoke a quiet word or two with Grady before turning back toward camp.

They hiked two days through the crumbled black rock in near silence, enduring the baking heat without complaint. The group slept crowded together in a cave the first night, though Mason preferred sleeping outside. The second night, he camped under the blanket of stars, close to another cave system where they'd replenished their water. The wasteland was deceptive, with hidden water in numerous pockets protected by stone.

Tonight, Mason set up away from the others. It was clear and overnight would be cold, but though he was welcome among them, he craved the peace and solitude of his own company. In the morning, he and Caitlyn would split off from the others and continue toward the bunker entrance. He would feel better about Grady and the rebels' chances of remaining free if they had horses, but they'd brought none. Feeding horses in the desert would have been difficult where wild feed was limited, and only GreenCorps could afford to carry horse feed in quantity. Mason had to trust that Grady could evade capture; after all, the man had been a fugitive his entire life.

Mason started awake with a jerk at a faint sound on his right. His pulse throbbing, he peered into the darkness until Caitlyn emerged, a dim outline in the moonlight. He hadn't expected her to join him, though he'd hoped. He wasn't sorry for the company. He started to sit up, but she shook her head, kicked off her boots, and slipped in beside him. Her bare arms felt cool in the night air and he tucked her close to his chest, his arm wrapped around her shoulder. They could keep each other warm. Tonight, he was content with her company. Waking up next to her the other morning had soothed some of the jagged edges inside.

He didn't speak as she lay her head on his shoulder and rested her hand over his pounding heart.

"I want to give us a try," Caitlyn said in a whisper.

Her words spoke to his secret wish. He'd been right to be patient and let her lead this time. Her body became limp as she fell asleep almost right away. Mason's heart filled, and he was almost scared to sleep. What if he woke and found he'd been dreaming? He lay there a little longer, enjoying the smell and feel of this woman in his arms, before he found peace and drifted off to sleep.

* * *

Mid-morning, Mason and Caitlyn slithered through the sparse vegetation on their stomachs and forearms to the summit of a small hill overlooking the rubble of the University of Idaho. They'd circled the GreenCorps camp below and now watched from the north. It had been a week since Elsa and the others had locked themselves in the bunker. Jaxon still waited for her to exit. Without intervention, it was difficult to guess how long he'd stay. He must have other obligations in other parts of the GreenCorps empire—however, his personal vendetta against Elsa may supersede his responsibilities.

McCoy and a dozen GreenCorps soldiers under his command sprawled around a camp with half a dozen small canvas tents in an untidy clump. It had been easy to spot their camp from afar because lazy spirals of smoke rose into the air.

There wouldn't be much for these men to do besides wait, and they were most likely bored. Two looked like they were napping, another group half-heartedly played cards, and one poked at the dying campfire and watched the sparks rise. They'd eaten a cooked breakfast. Mason's stomach rumbled despite his breakfast bar, now hours in the past. Campaigning was hungry work.

Mason and Caitlyn stayed low, his heart thumping against his ribs in pre-raid excitement. He'd had this jittery feeling on dozens of occasions in the last ten years, but this was the first time Caitlyn had been at his side. While minor thoughts of concern crossed his mind, she was strong and capable. Working together as a team made this more likely to succeed. They belly-crawled to a better concealed hiding place behind a clump of thick sagebrush that spilled over the hill and settled in to wait.

About an hour later, a rider approached from the southeast at a gallop. Not long now.

The messenger's excited voice carried to their hiding place on the hill. "McCoy. Grady's been spotted nearby." The rider puffed his chest out as he pulled his horse to a halt. "He's on foot with less than a dozen men. They can't spare anyone from the garrison. This might be a trap, or a feint to draw them away from the lake. Grady can't take the reservoir or he'll control the potato crop this year. Orders are for you to take your men, intercept, and take him prisoner. They want him alive."

Jaxon cursed where he sat, leaning against a rock with a view of the bunker door, half-facing Mason on the mound above. "And the ones we have trapped?" Jaxon leapt to his feet. Scowling, he stared over his shoulder at the bunker door. "Other than my sister, the rest are expendable."

The horse danced with energy under the rider instead of standing still, indicating that the messenger hadn't ridden far—probably from the garrison stationed at the southern end of the reservoir. Everything was going to plan so far. Mason kept his eyes riveted below. Would Jaxon take the bait or insist his vengeance was more important?

"Isn't there anyone else who can go?" McCoy said with a growl.

"The order comes from your father," said the messenger, swallowing. Perhaps he'd been the target of Jaxon's frustration on another occasion.

McCoy flung the contents of his mug onto the ground and spat on the dry ground. "Bill and George, you're staying here."

The soldier by the fire and one of the men playing cards nodded, then smirked as the others threw down their cards in a heap.

"Wade, you and the rest, be packed and saddled in five. If we capture Grady, your careers are made. If we do this, they'll let me stay here for five years, if that's what it takes to catch my bitch sister-in-law." McCoy drummed his fingers against his thigh as he spoke, glaring at the bunker once more.

The man must hate leaving with Elsa so close to his grasp.

"Yes, sir," said a bearded man. Everyone scuttled around, getting ready to leave. "We can get Grady and still be back tonight," said the tough that McCoy had identified as Wade. "Travel light," he shouted to the others. He kicked one man who was slow to rise.

Mason watched as the men saddled their horses. To his satisfaction, there were three extra horses, including the one he'd ridden last week. With the horses of the men left behind, there would be five remaining. He and Caitlyn would have to neutralize the men quietly, so they didn't bring McCoy and his men rushing back. The sound of gunshots would travel.

The GreenCorps soldiers thundered away with the messenger, leaving the two men behind.

When the riders were out of sight, he and Caitlyn crept closer.

"Think they'll catch Grady?" said one of the men. He speared a piece of processed-looking meat from a pan set at the edge of the fire. Blowing, he ate it off his knife.

"About as likely as we are to catch the girl in the bunker," said the second man with a yawn. He pulled his hat lower over his eyes. "Whole fucking country is one wild goose chase after another. At least we get paid."

"Too bad that blonde got away. I chased her and that fellow for hours. All we found were the stolen horses. She looked tasty, and I bet she would've squealed."

Mason and Caitlyn shared a look. So, they had been followed.

"Don't be an idiot. She's long gone. No good thinking about her," said the other man. "But I'll admit she was more my type than Jaxon's sister-in-law. That bitch looked bony and cold. Wait until we're back in town in a few days. There are girls at the pleasure houses. We're due to be rotated out this afternoon. Tomorrow at the latest, if this Grady thing causes a delay."

Mason spared a look at Caitlyn and clenched his jaw. Grady might be closer to more soldiers than he meant to be if another contingent of soldiers was headed here as replacements. The rebel leader might be forced to make a real run for it. Mason seethed at the casual way the men talked about rape and women he considered friends. Grady's men would have been dismissed for that kind of talk. GreenCorps didn't seem to care how brutal and unruly their men acted.

Caitlyn must have heard and seen worse on rebel missions when she'd rescued the unwilling pleasure house workers in Texas, but Mason didn't have to like it. He shook his head to refocus on what was happening right now. Both Caitlyn and Elsa were more woman than these cowards could handle.

Caitlyn whispered, "New plan. I'm going to talk to them. They'll run this way. We each knock one out, tie them up, blindfold them and leave them behind."

He didn't like her plan or the idea of her putting herself at risk. "Or slit their throats." Mason hadn't liked the recruits before they'd opened their mouths. Now he hated them.

"I'm not big on killing if we don't have to." Caitlyn looked at him with her blue eyes and he was lost. Leaving witnesses wasn't the best idea, but he'd try it her way.

"Unconscious might work. They can say we were here," said Mason, thinking of the upside of her plan. "Jaxon and the others will know Elsa's out, guessing she gambled on getting away when she couldn't hear them outside. They shouldn't cause additional harm if they can't see us leave."

"Too bad we can't get him to stay here waiting for another week." Caitlyn's eyes sparkled. With no further talk, she stood and waved with both arms at the men below. "Hello. Can you help me?"

Mason resisted the urge to snort. They wouldn't be dumb enough to fall for that. It was so desolate out here—there was no believable reason she should be here.

Both men jumped to their feet, reaching for their guns, but seeing a solo Caitlyn, they put down their weapons. Stupid move.

"I've gotten turned around and I lost my friend. I was hoping you could point the way back to Pocatello." She stood skylined with her hand on her hip, showing off her incredible figure. The men wouldn't be able to make out her face with the bright morning sun behind her. She'd chosen the perfect position.

The men below looked stunned, first staring at her speechless, then at each other.

"Mine," shouted one, running.

"I get a turn too," said the other, springing after him.

"Stop right there," she said, stepping back, looking like she was going to bolt. "That's far enough. I just need directions."

The soldiers kept running. Mason unsheathed his knife. In his other hand, he gripped a solid chunk of stone. With the front man fifteen yards away, too close for Mason's comfort, Caitlyn lunged at last and ran. She passed where he crouched behind the sagebrush. He held his breath, letting the first man pass. She could take care of one. His turn came moments later.

He tackled the second man to the ground, smashing the man's head with his chunk of black rock. The GreenCorps recruit went limp and his eyes rolled back. His chest rose and fell. Mason looked up as Caitlyn threw her opponent to the hard ground. The soldier landed on his back, his breath rushing out with an oomph. He struggled to move, but Caitlyn kicked him in the groin, making him curl into a groaning ball.

In this vulnerable position, she smashed his head with a rock and he stopped moving. Mason liked her tough.

They rushed, tying the men together, sitting up behind the ridge where they wouldn't be able to see the camp or the bunker door. Mason made blindfolds from their socks and lengths of cord, then rolled their second sweaty sock and stuffed them into their mouths. He grimaced at the smell, but the soldiers could breathe, even if they wouldn't be coherent until the gags were removed.

He and Caitlyn returned to the bunker door.

With the GreenCorps men secured, Caitlyn pounded on the heavy metal. "Elsa. It's Caitlyn." She banged again. "It's safe. Jaxon's gone."

There was no answer from within. "This might take a while," she said with a shrug. "We couldn't expect they'd be sitting by the door waiting to be rescued." She thumped on the door again a minute later, while Mason kept watch and checked the prisoners before making himself busy. She continued at regular intervals.

He saddled the remaining horses in preparation to ride and scavenged what he could from the belongings left scattered in camp. Though they were alone, it was challenging to keep from jumping at every sound. He and Caitlyn were exposed and in the open. While there was no indication of the men regaining consciousness, waiting for the plan to work was nerve-wracking. He wasn't sure how much longer they should wait. An hour? Two tops. He didn't think Jaxon's company would find Grady, but there was always the chance that the GreenCorps forces might get lucky, but he couldn't spare worry for his father. Grady knew the risk.

Mason's head remained on a swivel, acting as lookout. Leaving here, the group would need a head start. He didn't want to chance immediate pursuit with a bunch of inexperienced riders.

He threaded a rope between three of the horses, attaching them to a lead. He hoped Caitlyn's banging paid off. They would stay as long as possible, but at the first sign of the soldiers, they'd leave. Elsa or no Elsa. His number one rule was, *'Don't get caught'*.

Mason's jaw almost dropped when fifteen minutes later, the bunker door opened inward with a scraping sound. A backpack came shooting out, with Elsa right behind, carrying another pack against her chest, her arms looped through the straps. She blinked in the bright light, looking in every direction. She must want to be sure it was safe.

"You heard," said Caitlyn with a wide smile.

The door ground open a few more inches and Tatsuda, Ginger, and Walker exited the bunker.

Caitlyn hugged Elsa. "I wasn't sure you'd get to the door in time."

Walker hauled the door closed, then double-checked the handle, shaking it to ensure that it was locked. Nice. GreenCorps was out of luck. Mason might have liked to see inside, but they'd been successful. Hopefully, their full packs were worth the trip.

"Thanks. We watched most of the men leave and when you distracted the others, we hurried up the stairs. What did the rider say to make the others follow?" Elsa tugged up her UVee goggles.

"How'd you watch?" said Caitlyn. "You were underground?"

"I'll explain later, but the quick version is that Walker pulled the focus back on the satellite when the riders left, so we got a clearer picture. We'd left everything we wanted, packed and ready at the top a few days ago."

Satellite? He wanted that explanation, just not now. Mason approved of their readiness. The less time here, the better. He edged toward the horses.

"Nice work." Walker nodded to Mason. "Those two still out?" He waved at the bound soldiers on the far side of the ridge.

Mason nodded. He didn't know how Walker knew where the men were, but Elsa was right. Someone could explain it later. They needed to leave.

"It's great to see you." Elsa handed Mason the spare backpack she carried. It had some weight to it. "We brought you one."

He looked down, touched. He hadn't been given many gifts. The pack was better than what he was using, and he'd bet whatever she'd put inside would be useful.

"Thanks." His eyes met Elsa's, and she gave a small smile before she turned away.

"Good to be outside again." Walker took several deep breaths, as though relishing the fresh air while he looked around.

If Mason had been cooped up underground for a week, he'd appreciate fresh air and blue sky too. "Anyone know how to ride?" said Mason, getting back to the practical.

"I've been on a horse a couple of times," said Ginger, tossing a long red braid over her shoulder.

Mason suppressed a smile. He'd seen Caitlyn do that toss a thousand times. Seems she had another admirer. He couldn't blame the girl. "You and Tatsuda can share this one," Mason said, patting the flank of the second to last horse. He turned to Walker and Elsa. "You two able to get on? We'll go north; head for Idaho Falls and the station before Pocatello. Looks like it doesn't stop again until Boise, then Portland."

"Riding will be a first." Walker strode over to the last horse. He hesitated and looking a little tentative, he swung himself into the saddle and sat. He hadn't ridden, but at least he must have paid attention when others mounted.

Elsa bit her lip and shrugged. She took the horse right behind Mason.

"Left foot in the stirrup," he said. "Then hop up."

"Like a train," said Walker, with a nod of encouragement.

She followed directions, swinging up. Mason had guessed the stirrup length, but hers were too long. Elsa always seemed larger than her actual size. In that way, her confidence and fierce gaze reminded him of his father.

"I'll be leading, and your horses will follow. Grab the horn if you feel unsteady and pull back on reins hard to make them stop." Mason showed them what he meant while they shifted to get settled, then he readjusted Elsa's stirrups with another pat for the patient horse. Ginger and Tatsuda watched, the two of them side by side, holding hands. It looked more like comfort than attraction. He'd like to hear more about

Ginger's story, if she was willing to share. Her life must not have been all roses or she wouldn't be here, but that was the same for all of them.

Mason checked the two soldiers for a final time. They were still unconscious, but one groaned like he might wake soon. With a last glance in the direction the GreenCorps riders had gone, he trotted down the hill. Mounting the lead horse, just before Caitlyn swung up onto the rear horse, he was ready. She nodded, and he kicked his horse, leading them away.

He missed his gray mare, but it felt good to be in the saddle again. He aimed to get far away so that they wouldn't be visible to returning riders. With the horizon clear, he allowed himself to hope that this venture had been successful. Still, his shoulder blades twitched as he left enemies at his back in an unknown position and headed toward their destination.

It was sixty miles to Idaho Falls and the next train station, and he hoped to cut the traveling time in half by riding. They'd leave the horses at a point along the way where it would be confusing, hoping Jaxon, or whoever else followed, might think they'd headed for Pocatello and take the wrong trail.

Sixty miles was two long days if they walked the horses to keep them fresh and moving. He'd love to ride faster, but it wasn't a sprint, and the horses would do them no good if they dropped from exhaustion. He looked back, checking on the inexperienced riders. They'd be sore tonight after riding astride when they weren't used to it, but horseback was faster than on foot. Ginger, especially, would find walking difficult. Still, the new kid was plucky, even if he made her nervous.

Despite the hurry-up feeling in his chest that made it difficult to breathe and want to gallop, he limited his horse to a quick walk, a pace these hardy campaign horses should be able to sustain. His head swiveled, checking the horizon and watching for the unexpected as they rode north. He was uncertain about what lay in this direction between here and Idaho Falls, but it was best to be prepared.

CHAPTER 22: GINGER

Ginger's legs ached from hugging the horse's wide back, feeling very out of shape. She couldn't wait to get off. Her butt felt bruised after a day and a half on a horse, making her glad she'd hopped a train in Denver and not stolen a horse. Though she'd been clean after the bunker, now she was dirty and sweaty from riding horseback. She'd never imagined the smell associated with close proximity to horses. It wasn't exactly unpleasant, just pervasive. Easy come, easy go.

Riding was harder than she'd expected, especially crowded behind the rigid seat of the saddle, clutching Tatsuda's middle. She tried not to stare at Elsa or Mason, who made her nervous, instead took the time to appreciate the wide-open space of the land through which they traveled. So much better than watching from her upstairs window in Denver. There, to the west, the rugged mountains had closed off the view, like a fortress had enclosed that side of the city. Here, it stretched forever and felt limitless—like her new life.

Everything felt more alive, including herself. She'd spent so much time going through the motions, but every day had been boring and she'd been of no importance. She squeezed Tatsuda a little tighter, happy to be here with him. She looked around once more. It was like the air tasted like freedom. She smiled to herself. That seemed ridiculous, but somehow, it seemed true.

The world was beautiful, even where dominated by drab gold and faded brown. If you looked carefully, there were flowers and birds and a pleasant breeze. At last, she was living. So what if she was covered in dust and a little sore? It was worth the discomfort of having an adventure to be free.

Several times, Mason had passed the lead to Caitlyn and ridden up a nearby ridge or hill to scan back the way they'd traveled, always on the lookout for pursuers. Her brother was likely to be on their trail at some point. She tried to picture Jaxon's reaction when he arrived at the bunker to find his men tied up and his prey escaped. He'd be livid. Would he have taken his anger out on his horse? She hoped not, absently patting the butt of the one where she rode.

She watched as Mason returned from the rise on the left.

"Still clear," he said with a nod. Her horse seemed willing to follow wherever the others went. Without the need to direct her horse, riding seemed easy.

Ginger appreciated Mason's caution, noting that he seemed to like the viewing glasses Walker and Elsa had brought for him from the bunker. It gave them the ability to see much greater distances. Before the light had disappeared in a brilliant blaze of color yesterday, they'd all taken turns looking.

Ginger hadn't mentioned she'd used a pair much like them from her room to see into town. Jace had given them to her when she was ten. She swallowed the apple-sized lump in her throat and flicked a glance at Elsa, who rode just ahead in line. Since her brother had died, it had been easier to only remember the positive things, but she couldn't fault Elsa for defending herself, either. It was just a shame that he'd died and she was coming to grips with his death. Maybe people weren't always all good or all bad, but somewhere in between and capable of both kindness and cruelty. She'd read somewhere that the world wasn't all black and white, but shades of gray. This might be what the writer had meant.

Ginger turned and scanned for Jaxon and the GreenCorps soldiers who could be out there, but like Mason, she didn't see anyone else. They all checked compulsively. Here in the open plains, pursuers would be hard to miss, but it was also difficult to hide. What would they do if someone appeared on the horizon? Gallop?

Now that she'd fallen in with this group, it seemed like she had a chance to survive out here in the world. On her own, she hadn't been doing great. She'd been starving, dependent on stolen water, and almost raped. She just had to convince them to let her stay with them. After what she'd seen in Pocatello and how she'd been attacked near the tracks, she wanted nothing to do with GreenCorps. Too much of what her father and brothers had said seemed to be wrong or lies. If things didn't work out with Elsa, Ginger might join the rebels mentioned by others. She remained determined to make a difference.

What this group was doing after hopping the next train hadn't been explained. They didn't fully trust her with their plan. She understood that, though Tatsuda seemed to have no reservations. In the bunker, they'd had long conversations well into the night, or at least hours after the lights had gone out in their room.

Left to his own devices, he'd probably would have explained what was going on, but he wouldn't go against what Elsa wanted. Ginger would like to stay with them for a long time. Even Elsa. She imagined that her father's GreenCorps partners would kill to get their hands on the seeds and equipment in the bunkers. They'd keep these fertile seeds for themselves and continue to only sell terminator seeds. Keeping them from accessing the bunkers was noble and important.

From what Elsa had shared from her findings in the history books, previous leaders hadn't shied away from killing to get what they wanted. They'd withheld water in their work camps or corporation towns to quell uprisings. Even the soldier by the tracks in Pocatello had bragged about GreenCorps doing that in SoCal earlier this year. It was something current, not just something from the past. Ginger sympathized with those poor people, especially the poor children.

Walker had described what previous GreenCorps leadership had done as crimes against humanity, genocide of the poor, and perpetuating a have and have-not class system. Ginger didn't understand some of those words, but things needed to change.

"Time to leave the horses," Mason said, interrupting her thoughts.

They were near the Snake River, which was on their right as they worked northward, and grass grew on its banks. No matter how much her legs hurt from being on a horse, she would miss riding when she had to walk in this heat. She looked down at her new durable tan pants and boots. She'd enjoyed 'shopping' in the bunker with Tatsuda, replacing everything she'd lost when she'd been assaulted by the train tracks. She didn't like to dwell on what could have happened if Tatsuda hadn't interrupted. She'd been saved, and that was enough.

Mason reined his horse to a stop, saying, "Whoa." He dismounted and unpacked his gear.

Ginger squeezed Tatsuda again before he slid off the horse and he shot her one of his shy smiles. She scooted forward and followed him to the ground, remembering to use the stirrup this time. It seemed strange to stand after so long on the horse, and she swiveled her hips to loosen them, wincing as each movement revealed another ache.

It didn't take long until they unpacked the horses, their saddles loosened, and the lead rope disconnected. Mason pulled their harness things loose on their heads and took the metal bars from their mouths before he set them free. The trio of animals headed toward the water before splitting apart as they meandered toward the thicker light green and golden grass, ripping off chunks to eat.

Mason led his horse and Caitlyn's down to the water, leaving muddy hoofprints and one deliberate boot print on the bank. Jumping from rock to rock, he left the river and returned.

She turned to Tatsuda. "What's he doing?"

"He wants our path to be confusing for trackers." Tatsuda watched Mason. "At least enough to slow them down or force them to divide and search multiple places."

She nodded to show her understanding, though she didn't see how a boot print and a few horse tracks might be enough for anyone to follow, though tracking anything was far from her experience. Marks on the ground looked pretty much the same to her eyes.

Falling in line, the group continued on foot, traversing the hard ground above the river on the plain. Once walking, Ginger's pack seemed heavy, but that was reassuring. She enjoyed having clothes, a warm sleeping bag for the chilly nights, and some of her own food and water. If she got separated from the group, she wouldn't be as desperate as the last time she'd been on her own.

Even with the group, a certain amount of independence was expected; it was important not to be a burden. Maybe they would let her come with them further than Boise and the next train. It sounded like Walker was a real hopper and she could learn how to do it from him. She also didn't want to leave Tatsuda. She'd never had a friend before, someone who looked out for her as a matter of course. Someone she could talk to and tell her secrets.

They hiked for hours in the blistering sun while sweat ran down her back and pooled between her breasts, leaving her sticky. They stayed close enough to the meandering river they might camp near it tonight. Maybe she'd wash up once it was dark. Plus, it would be good to replenish their water before trying for a train. She congratulated herself for thinking like a hopper. With a little luck, they'd be aboard the train and headed to Boise tomorrow. The others didn't plan to stay there, but she didn't know their final destination.

Caitlyn's voice interrupted her thoughts. "Where are we going to cross the river? We should be only a few hours south of Idaho Falls, and the railroad tracks are on the far side."

Everyone stopped and Tatsuda pointed. "Check those out."

Ginger stared at a bison herd across the river. She'd seen nothing like the massive prehistoric-looking creatures. "Are those buffalo? I've read about them."

Mason gave her a quick nod.

Nobody could take their eyes off the herd as it moved northeast in an undulating mass, almost like an optical illusion.

At the river's edge, a flicker of movement caught Ginger's eye. A lighter patch stood out against the golden-brown land. She focused and found two more. They were much smaller animals than the bison, but she didn't know what they were. They looked like gray dogs.

"What are those?" She whispered to Tatsuda as she pointed.

He shook his head. "Mason?"

Mason turned and saw where she'd indicated. "Wolves." He didn't seem concerned, but her breath caught in her throat. He took off his hat and mopped his face and forehead with a handkerchief.

"They shouldn't bother us," said Caitlyn, tugging on her braid. A crease appeared on her forehead between her eyes.

Was she lying? Were wolves dangerous in real life the way they were in stories? Ginger had thought them something from the past, something just in fairytales and children's stories. Her life before now hadn't prepared her for much. She looked back and forth between Mason and Caitlyn, and a pit of dread bloomed in her stomach.

"I heard they aren't dangerous unless they're starving," said Elsa, glancing at Walker, the probable source of her information. She turned to Ginger. "This time of year, they should keep their distance."

"They shouldn't be a problem," said Mason, shading his eyes once more with his battered old hat. He indulged in a long pull on his canteen and started walking once more.

That must signal the end of the conversation.

"Where are we planning to cross the river?" asked Elsa, repeating Caitlyn's unanswered question.

Ginger looked out at the expanse of swift-moving water below. She didn't know how to swim. Was that how they planned to get across?

"Not until Idaho Falls. There's a bridge in town." Mason said, "We'll stop and have dinner in an hour or two, then finish the trip in the dark."

"Will that be safe?" Elsa frowned, her piercing yellow eyes directed at Mason's back.

He continued forward without glancing behind. "No, but we'll figure something out. I know someone in town who might help."

Something in his tone seemed different and made Ginger pay particular attention. He flicked a glance over his shoulder at Caitlyn. Was there something about his friend in town that might affect her? Caitlyn walked on without seeming to notice anything amiss.

Ginger put one foot in front of the other, forcing herself to keep up.

CHAPTER 23: MASON

Mason stared at Caitlyn across the rock-lined sunken fire pit, the flames licking the edges but staying below ground, giving her hair a glint of gold. Her gaze met his, daring him to sneak into the plains with her. He hesitated, even though Elsa and Walker had already excused themselves after they'd eaten. Dinner consisted of hot water added to bunker food pouches. He didn't understand how gray and tan powder became appetizing food, but appreciated it all the same. The bunker rations were light and easy to carry.

He finished the last of his dinner and stacked the empty pouch with the others. His glance lingered on Caitlyn, remembering her whispered words before they'd eaten.

"You two fine on your own for a bit?" said Caitlyn, speaking to Tatsuda and Ginger.

He wasn't sure about leaving them on their own out here. Two city kids on the plains, but they weren't small children—and he'd seen Tatsuda handle himself. If he and Caitlyn didn't take this opportunity, it could be a while before they had another chance to be together and he ached to touch her again. Now that he'd started, it was impossible to keep his hands to himself. With luck, they'd be on a train tomorrow. The next day at the latest and there'd be little chance for privacy.

Tatsuda nodded, his glance flicking to Mason. Caitlyn stood, and Mason followed her example. The slight smirk on the boy's face made it clear that it wasn't lost on him, that the adults were sneaking out into the cover of the dark, acting like teenagers while the teens guarded the campfire.

"Whistle if you hear anything you shouldn't," Mason said to Tatsuda before he'd gone more than a few paces. The kid nodded again, his eyes gleaming in the firelight.

Following Caitlyn into the velvet night, the light of their small fire disappeared. They strolled by moonlight while Ginger's voice came in snatches of sound. When that faded, Caitlyn stopped. After the sound of water gurgling along the bank of the river, the night on the plain was silent.

The evening was still warm, but his flesh broke out in goosebumps when Caitlyn turned and lifted his shirt over his head. He cooperated, but let her take the lead. He liked when she took charge. They made love in the grass, keeping their voices quiet but enjoying themselves nonetheless. His heart was still hammering rapid fire where they lay in the blissful aftermath, naked to the cooling night air, when a piercing scream rent the night air.

Caitlyn shot up, grabbing for clothing while he did the same, his heart racing for a new reason. "That was Ginger, I think." Caitlyn's voice was breathless as she groped on the ground for her shirt.

Mason had his pants on in record time, grabbed a pistol from the holster nearby, and ran barefoot back to camp, ignoring the pebbles underfoot. He skidded into camp, arriving seconds before Walker and Elsa. The night hid their expressions, but anxious energy surrounded them as they adjusted their clothes. Caitlyn was last to arrive, fully dressed and carrying his things, his holster draped over her shoulder.

Ginger was nowhere in sight.

Tatsuda stood staring at the river by the embers of the dying fire. His widened eyes looked upset. "She went down to the river. She said she'd be right back."

"I'll stay here." Elsa put a hand on the boy's shoulder. "You can go."

Tatsuda tore off down the bank with Walker and Caitlyn close behind. Mason pulled his boots out of the pile Caitlyn had brought and shoved his feet into them.

"She might have fallen in the river. If that's the case, she'll be long gone."

Elsa shook her head, her eyes glinting in the dim light. "My gut says she's fine. Something just scared her." Her confidence and optimism made him stop.

"Your gut?" Her words had resonated with him; her certainty seemed more than a casual observation.

It was too dark to see Elsa's expression, but her tone changed and her voice lowered. "It's something I inherited from my Granny. It's not just a vague feeling, it's strong." She hesitated, perhaps deciding if she wanted to confide in him. "It's more like trusting an instinct and when the feeling is strong, I listen. When I've ignored the feeling, I've had problems. Like almost being beaten to death."

"That happens to me, too." Mason's surprise made the words pop out. It wasn't something he'd ever talked about, but his sense or feel when things were off had always been right. Good instincts, even if he wasn't always aware of his reasons for making certain decisions. He'd never heard anyone describe the sensation in a way that was so close to his own.

"Grady too, I think." Elsa stared after the group. Her body remained tense and at attention until a smattering of voices came to them from below.

Interesting that it was something he, Elsa, and Grady shared.

Walker was the first back at the fire. "Just a scare. Saw something. Probably a coyote, maybe a wolf. Thought it was going to attack her. Her scream scared it away." He stuffed the cooled pot from dinner into his pack.

Ginger came next, climbing the bank, Tatsuda and Caitlyn on her heels.

"What were you thinking of, going off alone?" Elsa's words were snappish and Ginger shrank into herself.

"I wanted to get clean," she said, her eyes downcast.

Elsa took a deep breath. "Next time, wait. One of us will stand guard." She softened her voice as much as the abating fear would allow. "I'm sorry if I was abrupt. You scared us. Get your stuff. We have to leave right away."

"Already?" said Ginger, looking around. "I thought we had a few hours to wait."

"If anyone else is out here, they heard you scream too," said Caitlyn.

Her tone was patient. The girl needed to learn, but harsh words would just spook her.

"Pack up," said Elsa, grabbing her backpack and hefting it onto her back.

They scrambled to grab everything and Walker doused the fire. The night plunged into a deeper darkness as the embers hissed and he refilled the pit. Mason's eyes readjusted to having only the light of the half moon and pale stars, but it was enough. Following the riverbank, they headed north again, remaining alert for anyone else attracted by Ginger's scream.

It wasn't long before the rolling sound reached them; horses headed their way. The group flattened themselves on the ground below the lip of the riverbank. Mason risked a quick peek above.

A pair of GreenCorps riders with lanterns rode past them above the river on the open plain. They must have been posted nearby. Good thing the fire was out.

Mason looked away from their lights so he didn't wreck his night vision entirely. When the riders disappeared downriver, Mason hurried onward, leading the group toward town. It should be about an hour to Idaho Falls and the bridge. He hadn't wanted to be closer and discovered by accident, but it was time to make their move.

They stayed alert as they walked, but there were no further riders, though they listened for the first set to return from behind. They had almost reached Idaho Falls when the thud of hooves signaled it was time to hide. They jumped back down below the riverbank and stopped while they let the soldiers pass.

The light of town spilled from the clustered buildings across the river while noise poured out of the rowdier bars near the train station.

The bridge's silhouette was illuminated enough to see either end. Mason stopped everyone with a quick raise of his arm when he determined they were close enough. He pointed up to the bridge, then to himself.

The others nodded. They understood. He left to scout on his own.

Regulating his heart rate and quieting his breathing, he slipped over the edge and onto the deck of the old concrete bridge. He placed each step with care, determined to make no sound. GreenCorps hadn't maintained the old road it had once been part of, which had crumbled and been reclaimed by the wild, but they'd kept the bridge itself in good repair. If they were following their usual protocol, guards should be stationed at either end.

Mason waited until he spotted both in the shadows before proceeding. He scoured the bridge with his gaze, unable to locate others. He needed to take them out one at a time without making noise that would alert those at the next post.

He waited as the night cooled, watching for an opportunity to strike. From the town, shouts and murmured voices broke the stillness on occasion. Mason jumped when a dog barked in the distance, but relaxed when it didn't come any closer. The watchful recruit at the close end looked in both directions and ambled to the edge about ten feet from Mason. The man unfastened the fly of his pants, the zipper loud in the quiet night.

Mason let him relieve himself, then as the man fumbled at his pants, he struck. Mason grabbed him from behind and choked the man with his forearm until he slumped to the ground, unconscious. Hearing a man's last breath was never easy. He held on for a few extra minutes, then snapped the man's neck. He'd have preferred not to kill anyone, but if the man woke too soon, he'd alert everyone. Mason dragged the body farther into the shadows and left it obscured by rocks, bushes, and the bridge piling.

He stripped the GreenCorps jacket from the former guard and took his rifle. He forced it on, though it was tight across the shoulders and too short through the sleeves. It wouldn't work as a disguise in daylight, but at night he should be able to get close enough to neutralize the other guard, if he was quick.

Sliding back down the bank, he whispered his updated plan and motioned the others to follow several yards behind. He waited while they scaled the bank and hid in the shadows at the verge of the bridge. He winced every time they made noise, even a snapped twig or rustle of grass, slight as they were. This depended on stealth. Only Tatsuda was as silent as Mason wanted. He waved them to a stop and then he strode down the center of the bridge, rifle across his body like the guards. He acted as if he belonged.

He called out to the second guard in a loud whisper. "You see anything?"

"Nothing," the man said in disgust, spitting onto the bridge deck. "I'm sick of this high alert shit. I'd rather be sleeping. Night-time guard duty is the worst. They don't tell us anything."

On cue, Ginger yelped. Not the full scream she'd given by the river, but enough to make Mason dash toward the sound. He smiled when the second guard left his post and followed at a run. When Mason stopped and stared into the darkness below the bridge, the guard skidded to a halt beside him.

"Sounded like someone by the water," Mason said. "Hello, anyone down there?"

Walker slid out of the shadows and knocked the guard out with a blow to the temple. Between them, they dragged him under the bridge and lay him next to the first. Walker raised a brow and hesitated with his knife. Maybe he'd never killed anyone. Mason waved him away. He could do it.

Once more, Mason twisted the man's neck, killing him so he couldn't turn them in. He drew in a deep breath. No point in regretting necessity. Walker's look filled with compassion, but he turned away without a word. The guards had just been following orders, but they would have shot first and asked questions later. While it would be suspicious to find their bodies later, having them report activity on the bridge tonight would be worse. With luck, the bodies wouldn't be found until their group was aboard the train and long gone.

Mason and Walker returned to the others.

"Where's the train station?" Tatsuda said, keeping his whispered voice low.

"Several blocks that way," said Mason with a jerk of his head toward the busy part of downtown. "Watch yourself." The houses in rows in this section were dark and silent at this hour—well past curfew for all except railroad workers and GreenCorps recruits.

Tatsuda melted into the darkness.

Walker kissed Elsa. "I'm going to scout too. He's sneakier, but I know more about trains and getting schedules. Where should we meet you?" He looked at Mason for the answer.

"We're going to wait behind the last brothel on the left before the warehouse district. The alley at the end of the street."

Mason hadn't warned Caitlyn, but his friend, if she was still here, worked at a pleasure house. He didn't think Caitlyn would be jealous of his past, but Charise had wanted to be more than casual, even if Mason hadn't. His contact in the kitchen would know if someone had captured Grady. Mason had hidden at the brothel before and they would need somewhere safe if the train didn't come until tomorrow.

Time ticked by slowly while they waited beside the brick building, sitting against the wall in the quiet alley. The odd patch of light slanted down from the windows above, but most had shades pulled down or had gone dark and quiet. A couple of rats rummaged in the garbage a couple of doors back, but the night grew quieter as the brothels closed and the bars shut their doors. They needed to be certain all the patrons were gone. It must be close to three a.m. but there was still no sign of Walker and Tatsuda.

* * *

Just before dawn, from the far end of the street near the bridge, came angry shouts. The missing guards had been discovered—probably at the shift change. They couldn't wait outside anymore. It was still dark, but Mason couldn't sit any longer. His butt was numb, and they needed a place to hide. Caitlyn slept on his shoulder while Ginger had curled up, her head in Caitlyn's lap, also asleep. Elsa nibbled at the inside of her cheek, staring after where Walker and Tatsuda had gone. She hadn't closed her eyes, nor had Mason. It had been a peaceful silence as it seemed neither had felt the urge to fill it with unnecessary words.

"Time to hide." In the pale light approaching sunrise, her yellow eyes looked fierce. "Hope your idea is solid." She adjusted her hat, obscuring her recognizable features. The girl was sharp.

The pleasure house had been quiet inside for some time, but the kitchen help slept by the back door and probably had to get up soon to prepare food. Squeezing Caitlyn's arm, Mason woke her and kissed her temple, noticing Elsa's slight smile. The change in his and Caitlyn's relationship status hadn't been discussed, but clearly noticed. Ginger yawned and stretched as Caitlyn woke her in turn. Mason stood up and tapped at the wooden door while the others slid away opening and hid behind the garbage dumpster.

A young man poked his head out the partially opened back door. "The kitchen's still closed. No scraps yet." The bleary-eyed young man appeared to be about Tatsuda's age and had blotchy red skin, visible in the faint light from inside the kitchen. He was older, but he was the same youngster who Mason had expected.

"I'm not begging. There's thunder on the plains." Mason gave the code words.

The boy perked up, his eyes taking on a serious glint. "And lightning in the sky." He stretched out his hand and showed the dot of tattoo ink in the webbing between his thumb and index finger. Mason did the same.

"Any news from the boss?" If Grady had been taken, it would have been reported.

The kid shook his head. "Sighted south near Pocatello a few days ago, but they lost him when he vanished into the desert. Forces stationed in both towns. Something's going on. But I'm guessing you know that."

Mason shrugged. Last time, the boy had been trusted, but not well-known. "Is Charise here?"

The boy hesitated. "She's with Master Gil. In his room." At Mason's blank look, the boy added, "The owner."

Charise was moving up in the world, which might make things easier. Gil had been sympathetic to the cause and shouldn't be trouble.

"Tell her Mason's here." He glanced at Caitlyn. He didn't want to make her uncomfortable, but this might be awkward. He'd never have called Charise a girlfriend, but she'd tried to get him to take her with him when he'd left town a few years ago.

The boy nodded. "I remember you now. I'll get her." He closed the door and his quick footsteps retreated. He wasn't gone long before the back door flung open and a busty blonde in a flimsy nightgown flung herself onto Mason, her arms wrapping around his neck in her enthusiasm. His stomach lurched. Maybe this hadn't been a good idea.

"Mason, you came back. Give me a kiss."

"It's nice to see you, Charise, but it's not like that." She didn't let go and wiggled against him. He pulled back, removing her arms. "My girlfriend won't like me kissing another woman." Best to get that said right away.

The young woman's smile disappeared, and she crossed her arms under her breasts, pushing them up, making her dark nipples more visible through her sheer clothing.

"You aren't happy to see me? It's been so long." Charise's smile had become a pout.

He took a deep breath and maintained his lifted gaze. "Rebel business, not personal. There are six of us. Can we have the storeroom for the day?" He flicked another furtive glance at Caitlyn, who had stepped forward with an amused glint in her eyes.

Mason was uncomfortable, but she didn't seem threatened or upset.

She rested a proprietary hand on his shoulder. "Can you help us or not, Honey?"

Charise's eyes narrowed, but she nodded. "I'll be right back." She went inside and returned with a jingling set of keys. "Follow me."

She stepped out of the doorway and brushed past Mason, her breasts grazing him on the way by. His cheeks flamed, but once more Caitlyn seemed amused rather than offended. This wasn't going how he'd expected and put him off-kilter. Mason motioned Elsa and Ginger to follow his friend while he brought up the rear, scanning the otherwise empty alley. Ginger's mouth was pursed, and she shot him a pointed look while Elsa shook her head in mock dismay.

"If I can deal with your friend's disappointment, so can you." Caitlyn patted Mason's butt before following Charise.

Elsa whispered before she turned. "Something's not right. We should wait for Walker and Tatsuda."

Mason, too, sensed something wasn't quite right, but chalked it up to his discomfort.

"What was taking Walker and Tatsuda so long? Had they found trouble? His senses agreed with Elsa, but this had been his idea. He'd just have to be vigilant.

At the end of the alley Charise looked back, causing Mason to check too. There was nobody in sight watching, so she unlocked a storeroom where he'd hidden before. It was deeper than it looked and had a tap for water. She held the door open and raised an eyebrow. Her glance skittered away, not meeting his eyes as she glanced at the others. Was she upset? The others went in ahead of him. Elsa's hand had drifted to the haft of her knife. She gave him a pointed look and glanced at the door. At least, she was thinking.

He stopped in the doorway and stretched out his hand. "I need the key. There're two more of us coming back anytime. I'll let them in." He didn't know or trust anyone in Idaho Falls well enough to put himself entirely in their hands. Rebels or not.

Charise looked like she might refuse, then grumbled to herself as she unhooked one key and pressed it into his hand. "Do you need anything else?" She paused and leaned forward to whisper, "Maybe a key to the main house for later?"

He shook his head. Once, he'd have been tempted. To be honest, that was how he and Charise had met both times before tonight. Once he'd stayed a week, hiding in her room while she pretended to be sick. He was no longer interested in anyone except Caitlyn.

"We just need a hiding place until we finish some business. I'll leave the key in the usual spot before tomorrow night." He wasn't about to tell her they needed the train or who was searching for them. The less she knew, the better.

Her dark eyes flashed as she left, slipping back up the alley to the kitchen door. She tossed her head and went inside with a final check over her shoulder. Had she displayed a sour expression on her face at the end? Coming here had been a poor idea.

"I'll wait for Walker and Tatsuda." Dropping his pack inside, Mason remained outside.

"I'll wait with you." Caitlyn stepped back into the alley.

He didn't know what to think. Had he been presumptuous in calling her his girlfriend? She'd grinned at the time. Whatever this was between them was still new.

He closed the door. Elsa was safe, but he might be in trouble.

Caitlyn rested her palm on his chest and his thoughts flew out of his head.

"You don't have to explain. That was before. But should I expect us to be casual, or can I count on something serious?" Her eyes met his in a forthright manner.

His mouth became dry. No games. He appreciated she cut to the chase. He'd expected jealousy or an argument. Instead, she was calm and reasonable. It made him more certain than ever that he'd fallen in love with the perfect woman.

"I want only you." His eyes met hers, hoping that was enough.

"Good," she said, wrapping her arms around him and tilting her face toward his. Her soft lips made his every nerve-ending tingle and dance with excitement. "That's what I thought."

"What was that for?" His heart hammered in a way that was distracting.

"A reminder." Her soft smile made him wish they'd had more time on the prairie.

"I don't need one," he said, returning her kiss. "You're all I think about."

She kissed him again. "You shouldn't say anymore or you'll make Walker blush." She stepped back, and Mason missed her warmth at once. He must be off tonight if he'd missed the big man's return.

Walker cleared his throat and stepped into the last patch of light in the alley.

"Tatsuda's waiting near the tracks in a small hiding place. Not big enough for all of us. Security is top level at the station, crawling with GreenCorps uniforms. The train we want comes through in six hours. They'll load the potatoes and then it carries on to Boise, leaving after noon."

"Damn. Broad daylight." Mason clenched a fist in disgust. Elsa couldn't stroll through town once it was light. Not her fault, just a fact.

"I came to get Elsa now," Walker said, thinking along the same lines. "We'll wait at the far end past the station as the train heads out of town, by a broken-down building. It's open on three sides and not much cover, but it's better than nothing. It's too cramped to fit everyone, though. You three join us just before the train. Hang back until you hear the cars move, which is when you'll see our location. You know the crashing?"

Caitlyn nodded. "I remember it well."

Mason nodded. He'd only ridden a train once, but the sound was unmistakable.

"You'll have to be close enough to see when they're done loading. Can you do that?"

Mason nodded again. Ginger would need to hide her flaming hair before marching through town in broad daylight, but at least they could rest. The others wouldn't get much, even if they took turns. It felt like a bad idea to split up, but he didn't have a better idea. Not with GreenCorps forces everywhere and limited cover near the tracks.

"Anything else?" Mason hated being unable to scout, but he trusted Walker's judgment.

"We should ride in pairs. You hopped before?" Walker said.

"Just once," Mason said. "But I can get on if it's moving, as long as it isn't too fast."

"Mathew and I hopped trains regularly to get to Texas and back," said Caitlyn.

Walker nodded. "And Tatsuda will help Ginger."

Walker swung the door wide, motioned to Elsa, and she joined them outside, trading places with Caitlyn.

"See you in a few hours." Walker and Elsa left, hurrying toward the railroad tracks before day broke. It was no longer fully dark, but they flitted from shadow to shadow. Walker knew how to move through a town and stay unseen.

Disquiet spread through Mason's chest, making it tight. He took a deep breath and downplayed his unease. He went inside and locked the door, unable to shake the feeling that something was wrong.

Chapter 24: Mason

Mason sat up from where he'd snoozed, leaning against lumpy sacks of potatoes, his head shaking. Caitlyn had slumped onto his shoulder again, but something had awakened her too. She met his eyes and nudged Ginger. The girl's hazel eyes sprang open, and he held his index finger to his lips. He listened. Footsteps stopped outside the door. The door was at the end of a dead-end alley. There shouldn't be foot traffic here. Caitlyn and Ginger got up and slid to the corner in darker shadows while he stood behind the door, so whoever opened it wouldn't see anyone with their first glance.

"He said there were six of them," said Charise's voice. "They aren't all here, but I saw the redhead myself."

"Fuck." The word came out as a quiet hiss. Ginger looked at Mason with tears shining in her eyes. She shook her head, gathering her braid in her trembling hands. She'd said that she didn't want to go home, but she might not have a choice. No. He wouldn't let them take the girl against her will.

"You better be sure," growled a male voice, still fiddling with the keys. "I could use the coin, but I'm not looking to upset the rebels."

"You should have come to me sooner," said the voice. "This is my place."

Her boss then. They must have decided to collect the reward for Ginger, figuring she wasn't actual rebel business, which was true.

It didn't seem like the whore to run to GreenCorps—she'd been sympathetic to the rebel cause. Mason flexed his muscles to get ready, then swung his arms back and forth—he might need to fight. The key turned in the lock. That damn Charise must have another copy. Good thing he was a light sleeper. One hand touched his pistol on the left.

The storeroom door opened a fraction at a time. The room would appear empty.

"Come on out," said the boss. "I'll rip the place apart if you don't. I just want the girl. I don't care about the rest of you. I don't want trouble with the rebels."

"Grady won't be happy if you turn her in," said Mason. Maybe they could talk their way out. Alone, he might have fought, but with the others here, he needed to stay cool.

"Grady isn't here to ask, now is he? A couple of weeks ago, he spread the word to keep our eyes out for her."

That would have been before Tatsuda had found Ginger and she'd joined their group.

"Watching for her is not the same as turning her in." Mason's lip curled as he spoke, a heaviness settling in his chest.

Good thing Elsa wasn't here. She would have been recognizable by day and they'd want her too with the price on her head—one hefty enough to be worth almost any risk. Mason stepped out, his hands up, away from his guns. He motioned for Ginger and Caitlyn to come out of the corner.

Charise's owner was a brute, perhaps a retired bull, and he was armed with a long knife—probably from his kitchen. Mason's hands itched to reach for his gun, but as long as they were trapped in this room, he didn't dare. They stepped into the alley, with Mason staying in front of Caitlyn and Ginger. His heart sank as he reassessed. The odds weren't a lot better outside. Three heavily muscled men, probably the bouncers, stood behind their boss.

"Where's the rest?" Gil's hard eyes met Mason's. "There's supposed to be six."

"They left." Mason kept his tone even.

Gil's eyes flicked toward Mason's guns. "We just want the girl," he repeated, looking more confident now with clear odds in his favor. His gaze settled on Ginger and her flame-bright hair.

"Not going to happen." Mason didn't dare look at Caitlyn, but knew she'd be ready. He needed her help, and they might underestimate her. Gil's toughs were going to rush him together. She'd need to take care of the boss when they did. Gil lunged first, his knife swinging for Mason's head, but Mason dodged with ease. The bar owner was past his prime and not the real threat.

The rest held back, unsure of what Mason was capable, giving him a chance to assess. He caught Charise's gaze.

"What's in this for you, Charise?" Mason asked without taking his eyes from the waiting toughs. Gil swung again and went down on one knee. Winded.

"I'm sick of being a whore," said Charisse. "With my cut of the reward, Gil says I can buy my freedom."

Sharing a look, all three bouncers rushed him. Mason feinted left and smashed the bouncer on the right with his elbow. The man's nose crunched and Mason stepped back, pulling a knife from his boot. Caitlyn tripped one man, and the other stumbled, giving Mason time to return to position. The two remaining men charged, and Mason sliced the second man across the chest and shoulder, hard enough to draw blood. The man went down, pressing his hands to his chest, bright red blood spreading in a pool on the ground while he wore a surprised expression on his face. His eyes rolled back, and he slumped against the wall. Mason had reduced the odds, but this wasn't over.

The boss returned to his feet and attacked with a yell while the final bouncer circled, waiting for an opening. Mason kicked Gil on the side of the knee and the former tough guy crumpled, dropping his kitchen knife to the dusty, hard-packed ground. He got up and backed away before limping down the alley toward his kitchen door, perhaps for additional help.

Mason needed this to end fast.

Turning to face the final man as the first bouncer got up from the ground, his face covered in purplish-red blood and already swollen. Mason had probably broken his nose. Caitlyn stepped forward and shot the first man before he reached for his weapon. Mason winced as the sound reverberated through the alley. Noise was going to attract attention. The last man rushed Mason, pinning him against the wall.

Caitlyn's gun appeared next to the man's head.

She met Mason's eyes. "Step away. Nice and easy. Keep your hands out."

The bouncer nodded and moved back, checking the body of the man Caitlyn had shot—perhaps knowing when to quit.

It looked like they might get out of this unscathed, but Mason hadn't bargained on Charise. She snagged the kitchen knife from the ground and grabbed Ginger as a shield. With wild swings, chopping back and forth, she charged Caitlyn's back as she attempted to even the score.

Mason didn't think. He blocked her blow from striking Caitlyn, the knife slicing his arm with a burning sensation. His hand stopped working and his arm became weak. He staggered with the sensation, heat enveloped his arm and he lost track of Caitlyn as his vision blurred. He wasn't sure what was happening as time slowed to a crawl. Ginger became rag-doll limp and collapsed to the ground, escaping Charise's hold.

A gunshot rang out, and he squinted to focus on the damage.

A dark hole appeared in Charise's chest. Blood blossomed around the edges and spread, staining her clothes like a fast-growing flower. Her mouth opened and closed twice, and then she stumbled and fell to the ground. She didn't move. Crimson soaked the alley as the last man staggered away. Three bodies littered the ground.

"Are you okay?" Caitlyn's face swam before his eyes, his vision blurred more and her voice came from far away. "How bad? Let me see." She reached for his arm. "Shit. You're in shock."

"We have to go. Right now. They'll be here any minute." His voice sounded remote, detached. Unconcerned. His arm burned with pain, but leaving had become urgent.

Mason shook his head to clear the fog. To get out of here alive, he needed to concentrate. He unbuttoned his shirt and tied it around the scarlet slash on his arm, which continued to bleed. He'd need to bind it better soon, but crowds, likely GreenCorps men, would be attracted to the gunshots. They had to go. He couldn't move his arm, but with Caitlyn's assistance, he stuffed it back into the borrowed jacket, hoping its dark color would disguise the blood for a few minutes, or at least long enough to get away from the dead.

Grabbing their stuff, he, Ginger, and Caitlyn ran from the alley to the main street, where they dropped to a walk and headed toward the train station. Periodically, he checked over his shoulder to ensure they weren't followed. A few blocks from the brothel, when he looked back, there was a trail with drops of blood. They'd have to find somewhere to deal with his wound. Soon. That wasn't the only problem. Hopping a train with one arm would be a challenge.

Chapter 25: Elsa

With the proximity to the river, Idaho Falls was greener than Pocatello and many of the towns Elsa had seen. She found the color relaxing and beautiful. Not that she could see it now. She lay sandwiched between Walker and Tatsuda beneath a once-spruce green, now grayish tarp that smelled of dust and dried mold. With the sun, their hiding place had grown stuffy and hot, making it difficult to take a normal breath.

She dozed several times but hadn't dared to fall asleep for long. They couldn't afford to miss the train to Boise or they'd be waiting an extra forty-eight hours—time they couldn't afford if they were going to stay ahead of Jaxon. Taking his sister was a complication, but Ginger seemed like a nice enough girl. Naive in lots of ways, but knowledgeable in others. Tatsuda wouldn't want to leave her behind—they'd become fast friends.

North of the trainyard had been the first place Walker had scouted, but there'd been nowhere to hide. The sightlines to the tracks were open and exposed at all times. In all likelihood, he still would've tried to hop a train there if they'd been alone.

The train station swarmed with GreenCorps forces, but this far out, it was quieter, with fewer patrols. Walker had located a sharp bend in the tracks where they cut south. The outbound train wouldn't be able to pick up full speed until after that corner. That's where they waited to get on, at the peak of the bend.

On her right, Tatsuda slept with deep, even breaths, looking peaceful. She'd spelled Walker off, allowing him to get some rest, but they were both awake now. She stifled a yawn; the temperature was making her drowsy.

At regular intervals, uniformed men had walked past the tumbledown building beside which they hid under the tarp, disguised with the junk beside the collapsed shed. Twice, she'd lifted the edge just enough to peer at the boots of the patrols. Snatches of their conversations had been all she'd been able to make out. Other than the excitement about the bodies by the bridge, there had been no other news. Some said she'd done it, others blamed Grady. Either way, the search was on and she remained statue-like, holding her breath until they passed.

The inbound train had arrived at noon and burlap sacks of potatoes had been passed into the depths of the cars, waiting to take them to market where GreenCorps would make huge profits for their crop. Soon it would be time to go.

The bustle at the station behind them seemed to lessen and the muffled voices retreated while boxcar doors scraped closed with a series of clangs. Elsa's palms grew sweaty.

It shouldn't be long now.

Walker's eyes gleamed beside her. "Tat, time to wake up. They're done."

The boy's eyes popped open, and he rolled out from under the tarp. Walker and Elsa hunched beneath the cover, clipped their packs, and checked for stray straps.

"The motion will be the same," said Walker. "Hand, hand, step, hop, starting with the right. But we aren't waiting for the last car. You and I will be the front pair. We won't get a covered hopper this time. They look like they're all too close to the engine. Lots of boxcars and a few open-haul cars called gondolas in the back section, from what I can see. They're like boxcars cut in half, open at the top. I can't tell if they're empty or full. We'll deal with what we find."

Elsa nodded and swallowed. She worried about her shoulder, but had to trust that she could do this. She needed to get to Canada with knowledge of the bunkers and the key. This was what all the pain and stress of the last few months had been leading toward. A chance to get out from under the thumb of GreenCorps for everyone.

The train cars at the station jolted, crashing one after another as the train advanced from the station, slowly gaining speed as it left the trainyard, passing through the edge of town and south, back toward the bridge.

From their hiding place, she and Walker watched, the tarp no longer covering their heads, but they remained crouched behind the building debris. Tatsuda had disappeared from sight. Perhaps he'd already gone looking for the others, as he was responsible for getting his friend on the train. Elsa's stomach lurched. All day something had seemed off.

The engine roared past first, followed by two passenger cars filled with recruits. Elsa grimaced and cursed under her breath at the sight of a familiar figure seated by a window. Jaxon was on board, headed west to Boise. They'd have to be extra cautious not to be recognized or caught. She returned her attention to the task at hand. The next cars were stock cars, probably carrying horses for the soldiers.

"We're still going," said Walker, perhaps responding to Jaxon's presence or her expression. "This place is thick with GreenCorps. We can't stay."

He squeezed her sweaty hand as they waited until the middle engine passed. A couple of water tankers came next, but most of the cars were boxcars, like Walker had predicted. At the end were half a dozen flatter cars—the gondolas, open-topped rectangles. They'd have to climb up, jump in, and crouch or sit out of sight. There'd be no protection overhead from the mid-day sun, but once onboard, they'd figure something out.

"Back there," said Walker, nodding to the gondolas. He glided away from the ratty tarp and collapsed building. Elsa followed, being just as cautious. No GreenCorps, no bulls, and no sign of the others.

"Where are they?" Elsa scanned the face of the broken building and the shed on the opposite side of the tracks. Was something wrong? Tatsuda wasn't there either. Her chest constricted. Had they had caught him? She didn't want to abandon him. He'd become family.

"If they don't get on, we'll wait for them in Boise. Let's go." Walker's infectious enthusiasm for hopping trains infused her as she followed at a jog, her adrenaline increasing with her heart rate. They dashed at an angle to intercept the tracks. The packed dirt and gravel were uneven under her feet, but she was careful not to fall or twist her ankle. She'd only done this three times previously, but all under Walker's expert guidance. He'd traveled this way year-round for eight years before they'd met.

The train grew louder, though the crashing almost ceased as the train picked up speed. She tried to count the spokes on the wheels as they pulled up next to the train, but she was too close to be accurate. Was it already too fast?

Arms and legs pumping beside the train, the vibration in her chest and feet, she got ready. Walker grabbed the nearest steel ladder on their right and scrambled up with ease. Taking a deep breath, Elsa launched and grabbed, hauling herself up. Her shoulder twinged, but didn't give way as she clambered up, swinging over the ladder at the top. Walker stood in the metal bottom of the gondola but was tall enough to see out. They shared a grin.

From the corner of her eye, a streak headed for the train, leaving the shadow just past the bend. She turned to watch. They'd left it later than she would have thought was safe—Tatsuda and Ginger ran holding hands. Like Walker, Tatsuda climbed first and half-pulled Ginger, who caught the ladder on her first try. They disappeared over the top edge into their open car. Safe on board. Some of the tightness left her chest. Where were Mason and Caitlyn?

Movement by the bend showed them at last, coming up on the final car. Caitlyn supported Mason, who ran with a shambling gait, favoring his arm. Was this what she'd been uneasy about all day? What had happened?

Elsa broke out in a sweat. What if they didn't make it? They only had one shot.

Already the train's speed had increased with most of the cars around the last bend before it headed south back down the river, mirroring their travel on the far bank yesterday. Elsa crouched on top beside the ladder, holding on and watching. Walker gripped her leg, providing stability as the rushing air whipped her short dark curls away from her face and water streamed from her eyes. The roar of the train over the tracks made it impossible to hear.

With her eyes riveted on her friends as they raced for the rear of the train, she stuffed in her earplugs, muffling the screeching sound of the train and the press of the air.

Mason jumped first and caught the ladder using just one arm. Caitlyn followed immediately. She passed him and swung over the top ahead of him. He half climbed and was half pulled to the top. She dropped her pack into the gondola car, meeting Elsa's eyes with a nod. She steadied Mason as he climbed over and dropped into the final car. Six cars away, Elsa could do nothing but hope he was okay. Mason's arm had been blood-soaked. Good thing Caitlyn was a medic.

With everyone on board, Elsa dropped with a thud onto the steel box. A skiff of sharp gravel covered the bottom, making walking without skating difficult. The steel vibrated more here than on the hoppers where she'd ridden on previous occasions.

"Must have had trouble in town," Walker shouted. His gray eyes looked subdued. He liked Mason. "At least they're on."

She nodded, settling in, her back against the car, chewing on the inside of her cheek. As soon as she realized, she stopped.

Seated next to her, Walker pulled out his blue tarp to use as a sunshade. She admired that he always prepared for any contingency.

"We'll find somewhere safe to get a good night's rest before the next train. I know a place." He sounded tired, but they all were. The last couple of days had been long and exhausting, with very little sleep.

"Four hours to Boise. Then twenty-eight more to Portland." She fell asleep on Walker's shoulder, trying to ignore intrusive thoughts of Jaxon.

CHAPTER 26: MASON

Mason's head spun. He couldn't believe he'd gotten onto the train. Damn good thing Caitlyn was strong. She'd manhandled him up the ladder and into the last car. They almost hadn't made it. He'd been running on willpower alone. The exertion had made him winded and light-headed. He slid down the side of the warm metal car in the front corner where it was most sheltered and closed his eyes, his arm throbbing with a dull pain.

"I need to see your cut." Caitlyn's eyes looked bluer than the summer sky as he forced his eyes open. "You're bleeding again."

Why was she so pale?

He, Caitlyn, and Ginger had hidden under a porch of a house close to the railroad tracks after the incident in the alley. In the limited light filtering through the slated boards of the floor above, they hadn't been able to see much, and they'd had to remain quiet as mice because the house they'd chosen was occupied. While Caitlyn had bound his arm to staunch the worst of the bleeding, it had seeped. It had frustrated her she'd been unable to clean it, other than a quick rinse.

He shrugged to peel off the blood-soaked sleeve of the GreenCorps uniform, though the motion sent shooting pains up his injured arm and he clenched his jaw to muffle the groan.

"Stop. Let me help." Caitlyn tossed the jacket aside without a second thought and it skidded on the loose gravel, leaving a bloody swath on the scuffed metal. It looked more like rust than blood.

Mason took a deep breath. He'd never ridden in a box like this and he couldn't see much of the countryside; he would have preferred to see where they were in relation to the river and mountains. He didn't like feeling disoriented, and it was difficult to stay focused. He must be feeling the blood loss. It had been six or seven hours since he'd been injured.

Caitlyn's hands were gentle as she pulled his shredded sleeve away from his skin. His stomach lurched, and he sucked in his breath. Charise had done a number on him. She'd sliced his forearm from his wrist to his elbow. The blade had glanced off his wrist bone where it was deep, while the rest of the slash tapered off to become superficial. But it had split open again.

Caitlyn's finger traced the length of the cut and grimaced. "I wouldn't have been in time. I didn't expect the whore to jump us with a kitchen knife."

Was she blaming him for the situation? Rebel sympathizer or not, he never should have trusted Caitlyn's safety to someone he knew only because he'd slept with her years ago.

"I'm sorry," he muttered, his head spinning. "Stupid to take you there." He rested it against the metal of the train car, ignoring the added vibration coursing through him. At least down here, the thick metal of the gondola blocked most of the wind. Despite the scorching sun and warm metal, he shivered. Perhaps he was in shock.

"I'm saying you saved me, you ninny. Don't apologize. You need to do one more thing for me." Caitlyn's insistent voice made him force his eyes open again. Her form was a blur. "Don't you dare die on me," she growled.

He concentrated on her eyes until he saw only a single set. "I'll do my best." After what had happened to Mathew, she must need reassurance.

She released his arm, dragged her pack closer, and dug through it to find her med kit. He watched, if only to make her happy, but he wanted to sleep.

Grabbing his arm again, she rinsed it with water, then with something from a bottle in her pack that stung. He cried out and his eyes widened in alarm as the solution fizzed and burned. His cheeks flamed, and he clamped his lips together, determined not to let that happen again.

"The train is loud enough, nobody can hear." She rummaged in her kit. "Scream away."

He sucked in a breath when she lit a match and sterilized a needle in its flame. This was going to hurt.

With steady hands, she threaded it with fine black thread, pushed the raw edges of his wound together, and stitched the deep section. Despite permission, he didn't make a sound, but was sweaty and shaking when she finished. It took more than two dozen neat stitches.

Her face was intense, but her hands were careful as she smeared a gel on the surface of his wound after blotting away the remainder of the blood and fizzing solution. She wrapped the whole thing in gauze, winding it around and around his arm. After she fastened it with tape and fashioned a sling for his arm, she sighed and crouched back on her heels. His stomach lurched again as the train rocked. Her eyes looked enormous in her pale face.

"I'll be fine in a day or two." He squeezed her hand.

She gave him a tired smile that took his breath away. Filthy and exhausted, covered in smears of blood, she was still beautiful.

Opening his canteen, she handed it to him with the lid off. "Sip it."

He nodded to show that he understood. Taking small mouthfuls, he followed orders, wishing it was whiskey. He could have used something stronger to numb the pain. What he wanted to do was lie down and sleep. "I need to rest while the train is moving. Getting off might be tricky." He didn't feel fine, but he wanted to offer reassurance. Mathew had died of a festering wound. It had to bring back terrible memories.

He'd just pulled a blanket from his bag when Tatsuda slipped over the front side of the train car, landing lightly on the bottom like a cat. He must have traveled, jumping from one of the previous cars. The others had to be worried and want news. Mason closed his eyes.

Caitlyn's voice came from far away. "As long as it doesn't get infected, he'll be fine."

He didn't hear Tatsuda.

He woke once to find that Caitlyn had shifted him so that his head lay in her lap. She smoothed the hair from his face and his awareness fell away again, rocked to sleep by the motion of the train.

* * *

Mason woke to the jolting crashes that signaled the train was coming into a station or approaching city limits. He'd been to Boise three times with the rebels, but always by horseback. It was a bustling city with about twenty thousand people—a similar size to a dozen other GreenCorps towns scattered throughout the West. Boise wasn't as large as Salt Lake City, at two-thirds the size. The inhabitants had scavenged building material from the long-ago wreckage and built a grid-like brick city nestled on a narrow uplifted bench of land against the rolling foothills and mountains on the northern side. The rest extended below on the flat plains with hundreds of mid-size leafy trees that broke up the red and orange expanse of downtown, which should create an attractive view from the train.

He couldn't remember much about the train station, other than that it was on the upper bench, above the main downtown section. He wasn't a hopper, so he'd paid little attention. He hated being so helpless. The plan would be up to the others. He sat up and took an extended drink, his throat parched and his arm throbbing.

Instead of standing up to check their surroundings, he asked, "How long do we have?" His dry throat hurt from speaking over the train noise.

"A few minutes." Caitlyn crouched down to collect both backpacks.

Her radiant face still looked tired and had a flaky patch of dried blood on one cheek. She must have watched over him all afternoon, despite her exhaustion. She really was something special.

They'd just pulled a fresh shirt on him and fixed his sling, when one-at-a-time Tatsuda, Ginger, Walker, and Elsa dropped into the car from farther up the train.

"Nice to see that you're awake," yelled Elsa, direct as always. "Tatsuda passed us word that you'd been doctored and gone to sleep. We'll have to hear the story later." She seemed re-energized and ready to take charge. Good that someone had energy.

Walker pulled earplugs from his ears, as did Elsa. They stuffed them in their pockets. They'd been prepared.

"What are you all doing here?" said Mason, yelling over the train's noise.

"We're getting off at the back," said Walker as he peered ahead over the left side.

"Jaxon's on the same train. He's near the front with his company of men, plus Boise will have its own garrison and trainyard security." Elsa's gaze flicked toward the front of the train. She might be tough, but she didn't want an encounter with her brother-in-law.

"We're going to have enough trouble getting back on the train, but this one isn't going on to Portland. It's turning to head south toward Salt Lake City instead of continuing west. The one we want is tomorrow night," said Walker.

"Since this is the final car, thought we'd slide off the back with the train to hide us from the soldiers. That's how I did it the last time I was here," said Walker. "There's a spot in the hills where we can sleep. Not too hard a climb."

Walker looked at Caitlyn, who nodded.

"I'll be fine," said Mason, irritated that he was being treated like an invalid. It made his teeth ache.

Caitlyn raised an eyebrow, giving him a direct stare, as if daring him to prove them wrong.

He took a deep breath. "I'll keep up. Medic's orders. It's my arm, not my legs." He might not feel confident, but he did his best to sound convincing.

The train rattled into Boise at a slow pace, but ahead the crashing resumed as it slowed further. They'd need to get off soon.

"Middle track of five," said Walker as he peered over the edge on both sides. "Off the back, down the track, then fade left toward the hills after about a hundred yards. Follow me once we're all on the ground."

Mason put on his hat and struggled to his feet, clenching his jaw at the fiery pain that shot down his arm with the slight movement. It hurt more than he'd expected. He'd gotten stitches only once before and the rebel medic must have used a numbing agent. Caitlyn had used nothing. He'd felt the burn and tug of every single one of the twenty-five stitches.

"No ladder," said Walker. "Those getting off farther up won't see us. It'll buy us time."

With that, the train shuddered to a complete stop as they braced themselves on an edge so they didn't topple over. Now that it was quiet, Mason's ears rang from the hours of noise. Tatsuda and Ginger shook their heads as if to chase away the ringing as well.

He met Tatsuda's eyes. "If you find earplugs for next time, get some for me too."

Mason would bet good coin the boy would have ear protection before the next extended ride. Mason hadn't had any years ago on his other train ride. He'd been under prepared and overwhelmed—much like now—but for different reasons.

Walker beckoned to Elsa and boosted her up at the back of the gondola. She turned and slid until her feet rested on part of the train. She met Mason's eyes, spun, and jumped. The crunch of the gravel below as she landed was obvious if anyone had been listening, but no alert sounded. Tatsuda and Ginger followed almost right away. Get the noise over with all at once and hope security and the disembarking soldiers didn't hear it. It should be covered by the clanking of the train and unloading far ahead.

Walker sent Caitlyn next, then boosted Mason to the top. He swung awkwardly, worried about balance without the use of his left arm. The ground swam beneath him, but he didn't hesitate. He focused on Caitlyn's anxious face below and jumped. He stumbled at the impact, falling to one knee. He wasn't usually so clumsy. Walker landed beside him and hauled him to his feet by the uninjured arm.

They all started down the tracks, checking over their shoulders every so often. He hoped they weren't seen, as he wasn't up for running unless his life depended on it. Walking on the uneven footing with mounded gravel and railroad ties was awkward, but they didn't stay on it for long. Walker led them unerringly to a gap in the bushes on the left. Behind them was a slim trail that led into the hills. It didn't look well-traveled, though the middle of the dusty path was free of grass in a single track.

The sounds of bustling activity behind them in the trainyard faded as they climbed. The hills were seared brown this summer and there were few trees, but the rolling landscape provided more cover than he would have guessed. They stopped hiking after twenty long minutes, now far above the city and out of sight on their winding route. As long as they hadn't been followed, they should be safe.

A vagabond campsite sat empty by a small stream where they stopped. Mason's legs shook. He needed food, water, and sleep to recover. Caitlyn filled his canteen and handed him water before checking the dressing on his arm. A frown pinched her forehead when she peeked under the bandages. The stitched part of the wound was an angry-looking pink with red edges around the black stitches and his entire forearm was swollen.

Caitlyn poked it twice. Her fingers cool on his fiery skin, that felt like it was burning from within.

"You have antibiotics?" A tightness grew in his chest and he became afraid that he knew the answer. She would have given him some already if she had a ready supply.

She shook her head. "I'm going to clean that part better. I don't like the look of it. It'll hurt like hell."

He met her direct gaze. There was fear behind her words.

"If that redness has spread in the morning and we can't get antibiotics, you could lose your arm." She hesitated. "Or your life. It isn't infected yet, but it isn't good. Blood poisoning can be fatal if untreated."

"Let's do it. Pity you don't have whiskey." He tried to sound like he was joking.

"You might feel it less if you drink," she said with her mouth flat in disapproval, "but you're dehydrated from blood loss, so it would be worse in the long run."

He clenched his muscles to prepare for the pain, looking up at the sky as she cleaned his wound again, cutting off some of the flap of loosened skin. It was worse than he'd imagined.

CHAPTER 27: WALKER

Caitlyn doctored Mason's swollen arm, but he still didn't feel well and couldn't choke down his dinner. Walker collected dried willow bark from his pack and brewed tea for his friend, as he'd once done for Elsa. Mason needed antibiotics, but Caitlyn didn't want to leave his side and Walker didn't blame her. Mason fell asleep, muttering and restless, while the others considered their options. Despite the danger, Walker volunteered to go into town even if the idea made him sweat. He was less identifiable than Elsa, and to his relief, Tatsuda offered to come with him.

Ignoring the panicked look that had passed over Elsa's face before she smoothed it away, he kissed her softly, savoring the feel of her lips before he promised to return as soon as possible. He trod the path with care in the dark, using moonlight as a guide until they reached the tracks. Here, it was more open and easier to see.

They walked the last stretch into town, avoiding the bulls and the empty train station altogether. Without a train on the tracks, the trainyard appeared deserted, though experience told Walker that security was there, even if unseen. They had twenty-four hours to get Mason in shape good enough to travel, or Walker and Elsa might have to proceed without him and Caitlyn. Neither of them wanted to leave their friends, even temporarily, but to make it into Canada and avoid Jaxon, it might be necessary.

Walker was inclined to wait, rather than risk an injured man on the rails. Elsa's impatience would mean she'd need convincing, but she was reasonable.

Ahead, Tatsuda flitted from shadow to shadow without making a sound, but he stayed close rather than wandering into town alone. Walker wasn't noisy, but the kid's ability to become a ghost was a gift.

From out of the dark, Tatsuda spoke, startling Walker. "Will we be leaving Ginger behind?"

Walker's steps faltered at the unexpected question. "You don't want to."

"I'm her only friend," said Tatsuda, his words quiet. "And she's mine."

"You've got us," said Walker. He'd grown fond of the rascal, as had Elsa. He'd become another younger brother, but, unlike Hayden, he was reliable. Walker pushed unwanted thoughts of Hayden down deep. It wasn't the time to worry about him. Perhaps someday, after their trip to Canada, he'd look for him. Or not. With a little distance, he could see now how much that relationship had become a toxic drain. Maybe his friendship with Hayden had run its course.

"It's not the same," the boy said, bringing Walker back to the present. Tatsuda's shoulder dipped in a shrug. "You're family, but Ginger and I talk. I haven't had that before and neither has she."

When Walker didn't answer, they continued in silence.

Tatsuda said, "Did you know they locked her in her room in their big, fancy house in Denver for three years? She wasn't even allowed outside."

Ginger's story was more interesting than Walker expected. If he'd been confined for three years, he'd have lost his sanity. He couldn't help but ask, "How did she get on a train?" It was a wonder that someone so inexperienced had evaded security.

"She found a secret passage in their house, explored until she found the way out, and ran. The train part sounds like pure luck. She climbed on and nobody found her." Tatsuda hesitated. "She doesn't want to go back. Even when she was thirsty and starving, she was certain. She doesn't belong there, and she'd never turn in Elsa."

"Why not tell this to Elsa?" said Walker as they drew near the lights of the town.

"I will," said Tatsuda, "but I want to know what you think."

Walker mulled over his next words. "If she isn't a liability, Elsa won't leave her. She wants to protect her from Jaxon and her father. That's a start." They walked another couple of hundred yards without talking, bringing them to the streets of Boise.

"What did Caitlyn need us to look for?" said Walker, as much to change the subject as a reminder of the importance of their trip.

"Penicillin or any other *'illin'* in tablet form. If that's not possible, anything that says sulfa," the boy recited. He stopped walking and Walker ran into his back, nudging him forward a step. Tatsuda pointed ahead to two shadowy figures walking in their direction on the right. They carried rifles and looked like soldiers on patrol. Walker and Tatsuda veered left and turned down a different darkened street.

Because they avoided downtown, the neighborhood streets were quiet, with few people abroad. It must be past midnight and curfew for non-GreenCorps employees except for those with specific passes to be out later, like bar workers and patrons. Strains of music and the odd voice from the distant, busy part of town floated on the air. With a large GreenCorps garrison here, the bars and brothels would be busy. Once Walker jumped as a cat crossed his path—a slinking black shadow with gleaming green eyes.

Caitlyn had directed them to look for a Med Center, marked with a red or green plus sign on a white background, or a medic office with a name and profession on a sign. Something official-looking. Tatsuda should be able to sneak in and out with the needed medicine without getting caught.

"What was the other thing she wanted?" said Tatsuda. "I didn't hear."

"Dexedrine or Adderall. A stimulant in case Mason needs a boost to get on and off the next train. Two doses." He hoped they waited a couple of days for hopping. Mason shouldn't rip his stitches again before his arm healed.

Walker and Tatsuda checked the buildings in a several-block radius without success. Twice they ducked into shadows to avoid GreenCorps patrols looking for those out after curfew. Then twice more. Too many GreenCorps soldiers around town. It seemed wrong. The tight feeling in Walker's shoulders increased. They couldn't stay in town much longer. Get the medicine and get out.

They came to the last section of the neighborhood before they reached downtown when at last Walker spied a medic sign propped against a front window of a shadowed house. He and Tatsuda jumped the fence and circled the premises in the dark, looking for a way in that wasn't as obvious as the front door.

The small two-story brick house sat second from the corner and had a back door opening off a small yard where three tomato plants grew, all ripe and heavy with fruit. The distinctive smell was enough to make Walker's mouth water. They'd been spoiled on Caitlyn's farm and hadn't eaten many fresh fruit and vegetables since leaving. His fingers itched to take a couple, but Elsa's head in his voice dissuaded him.

Once he wouldn't have hesitated to help himself, but now he admitted that regular people, like the inhabitants of this house, wouldn't be much better off than most, scraping to get by. Regular people didn't have surplus. Those three plants were part of their wealth, and stealing from them would be wrong.

Tatsuda pressed his ear against the back door, listening for sounds within while Walker regulated his breathing. After a long minute, the boy nodded and removed something shiny from his pocket, which he inserted into the lock, bending down to wiggle it around. From another pocket he produced his shear. Every scratch seemed loud in the silence, and Walker's palms became clammy with sweat.

It didn't take long for the lock to click and pop open. Walker let out a sigh of relief. Tatsuda swung the door open; the hinges squeaked, causing them both to cringe. Walker froze and held his breath, but no other noise emerged from within. Either the house was empty tonight or the inhabitants were sound asleep.

Before following the boy inside, Walker remained outside with the door ajar, searching the shadows again, listening and cataloging every noise, wanting to be certain that they were alone. Stealing from a medic would be considered a major crime, punishable by deportation to a work camp. When there were no sounds of commotion, he drew in a deep breath and entered the house, clenching his teeth as they stealthily made their way through the house, searching for the medic's office, the prime location for medication.

His footstep followed Tatsuda's, close to the wall. Without the bright light of the moon, the hallway seemed darker than outside, but the rooms with windows were brighter and easier to search with a glance. It remained as silent as a tomb, the only sound the quiet one of his breathing.

Caitlyn had said a locked cabinet with solid doors was common for most medics. In town, junkies might be a problem and break-ins regular, but few could pick locks like Tatsuda. Walker scanned the cramped office when they found the treatment room. The blinds were drawn and minimal light emanated from the rest of the house. Tatsuda must have better night vision than he did because Walker could see little in the shadowy room to cause excitement, though Tatsuda rushed ahead.

Tatsuda hissed, perhaps to get Walker's attention. Quieting his breathing, Walker followed the sound, passing an empty bed and two stools, almost tripping over them in the darkness. The boy had found a locked cabinet in the far corner of the treatment room. Walker held still, listening to the faint scritching sounds while Tatsuda worked on the lock.

Once it was open, Walker flicked on a small solar flashlight from the bunker and shone it inside of the cupboard. Dozens of small and medium-sized labeled jars lined four shelves in neat rows.

Jackpot.

This medic seemed well-stocked. Two large bottles labeled penicillin sat on the top shelf. Spying an empty smaller bottle on the bottom, Walker counted out ten days' worth of tablets for twice a day as per Caitlyn's instructions, filling the new container. With shaking hands, he fastened the lid.

He scanned the other shelves and located a bottle labeled Adderall and shook out two small pills and added them to the antibiotics. He returned both jars to the cabinet and nodded. Tatsuda locked the door while Walker placed a silver coin on the counter beside the sink and cabinet. If GreenCorps caught them, it wouldn't reduce the charges, but it made him feel better about taking the medicine. He clicked off his light, gave his eyes a moment to adjust, and followed Tatsuda toward the door where they'd entered, his chest still tight.

They hadn't gone far when a growling sound stopped them in their tracks. The medic or their family hadn't woken up, but their prowling must have alerted their dog. Tatsuda inched forward, making Walker swallow in nervousness. He grabbed for Tatsuda to haul him back, but he glided out of reach. Walker would hate for the boy to be bit; plus, they couldn't afford another injury.

The dog's growl deepened, causing Walker's hackles to rise. The dog's white teeth shone in the moonlight as its lips lifted and its shadowy form remained a vague outline while its narrowed eyes gleamed like sparks of fire. The head swivelled towards Tatsuda as he moved.

Walker stopped breathing as the boy stepped to his left and opened the chiller, which made a quick sucking sound as the seal broke around the edge. Walker prayed those sleeping above couldn't hear it. Tatsuda grabbed something from inside the chiller and tossed it onto the floor in the direction of the guard dog. The animal lunged, its toenails clicking and scraping on the floor as it snatched the food, and wolfed it down with wet chewing noises. Smart thinking on Tatsuda's part.

Neither Walker nor Tatsuda wasted time getting past the dog, and they scooted out the door into the night. Walker closed it without making noise, beyond the faintest clicking sound. Stepping into the yard, he glanced up at the second-story windows, which remained dark. They climbed the fence, landing on the street before heading back out of town, away from the raucous downtown noise from the next block.

They hadn't covered much ground when they encountered a patrol up the street.

Backtracking to avoid trouble, Walker and Tatsuda turned left and went around the block to the next street, trying to head north toward the hills. They didn't get far. Twice more, they detoured. Active GreenCorps patrols were everywhere at this hour. This wasn't a typical level of security, which made Walker uneasy.

Walker and Tatsuda met yet another dead end before deciding that they couldn't get through. Tatsuda was as silent as a mouse, but they were only a block from the still dark medic's house when the street filled with GreenCorps recruits. They seemed to be actively seeking someone, and he and Tatsuda couldn't get around so many without being noticed.

They stepped around a corner again to confer. Walker clenched his jaw, frustrated not to get through. "We aren't going to pass this far after curfew. They're everywhere." His mouth went dry as he whispered. "I'll cause a diversion. Pretend I'm drunk. You run. Get Mason the medicine."

"Elsa will skin me if you don't make it back." A slight frown lined Tatsuda's face.

"Advise her to take the train if I fail to return on time. If not tomorrow, the next express is in three days. Same evening time. I checked possibilities when I was in Idaho Falls. That one is just as good. Probably better. Maybe Jaxon will leave town when he can't find us."

"What will you do?" Tatsuda seemed reluctant to leave.

"If I can't return without giving away our camp, I'll hide. I have my canteen and a few rations. I'll be fine. I'll look for you near where we got off the train." Walker handed him the medicine container. His words projected more confidence than he felt, so Tatsuda would believe this solution.

"What if you're still not there?" Tatsuda seemed bothered by the idea as he stuffed the bottle into his pocket.

"Then I'm pinched and you should go on without me."

"She won't do that. I won't do that," said Tatsuda.

Walker placed his hand on the boy's bony shoulder. "I'll be fine. Take care of them for me. Don't let Elsa march down here on her own. You saw the posters everywhere."

"I won't," said Tatsuda. "This might help." He handed a small glass bottle to Walker, who unstoppered the bottle and sniffed. Some kind of moonshine, but it would do the trick.

Walker cocked an eyebrow.

Tatsuda shrugged. "It was in the medic's office, too. Mason wanted whiskey. This was close enough, but you might need it more to be convincing. I grabbed a bunch of foam for earplugs too."

The boy was quick, as usual.

Walker tugged on his hat, pulling it lower on his face, and splashed some moonshine onto the front of his shirt. He took a swig and swished it around his mouth before spitting it out with a grimace. He smelled enough like alcohol to fool someone briefly, hoping he could keep anyone from getting close enough to notice that he was sober.

"See you soon." He stumbled into the street with a loud curse, pretending to trip. Reeling from side to side, with a lurch, he attracted immediate attention.

"Halt," yelled several soldiers.

Walker stopped moving and glanced from side to side, as if confused. One man looked to be in charge of several others from the way they stepped back to let him through. The bearded man strode toward Walker with a scowl.

"What seems to be the problem, sir?" Walker lurched again and slurred his words.

Several men laughed, and the tension on the street dropped.

"Curfew was three hours ago," said the leader, continuing to hold his rifle pointed at Walker.

Walker swayed in place, not looking at the gun. He needed to look oblivious. "Didn't make it home the first time. I tried. Promise I'm headed there now." He belched. He was laying it on thick, but wanted to be enough of a spectacle that everyone would watch him and stop paying attention to everything else. Hayden had done this routine a dozen times. Only twice had he been locked up overnight to sleep it off.

Walker stared at the leader, squinting as he tilted his head. "Haven't I seen you before?"

"I think it's the same drunk as last week," said someone else. "From the other side of town."

"Na, the other guy was skinnier," said another of the GreenCorps recruits. Two others broke into the discussion, comparing the half dozen drunks in town. In a town this size, there were several.

From the corner of Walker's eye, a fleeting shadow turned the corner in the direction they'd been trying to go. North. Tatsuda was through. On his own, Walker had faith that the kid could sneak past anyone.

"Take him," said the leader, pointing to Walker. "We're doing a thorough sweep."

"Locking me up overnight?" Walker slurred his words, hoping to sell his act. His shoulders tightened as the patrol moved closer.

"Orders are that anyone after curfew is being shipped south in a few days. Good riddance to the lot of you. After that disturbance in Texas last month, they need new bodies fighting the fire."

Five weeks ago, Mason had left Texas just one step ahead of the law. That suggested a successful rebel operation. He'd never spoken about what he'd done, but Walker suspected he'd been part of the action. Good that the rebels had been successful.

The reality of the man's words sunk in. Fighting the ongoing tire fire was practically a death sentence. The black smoke and chemical guck filled lungs faster than they could get new men on site. Walker clenched a fist. He felt a sinking sensation in his chest as he looked around. He'd been hoping they'd escort him home or let him go with a warning. No such luck. He had to leave.

He took one step, hoping to run.

Someone in the distance shouted, "Stop or I'll shoot."

The guards laughed. "It's a busy night," one said as they all turned to look toward the action on the next block.

Walker held his breath, froze, and then stumbled again, moving toward the shadows, staying out of reach of the soldiers. His peripheral vision showed that everyone still looked relaxed and confident that he was just some drunk and not a wanted fugitive with a price on his head.

He couldn't let them lock him up and risk being seen by Jaxon or Wade. They might recognize him as the bouncer from the bar in SoCal—after all, they'd been regulars. They would know how he'd left town with Elsa. If they caught him, they'd scour every inch of town for her. He'd have to escape now, not later.

Walker took another deep breath and bolted, vaulting a fence on the right. A loud gunshot rang out behind him and the bullet whizzed past his head and struck the house, spraying chips of brick into the night. Close, but a miss.

"After him," the leader shouted from the street. Footsteps followed him as boots pounded on the cobbled street.

Walker didn't wait to find out how many or how soon. He sprinted for the far fence across the yard, vaulted it too, then tore around the corner of the house. He zigzagged across the street and hurdled another fence into a backyard. When he'd gained enough ground, he slowed and headed for downtown, which he hoped would be the last place they searched. Double-checking that nobody was behind him, he hid in a yard under a prickly pine tree with low branches. He'd be uncomfortable and sticky, but with luck, the search would move on. He pressed himself flat, his heart racing as he willed the soldiers away.

As daylight brightened his surroundings, the pounding footsteps receded, the GreenCorps voices moved farther away, then disappeared. He peeked out again when the back door of the house opened. With a sinking feeling, he recognized the tomato plants. He'd returned to the medic's house. A large black dog trotted into the yard and Walker froze, holding his breath and hoping the dog would leave. Instead, it finished its business and wandered the yard, sniffing.

Walker was unsure about how to proceed. If he ran, the GreenCorps search might still intercept him. Now that daylight was dawning, he wouldn't find a more secure place to hide. His head rose as the dog turned toward his hiding place with a snarl.

CHAPTER 28: ELSA

Elsa's eyes followed the retreating forms as Walker and Tatsuda headed down the path, soon losing them to the darkness. She took first watch as she would be unable to sleep knowing Walker was going into town. He'd downplayed the danger though he was also wanted and anything could happen—even if he was careful. As the night deepened, she identified many of the night sounds and took comfort in them, thinking of her time at the cabin near Lake Tahoe.

An owl hooted from the thicker treed area up the hill. The faint rustling in the whispery grass was probably just the wind or an occasional mouse. The light from the concealed fire pit died and she tucked her hands into her long sleeves to keep them protected from the chill night air as she waited.

The night wore on, stretching as thin as her nerves.

She drummed her fingers against her jittery leg, unable to keep still. Often on watch, it was difficult not to doze, but tonight she remained alert and decided against waking anyone else to take over, staying at her post.

Across the campsite, Mason lay stretched out, Caitlyn curled next to him. Since their trip alone, while Elsa and the others had been trapped in the bunker, they'd been inseparable. Elsa hadn't met Mathew, but if he was half the man Caitlyn described, her late husband would have been pleased to know that she wasn't lonely anymore. Plus, Mason seemed like a good man, even if he was hard to read.

Elsa looked around; the sky had brightened into a bluish color at the edges, instead of the true black of night, as dawn approached. Walker and Tatsuda had been gone all night. Her throat constricted and for a minute she pictured them caught, locked in GreenCorps holding cells. Her chest tightened, but she shook her head, trying to shake the negative thoughts loose. She stood and turned slightly, so she could watch the trail now that it was growing light. Her eyes strained as she stared at the path, willing them to appear, but there was no movement.

Walking closer, she found a new place to sit on a rock with a good vantage of the hillside below. The sky's colors shifted again—orange and pink stained the east and still no Walker. Something must have gone wrong to cause a lengthy delay. Her instincts indicated that he was okay, still, she fretted.

Behind her, the other women woke. Caitlyn sent Ginger for water while Caitlyn made a small fire to boil water for their breakfast. Mason sat up, glassy-eyed with flushed cheeks. Fever. Caitlyn left the fire to check his arm and replaced the bandage. She didn't smile this morning and her eyes seemed strained.

"How is he?" Elsa asked when Caitlyn wandered near to check the trail too.

"Hot," she said, a crease between her brows. "I'm concerned about infection. If they aren't back in a few hours, I'll go into town myself. He can't wait much longer for antibiotics."

After how Mathew had died, it made sense for Caitlyn to be extra vigilant.

It was full daylight with the sun almost overhead when Elsa's heart caught at the rustle of footsteps below and a flash of movement between the trees in the distance. She motioned to Caitlyn and Ginger to stop talking, and eased her knife from its sheath, hiding behind a tree until Tatsuda appeared, scrambling upward in a hurry. With a deep sigh of relief, she scanned the trail below, waiting for Walker. The trail remained empty.

When Tatsuda ran into camp, Elsa could wait no longer.

"Walker?" She tried to conceal the desperate sound from her voice, but failed.

"He's okay, last I saw," said Tatsuda, gasping for air. Leaning on his knees to catch his breath, he dug in his pocket and produced a small jar filled with white tablets. He tossed them to Caitlyn, who sighed in relief. The tightness and tension she'd held all morning seemed to drain away, and the set of her shoulders dropped.

"Thank you." She gave the boy a huge smile as she opened the container and handed a pill to Mason.

Elsa couldn't relax and her gaze returned to the empty trail as if willing Walker to appear.

"I could watch." Ginger didn't look at Elsa and instead picked at the raw edge by her thumb where the skin had flaked off and bled. "You can get breakfast and hear the complete story."

It was kind of the girl to offer. Ginger had picked the edge of her thumbs raw without Tatsuda around and been silent, clearly also worried for him while they were gone.

Elsa nodded. "My eyes need a break. Get me if you see anyone or anything." She halted and filled her lungs with air. "Thanks, Ginger." Her gut said this would work out, and she needed to calm down. That was easy to think, but her stomach roiled with uncertainty.

At the fire, Elsa handed Tatsuda a steaming pouch of food that they'd saved near the embers and took one for herself. "What happened?" She tried to keep the impatience from her voice. "Last you saw? How did you get separated?" She must have been successful, because he looked at her with sympathy instead of frustration.

He told her about how difficult it had been to find a medic, about the numerous patrols, and the tight security. "Even with Walker's diversion, it took me hours to get back safely. I had to hide twice and out-wait the patrols."

"Where was the last place you saw him?" Elsa stepped toward the trail, prepared to go after him. It was foolish, but she couldn't sit any longer. She needed to do something.

"You can't go down there." Tatsuda scrambled to his feet, his eyes wide. "It's broad daylight."

She stopped and raised her eyebrows. "Can't?"

The boy stood straight and didn't move under her gaze. "Walker said not to. He didn't want you to march into danger. Trust him. I'm not exaggerating how hard it was to get back without being seen. If it makes you feel better, Walker must have given them the slip, though, because they searched for him all night."

She was torn. What if he was hurt and needed her? But she'd help no one by getting caught too. She had to take the bunker key to the Canadians so the seeds could be distributed. A way for everyone to grow food was more important than her boyfriend. The decision still didn't hurt any less.

"Will we still try for the train this evening?" said Caitlyn, flicking a glance at Mason.

Elsa's eyes strayed again to the empty trail. "What do you think?"

"There's another express in three days," said Tatsuda, not looking up from his food. "Walker said to let you know."

"I say we stay, give the antibiotics a chance to work. It'll give Walker a chance to slip out of town and join us." Caitlyn tugged on her braid, then rested her hand on Mason's arm. He covered it with his hand and gave her an almost imperceptible smile. Caitlyn deserved a chance at happiness.

"I'll be fine," Mason said, conviction ringing in his voice. "I've got antibiotics now."

"What will I do with myself for three days?" Elsa muttered, half to herself, not expecting an answer.

"Read," said Ginger, turning from her post at the head of the trail. "Whenever I was stuck in my room without company, that's what I'd do. You brought a book or two from the bunker, didn't you? Or you can borrow mine."

Elsa hated to admit that everyone else was right and that it would be foolhardy to get caught because she'd been impatient. Biting her lip, she nodded.

"And try to get some rest," said Caitlyn. "You'll do the group no good if you exhaust yourself or make yourself ill." She gave Elsa a wan smile. "Medic's orders."

Elsa nodded and retreated to the border of the camp, rolled out her sleeping bag in the shade, and lay down on top of it. Every part of her seemed stiff as a board. She took a couple of deep breaths and imagined sinking into the softness and peace of sleep. She couldn't imagine that it would work, but drifted right away, falling into oblivion.

* * *

Elsa passed the next two days in a fog. After the first long nap, she'd woken that afternoon in a sweat, flailing and yelling at Jace. It was the first time she'd dreamed of him since the bunker. It wasn't the dream where she killed him. Instead, it was the memory of when he'd beaten her the night she and Walker had fled SoCal. She missed Walker's quiet words of reassurance after her nightmares. Her heart still racing, she got up to look for food. She'd slept little these past two nights, though she lay down, pretending for the sake of the others while she worried the insides of her cheeks raw.

The third morning without Walker, Elsa woke after a restless night. A heavy weight settled on her chest and it became hard to breathe. All the worry and fear for Walker, but also being left on her own with the task of convincing the Canadians to help, fell on her all at once. Her cheeks burned. There was a part of her that felt abandoned and angry towards Walker for not returning. She threw off her sleeping bag, stomped on her boots, and lunged toward the mountain heights where she could have some privacy.

Had something happened to Walker? No matter how careful he might have been or how competent he was, he was still a fugitive.

Anyone could have found him and turned him in, even if Tatsuda had heard nothing. What would she do if she were alone forever?

The sparse golden grass was covered in dew and the night had been cold, especially sleeping alone, but the brisk activity of scrambling up the mountainside soon warmed Elsa's muscles. It wouldn't be long now until the season turned. She surveyed the hillside where bits of bright yellow had sprinkled the canopy almost overnight. Walker had told her that in this country, away from the ocean, there would be snow in late fall. Maybe as early as next month. She shivered. It wasn't cold like that yet, but the air had a damp bite to it she hadn't noticed before. Mist rose off the river below in a clump of white, rising toward their camp on the mountainside.

The town below looked peaceful. Leaving today, possibly without Walker, brought her tears to the surface. Alone, there was no one to see them or to judge her, and Elsa couldn't stand the tight sensation in her chest any longer. It made it hard to think or breathe. She stared at the town, tears tracing her cheeks, letting them drip.

The enormity of it all hit her. If Walker didn't come, should she even leave? Instead of going on to Canada, she could hop a train in the other direction and head back to the cabin. If he was able, he'd return there, knowing it was a place they could connect, but she wished they'd discussed the possibility. The cabin was the only place she'd found peace, but without Walker, it would be different. She didn't want everything to be this hard. She didn't want to have to make this decision on her own. Sobs wracked her thin frame where she sat, the cold seeping into her bones from the ground.

If Elsa left, she could let Caitlyn and Mason off the hook. They'd probably go back to Caitlyn's farm and raise a family of little rebels. Now that Tatsuda had Ginger, the two of them might make their own way to a city and live by pick-pocketing. Ginger's book smarts and Tatsuda's street smarts made them a force to be reckoned with. Everyone else could go back to a different life if they were careful. Elsa had nothing to return to without Walker and without this cause.

Her body shook as the tears intensified again, scalding paths down her face. She couldn't breathe, the band in her chest clenching like a vice. She put her head down on her knees and wept. Crying not just for herself, but for Granny and her mother, who she barely remembered, for Avery and the girls, and for the life she'd left behind when she'd hopped her first train. Her life had been a dead-end of poverty and loneliness; she just hadn't seen an alternative.

If she didn't take these seeds and bunker key to the Canadians, it could be another two hundred years before anyone could break GreenCorps' hold with their monopoly on viable seeds and terminator seeds for sale. Her sense of responsibility to their cause came flooding back, washing away her self-pity. She had to do something, even if she didn't feel strong enough on her own. She needed to find that strength and do it.

After a few minutes, awareness returned. A songbird trilled off to the right and as she followed the sound with her gaze, a doe and spotted fawn stood at the brink of the clearing near the trees. They seemed aware of her presence, but unafraid.

Elsa wiped her tears on her ragged sleeve and sat up straighter, willing herself to be strong. Taking several deep breaths, she stared down at the quiet town. She could just make out the station to her far right, where the soldiers and workers unloading a northbound train resembled scurrying ants. Her gaze drifted into the neighborhoods of Boise. Walker was down there somewhere.

If he wasn't on the train tonight, she'd take the key to Canada, then come back and pick up his trail. Tatsuda would help. Even without Walker, she wasn't alone. She could do this. She stood up and brushed the dirt and pine needles from her pants and headed downhill to make breakfast.

Tonight, they had a train to catch.

* * *

Elsa watched as Tatsuda slipped down the hillside where he was off to scout the train tracks for this evening, check for news of Walker, and keep alert for GreenCorps forces who might discover their trail or hiding place. She worried at her cheeks until he returned; they didn't need someone else to go missing. So far, it had remained quiet despite the hive of activity at the train station each time a train came through town. Tonight, before he'd gone, Tatsuda had asked if Ginger could come with them when they left Boise.

"The girl belongs with us as long as she wants to stay," had been Elsa's sole comment.

Tatsuda had grinned, eyes sparkling before he'd whispered the decision to Ginger, who shot Elsa a real smile, not her customary nervous one.

There'd still been no sign of Walker. This evening, they'd all go. Elsa breathed easier when Tatsuda reported that Jaxon had left town. He didn't know what direction the GreenCorps man had gone, just that he'd left town without most of his men. While his whereabouts were a concern, it wasn't Elsa's priority.

Walker was the most important person in her life. He'd changed everything for the better, he was her everything. It was difficult to consider leaving him and the weight of her duty to the rest of the people oppressed by GreenCorps weighed on her, the burden growing heavier with each day that passed.

They'd been right to wait until today for the train. But they needed to go. Their campsite wouldn't remain hidden forever and their stock of rations was getting dangerously low.

Mason's arm had been a brilliant red by the time Tatsuda had returned with the antibiotics, but the potent medicine had worked by the next morning, the red fading to pink, then to normal skin tones. He'd slept easier after the first night, with less muttering, and he'd lost his fevered glaze.

When it was late afternoon, with the sun blazing down, they packed their camp. Elsa carried Walker's backpack in addition to her own. The train today was supposed to be an express, so it wouldn't come to a full stop in Boise. The plan had been to get on as it slowed to travel through town. They needed to get on before where they'd gotten off the last train. If they waited much longer, their run would take them too close to the station and they couldn't risk the train's speed increasing on the far side of town.

Guessing they might need extra running space, Elsa led them back along the tracks, away from town to the east. Though she watched carefully, still no Walker. She kept hoping he'd stride out of the bushes or the forested hillside and catch her up in an enormous hug. The world was lonelier without him. Somehow, when he was around, she believed everything would work out fine, not just relying on her instincts.

The tight feeling remained with her as they hiked along the railroad tracks. This would be the first train she'd be hopping without Walker's help. "We're getting on, whether or not he comes." The decision left a stone-sized lump in her throat and a yawning pit in her stomach. She swallowed. "He wanted me to get the key to Canada."

Mason tipped his hat. "Welcome to the rebels."

Elsa looked up, startled into meeting his steely blue eyes. "What do you mean?"

"I figured it was time you admitted it. You're doing this as part of a cause bigger than yourself. You've got the largest price on your head in the history of GreenCorps, other than Grady himself. You're one of us."

Elsa hadn't ever looked at it that way. "If I fail, or get caught, will someone else continue?" She looked at Mason and Caitlyn.

They nodded as confirmation.

Elsa fought the unexpected hot prickle of tears that overwhelmed her.

"It's worth doing," said Caitlyn. "Or we wouldn't be here."

Though Elsa had known to expect the train about half an hour before sunset, and they were in position early, it was still hard to feel the same level of excitement about hopping a train without Walker.

She ran through his usual instructions in her head and took a deep breath. "Okay, we'll go in the same groups as before. If Walker turns up, he can find me." She located the most level area possible for running beside the tracks and a hiding place where they could observe and listen to incoming trains. They waited on the high side where they would dash at the last minute as the train slowed.

The rails rumbled and vibrated as the train approached. Her chest heaved with another deep breath when the engine passed. This was it.

She couldn't believe how fast it traveled. This didn't seem slow enough to get on board, but the cars that passed soon crashed into each other around the corner with loud metallic clangs. The metal rails rang with the jolting sounds. It was slowing down to continue through town, but still too fast for her comfort.

Butterflies flitted through her stomach. She'd chosen a location where the train curved like a long snake hugging the edge of the hills, where she'd be able to see when the final few cars were coming. They could decide then which cars to hop. She wished she knew what to aim for in advance. That was the problem with choosing cars on the move before they came to the train yard, but with the non-stop GreenCorps patrols, they'd been unable to scout the other end of town past the station to know how soon the speed picked up again.

Like the previous trains, the front half had two passenger cars, half a dozen water tankers, and several dozen boxcars. Elsa stuffed in her earplugs and Tatsuda passed around several pieces of foam so the others were equipped. Sometimes his light fingers were an asset. The noise grew in intensity and the ground trembled as the train thundered past their hiding place at the treeline.

She swallowed. It would be obvious to anyone on board the train who spotted them why they were near the train, so she remained hidden until the middle engine passed their position. The remaining of the cars should be unmanned unless there were others hopping. To her relief, the back half of the train included several covered hoppers.

Pointing to the train, she held up four fingers rather than yelling over the din. They'd aim for the final four cars. That way, if a pair missed their intended car, they'd have another chance. As long as they didn't stumble. She'd never been in charge of this part of their traveling.

Elsa ran alongside the train from the right, going first, she replayed Walker's chant in her head, *hand, hand, step, hop.* The train's rumble filled her chest and ears, making it impossible to think of anything except the roaring train. Coming close to the ladder, she leaped and climbed, catching the rungs, which were hot from the sun. She made her smoothest ascent and pulled herself over the top, swinging onto the hopper. She braced herself, leaning to watch Tatsuda and Ginger as they hopped the next car. Ginger was a natural.

Tatsuda helped Ginger over the top and they took their seats on the train car just behind hers where they were no longer visible. Caitlyn and Mason hopped last but had no trouble that Elsa could see getting on board. They were an excellent team, and the extra days of rest had been beneficial for Mason. Elsa was certain his injury must still hurt like hell. She had experience with stitches and deep cuts, but at least it was clean and healing. If it wasn't for the missing Walker, this part of the trip would have been a success.

Unlike previous trains she'd boarded, this one wouldn't stop at the next station, but she needed to get into the covered part at the rear of the hopper and remain out of sight. They would stay on the mountain side of the flange that ran down the back of the porch and gamble that most of the station workers would be busy on the opposite side of the train.

She wished she knew which of the five tracks the express would use as it charged toward town. Hopefully, one of the ones farthest from the station buildings, so they'd be less likely to be spotted. The train wouldn't stop in Boise, but GreenCorps could phone from station to station to let someone know they were on board, which could make getting off in Portland difficult.

Elsa settled in, both packs tucked behind her. The others had taken most of the food pouches to lighten her load, for which she was grateful. She swallowed and hugged her knees to her chest. Leaving Walker's belongings behind wouldn't have worked if he'd met them onboard. He expected them to catch this train. She swiped at the pesky tears on her face. At least no one witnessed her crying. She took a few deep breaths and pulled herself together.

As they approached the station, the train slowed further, but rattled onward. She held her breath until they passed the close edge of the trainyard, where there was some kind of disturbance. A second train heading in the opposite direction was stopped between their moving train and the station buildings, blocking her view. The extra train should have made her feel safer, but her stomach roiled and the hair on her arms rose as midway a scream cut off—silenced by a gunshot.

She snuck a peek. GreenCorps soldiers milled along both sides of the other train. Twice more shots fired, and each time Elsa's heart leaped. Her hands trembled as she shrank into the train. A tremendous roar went up, then a boom that she couldn't identify, followed by deafening metallic banging.

The next train car she passed rocked back and forth on the tracks and GreenCorps soldiers scurried for cover as it tipped toward the next track, just missing the car that held Ginger and Tatsuda. Several men in black uniforms fired their guns, but a massive surge of people overwhelmed security. The uniformed men disappeared from sight, swallowed by the raging townspeople. There was no sign of Walker, but it appeared as though a group of women had resisted being loaded into the boxcars with the help of the majority of Boise.

Elsa had never seen such a huge mob or witnessed GreenCorps on the losing end of a skirmish. She cheered inside. They weren't invincible after all.

Wails and screams filled the air, and Elsa longed to join the fight. Instead, she tucked her head under and pressed herself farther into the metal recess at the back of the hopper, hoping the larger disturbance masked their passing. Further away, soldiers marched from the lower part of town—headed to the station. GreenCorps must have emptied the garrison.

The incoming soldiers fired a volley of shots before falling to the town mob. Her heart went out to the families of those in danger as the train rattled past the scene. A thick plume of charcoal-colored smoke rose, flames roared as the stationhouse caught fire, and an orange blaze danced skyward—illuminating the twilight. GreenCorps wouldn't let this be the final word, but for now, hope blossomed in her chest. Thousands of others out there were waiting for chances like this, for the right time to overthrow GreenCorps. It wasn't just a few rebels, everyone seemed willing to take a chance.

Chapter 29: Walker

"King, get back here," boomed a loud voice in a tone that expected to be obeyed.

The black dog stopped and Walker resumed breathing. He didn't dare move or he might attract attention from the man in the yard, who may or may not be the medic. Walker hoped to remain in the dense branches that hid him from both the yard and street until it was dark. He risked capture if he left sooner, so he'd planned to slip into the night before curfew, but if the dog flushed him out, he'd jump the fence and run. Elsa would probably insist they wait for the second express, the one in three days. Not just for him, but because of Mason's arm.

He'd said for them to continue without him, but he counted on Elsa waiting for the three-day train. He ached, picturing her quiet distress when he didn't return. She wouldn't let the others see her fear, but it would be there. She'd be efficient and cold, even if that wasn't the real her. There was no remedy for it, though.

In the last three months, they'd seldom been apart for more than an hour or two, and being away from her was odd and uncomfortable for him, too. They didn't always talk, but he was always aware of her presence. She'd become part of him in a way that Hayden never had, despite all their years on the road together. Not only did he love her, but he trusted her with his life. He'd had no one else he could open up to or depend upon until her.

Walker focused on the man at the edge of the backyard, hoping he wouldn't have to make a break for it in the other direction. The dog took another step in Walker's direction and the man gave another order.

"King. Come." The man's voice left little room for argument.

The dog listened, turning from Walker. It bounded toward the man, who gave the dog a pat before they returned inside the house.

That had been close. Walker repositioned himself under the branches and let his body go limp, and drifted off to sleep.

When he woke, he wasn't sure if it was day or night. The sky was an indeterminate shade of blue that could be dusk or dawn. Hearing the raucousness of day-end chaos, he determined it must be twilight. His stomach rumbled with hunger and he reached into his shirt for his jerky, breaking off a chunk to chew on. It wasn't quite dark enough to leave.

Walker shifted as the light dimmed, edging toward night. He was about to scramble out of his bristly hiding place that smelled of pine and sun-warmed sap, when a group of people marched in unison onto the street beyond the fence and their footsteps stopped nearby. It sounded like GreenCorps soldiers. He hadn't expected this area to be busy again tonight.

Damn. He should have left sooner, but his description might have been passed around today, so it wouldn't have been safe. The recruits would watch for him and with his distinctive size and no way to change his appearance, he'd be easy to recognize. Cursing his terrible luck, he stayed under the thick tree, listening.

Walker caught the words "round-up," and his blood ran cold.

He hadn't witnessed a thorough door-to-door search and seizure since he was young. Sweat ran down his face and from his armpits, making his clothes stick. This could be bad. He shifted once more as he clenched his fists. They planned to collect young women to send south. Perhaps this street had been chosen because of his activity last night. His stomach churned in his anger. GreenCorps must have decided that someone was harboring fugitives and were using this excuse to teach the residents of Boise a lesson about going against the corporation.

He should slip away, but with so many GreenCorps soldiers nearby, he would be too exposed. Walker crouched lower, flattening himself on the ground. He would stay longer. It was still a couple of hours until curfew. He'd have time after they moved on.

From the murmur of the crowd, soldiers lined the street. Several dozen at least. Marching in pairs, they knocked on the doors of the houses situated on both sides of the street. When the occupants answered, the GreenCorps men ordered them to move aside in order to conduct a search. Several times smashed glass and people's shouts broke the evening silence. All other noises ceased until the crying and shouting grew louder in the street as they forcibly removed several women from their homes.

"Let me go. I've done nothing wrong," one woman shouted.

A slapping sound followed, a distinctive noise of flesh against flesh. Walker winced as though the smack had hit him.

"Keep your hands to yourself," another woman said through the sound of tears.

"Don't touch me," said another.

Violence followed each protest and the number of women taken from their homes increased.

Walker tried to block out their words, the taste of bile in his mouth. It became almost impossible to do nothing.

The search and seizure advanced up the street for twenty minutes before arriving at the medic's house. It was now dark enough that Walker couldn't see beyond his branches, except for the light from an upstairs window and brighter ones beyond the fence at the neighboring houses on either side.

He held his breath as the soldiers pounded on the front of the medic's house. Inside, the dog barked and the back door opened, releasing the dog into the backyard.

"Stay." The medic's voice was low and urgent.

The dog, illuminated by light from within, sat by the back door, staring as it closed. The dog whined, but to Walker's surprise, it didn't move.

Thumping fists banged against the front door again. "Open up. We're conducting a search." The snarled voice at the medic's front door sounded familiar.

Recognition came to Walker right away. The voice belonged to Jaxon's new number one man, Wade. Walker had watched him through the video feed provided by the satellite when he'd been in the bunker. The man used to hassle Elsa in SoCal before Walker had arrived. Did this mean Jaxon was on the street, too? Walker listened for Jaxon's voice, which he should recognize at close range. Both men had been regulars at Ginny's bar in SoCal where Walker had been a bouncer.

Blood pounded through his ears and he was uncertain what to do. In a thorough search, he might be found, but at the other houses, it had seemed cursory, more like scare tactics and an excuse to take the young women. Bile rose in his throat again. He felt impotent to do anything.

The sound of the medic's deep voice was muffled, but the destructive sounds of the soldiers in the house grew. Someone screamed, glass smashed, and furniture crunched inside the house.

"Nobody here, except his daughter. She's about the right age," said a recruit, returning to the front.

"Bring her," said Wade. "Put her with the others. McCoy's orders were to make Boise pay for hiding the criminals."

"Daddy, don't let them take me," came the daughter's tearful voice.

"We haven't seen any fugitives," said the medic, his voice becoming louder as he followed the men with his daughter outside in front of his house. His deep voice seemed calm and reasonable, even with the soldiers smashing his home. "My daughter has done nothing wrong. I'm the medic the garrison often uses. Talk to the captain."

There was a thump, followed by a groan and another thump. The dog growled and scratched at the back door.

"You're not exempt," said Wade with a snarl.

"What the hell?" said the medic's strangled voice.

His voice came from lower to the ground; one of the men had likely bashed him with their rifle.

The daughter screamed. "Daddy. Help."

Walker covered his mouth, his teeth aching from the pressure of containing his fury. How old was the daughter? She sounded young and scared, someone like Ginger. Younger.

The medic growled and the noise of a disturbance intensified. There was more screaming and a series of thuds, including the sound of someone falling. The dog barked and left the door, racing in circles in the yard before launching itself at the tall fence. It fell to the ground but immediately jumped up, put its paws on the fence, and howled. Walker's heart went out to the dog. Its family was in trouble.

"Dad," the medic's daughter screamed.

"Shut her up," Wade growled.

There was the sound of someone striking her, perhaps a slap, and she went quiet.

Walker's blood boiled, and it was all he could do not to rush in and get involved. He closed his eyes and counted in his head, trying to remain calm. People shouldn't have to live this way. It was wrong.

"Stop your bawling. Don't make this worse than it has to be," said someone, probably another soldier.

"That will teach this arrogant asshole to get in our way," said Wade, his satisfaction clear. "What makes him think he'd get special treatment?"

Nobody answered.

Walker clenched both fists, wishing he could do something. There must be two dozen armed men out there. He didn't stand a chance if he rushed them. He couldn't save the young women. Not here. Not now when he was alone. He shook with impotent fury while the search moved on to the next house on the street.

The dog barked and whined, still trying to get through the fence. On the other side, someone banged the boards, and the dog growled, rushing toward the sound. Someone gasped and stepped back.

"Don't waste a bullet on the dog," Wade said. "It's locked up and can't hurt anyone."

Walker watched in horror as the butt end of a rifle swung over the fence and landed a glancing blow against the dog's head. It fell with a whimper and struggled to its feet. Thankfully, just dazed, but not injured. Hot rage filled Walker that someone would hurt a helpless animal. Taking the girls as sex slaves was worse, but this moment of casual cruelty was the last straw. His breaking point. Something had to be done about GreenCorps. Not just for Elsa, for everyone.

The collection continued for another block. Several more people were injured, the sound of their voices cutting off mid-sentence. Anyone who protested was silenced. At least there hadn't been gunfire, just a few beatings. Sounds of muffled crying continued down the street. By his estimate, they'd taken at least two dozen women by the time they stopped. Young women who would fetch the best price in the south. His stomach churned, and he resisted the urge to throw up.

"That'll do. Show's over," Wade announced to the neighborhood. Walker could picture the smug bastard's face. "Consider yourselves to have gotten off lightly. We could have searched the whole damn town. You have until tomorrow afternoon to turn over the fugitives or we'll pick another street at random and do the same thing. Somebody has to know what happened to the rebels that arrived by train."

"What about our daughters?" Said an angry woman's voice.

"They're the price of your stubbornness," said Wade.

"Will you set bail?" said another voice from somewhere closer. "I can pay to get my wife back."

"Take it up with GreenCorps headquarters. We're just following orders." Wade yelled, "Let's go."

There hadn't been a sound from the front of the house since the medic had been silenced. The dog had returned to the back door, where it barked and scratched. Walker crept out of the boughs where he'd hidden all day and stretched, his back cracking. At the sound, the dog turned and ran toward him with a deep growl.

"Good dog. I won't hurt you. I'm not a threat." Walker froze and spoke in a soft voice, holding his hands in front of him. The dog stopped six feet away and its lips lifted in a snarl as, stiff-legged, it circled Walker. He remained motionless. Sweat trickled between his shoulder blades as he waited.

The dog's hackles lowered when the threat level didn't rise.

"Good dog. It's okay. I'm here to help." Walker tried to soothe the upset animal. The dog stopped snarling, coming forward hesitantly to sniff Walker's hand. Walker held his breath until the dog licked his fingers. All the anger seemed to have leached from the dog and it whined, looking up at him with its dark eyes.

Walker knelt down beside the dog and scratched behind its ears. "Good dog. Let's check on your people." He kept his voice low in case neighbors were listening for out-of-place voices. He stepped up to the back door and rapped on the wood with just one knuckle. Trying to be loud enough that if anyone was inside, they'd answer, but not so loud that others on the street would hear. Everyone would still be on edge, and his discovery could end in disaster for him and the girls.

After the third knock, each one louder than the previous, the door remained closed and the house silent. Since no one had come, Walker turned the knob, opening the unlocked back door. He blinked when it was bright inside. Lights had been left on in the kitchen and broken dishes littered the smooth floor. What a mess.

"Hello," he called out. "Your dog wanted in." The dog rushed past him, running through the kitchen and down the hall toward the front of the house.

Walker closed the door and followed, his feet seeming loud despite avoiding most of the broken crockery. The house felt empty tonight. Emptier than last night when the medic and his daughter had slept upstairs while Walker and Tatsuda had searched for medicine, as though their breathing had filled the house. Now there was nothing but silence. Had they had killed the medic?

Walker passed the treatment room and the stairs to the upper level as he tracked the dog to the front door. A tall narrow window beside the front door had been smashed and Walker's boots crunched on shards of broken glass. He opened the front door a crack, unsure what he'd find out front.

At first, he couldn't see anything in the darkness and the street remained dead quiet. It seemed that everyone was hiding inside their homes. Doors were closed, blinds were down, and the night was hushed. He waited, but the silence remained. Holding the door open wider, he stuck his head and shoulders outside for a better look. Still quiet. No outcry over his presence. The only light came from the hallway inside the medic's house.

The dog pushed past him and bolted down the three steps to the front walkway, where the dim shape of a prone form lay on the ground near the street. The black dog nudged the man with its nose, whining. It looked back at Walker as if imploring him for help. Walker hesitated. Elsa would be worried, but she was safe in the mountains and he had no doubt that resourceful Tatsuda had delivered his message along with the antibiotics.

Walker couldn't help the young women on his own, but he might help the medic. It wasn't much, but it was something.

He checked both ways, expecting soldiers to appear or to leap from hiding, he slid out the door and jumped the stairs, leaving the door open behind him. He rushed to the man on the ground where he found the medic still breathing but unconscious. Walker grabbed beneath both of the man's arms and dragged him toward the house, the dog following.

The large-framed medic's dead weight was heavy, but Walker dragged him up the front stairs and into the house. He hauled him past the worst of the broken glass and into the treatment room before going back to close and lock the front door. The dog hovered by the man's side, unwilling to leave.

Walker turned on the light switch in the treatment room, hoping the electric lights worked here too. The medic must make good coin because an overhead light came on. Walker couldn't lift the man onto the treatment bed, so he left him on the smooth floor and tucked a pillow under his head while he fetched water.

Like the lights, the water was operational, so Walker filled his canteen before searching for an unbroken mug to fill. He grabbed a dry dishtowel from beside the sink and returned to the medic, where he cleaned the blood off the man's forehead. The cut itself didn't look too serious, though there was a lump. Walker wasn't a medic, but the bleeding had stopped. There was a good chance the man would wake on his own.

Walker debated leaving once more as it might be his only chance to get back to Elsa in time, but the abducted women had families, too. What if Elsa had been taken? The image of her shackled and forced onto a train, and shipped south, stopped him. If it was Elsa, he would do anything to get her back. In the end, he stayed.

He didn't have long to wait.

"Cora," the man muttered. "Cora."

The dog woofed and nudged the medic again. This time the man's hand found the dog's fur and held on as though hugging him with just his hand. The medic blinked his eyes and groaned, his other hand rising to his injured head.

"Where's Cora?" the medic said as he pushed himself to a sitting position

Walker handed him a fresh mug of water. Without his pack or supplies, he had nothing to give him besides water. In any case, the medic would know best how to treat a head wound.

"Who the fuck are you?" The medic's eyes narrowed as he surveyed the surroundings. "And what're you doing in my house?"

This was it. A sink or swim moment. "One of the fugitives GreenCorps is looking for. Hid in your backyard last night and couldn't get past the patrols. I was going to slip away tonight after dark, but they came door to door, taking young women."

"You took something and left me a silver coin," said the bearded man, cocking his head to one side, giving Walker a longer look. "You could have just stolen the medicine."

Walker shook his head. "We needed antibiotics, but I know what hard times feel like and wasn't willing to force someone else to struggle for our predicament. Cora's your daughter?"

The medic eyed him for a moment. He seemed to come to some conclusion about Walker because he nodded. "Yes." He pulled himself to standing by holding onto the corner of the treatment bed while he swayed. He took a deep breath. "The GreenCorps bastards took her."

"They did." Walker stood in the doorway, deliberating his next move.

"Why didn't you leave? This is none of your affair," said the medic. "GreenCorps has been looking for an excuse to knock us down. Too many rebel sympathizers in this town."

"Not just my fault, then." Walker might not be to blame, but this was intolerable. He couldn't leave those women to GreenCorps.

The man shook his head and winced at the movement. "No. Though the excuse may have been because of your group. Which one are you?"

"What do you mean? Which one?"

"The kidnapping murderer, a rebel, or the thief?"

"Can't you tell?" said Walker, suddenly finding himself amused. "GreenCorps invented most of the charges," he said, meeting the other man's eyes. "As they do."

The medic inclined his head as if in agreement.

"There was no kidnapping or theft. The rebels are helping, but I'm not really one of them." Yet. The unspoken word hung in the air between them. "Name's Walker."

"I used to be with the rebels," said the medic, showing Walker a faint dot of ink in the webbing of his left hand. "I left them soon after I became a father. My wife died and my girl needed me here, not in jail or on the run."

Walker considered his next words. "My Elsa didn't murder anyone. It was self-defense."

The medic nodded. "I'm not surprised. Good, that she got one of them. I've got to get my daughter back. She's not tough enough to fight like that."

"I'll help." Walker's words came slowly, almost against his will. He wouldn't miss the next express train and risk not getting back to Elsa, but this was important. He could stay two more days. "But if your town is full of rebel sympathizers, we need them. If there are as many as you say, maybe this anger can tip them over the edge. Fight back. Use the distraction to save the young women from being loaded onto the train."

"Next southbound train isn't for two or three days," said the medic, stroking his beard. "I wouldn't risk my life here for no reason, but this is my daughter. It's personal, and most of the other families in town will feel the same way. We can't take this anymore. GreenCorps made an error this time. They think to grind us down. Instead, they've lit a flame. We'd do anything for our wives and daughters. I know just who to talk to. Never you fear." His eyes remained fixed, staring towards the garrison.

"Your daughter can't come back here afterward," said Walker. "Do you have somewhere out of town to send her? Utah maybe? Or somewhere the two of you can go?"

The medic shook his head. "We have no other family. Can you take her with you when you leave? She can send word when she gets somewhere safe."

Walker shook his head. On the run wasn't the place for a girl not hardened to life on the road. Not if she had options. "We're leaving by train. Something secret, and probably dangerous. But if you can get her to Salt Lake City, Grady can find her somewhere safe. Mention my name."

The medic's eyebrows shot up his forehead at Grady's name, but he nodded. "We can do that. She won't be alone." He hesitated, perhaps sizing Walker up again. "My name's Kurt." He stuck out his hand, which Walker shook.

Walker nodded. He trusted the man enough to work with him. The man was motivated to get his daughter back and if he had help and contacts, so much the better. Elsa might be rubbing off on Walker because his gut told him the medic was trustworthy.

"Two days from now, I need to be on a train. Until then, I'll help." He drummed his fingers against his thigh. He would figure out a way to be on that train, no matter what.

CHAPTER 30: ELSA PLUS GINGER

The train picked up speed after leaving Boise; the air rushing past, whipping Elsa's hair into her eyes. She huddled into the train car, trying to stay warm but unwilling to pull a jacket from her backpack and get settled. She would soon, but she needed a few more minutes. Crushing disappointment still made it hard to do anything except sit. Elsa shifted and felt a distinct new vibration in the train's metal—like something had jolted the train.

Each car was separate from the others, and the train was immense, with fifty cars in total. The unexplained movement must have come from somewhere on the one on which she traveled. She unsheathed her knife, the long metal blade glinting in the orange glow from the sunset, reminding her of the reflected firelight on Jace's knife before he'd plunged it into her shoulder. She swallowed, getting ready for action, just in case.

She kept her eyes riveted upward on the top edge of the hopper as she waited, but nothing happened. Clutching the handle of the knife, she took one hand away and wiped it on her pants, then the other, remaining alert for whatever disaster might occur.

She removed her earplugs to listen, hearing only the train and the usual scraping and roaring as it sped toward Portland, twenty-eight hours away. A long time for many things to go wrong. Tatsuda had mentioned that Jaxon had left town, but he could have told GreenCorps to up security on this train. Maybe bulls were searching, car by car. Or someone had been spotted on board by the station and they'd radioed security on the train.

Tatsuda had reported that Wade had been left in charge of Jaxon's men in Boise. She fervently hoped he wasn't here. Wade was as bad as Jaxon. Worse perhaps because he was always looking to prove himself to his GreenCorps superiors—men like Jace and Jaxon McCoy. Elsa had only escaped being raped by the man last year when his sister Janna had intervened. Elsa swallowed the hard lump in her throat. Janna had been sold south this spring. It didn't do to dwell, but that was another crime she'd make GreenCorps pay for one day.

From above, came a quiet scraping sound. Like someone moving on the roof of the train. Whoever was up there would have to be crazy or desperate, because moving across the high point of the train seemed dangerous. It would be easy to lose balance or fall. Transferring from gondola to gondola had been risky enough. She couldn't believe anyone would move between full-height train cars unless they had no other option. Her mouth became desert-like, and she gnawed the inside of her cheek, listening again. Straining to hear anything beyond the constant roar of the metal wheels on the iron tracks.

A muffled boom, like bending metal, followed by another scrape, and her heart raced. She stood and braced herself, watching the ladder that led to the roof. Should she climb up and check if someone was there? Could the sounds be products of her imagination? She didn't think so. Someone was on the roof of the covered hopper.

She'd taken only two steps when a whisper carried on the wind. It sounded like her name. Was Tatsuda trying to get her attention? She turned, peeking behind, tilting her head to find a place where the moving air didn't steal sound. Her eyes watered from the wind, but there was nothing. She pulled back, worried that she was hearing things. She looked up and gasped.

Walker peeked down from the roof of the train car where he lay, his long body pressed against the metal.

"Found you." He grinned, and then swiveled his body, climbing down the ladder.

Elsa shoved her knife into its sheath with shaking hands. Walker was here. She hadn't let herself hope he would hop the train somewhere else. She'd tried to be strong, to continue her mission, but right now, all she wanted was her boyfriend.

He climbed down and braced himself on the grated metal platform beside her, his back against the railing. He held his arms out, and she launched into them, unable to keep her tears at bay as she squeezed his muscular frame, almost unable to believe that he was here. Her eyes streamed as Walker's muscular arms closed around her, holding her close. With her ear pressed against his chest, his rapid heart hammered in her ear, beating as fast as hers. She inhaled the outdoorsy yet sweet smell of him, basking in the feel of his strength. When at last they relaxed their hold on each other, she stepped back. The ground beneath the train was a blur—full speed toward Canada.

Her cheeks flamed. Without Walker, she'd been missing a limb. Instead of making her weak, their reliance on each other strengthened them—more than either of them was apart.

Walker tipped her face up and, cupping her face between his huge hands, kissed her like she was precious. "I missed you," he said at last.

Even with the roaring of the train, his words were clear. He kept one arm wrapped around her as they moved into the protection of the train car under the covered porch. She couldn't release her hold.

His eyes twinkled. "Maybe you missed me, too." He bent to kiss her again, and she wrapped both arms around his neck, her eyes meeting his warm gray ones.

"Nothing was the same without you," she said. "I almost didn't get on this train. I wanted to look for you."

"I know, love, but I stayed away for good reason." Seriousness returned to his face while his thumb traced circles on the skin of her hand. It didn't seem like he could let go any more than she could, which made her smile. They were so similar.

"Tatsuda told me what happened the night you two got separated." She rolled her earplugs in her hand, debating if she should put them back in.

"I slept under a tree, planning to return the next night."

"What changed your plans?"

"Before I slipped out, GreenCorps came door-to-door, ripping young women from their homes. I worked with one man, a former rebel, to plan a rescue. The other families needed a little convincing, but they charged the station when the girls were being loaded onto boxcars." His voice shook and his eyes hardened as he spoke.

"I didn't know that the train would still be there when our express came through. I left before the fight started, running for the opposite end of town to catch the train, and Wade spotted me. The train was almost too fast, but I climbed on. He fired a couple of shots, but nothing that came close. I had Wade on my trail and couldn't wait for the final cars where I knew you'd be." He smiled. "I taught you well. Everyone's on board?"

She nodded and took a deep breath. "I considered waiting longer."

"Knew you'd be on this one. I was counting on you," he said with the smile that made her heart flip-flop. "What else do I need to know?"

"That I love you. That I hated worrying about you." Elsa bit her lip.

"I'm sorry I worried you, but it couldn't be helped. Not only did I help plan an insurrection, but I didn't dare want to lead anyone to your camp. I liked knowing you were safe." He kissed her temple.

"Tatsuda said that was probably why you didn't return," said Elsa. "To keep us safe."

His lopsided smile made every moment without him worth it somehow.

"How's Mason?" said Walker. "The antibiotics were in time?"

Elsa nodded, putting her earplugs back in. "He's on the mend. Caitlyn gave him a stimulant to get him on the train, but he'll be fine."

Walker nodded before kissing Elsa again, this time more forcefully. "There's something else I've always wanted to do on the train," he said into her ear. "We're alone for the next twenty-eight hours." He slid a hand into her shirt, stroking her breast.

She gasped, but leaned into his touch.

"I missed all of you." He nuzzled the sensitive skin of her neck, sending shivers racing through her. Her tiredness fell away as her skin tingled at his touch.

"However, shall we pass the time?" she said, once more trembling, but for a much different reason. Her hands found his hot skin beneath his T-shirt. She needed him, too.

* * *

The journey on the train took longer than the others Ginger had been on before, but with Tatsuda beside her, she was never bored. They also had proper supplies. This was riding in style compared to her previous experience. Much of the time, she had the foam bits he'd given her stuck in her ears, which muffled the majority of the din and she watched the mountainous countryside pass by. The jagged mountains reminded her of a giant's teeth and Denver. She wasn't sure what they'd find ahead.

Once underway, Tatsuda had finally explained why Elsa and the rest were heading towards Portland—taking the bunker key to the Canadians. It didn't surprise Ginger their journey was about the bunkers. She'd figured out that much on her own. They were a prize.

Ginger cast her mind back as the landscape rolled by. She'd heard something about Canada when she was listening to her father's phone calls through the wall of the secret passage, but she couldn't remember what. It hadn't been relevant at the time and hadn't stuck with her. But there'd been something. Some missing detail niggled at her, something just out of grasp. Why couldn't she remember? She sighed. Maybe it would come to her later.

Her stomach rumbled, and she reached for a granola bar. Without a way to heat water, she and Tatsuda were back to eating dried fruit and nuts, processed bars, and strips of iron-like jerky that Mason and Caitlyn had purchased in Pocatello. Still, it was worth it to be here and part of something significant.

They hadn't seen the last of her brother. If she spoke to him, would he listen and at least try to understand why she didn't want to go home? Probably not. Though family, he wouldn't give her a chance to explain.

What would happen when they reached Portland? She'd never been to Canada, but from the bits and pieces she'd picked up over the years, it would be different. People there drove cars and all the young people went to school, not just the rich. Children weren't allowed to work and everyone had access to free medical care. Many of her books and most of the medicine in GreenCorps territory had been imported from Canada. These all sounded like great things, though from her father's rants, he didn't share that opinion.

The idea of traveling to a foreign country should make her nervous, but her heart beat faster with excitement. They should arrive soon.

"We're slowing down." Tatsuda shoved his loose belongings into his backpack, preparing to disembark. He handed back one of her books. They'd spent some of the trip reading.

In the bunker, she'd been appalled to discover that he couldn't read, but it had nothing to do with his intelligence. He'd never had the opportunity to learn or had anyone who would've taught him. When they'd been trapped underground, she'd coached him on the alphabet and to recognize the letters in her book. They'd practiced yesterday, then after the lesson, she'd read to him. Her voice had become hoarse from yelling over the train noise, and they hadn't read for long, but it had helped to pass the time.

"How will we find them when we get off?" She gathered her gear as well, tucking the book into a separate front pocket.

"We'll all jump down at about the same time, on the side farthest from the station as agreed, no matter what track we are on. That's the best plan because we should see each other. We'll head back down the tracks at a run. That's how we've done it before. That's what Elsa was taught." His eyes looked serious. Perhaps he, too, was worried that they'd left Walker behind.

The train's speed decreased as buildings grew more common on both sides of the tracks. Ginger's jaw dropped when they came around a corner and an immense city spread out before her. She couldn't see the far side, and a forest of tall buildings dominated what must be downtown. The train ran beside a wide river with a second city built on the far side. Colorful brick and wood houses stretched beyond her sight. Roads criss-crossed the land, as well as at least three massive steel bridges that spanned the river. Fast-moving vehicles with bright spots of white and red lights sped along.

As darkness claimed the city, the expanse filled with lights that sparkled like jewels. Ahead, the train cars jolted with a series of loud crashes and she and Tatsuda braced for impact as the sensation wove down the train in a crescendo, building then waning. The sudden jerks matched the slowing of the train. Tatsuda checked first the right-hand side of the train, then the left, to determine track position relative to the station. His actions made her hands clammy. Even he wasn't sure where they'd get off or what their reception would be.

At last, the train shuddered to a stop. It was dusk, but the trainyard ahead was lit by a long row of overhead lights on curving metal posts that overhung the tracks. Elsa hadn't been here before but said Walker had coached her on what to do with the heightened security in a new country. Get off, find an official, and say they needed to speak to someone in charge. The opposite of how they'd operated as hoppers in GreenCorps territory.

"I'll go first. Come right away," said Tatsuda. "The sooner we're together, and away from the train, the safer it is." His long hair flew in his face as he swung over the top of the ladder and clambered down. She didn't wait for his feet to hit the ground, but followed as soon as the top of the ladder was free.

He dropped to the gravel with a crunching sound, and she landed seconds later. Without warning and before she could move, there was a snapping sound, and blinding lights shone in her face. She blinked and her eyes watered as she stumbled, unable to see. Tatsuda grabbed her hand.

"Stop right there," said a loud voice from a speaker. The sound seemed to come from several sources.

Ginger froze, her chest tight and her hands instantly like lakes.

An alarm rang—a continuous buzz that hurt her ears. Were it not for her grip on Tatsuda's hand, she would have covered her ears to block the sound.

"Don't move," boomed the voice above. "All illegal entrants into Western Canada must proceed through customs and immigration where you will be processed. You will be assigned a file number and your case will be heard in order of arrival. Do not attempt to flee."

Ginger looked around, still unable to see past the blinding light. They'd been caught like mice in a trap. Elsa must be fuming. She'd mentioned the possibility of being met train-side, but knowing and experiencing it were two distinct entities. Ginger shivered in the crisp air, despite wearing her jacket. They didn't wait long.

A man in a navy blue jacket and tan pants approached from the direction of the station. Perhaps he worked here, as he appeared to be in an unfamiliar uniform. "You two, come with me," he said, showing with a wave for them to walk. He fell in behind them. The floodlights dropped and in the dimmer light, Ginger made out two figures under escort ahead. One towered over the other. Had Walker been on the train? Elsa must be ecstatic.

Other uniformed people spoke to Elsa ahead and to Mason and Caitlyn behind. They had caught their entire group. Blinking her eyes, Ginger couldn't make out more than their forms, but their voices were clear and calm.

Ginger tried to figure out from the man's tone if they were in danger. Her feet itched to run, but she glanced at Tatsuda, who squeezed her hand and shook his head.

"That's them all right," said a familiar voice just before the station. The words sent chills skating down Ginger's spine. "They kidnapped my sister, stole GreenCorps property, and murdered my brother."

"Thank you for tipping us off, Mr. McCoy," said one official.

"I've got documentation, including multiple warrants for Elsa Lee. She's the ringleader. We want her extradited to face trial in Denver." Jaxon's smug tone reminded Ginger of home.

With his words, memories of her father's conversation washed over her. Every year, they'd sent Jace to Canada for diplomatic purposes, though his chief interest had been commercial and about trying to expand the business. The Canadians had resisted making concessions of any kind for GreenCorps. Of course, Jaxon would have been sent in his stead. GreenCorps had contacts here and knew people. Ginger's heart plummeted like a rock to the pit of her stomach. Jaxon had been here long enough to have a plan in place and would have paid people to be on his side. Her brother used bribery as an everyday weapon.

Jaxon handed a crinkled piece of paper to one of the border guards. A wanted poster with Elsa's likeness. From inside his pocket, he produced several crisp white documents folded together and handed them to a security guard.

The man opened the stack and scanned the first before taking a quick look at the others with a nod. "Everything seems to be in order."

"You have the right to remain silent," began one uniformed man from the line near Elsa. "You have the right to an attorney."

"I didn't do any of those things." Elsa's tone was heated, but at least outwardly, she remained calm. Walker's big hand wrapped around her forearm. Without him there, Ginger guessed Elsa might have lost her temper. As it was, hectic patches of red dotted each check and her posture was as rigid as a board.

"We'd like to see our lawyer," said Mason, coming up from behind with another escort and Caitlyn.

"Elsa here doesn't have a lawyer, and we were just leaving," Jaxon sneered. His gaze traveled up and down Elsa in a way that disgusted Ginger. Wasn't he married? He was repulsive.

"Our officials have taken the accused into custody," said the Canadian. "You can't just take her with you. There are protocols that must be followed."

Jaxon's face turned beet red as he reached for Ginger. "I'll take my sister at least."

She side-stepped him with a quick glance at the officials. "I'm eighteen and they didn't kidnap me. I left home and these are my friends." She stepped closer to Elsa.

The men in navy uniforms exchanged looks and nodded.

"I'm afraid she can't go anywhere either. She entered a foreign country without legal documentation. We have procedures to uphold," said another guard, who stepped forward.

Jaxon pulled his gun and aimed it at Elsa.

The Canadian border guard went into immediate action. Several stepped between Jaxon and where Ginger stood with Elsa, forming a wall of bodies. What was wrong with her brother?

"Drop your weapon," said one of the Canadian officers as another man came from behind a locked door to meet them. The newest arrival was armed, unlike the other Canadians.

Jaxon wore an annoyed expression, like he hadn't expected opposition. His expression darkened and his mouth gaped open and closed while he searched for words. His nostrils flared, but he lowered the gun. He trained a dark look on Elsa, one filled with hate. Ginger had seen that look before. This wasn't the end.

"We're seeking asylum as political refugees," said Caitlyn.

Mason nodded and took her hand. "We are an envoy sent by Ryan Grady. Our lawyer is expecting our call."

CHAPTER 31: ELSA

Elsa hadn't been able to stop sweating since getting off the train, and her eyes hurt from the glare of the lights that flooded the station. Her clothes stuck to her clammy skin, and she'd never been more aware of her scruffy travel clothes and wild curly hair. It had come loose again on the train and she smoothed it back with her hands, tucking the front behind her ears. Maybe if she'd looked like one of the official envoys from Grady and the rebels, she'd be taken seriously. Perhaps not.

She hadn't been prepared for the official welcome in Portland or given their arrival much thought. She'd assumed they'd get off and go in search of Grady's contacts who would take them to an official. She kicked herself for not counting on security being this efficient. That's what she should have been preparing for the last few days, instead of feeling sorry for herself that Walker was missing. She should have guessed where Jaxon had gone.

Frustrating as it was, grudgingly, he'd earned some respect for figuring out that she would head to Canada instead of back to Salt Lake City and the rebels. Nor could it surprise her he'd brought a poster with her likeness and warrants for her arrest. She hoped Grady's lawyer friend, Alexander Campbell, was as influential as Mason believed.

Elsa flicked a second glance at Walker. He towered over the men here, but he hadn't tried to run or fight. Inside, he was probably as upset as she was, so she took her cues from him and concentrated on controlling her fear. Walker must still think this would work. She needed to be patient.

Despite the late hour, workers filled the bustling station outside while pale electric lights lit up the stark interior of the station office. A stenciled black on white sign hung overhead at one end of a long counter, *Customs and Immigration.* The tall white counter separated strange machines with screens like those in the bunker and uniformed station workers from the public, while an area with several doors to offices lay behind the counter.

Each door had a separate keypad by the side, and one was marked *Private.* She restrained from biting her lip; but she didn't like not knowing what lay behind their immediate area. The tiled floor was polished to a perfect shine, making her hesitant about walking on something so shiny.

Elsa took a deep breath as the six of them were marched across the sparkling clean room. Dozens of eyes turned in their direction. There was no sign of Jaxon; someone must have ushered him elsewhere. He could have seeded lies to everyone they might have to speak to. She wouldn't be surprised if he'd bribed people here, the way he did back home.

Every step echoed in the cavernous room as they were herded toward a man wearing glasses who stood behind the counter while security remained behind them, blocking the exit. She looked back, but running was no longer an option. She swallowed, hoping they'd seen the last of Jaxon, but she couldn't shake the feeling there would be more trouble. He wouldn't give up any more than she was.

"Passports or travel documents," the counter official said, barely glancing up. He didn't seem interested in their fugitive status or his job. She'd met bored clerks before in SoCal. Same problem, different country.

"We don't have anything." Elsa unclenched her hands and flattened them, resting them on the cool counter.

The man's head jerked up and his pale eyes stared at Elsa. She didn't back down.

"They're seeking political asylum," said the man leading their escort.

Elsa wasn't sure what that meant, but based on the Canadians' reaction, she was grateful for Caitlyn's quick thinking. Jaxon's claims must need to be verified and the asylum claim handled. The Canadians seemed willing to investigate both, which was an improvement on how GreenCorps operated.

"Name please," said the man behind the high counter. "Then state your city of origin. I need to record something about who you claim to be and where you're from."

Elsa glanced at the others and then spoke up first. "Elsa Lee, Long Beach, SoCal." Her fingerprints were recorded and her eyes were scanned with something called a retinal scanner by someone further along the counter. What these things did, she wasn't sure, but she cooperated. Her chest constricted as one member of the security detail removed her backpack. They took her belongings further down the counter, where they were spread out and examined.

She ground down on her molars as they pulled out item after item, including the seeds she considered essential for the future and as evidence of her mission. The guards seemed most interested in the foil packets, placing them into a separate bag where she couldn't see them. Her hand was tempted a thousand times to touch the bunker key concealed around her neck, but she resisted, not wanting to draw attention to something so important. She still wasn't sure who to trust.

One by one, the others were registered, their belongings searched and catalogued. The ration pouches from the bunker were also separated from their clothes and put in a separate bag.

"You've been here before," said a second man behind the counter when he entered Walker's data last. He looked up, surprised. "Are you the same Walker Sullivan who was here four years ago with a Hayden Brown?"

At Walker's nod, the clerk continued. "You spent three days in custody before disappearing after your release. I assume that means you returned to GreenCorps territory."

"Coming here last time was unintentional," said Walker, his voice calm and steady. "We didn't mean to cross the border. We came because this is where the train stopped. When we were freed, we left on the next train."

"This time your arrival was intentional?" said the Canadian, peeking at Walker over the top of his glasses.

At Walker's nod, the pale-eyed man with the computer device made additional notes with his keyboard, his fingers clicking rapidly. Elsa wished she could see what he'd written. Her stomach ached, and the air felt too warm; she hoped nobody noticed her discomfort. Strength was now key.

After processing, a tall woman in a headset wearing the same navy and tan uniform as the rest of the Canadian border workers led Elsa's group down a hallway to another room, the security force trailing behind.

"Our facilities are divided," the woman said as she came to a halt. "Women to the left and men to the right. If you identify with neither gender, pick who you'd rather stay with."

Elsa's stomach clenched as a bad feeling about being separated crept over her. It wasn't just because she and Walker had only just reunited on the train—she didn't want to be split from any of the others. They were a team.

"Isn't there somewhere we can wait together?" Elsa said, her gaze flicking to Walker's steady gray one. He reached out and squeezed her elbow.

"I'm afraid not," the woman said with what looked like sympathy in her eyes. "I have orders."

As she finished speaking, there was a faint beeping noise, and the officer tapped her right earphone. "Officer Williams here," she said. "I see. Yes. We'll take care of it." She tapped her headphone again and refocused on their group.

"We have separate holding areas for men and women," she said, continuing as if she hadn't been interrupted.

Officer Williams no longer met Elsa's gaze, and her unease ratcheted upward. What had the woman been told? Was this related to Jaxon and his interference?

"What about our asylum status?" said Caitlyn. "When will we find out if our application is accepted?"

The woman looked toward Caitlyn, but it didn't look like she met her eyes either as her gaze skidded toward the door. "Your status isn't official yet. You will be comfortable and considered guests of our government until a judge can make a preliminary examination of your papers and determine if there is enough evidence to continue the process."

"Preliminary?" said Mason. "How much longer will this take?"

"At least a week," said Officer Williams with a sniff. "I'll give you a minute to say goodbye, but make it quick."

Walker grabbed Elsa and kissed her hard. He whispered, "Hang in there. We'll figure this out." He stepped back to say a quick goodbye to the others when Tatsuda unexpectedly threw himself into Elsa's arms.

"Take it," she whispered while he clung to her. She pressed the silver key into his hand, hoping he could hide it better than she could. It had been an impulse, but her instincts told her it was the right move. She didn't have time to check if he'd been successful as they escorted the men to an open door on the right. A long corridor stretched into the darkness and they were swallowed. The door clanged shut behind them and Elsa winced. Would she see them again? A hotness developed behind her eyes, but she smothered them.

Her stomach lurched again. Something still wasn't right.

"Ginger, Caitlyn, your accommodations are this way," said the officer, turning to the door on the left, which she unlocked with a swipe of a white card.

Elsa swallowed. "What about me?"

"You've been declared dangerous and a flight risk." Officer Williams tapped her headset and looked at Elsa. "I've just gotten word that you will be kept in solitary for the duration of your stay."

"What?" It was as though a hole opened in the floor and Elsa found herself sliding into a bottomless pit. Away from the others, anything could happen. This was because of Jaxon.

Several uniformed men stepped up from behind and forced themselves between Elsa and Caitlyn.

Caitlyn's eyes met Elsa's through the screen of bodies. "They waited until Walker and Mason weren't here. Jaxon is behind this, too. It stinks of corruption. Be careful, someone here listens to him. I'll keep reminding them they can't do this."

Caitlyn might have said more, but they shoved her through the lefthand door, slamming it from the other side, leaving Elsa alone with a dozen soldiers.

"Now what?" she snapped, turning to face them. She swallowed and her pulse raced. None of them would meet her eyes. Chills raced down her spine. This was bad.

No one spoke, and the ticking of a clock on the wall became the only sound in the room. She wouldn't ask again.

The door through which she'd entered opened with a click and she turned.

Jaxon appeared, his expression smug. Rage fogged her brain. Was there any place she could get away from the McCoys?

"On your knees, Miss," said one of the security men. "Lace your fingers together and put them behind your head." He gestured to the floor.

She bit the inside of her cheek. Fuck them. She wouldn't make it easy.

"What have I done?" she said, spitting out each word. "You're taking that GreenCorps piece of shit's word over mine?" It was impossible to keep incredulity and outrage from her voice. She'd thought Canada would be different.

"We have corroboration that the warrants are genuine. A special statement issued by Malcolm McCoy, managing partner and majority shareholder of GreenCorps."

"His Daddy? I haven't done anything," said Elsa. "They're lying. I've been framed."

"Mr. McCoy claims you have stolen GreenCorps property of a sensitive nature that must not fall into the wrong hands."

"He's a liar," said Elsa.

Something hard smacked against the back of her legs and she dropped to the floor, bashing her knees against the polished concrete floor. Ignoring the pain, she tried to get up but was instead shoved from behind. She lost her balance and the next thing she knew, Jaxon shoved her cheek against the cold floor. She shook all over, but bit back her words as they wrenched her arms behind her back and fastened metal bracelets over her wrists. A metal chain connected the cuffs and prevented her arms from moving. They'd trussed her up like a chicken before the slaughter.

With Jaxon pressing on her head, she couldn't see anyone, but footsteps moved toward the door. It opened, and the guards left. She was helpless and alone with Jaxon.

His hands pressed her shoulders down and she couldn't move. The pressure let up and a pair of black boots strode into her hazy field of vision. Jaxon crouched beside her and stroked her hair. Bile rose in her throat at his touch and she flinched.

"Get your filthy hands off me. You pay the guards? Spending Daddy's money because you can't get people to listen otherwise." Rage filled her tone, cover for her fear.

"Elsa, Honey. For once in your goddamn life, do this the easy way. You have something I need." He caressed her cheek, and she resisted the urge to vomit.

He wanted the key. The only way he was getting it was over her dead body.

"They didn't find it in your pack. Is it on you?" He grabbed her ass and fumbled in her pockets. He came up empty. Spotting the loose cord around her neck. He yanked it with a twist, leaving a fiery red burn trail around her neck before it snapped. There was nothing on the cord and he threw it across the room. "Where's the key, bitch?" snarled Jaxon, leaning into view.

He smelled of sweat and alcohol and was close enough that she got a close-up of the dirt-filled pores of his handsome, though self-important, face. She choked back her words. He'd get nothing from her. Not a single clue.

"Whoever has it, I'll find it." Had his eyes always been this dark?

She glared, still pressed facedown on the hard floor, her cheeks flaming. Relief that the key was no longer in her possession settled in her chest.

Jaxon patted her pockets again and groped the sides of her breasts. "Where's the key?" he asked again. White foam appeared at the corners of his mouth.

She smiled at his frustration—which may have been a mistake.

Her act of defiance cost her when Jaxon retaliated. She lost sight of his foot a fraction of a second before the impact, but braced herself. The point of contact was her ribs and something crunched. It hurt to breathe, but she remained silent, refusing to let on how much it hurt.

Someone new entered the room and a gust of cooler air swept over Elsa.

"Mr. McCoy, step away from our prisoner," someone said in shocked tones. "If she has your property, we will find it. That isn't how prisoners are treated in Canada."

"I'm not giving you anything, you impotent GreenCorps lackey." Her muscles quivered with suppressed rage. She wished she hadn't spoken and braced for his retaliation.

He'd taken a step back, but now something warm, wet, and sticky landed on her face. Her skin crawled. His saliva slid down her cheek and pooled on the floor, its slimy track burning like acid.

"I'm going to kill you one day, bitch."

"Mr. McCoy. You need to come with us. Now." The officer at the door held it open.

Jaxon hesitated and Elsa waited. The guard was too far to help if Jaxon struck. His hate might override any common sense he might have. His vendetta had become personal.

She cringed as he delivered a final kick. This time, she couldn't remain silent. She didn't want to give him the pleasure of seeing her pain, but she shrieked in agony at the fiery stab of pain in her ribs with each breath. She writhed on the floor, her hands still cuffed behind her back.

He grabbed her by the hair, pulled her neck at a painful angle, and slammed her head against the floor—stars danced in a circle as her vision dimmed. He let go suddenly, as though grabbed from behind. From far away, shouts cut off as everything faded to black.

Chapter 32: Mason

"Do you think they're okay?" Walker asked for the second time. "It was her voice. I know it was." The big man sat on the thin mattress of one of the four beds in their holding cell while he leaned against the bars facing Mason, Tatsuda… and the door. The three of them had been caged together. Alone would have been harder, with only his own thoughts. Mason was glad that Caitlyn, Elsa, and Ginger would also have each other for company.

Only Tatsuda had slept much. Mason's stiff muscles ached and his healing arm itched; despite knowing the women had each other, a faint sense of unease looped through his mind. Walker had insisted that he'd heard Elsa's screams. Could he be right?

Mason's brow furrowed. Rebels were often locked up together; splitting them had been an unusual move, no matter what they said about divided facilities. Trying to gauge the time, he looked at the one wall in the outer room that had windows high near the ceiling to let in light. While early, it was no longer night.

The Canadians had let him keep his bottle of antibiotics, but he wanted to take one with food. If they didn't feed him soon, he'd have to take it on an empty stomach, which Caitlyn had recommended against.

Mason's stomach rumbled in anticipation of food and he looked up as Walker's own stomach answered. His friend's usual pleasant expression had vanished, and in its place was a clenched jaw and a deep crease between his brows. Dark shadows that ringed his eyes suggested he may not have slept. He'd paced for hours.

"She's fine," said Mason, trying to put conviction into his words.

"That was her screaming last night." Walker flexed his fingers and winced at the loud cracking sound. "I know it was."

Mason was about to protest when Tatsuda sprang from his bed. He'd looked asleep until one second earlier, but was now alert, his almond-shaped eyes fixed on the door.

The entrance to the rest of the building opened into the narrow hall that ran in front of their cell and in walked Jaxon. Mason hadn't met him or seen him close up until last night, but there was no doubting who he was. Jaxon looked like the rich, arrogant, GreenCorps company man that he was. Well-fed, self-satisfied, and used to getting his way. No wonder Elsa had never liked him. The only resemblance to Ginger was the shape of his eyes.

The two guards accompanying him exchanged glances, and one nodded.

"You have two minutes," the one on the left said before the guards left the room, clanging the metal door closed on the way out.

The room seemed to shrink as Jaxon stared through the bars of their cell.

"What did you do to Elsa?" said Walker. "I heard her last night."

"What are you going to do about it? Big man behind bars. I could have done anything I wanted to your little whore and you couldn't stop me? Doesn't matter that I'm in a foreign country, there's always people willing to take a little extra cash."

Walker sprang up from his bunk, his muscles tense and his voice shaking. "What did you do?"

Jaxon smiled as he didn't answer the question. "Which one of you did she give it to?" He stepped forward to stare at each of them.

Mason's molars ached from pressing his mouth closed so he didn't say something unfortunate. Walker had been right about the screams. This asshole must have hurt Elsa, searching for the bunker key. Interesting that Jaxon hadn't found it. Would she have swallowed it?

Unless it happened after he, Tatsuda, and Walker had been removed, he'd missed that move. Mason wouldn't put it past her.

He glanced at his companions.

Walker's fists had clenched, rage tensed in every line of his massive frame. Mason wouldn't want to mess with him right now. Jaxon should be glad there were bars between the two of them. In a fair fight, Mason would pick Walker every time—angry it would be no contest.

"What did you do?" Walker's voice became whisper soft, which made it more frightening.

Jaxon still didn't answer, his gaze flitting from person to person as he searched for a sign of what he wanted to learn.

Tatsuda looked confused, tilting his head to one side as if trying to figure out what was going on. It might be an act. He was a hard kid to read.

"Give what to who?" Mason stood, feeling Walker move beside him. The air filled with menace, and Mason's hackles rose as energy crackled inside the small room.

"You will regret the day you laid a hand on her." Walker hissed. This time, Jaxon stepped back from the look in the big man's flinty eyes.

"She's still got quite the mouth on her," said Jaxon, his gaze returned to Walker, his eyes narrowed with suspicion. "My guess is she gave it to you, Lover Boy, but whoever gives me what I want or tells me where it is, goes free. Today. You hand over the key, I'll leave her alone."

"I won't be locked in here forever." Walker stepped closer to the bars and Jaxon flinched, wiping the sweat from his forehead.

Shit. Angry Walker was terrifying. Although, if Jaxon had hurt Caitlyn, Mason would have been the same.

As if to make up for his involuntary movement, Jaxon's next words seemed designed to wound. "She spent the night in the infirmary, I understand. But I can get to her anywhere in this building, with a little help from my money."

Mason interrupted. "You're worthless scum. Bullying young women just because you can." He turned to face Walker. "Don't let him get to you. He isn't worth it. He didn't get what he wanted, or he wouldn't be here." Mason turned back to Jaxon as the door to the hall opened once more. "Looks like time is up. No point in coming back. There's nothing you can offer to convince us to help you."

"Mr. McCoy," said the guard with a furtive glance back the way he'd come. "My supervisor and breakfast are on the way."

Jaxon spun on his heel and marched out.

The guard's timing had been accurate because it was less than a minute later that the door from outside opened again. An older woman with short black hair and two different guards arrived, each carrying a metal breakfast tray. She slid the trays, one at a time, through the slot on the cell door and Tatsuda passed them around. They returned to their beds to eat, placing the tray on the mattresses like they were tables.

The scent of bacon, fried eggs, and slices of oranges filled the air. Mason's mouth watered. He glanced at Walker, who still radiated fury.

"What happened to Elsa last night?" Mason directed his words at the older woman, who he guessed was the supervisor.

Her eyebrows shot up her forehead. "News travels fast." Her mouth turned down at the corners. "I'm Captain Chan. I'm in charge of Immigration here in Portland, Canada. I only heard about your friend's condition this morning upon my arrival." She hesitated. "How did you?"

"Jaxon McCoy paid off at least two of your guards and just left here after threatening us. I assume that means he got to Elsa last night. That should prove to you how much we need asylum. It isn't safe for us to go home. Apparently, it isn't even safe for us here. Especially Elsa, because she has something they want. Not stolen. Something that's hers."

"How bad is she?" said Walker, dropping his fork with a clatter without having eaten anything, though Tatsuda's tray was almost empty. The boy watched but kept shoveling his food.

Captain Chan still hesitated, perhaps deciding what to share. "My trusted guards pulled him off Elsa last night. He interrogated her illegally, breaking three of her ribs, and he gave her a concussion."

"How the hell did he get anywhere near her?" Walker's words burst out as if he couldn't contain them. He leapt to his feet and his hands shook with the effort to unclench them. He paced the cell, five of his giant steps in each direction. Back and forth. Officer Chan's eyes followed his motion.

"He shouldn't have been in the building then, or now, but we can't hold him as he has diplomatic immunity." Her expression seemed annoyed. She must be upset about the corruption of her team. She seemed a straightforward, rule-following sort, like many of the Canadians so far. The breach in security must be a slap in the face.

"You need to do something about him. Is the hospital secure?" Walker stopped beside Mason, facing Officer Chan with an intense look.

"I'll double the guard and be sure my most reliable people are there," the woman said. "McCoy should never have been alone with her, and I'll make sure that he isn't again." She met his eyes in a forthright manner.

"Can you send a message to our lawyer?" said Mason. "We were instructed to contact a lawyer in Vancouver, BC named Alexander Campbell at Campbell, Maharaj, and Yu." He hesitated a moment before continuing, playing his ace card. "My father, Ryan Grady, said that his friend Alexander would help us."

"The Ryan Grady," the woman said, pursing her lips like she was thinking. At Mason's single, sharp nod, she said, "I'll have someone contact your lawyer's office and let him know that you're here. If this is all legit, you'll get your lawyer and have this resolved as fast as possible. Grady's name carries some weight, even out here beyond GreenCorps' territory."

"What about Caitlyn and Ginger?" From the corner of his eye, Mason saw Tatsuda's head shoot up.

"They're in a cell much like yours. I personally delivered their breakfast ten minutes ago. They're fine. Like you, their primary concern is Elsa Lee." she turned to one of the guards accompanying her. "Lieutenant, check that their companions are alone. I don't want Jaxon

McCoy interfering with them, too." She turned back and tilted her head. "What is it that Mr. McCoy thinks Elsa is in possession of?"

Mason appreciated that the woman seemed decent and his gut said she was trustworthy, but that only went so far. "Not our place to say, ma'am. That's Elsa's story."

The supervisor's lips pinched together, and she shrugged as she turned for the door.

"Can I see her?" said Walker. "Please."

Officer Chan stopped and looked back over her shoulder. "I'll see what I can do. I'm thinking you all need a medical check-up. Your friend is hurt and alone, and I wouldn't wish that on anyone. I'm sorry Mr. McCoy injured her on our watch."

With that, she signaled to the remaining guard, and they exited, leaving the narrow room outside their cell empty once more.

* * *

Two hours later, two guards escorted Mason, Walker, and Tatsuda to the infirmary. Tatsuda's medical exam declared him healthy. Walker too. There was no sign of Elsa in the main treatment room where the doctor examined them. He scrutinized Mason's arm, pressing the ends of his stitches. It was free of pain. Under the bandages, the pink skin had healed, except for a thin purple wound under the deepest section, and most of the swelling had gone.

"How long have your stitches been in?" said the gray-haired doctor, peering over his glasses. Mason counted the days since the morning of the incident.

"A week." The black line of even stitches itched like fury, but the edges looked neat and clean. Caitlyn had done excellent work. With the danger of infection past, soon it would just be another scar.

"I'd like to take these out. Your previous doctor did a marvelous job."

"The medic is the blonde in the other holding cell." Mason ached to see Caitlyn and check for himself that she was safe from harm.

"She's been trained?" At Mason's nod, the doctor said, "I'll let her know it's healing well. You have antibiotics?"

"For a few more days," said Mason.

"That should be enough," said the doctor with an approving nod. He reached for his scissors and snipped the stitches, pulling them out with care.

Now that the examinations were over, it was time to ask their question.

"How's Elsa?" said Walker, glancing over his shoulder toward the hovering guards.

"She hasn't woken up yet." The doctor's voice was calm, and Walker's head swiveled back to him. "It allowed us to set her ribs, as well as tape and bandage them without additional pain."

"Can I stay with her? Please." said Walker. The poor guy was hanging on by a thread.

One of their escort guards shook his head. "We should take you back. You're finished here."

The doctor checked over his shoulder toward the room where Elsa must be. Two additional guards stood outside her room, as promised. "I think it would help my patient's recovery to have her friends sit with her for a while. I'll arrange it with Captain Chan."

The helpful doctor went into his office and made a phone call while everyone waited. The lieutenant's headset beeped as he got an incoming communication and he tapped it to answer.

"Mr. Sullivan can stay," the guard reported after listening to the captain. "For an hour each morning and an hour each afternoon until your hearing." His gaze flicked to Walker, perhaps measuring his strength or how much trouble he'd make over the decision.

"Come with me," said the doctor, opening the door to the guarded room beyond.

Elsa lay in a raised bed on wheels that angled upward on the top half with two fluffy pillows propping her up. One side of her forehead was a livid purple lump while the rest of her skin was pasty white. Several unfamiliar machines with screens stood watch over where she lay. A clear tube came from one of them and attached to her arm. Mason had seen an IV a couple of times in larger med centers. It looked like she was in capable hands.

Walker made a strangled sound and lunged forward, ignoring the guards at the door. He pulled a chair closer to her side and sat, taking her small hand in his larger one as though the rest of them had ceased to exist. He only had eyes for Elsa.

"You others need to return to your cell," said the guard, motioning toward the outer door.

"Thank you," said Mason to the doctor, who gave him cream to help with the itching. The new lighter bandage on his arm was an improvement, too. He checked Walker, who was oblivious to everything but the woman on the bed.

"I'll figure out something better than an hour at a time." The doctor winked at Mason. "It'll keep him out of trouble and give her extra protection. Plus, when she wakes up, a friendly face will keep her calm and aid her recovery. My guess is that you lot have been through more than your share of trouble."

"Thanks again," said Mason, nodding to the doctor as he followed Tatsuda and the guards out the door.

CHAPTER 33: ELSA

Elsa struggled to wake from her dream, gasping for air. She'd been running again and her muscles protested with a stabbing pain along her ribs. She'd come so far and was almost at the limit of her strength. She tried to hide several times, but Jaxon always found her and she had to sprint away again. Somehow, he was lurking around every corner. With her energy waning, almost unable to run, she leaned against the wall. She turned to face Jaxon, but Walker's voice penetrated her fear, making her pause. It was this detail that finally clued her in that this must be a dream. Jaxon couldn't really be everywhere. Waking, she followed the sound, pushing through thick fog until she found Walker.

At first, she couldn't open her eyes. She fluttered her eyelids, but they were so heavy. Was it worth the effort to wake up all the way? Jaxon's image flashed through her mind, flickering, then fading as she left him behind. She blinked several times at the bright light. Walker sat beside her and squeezed her hand. She smiled, her heart filling with gratitude that he was here.

"Walker," she croaked. Her throat was parched. "Did Jaxon get the key?"

"No, Love," he whispered. "It's safe."

The lines on her forehead smoothed as he stroked her forehead. "What's happening? Where are we?" She didn't recognize the white room where they were, and the air smelled of medicine and disinfectant, the second reminding her of the bleach smell of her sister's spotless home. "I remember the train and security. Not much else. How did I get here?"

"We're with the Canadians. Jaxon bribed a couple of guards and searched you, looking for the key. He got carried away when you didn't cooperate. Security stepped in and stopped him. The doctor says your head injury is healing."

Her hand reached up, shocked to find needles and tubes dangling from it, and touched the lump on her forehead. She grimaced. "Purple again, isn't it? I thought I was done with that." She shifted with a grimace. "My ribs ache too."

"The bastard cracked them." Walker scowled.

Her eyes become slits and her voice hard. "I remember now. He had them take you all away and cuff me first or it wouldn't have been so uneven."

"There's going to be a hearing in a few days. Mason claimed he was an envoy sent by Grady. He's sent word to Grady's lawyer friend. We haven't heard from him yet, but they've kept Jaxon away."

"How long have we been here?" she said.

"Four days." Walker smoothed her loose hair from her face, shadows so deep around his eyes that they were almost bruises. "I hated seeing you beaten again, but at least you have top-notch care this time."

She smiled with a warmth given only to him and he returned with a weary one that matched. She needed him to know how much he meant to her. "I had good care both other times, too. Have they said anything about our application for political asylum?"

Walker picked up her hand again and shook his head. "They let me stay with you most of the time and supposedly sent word to the lawyer that we're here, but I don't know any more. We haven't been allowed to see Ginger and Caitlyn, or speak to the captain for several days. Imagine she's busy."

"Mason must be frustrated," said Elsa. "Caitlyn will be livid. She doesn't enjoy being told what she can and can't do any more than I do."

They sat together for another hour while the doctor checked her vitals and examined her pupils. He tested her memory and looked at Walker for confirmation of some details Elsa provided. He declared her fit and recovering and had a tray brought with broth and baked wafers like crumbly flat chunks of bread that he called crackers.

"It's time for Walker to leave for the night," said the doctor with a kind smile. "I reported that you're awake." He hesitated and looked around. Lowering his voice, he said, "I'm not supposed to say anything, but your lawyer has arrived and scheduled a meeting for tomorrow. It's good you can participate. Officer Chan is most interested in what you have to say."

Walker kissed her, soft and tender as only he could, and then left with a last look from the doorway, as if to reassure himself that she was recovering. She wished he could stay longer, but it was selfish. A pang pricked at her; he must have been worried. Now that she was awake, he might sleep better; he'd looked haggard with stubbled cheeks and dark shadows around his eyes. Once she was alone, she yawned. Though she'd slept for most of her time here, she found herself nodding and resettled for the night.

The next time she woke, Walker returned wearing different clothes, ones from the bunker, and the doctor brought some clothes from her backpack, leaving them stacked on a chair. They'd been cleaned and smelled like lemons. Walker helped her get dressed, so she didn't strain her ribs. Because of the strapping tape and tight bandages, they weren't very painful, but her movements were stiff and limited.

Butterflies danced in Elsa's stomach as they were led to a room in a different section of the building with two dozen chairs facing a tall, raised desk in a carpeted room with wood paneling. While built for a specific purpose, this workspace was nicer than most homes she'd seen, except where her sister lived with Jaxon.

Mason and Tatsuda joined them a minute later. Mason's arm was no longer in a sling. Tatsuda slipped Elsa the key when he gave her a ginger hug. They, too, had been given a chance to clean up and change their clothes.

"Thanks." Elsa looked around with caution, but the group appeared to be alone. Walker nodded when she returned the key ring to the cord around her neck, remembering the burning feel as Jaxon had twisted it from her.

Mason noted the exchange with a twitch of his lips.

They'd just settled in chairs to catch up when Caitlyn and Ginger arrived, flanked by guards, who let them in and left. After another round of careful hugs and quick bursts of speech to update each other, they sat in pairs.

The next person to join them was a stranger in a formal-looking suit of gray. He wore the shiniest shoes Elsa had ever seen.

"I'm Alexander Campbell," he said, shaking hands with each of them. He set his briefcase on a narrow table in front of the chairs. "We only have an hour before the judge is due. The man petitioning the court to have Elsa extradited back to GreenCorps jurisdiction to answer for her crimes will be here, too." He shot her a look, as though sizing up her reaction to the news about Jaxon. "The Canadians are quite flustered about his attack on her, which is in our favor. If this doesn't go our way, I'll file a countersuit."

Elsa and Walker glanced at each. Their lawyer had gotten right to it, but she didn't understand most of what he'd said. Walker shook his head. Apparently, he didn't either. She reached for Walker's hand, needing that small reassurance that this was going according to plan.

"I don't know what most of that means." She took a breath and exhaled.

"Sorry, I was talking legal nonsense. The short version is that the Canadians want to let you stay, but we need to prove that it isn't safe for you to return to GreenCorps territory for your trial. How valid are the GreenCorps charges?"

She looked at him. "Which ones?" He might be Grady's friend, but she needed him to be specific or he wouldn't be helpful.

"Did you steal GreenCorps property?"

Elsa shook her head, her curls swaying. "I scavenged the Heap in SoCal and found the tube last spring."

Alexander Campbell didn't have anything to take notes with at first, but he seemed to file this information away with a slight frown. "SoCal is a work camp. How long was your sentence? How many prior convictions?"

Sentence? She'd never been convicted of anything.

"I was born there," said Elsa, as she tried not to clench her jaw. Her hands trembled as suddenly she saw her previous life in a different light. Her tone sharpened. "Before you ask, my mother was three months old when she was sent there with her grandmother as her guardian. My mother didn't do anything illegal either, though my great-grandmother was a rebel leader."

"Let me get this straight. You're saying you were born in a generational prison camp. When you left, it was with your own property. Nothing else." Alexander's face changed, as though suddenly he too saw everything in a new light.

She nodded, gritting her teeth, anger infusing each new word. "We weren't supposed to leave, but we escaped."

His voice deepened as he leaned in, and the crease deepened between his brows. "You aren't a convicted felon?"

"Convicted?" she said with a frown. "GreenCorps said I stole the tube, but they never proved it. They had someone steal it from me and after a few days, we got it back."

"The tube was the GreenCorps property that they allege you stole?" Alexander said with a deeper frown. At her nod, he continued. "When I ask you to, I want you to tell the judge about finding it. What do you remember about that day? The specifics will make you believable. Include details about the Heap and who was entitled to what they found. Does everything belong to GreenCorps?"

Elsa shook her head. "Granny and I had a registered and licensed salvage sector and everything we scavenged was ours to keep, trade, or sell. Of course, the only places we could sell or trade things were owned by GreenCorps."

"Okay. You found it. They wanted it. Then what?" Alexander pulled paper and a pen from his briefcase and leaned the notepad on his knee as he made notes. He now seemed to take this seriously.

"Jace McCoy, Jaxon's brother, attacked and beat me." She flicked a glance at Ginger, who sat beside Tatsuda. She'd given the outline of what had happened before, but never shared the details. Ginger nodded, as though encouraging her to continue. "Walker intervened and saved my life, smashing a chair over Jace's head. He knocked him out, and we escaped by hopping a train."

"Ha. Life-threatening injuries?" the lawyer smiled as he looked up. "You're pretty tough, you know."

Walker shook his head. "She was lucky. Just bruised and sore."

"Not her," said Alexander. "This McCoy person claims she left his brother with life-threatening injuries."

Walker shook his head again. "First of all, it wasn't her. *I* left him with a headache. Nothing more than a lump on the back of his head."

"When did you next see Jace? You are both charged with his murder." The lawyer's eyes were alight with excitement as he scrawled several pages of notes.

Elsa took over the tale again. "He hired Walker's brother to steal the tube, which he did outside Reno. Tatsuda stole it back in Salt Lake City, but Jace tracked us back to the house where we were staying. He set the house on fire to flush us out, held Tatsuda at knifepoint, and threatened to kill him if we didn't give him the tube. I gave it to him, but he attacked us, anyway. The three of us fought. He stabbed me and I stabbed him back."

"It was self-defense," said Walker, draping his arm around her.

Elsa slipped her shoulder from her shirt and showed Alexander her scar.

His eyes widened. "You really had a knife fight."

"It wasn't my idea," said Elsa dryly.

Walker said, "That time it was life-threatening injuries. She almost bled to death."

"Grady got me to stitch her up and sent her to my farm to recuperate," said Caitlyn from her chair to their left. The others had been listening intently to the story.

"Jaxon eventually found us, and we've been on the run since," Elsa said.

"What was in the tube and where is it now?" said Alexander. "Grady said you'd explain, and that it was a game-changer for GreenCorps territory. He mentioned that talking to you could give us evidence of GreenCorps corruption by the leaders for the first time. That their everyday policies are crimes."

Elsa inhaled, feeling her sore ribs move. Her instinct was to trust this man. He seemed genuine, and Grady had vouched for him. Though he'd been a stranger less than an hour ago, she surprised herself by being willing to put her life in this man's hands.

"Maps to six seed bunkers from before the Collapse almost two hundred years ago. With seeds for food species that are extinct or controlled strictly by GreenCorps. Original varieties, not terminator seeds," said Elsa. "We lost the maps in the fight with Jace. Either they burned with his body or Jaxon found them. I think he found them though because he was waiting with GreenCorps troops at the bunker we visited."

"Where are the bunkers located?" said Alexander, flipping his paper to the next page.

"One in Riverside, SoCal, but we didn't look for it. We went to Davis, near Sacramento in May, and now Aberdeen, Idaho. There's a fourth near Pullman, Washington, and another near here in Corvallis, Oregon. The last one is near Fort Collins, but the map shows that beside Denver, so we didn't dare go there. That's practically at GreenCorps headquarters. They may have known about the others from something that was there."

"If they have the maps, why do you matter?" said Alexander with a slight frown.

"I have the key," said Elsa. "They can't get into the bunkers without it." She pulled the key and cord from her shirt.

"Could you take people here to the bunker in Corvallis? Let them see inside?"

Elsa nodded. "It'll be under the ruins of the Oregon State University. That's not too far, correct?"

Alexander nodded. "About eighty miles. My advice. Share the key with the Canadians. Show them the bunker and they'll protect you from GreenCorps. With your story about unfair treatment at the hands of GreenCorps and information about how people are treated under their control, I think our government will finally have a reason to interfere with GreenCorps. It's been hard to get proof of what happens down there." A sudden shrewdness entered his eyes. "Your testimony will change that."

Had she underestimated him or gambled wrong? Was he out to help or destroy GreenCorps? Maybe his reason for helping didn't matter.

"Okay," said Alexander, checking a small flat device with a screen. "It's almost time. I'd like all six of you sitting in a row here in the front." He pointed to the chairs on the left-hand side of the room. They got up and moved into the indicated chairs. "When the judge enters, everyone stand, and let me do the talking. If the judge tells you to speak, stand up, look her straight in the eye and tell the truth." He looked at each of them and they nodded.

Alexander had become so serious that Elsa's chest tightened again. What if the judge didn't believe her account? Could Jaxon force her to return to GreenCorps territory? They would take the key and kill her. She clenched her jaw. He could try, but she wouldn't go. She looked at Walker and her friends. None of them would let that happen.

Elsa folded her hands together in her lap until Walker held out his hand for her to take. She grabbed it with a deep breath, comforted by his solid feel, and nodded. They could do this. She wanted to get this over with.

CHAPTER 34: ELSA

They hadn't been in position for long when a couple of people entered the room, including Captain Chan, who stood beside a door that led deeper into the building. Elsa took another look around the room, happy to be with all of her people again.

A Canadian flag on a metal pole stood beside the raised area for the judge, its crimson, many-pointed leaf in the middle on a field of snowy white bordered by a stripe of blue with a white star on either edge. A similar flag with the same bright red leaf in the center and wide bars of red along the sides hung on the other end.

At the back of the room, the door opened and Jaxon strode in. He didn't look at Elsa, just stared straight ahead. With him was another man that Elsa guessed was his lawyer, dressed in an outfit like Alexander's, except navy blue. He carried a briefcase, and they marched down to the slim table at the front on the right. The air crackled between Elsa and Jaxon, though neither spoke.

No sooner had they got settled, when the entrance at the front opened and a man dressed in blue and tan announced, "All rise, the Honorable Judge Nakamura presiding."

The judge was fine-boned and tiny but exuded a sense of power. Like a bird of prey.

Elsa and the others got to their feet at once and, with a scraping of his chair, so did Jaxon and his lawyer. She kept her eyes glued on the front, but watched Jaxon with her peripheral vision. She didn't trust him to behave if things didn't go his way. With every fiber of her being, she just knew that he'd make trouble.

The proceedings began exactly as Alexander had explained. They all sat and the judge spoke.

"Elsa Lee, how do you plead to the charges of theft, murder, and kidnapping?"

"Not guilty, Your Honor." She looked the judge in the eye, her voice clear and confident. The lawyer's reaction to her story had renewed her confidence to do what it took to take down Jaxon and GreenCorps. She was through being bullied.

Under his breath, Jaxon whispered, "Liar." His lawyer elbowed him to silence.

Elsa breathed slowly and calmly, wiping her damp palms on her pants once she sat. She hoped this would be over soon.

Alexander handled most of the speaking and some of it blurred together. She found it hard to concentrate on what was being said, but he presented their case well. He claimed the charges were false, and he explained that Elsa and her group had fled, fearing for their lives, claiming that they were political refugees seeking asylum.

First, the judge dealt with Ginger's status.

"I'm eighteen years old," Ginger said, standing straight, for once not picking at the rough skin on her hands. "I'm old enough to make my own decisions. I didn't want to enter an arranged marriage without my consent, so I left home. I don't want to return to Denver with my brother. I am free."

"Petition to transfer custody of Ginger McCoy, denied." The judge banged her wooden mallet. "She is not a minor, has not committed a crime, and is competent to make her own decisions."

Jaxon glared at Elsa, as though the decision was her fault. She hadn't changed his sister's age or influenced her to leave. Ginger had left on her own.

The judge asked Elsa about the charges of theft, so she stood and explained how she'd found the tube. She explained that she'd known it was important and had decided not to sell it. She talked without interruption, telling how she'd shown it to the storekeeper to ask if he'd seen anything like it before, but had otherwise kept it private.

From time to time, the judge asked clarifying questions but was content to let Elsa speak. When she came to the night where she had left SoCal, Jaxon interrupted.

"You're going to take the word of a whore?" he said.

Elsa took one step in his direction and stopped. She turned, sparks practically erupting from her eyes. She took a deep breath and Walker steadied her again, just resting his hand on her lower back, the tingling from his hand like a soothing balm.

She told how Jace had sent Jaxon home and cornered her, attempting to rape her and beating her within an inch of her life. "I expected to die," she said, looking the judge in the eye. "The only reason I am alive today is because Walker intervened, smashing a chair over Jace's head. He knocked him unconscious, and we fled. Jace's injuries were minor, so we hurried. We hopped a train and left town. I took the tube because I owned it."

Alexander explained about her sector license, and the trading and selling in SoCal at the corporation store.

"What happened next?" said the judge, her unfathomable gaze staring at Elsa. The judge's impassive face was difficult to read, but she was a good listener who asked astute questions.

"We took a side trip, following one of the maps in the tube to a bunker near the ruins of Davis, California, outside Sacramento. The seed packets in my backpack for apricot and almond trees were from that bunker, as are most of my clothes, my gear, and the pack itself."

"I'd like to see these items," said the judge, motioning to one of the minor court officials standing by the wall.

Officer Chan whispered to him. He nodded and left. Elsa hoped the packets weren't far away and would be convincing as something from long ago, even if they looked ordinary.

"Please continue," said the judge.

"By the time we returned to town, there were Wanted posters for me everywhere accusing me of theft. We couldn't stay there either."

"What sum was the reward?" said Alexander.

"Ten gold," said Elsa.

The judge furrowed her brow. "For an alleged theft? And escape from a work camp you'd never been sentenced to? That doesn't seem fitting. If I'm not mistaken, ten gold coins is rather a fantastic amount of money. Mr. McCoy, can you account for this incredible sum?"

"Elsa Lee is a dangerous criminal." Jaxon's sullen expression made him look like a defiant youth rather than a grown man.

"If I'm not mistaken," said the judge, her dark bird-like eyes flashing as she pinned him with a stare, "I understand Elsa Lee is your sister-in-law. Your attitude regarding your relationship with her is rather harsh and unforgiving."

Hope surged in Elsa's veins as the judge turned away from Jaxon. "Please continue."

Elsa explained how Hayden had been hired to find them and steal the tube and how they'd followed him to Salt Lake City, where Tatsuda had recovered the tube. Her word choice was deliberate at Alexander's suggestion.

Jaxon squirmed at the table, twice looking over his shoulder toward the back of the room as if he wanted to escape. Or looking for help from outside. Elsa's sense that something was off grew despite how well the hearing seemed to progress.

"What about the murder charges?" said the judge, glancing down at her notes.

Elsa explained about the fire and the knife fight, keeping anger from her tone.

At that point, Alexander Campbell took over and summarized, saying that Jaxon had not witnessed it, but that Jace's death had been accidental, and that Elsa and Walker claimed they had done it in self-defense.

With another bang of the wooden mallet, Elsa and Walker's innocence was proclaimed. Jaxon's face flushed red.

Then Alexander asked Caitlyn to explain her role.

Caitlyn stood and in a clear voice spoke about how her farm had been a refuge and how Hayden had betrayed them, bringing Jaxon and the GreenCorps soldiers there, as well as the doubled reward, and how they'd fled for their lives.

"I've heard enough," said the judge with a pointed look. "I'm granting political refugee status and asylum to Elsa Lee, Walker Sullivan, Caitlyn Dawson, Mason Grady, Ginger McCoy, and," she paused, checking the sheet—perhaps for his last name—"Tatsuda."

She turned to Jaxon. "Mr. McCoy, your petition is denied." She banged a wooden mallet on her tall desk and stood.

Elsa's hands shook. They'd won. They'd told the truth, and Jaxon had lost.

Elsa and her friends rose as the judge turned to exit. Elsa felt dazed that it had been that easy, that it was over. She couldn't believe they'd won. Alexander shook her hand and stepped down the line, shaking hands and giving them his congratulations.

Her stomach clenched with the instinct that something was going to happen. She turned toward Jaxon just as he pulled a pistol from his pocket with a murderous look in his eye.

She screamed, "Get down," and dove for the floor, praying that everyone listened. Keeping her eye on Jaxon, his first two shots went wild, one flying over her head, hitting the floor behind her. She rolled to the left, and the second lodged in the polished floor in the spot she'd just vacated. Splinters flew. She bounded to her feet, crouched, and prepared to run, but another quick shot rang out and the smell of gunpowder filled the room. She flinched, expecting to feel pain, but instead Jaxon staggered back, bleeding from his shoulder.

Officer Chan and her guards ran forward and grabbed him before he sagged against the wall, the gun dropping from his blood-soaked grasp and clattering to the floor.

"You'll pay for this, bitch," he shouted, his twisted face almost unrecognizable. "The joke's on you. You can't stay here where you think you're safe. You'll have to go home. I turned out Avery and her brats two weeks ago. Your sister is soft, not like you. She can't look after herself without my money."

With that parting jab, the Canadian guards wrestled him from the room.

Blood drained from Elsa's face as his nasty words sank in. The bastard would have done it too. It hadn't sounded like an idle threat or boast, but fact. Her throat constricted while she tried to play out scenarios in her head. Avery would have returned to the shack they'd shared with Granny. Her sister had sworn never to return to the Heap, but with luck, the water tokens Elsa had stockpiled working at Ginny's, and the sale of the scavenging license might feed them for another month or maybe two.

She hoped Avery remembered the hidden floor safe. Elsa wished there was a way to contact her, to let her know that help was coming. Her nieces had never gone hungry before or lacked for anything. Their lives right now wouldn't be easy. Avery wouldn't be able to work with the little ones depending on her and no childcare. She would be dependent on Elsa's stash. Elsa took a deep breath. She would have to trust that Avery could survive a little longer on her own. This was bigger than all of them, even her family.

CHAPTER 35: MASON PLUS GINGER PLUS ELSA

In the hours after the courtroom shooting, their group had been reunited for good and freed from custody. Mason paced, waiting for Caitlyn. It had been a long week away from her. He'd missed how she smelled, her smile, and her no-nonsense manner. The jail cell hadn't bothered him as much as her absence; that and worrying that Jaxon would get to her the way he'd gotten to Elsa.

With the change in their status to political refugees, they'd been given a house for the six of them to stay in while Alexander worked on setting up an excursion to Corvallis. The prime minister of Western Canada would arrive in three days to join them for a day trip. Alexander had impressed upon them the importance of this visit. Mason had never imagined the head of their government would come in person.

Mason hadn't seen inside the other bunkers, and he wasn't crazy about going so far below ground, but he was getting a chance next week. He preferred to be out in the open. It turned out that the Canadians had noticed the satellite Walker had moved and had redirected one of their own to the exact coordinates and had witnessed an epic tantrum when Jaxon had found his men tied up outside the bunker and Elsa gone. By tracking Jaxon and his men from space, they'd also witnessed some of the GreenCorps' actions in Boise.

The Canadians had been relieved to discover the reason for the satellite's return to being operational. They'd had been worried that GreenCorps had gained access to the satellite network, and had become concerned about the sudden advance in GreenCorps technology. They'd worked hard to keep the corporation from having certain telecommunications and scientific applications, hoping that the regime would change or develop into something more like the democracy that had once existed on GreenCorps lands.

Alexander had stayed for several more conversations with Elsa and Mason. He took copious notes about the women being sold south as sex workers. It turned out that several trains' worth of Canadian women had volunteered to help in GreenCorps lands in the last couple of years, citing humanitarian relief. They'd disappeared without a trace. Mason had nodded when he'd learned about the missing women. There had been a couple of battered Canadians among those he and the rebels had helped in Texas. Elsa's story about SoCal, Walker's recent experience in Boise, and Mason and Caitlyn's missions with the rebels gave the Canadian government the fuel they needed to investigate.

When Mason returned to GreenCorps territory, he would have backing from the Canadians. They hoped to help the rebels from within as well as put financial pressure on GreenCorps from the outside. He surveyed the yard outside where Elsa and Walker sprawled on the grass, his head resting on her stomach. They hadn't said it, but they'd be heading back south with him and Caitlyn once Elsa was healed. Tatsuda too.

Bringing the key to the bunkers here to Canada had become only another step in Elsa's actual mission—to break GreenCorps. He'd seen that about her as soon as they'd met, recognizing that drive. He could believe they were related. They had a lot in common. The rebels needed people like Elsa and Walker.

The last Mason had heard, the Canadians had given Jaxon medical attention for the bullet to his arm, escorted him to the train station, and sent him home in disgrace. Elsa had almost frothed at the mouth in her fury that he hadn't been detained or imprisoned despite his actions. He wouldn't be allowed to return to Western Canada. Diplomatic immunity only stretched so far.

* * *

Ginger came out of the bathroom, her long red hair tucked into the towel wound around her head. It was fabulous to have water whenever she wanted again—even hot—and access to a variety of clothes, stores, and books. There had to be a way to bring these small luxuries to the people back home. The inequality made her sick.

She stared out the window to the street where several cars were parked. She wanted to learn how to drive so she could get around wherever she wanted. Portland was an advanced, modern city with so much to offer and she could see herself staying here and building a life.

Except for two things.

The others would leave when Elsa's ribs healed, headed south to stir up trouble for GreenCorps and to help the rebels bring them down, once and for all. She could be part of that. If they went without her, she might never see them again. They'd become her first real friends, people she could count on. Especially Tatsuda. The second was the image in her mind of her little nieces, trapped in SoCal, cast adrift by her brother. That wasn't a life she wanted for them. Didn't they deserve a chance at a better life? Didn't all the children? She didn't know what she could do, but helping her nieces would be a first step.

Elsa assured her that Avery wouldn't starve right away. Before Elsa had left town, she'd stockpiled supplies and plastic GreenCorps tokens as a contingency plan, expecting her Granny to need them. While that might be true, Ginger had observed how quiet Elsa had become and that she'd returned to the constant chewing of the inside of her cheek. Elsa would return soon to make sure they were safe and provided for. While Ginger surveyed her luxurious bedroom in the four-bedroom house they'd been provided with, she couldn't dispel the feeling that many of the things that made it nice were unnecessary. She no longer fit a life of plenty. She hadn't earned the things in this house.

When the others hopped trains, returning south, she'd be with them. If not for herself, but for the children; her goal was unchanged.

* * *

Four days later, standing outside the bunker at Corvallis, after her third trip deep into the earth, Elsa stood blinking in the sun. With a racing heart, she clutched the silver key hanging around her neck. Alexander Campbell, Walker, Caitlyn, Mason, Ginger, and Tatsuda were at her side, as were the special guests—namely the contingent from Western Canada, including their elected prime minister.

She could feel their eyes on her, watching to see what she'd decided to do. The bunker had been set up the same as the others and hadn't been a surprise to any of them that had already been in one.

Walker had shown everyone the satellite control room and Elsa had given a tour of the seed room, explaining that different species of plants were housed at each bunker. The Corvallis bunker had seeds for species such as hazelnuts, hops, and mint, but the primary focus was berries, such as blackberries, raspberries, cranberries, grapes, and currants. She'd never tried any of the berries but was determined that one day, she would.

Taking a deep breath, she looked the prime minister straight in the eye and pulled the cord from her neck. Despite working toward this for months, it was harder than she thought to relinquish control of the bunkers to anyone else, even someone important who should be able to make her dreams of food for everyone a reality. Her hand shook as she passed the bunker key to the Canadian leader. A stab of uncertainty ran through her, but it was the right decision.

"Thank you, Elsa. You won't regret this. We will take care of the seeds and share them everywhere as fast as we can. I promise we will treat the people of your country as well as the people of ours. They will have fair access to food, water, and medicine." The prime minister seemed sincere as she spoke.

Elsa stared at Walker, and he nodded. They'd done what they'd set out to do, but this was far from over. She might have passed on the responsibility for growing food, but there was so much more to do to redistribute wealth and free the people enslaved by GreenCorps by circumstance and lack of equality. There could be more crimes against humanity that they would unearth and share with their new allies here in Canada.

This was another beginning, and she was glad to have trusted friends to help achieve their goals. Not just friends. Family.

Acknowledgments

I've always been a reader. Well, almost always. I learned to read the summer before I started kindergarten. My mom had been warned that I might be bored at school if I already knew how to read. So, though she'd spent years reading to me, had taught me the alphabet and letter sounds, and provided me with easy-to-read books, she'd held off on taking that final step where we put it all together.

Her plan was foiled. One August evening, my six-and-a-half-year-old cousin and I had been banished from the party our parents were having. We'd been sent upstairs, but we snuck back down to the landing, just off the kitchen, where we could listen to Fleetwood Mac's Rumors and be near the action. Technically, we were still apart and following orders. Cristine and I had a coverless, discarded library book about Dick and Jane.

She showed me how to sound out the letters together to make words. We turned the page and some of the same words were on that page—and I knew them. I turned another page and knew most of the words there too… then I sounded the ones out on the next page. There wasn't just a lightbulb a-ha moment, it was like fireworks exploded in my brain. I could read. Reading changed my life, opening vistas into incredible worlds in the past, in the future, and into imagination. Thank you to my cousin Cristine Jennings (now Lewis) who gave me the gift of reading.

The next milestone came when I was in second grade. My teacher put a copy of Laura Ingalls Wilder's Little House in the Big Woods in my hands and my reading skyrocketed. I became a voracious reader from that point onward. I wouldn't be a writer without having first been an avid reader.

The last year (and a day) since I received my first contract offer from Black Rose Writing to publish my first book, The Edge of Life: Love and Survival During the Apocalypse, has been quite a ride. I want to thank everyone at BRW for their talent, patience, and dedication to hard work, especially Reagan Rothe, who always makes time for my questions. I also want to thank BRW for creating a community of Black Rose authors that provide support, tips, a book club, review swaps, and blurb writers.

Special thanks to the BRW authors who have volunteered to read all of my books, including Karen K. Brees, David Buzan, Gail Ward Olmsted, and Cam Torrens. Several others have read one or two titles, and since my first four books have come out so close together, I appreciate that even more.

I also want to thank all the readers of my first three published books—those that read when I asked, those that volunteered, and those that found my books on their own or from a friend. Your interest and positive comments feed my soul. Knowing that my stories have touched people and brought them along for an adventure makes all the time invested in writing worthwhile. Every positive review has been read multiple times. Thank you from the bottom of my heart.

As always, I want to give a special thanks to Tracy Thillmann. She has become my friend, my critique partner, and my editor. Her contribution to every one of my published books is immeasurable. One of these days, I might even get the hang of connecting my thoughts without her prompt asking, "How do these two thoughts connect?" Maybe. I figured out how to use an em dash after all.

I also want to thank the Creative Academy for Writers again. They've managed to create and foster an online community of writers where we can get support, feedback, beta readers, launch attendees, and most of all, a place where we know others will help celebrate our successes, small and large. Writing can be such a solitary activity that having others there, going through many of the same challenges, matters.

Thank you as always to my wonderful husband, my daughters, my mom, my friend Julie, and several of my cousins who have helped spread the word about my books. Every person who has bought one of my books and finished reading it has my gratitude.

I also want to thank my friend Diane Kamagianis who has helped to host my first two Book Launch parties at the school where we teach. She buys terrific food, helps set up, and is an awesome cheerleader for my writing. She keeps asking for the sequel to The Edge of Life, so the snippet of *Aftermath: Into the Unknown* (Love and Survival #2) which is at the end of this book, is here for her. Publication Date for Aftermath: Into the Unknown is December 19, 2024. Until then, keep reading!

Keep reading for a sneak peek into the long-awaited sequel to

The Edge of Life: Love and Survival During the Apocalypse.

Aftermath: Into the Unknown

CHAPTER 1: ROBIN

Robin's youth ended three years ago when the asteroid smashed into the Earth. Everything she'd taken for granted in her previous life was gone, and to stay alive, she had additional responsibilities. Like scavenging for food and taking care of her grandfather. She looked around her sparse surroundings and a sense of unease crept over her as she finished dressing in the cold, windowless room, the odor of wet concrete stronger than that of her meager breakfast. Something was wrong, and the feeling persisted while she ate. Something more than the regular struggle for survival.

Maybe it had to do with the numerous flocks of geese flying south yesterday. The changing seasons lent urgency to her daily errands. It might be autumn, but with winter imminent, she had further preparations to make, so she and her grandfather didn't starve. Poking her head through the small crack she'd made with the door, she scanned the empty parking garage on the P3 level under the Towne Square Mall. She dashed out from the secure windowless room she now called home, headed for her shortcut upstairs. Afterward, she'd proceed outside for a gathering excursion in town.

She peeked around a cement column on P1. It was lighter here than the gloomy lower levels, and she stared at the sky-blue door across the final stretch of gritty pavement. This last open expanse before the stairs was the most nerve-wracking. Only the faint drip, drip of water, and the faint sound of her breathing met her ears. Waiting for the pounding of her heart to subside, she glanced back the way she'd come. If someone saw where she came from, she and Grandpa could lose their secure hideaway—they didn't have the strength to protect it, so she was always careful.

Her pulse normal, Robin dashed the last fifty yards along the cement wall toward the blue metal door—another quick check. Nobody else was around. With the key clutched in her sweaty hand, she inserted it into the lock and eased the door open. The interior was as black as the inside of her eyelids, but she didn't flick on her lighter until she closed the heavy steel barrier.

Lighting one of her two half-candles, she climbed the stairs by its amber glow, careful not to clink against the metal rail with her backpack. She always listened for out-of-place sounds—people could be anywhere—but there was nothing. Still. Best to play it safe.

On the top landing, she opened the door with the same key, closing it with a faint click as she stepped into the windowless hall that connected the mall service areas. With no natural light, it would have been in total darkness without the warm glow of candles that lit a path for her quiet feet. There was less chance of discovery here, but the most dangerous part was ahead. The mall itself.

Last fall, she'd discovered the desiccated corpse of the security guard in the main concourse, still clutching his key ring. That gruesome find had opened up a world of possibilities. The keys allowed Robin and her grandfather access to the little-known places in the mall they'd never have found otherwise. It had surprised her at how much space was behind the scenes and not intended for the public. The stock rooms had been incredible treasure troves.

The air in the hall was warm and stale, but not a concern as she walked, the smoke from her candle the most pervasive scent. She hadn't been upstairs for a few days, but it appeared undisturbed. One needed keys to access this hall, and as far as they'd been able to determine, they had the only set. Several locked doors branched off in either direction, but there was no point in opening them. She and Grandpa had already cleaned out anything useful.

She turned left, heading for the exit at the other end, ignoring the openings in this section. There had been little of value in the old kitchens and prep rooms on the right, behind the food court. Without electricity or refrigeration, most of the food had spoiled long before they'd arrived and they'd eaten the remaining cans last winter. Some offices upstairs had held surprising treasures: stashes of stale candy and snacks, a handgun with half a dozen rounds of ammunition, and a bottle of whiskey Grandpa had savored, a tiny glass at a time, eking the alcohol out over several months.

The two of them had lived in the parkade below the Boise Towne Square Mall for close to a year now.

At the end of the dusty hall, the pale glow emanating from the main concourse shone through the window inset in the last door. Beyond this lay the part of the building where anyone could have wandered around, long ago. This mall had been like hundreds of others scattered across the country, filled with high-end clothing shops, designer handbags, and jewelry stores that fit a lost lifestyle. Most of the merchandise had little value now. Well, diamonds and gold might be worth something, but she'd need to interact with people to find out, and that was a task they avoided.

Robin laughed aloud, the sound startling her as it echoed through the confined space. Three years was now long ago—a different life. Not that there were many people left in Boise since the final evacuation order. Or Idaho, it seemed. Once the military had pulled out, it had gotten quiet.

Here in the city, they'd seen half a dozen sets of travelers in pairs and a few family groups at a distance on separate occasions. There'd also been a few additional lone wanderers on the road since leaving the farm. Gangs and convoys were the greater danger. Several had come, but luckily they were just passing through.

She grabbed the plastic milk crate she left stationed by the door, climbed up, and peered through the window. They'd seen no one else in the mall, but twice they'd encountered people close to the Walgreens up the street. She preferred to avoid that part of town if possible, making this shortcut useful. As pickings became slimmer, it was only a matter of time before others risked the upscale mall, even if it had few shops carrying practical items.

Looters targeted and gutted the big box stores in the early days of the apocalypse. Opportunists grabbed the alcohol, junk food, and valuable items first. The next wave had been more practical, taking non-perishable food, equipment from sporting goods, and everyday medicine from pharmacies—things now in short supply, unless you knew where to hunt.

By the time Robin and her grandfather had left his farm, those kinds of stores had been stripped of anything useful. Still, they'd made do by thinking on a smaller scale. She and her grandfather hadn't boarded up the smashed plate glass entrances of the mall, but they'd lowered the security grates and dividers where possible. The barriers wouldn't hold back someone determined to enter, but they made the Towne Square look closed and inhospitable, discouraging the casual intruder.

She watched for several minutes before determining that the coast was clear. No sign of movement and no strange sounds. She jumped down, returned the crate to its storage position, and unlocked the door. Taking a deep breath, she slipped the key into her right pocket and checked she still had the second one she needed—an inside master key, which provided access to the individual stores of the abandoned mall.

She blew out her candle and shoved the door open, relying on natural light filtering in through the dirty overhead glass that comprised the leaf-covered roof over the food court, proof it hadn't seen maintenance in a long time. Though she and her grandfather had spent a year living below and venturing inside the mall, it appeared as though it had been undisturbed for years—a thick layer of dust had settled everywhere. She stuck to the edges by the wall where they'd made a footpath so they didn't leave obvious footprints.

Still in a reflective mood, Robin worked her way toward the far mall exit, considering her life. Not everyone could pinpoint the pivotal moment when they transitioned from teen to adult. For some, it might have been losing their virginity to a high school sweetheart, graduating, or leaving for university. Those were typical landmarks that separated childhood from adulthood and responsibilities. None of those things had happened for Robin.

Before the asteroid, this change would have been gradual, but in one fell swoop, civilization had died and obliterated her innocence. She'd been one week from high school graduation and had secured a full scholarship to Yale university before the chunks of NR 2025 collided in a series of destructive strikes across North America, changing her life forever—so much for a lifetime of straight A's. In the end, they hadn't mattered. She should be bitter, but there was no point. Everyone had lost everything normal.

After the asteroid, she'd become just another survivor. And she'd like to keep it that way. The initial brutal and lonely months of the apocalypse, back in the spring of 2025, had been the worst. She hadn't owned a vehicle, but a friend fleeing the city had dropped her and her sister Shelby off outside the Portland city limits a few hours before the first strike. The friend had disappeared, driving north, heading for Canada.

For a while, part of Robin wished she'd gone, too. She learned later from the Emergency Broadcast System that volcanic activity had almost wiped-out California and decimated all the cities down the Pacific coast. The only home she'd known had been eradicated. The largest chunk of the meteorite had taken out ninety-five percent of the population of southern California, while subsequent environmental problems and flooding plagued the coastline.

Cell towers had been destroyed and most power grids had sustained damage that had never been repaired, so they'd had no way of reaching anyone they knew, including their mother. On the second day, after the asteroid and thirty hours of silence, Robin had sent a Hail-Mary text with the last two percent of her iPhone battery to her grandfather—who lived inland on his farm—letting him know she was alive. To her relief, he'd replied, giving her a destination and hope.

She and Shelby had hiked west, into the mountains, heading for his place. After twenty-four hours, they'd come across an empty log cabin with a supply of canned goods. When the coastal mountain range had shaken with seismic and volcanic activity because of the asteroid strikes, they'd sheltered there for over a week. Their trip had stalled with everything coated in thick chunks of black cinders, and powdery ashfall like snow. It hadn't been safe to venture outside, and traveling had been a bitch.

Then the bikers had come.

Robin's throat constricted. She couldn't cope with those thoughts and returned her focus to the present, pushing aside the past. Today was unusual. She seldom thought about those days, and she tried not to think more than a week or two forward or back. Live in the now. Sometimes it worked. The farm had been good while it lasted and the parkade and mall were better. Or they had been until her most recent worry.

She sighed as she slipped out through the east entrance of the wall, using her key once she'd determined that she was alone. She couldn't be too careful because, despite its unkempt look, the mall was a gold mine. Walgreens, six blocks north, had been gutted. Fred Meyer, several blocks south, was no better. Most survivors hadn't cared about designer clothing and health food supplements, so they had mainly ignored the shops in this mall.

Last fall, she'd scouted around the mall in widening circles until she'd found a smaller, almost undamaged drugstore. Someone had removed the signs in the front, making it blend in with the small real estate offices and stationery store that were its neighbors. Her grandfather had shown her how to pick the lock with bent wire and a wrench to align the inside mechanism. They'd stockpiled antibiotics, various vitamins and supplements, basic first aid supplies, and all the extra soft toothbrushes they could find.

Today she had three missions. Her grandfather's cough had worsened in the last six weeks—as the nighttime and early morning temperatures dropped—becoming a deep rattle in his chest. His seal-like bark had her concerned, especially knowing colder weather was just around the corner.

She frowned as she walked, unable to shake her uneasy feeling. Twice now, she'd glimpsed blood flecks spotting his handkerchiefs, and her fear was that his condition was serious. He'd started asking her questions, as though testing her survival knowledge. Her chest tightened at the thought. He might not think he had much time left.

If her grandfather died, she'd be alone.

Living in a dank basement didn't help his health, no matter how homey they'd tried to make it, with carpets and bedding. Perhaps they should move upstairs into the mall offices on the third floor. Less secure, but there would be better light and it would be less damp. That, however, was a not-yet problem. For today, she would look through the cough remedies again to see if there was anything she could give him, at least to relieve his pain or help him sleep.

She would end her trip inside the mall on the way home. There was an Eddie Bauer with durable clothing, hiking shoes, and camping equipment. She'd already outfitted herself with the backpack she now wore, as well as her pants, but the chill mornings and leaves turning red and yellow had reminded her it was time to choose a proper winter jacket. The mall supplied a lot of their needs, but she couldn't only live indoors. Last winter, they'd stayed inside to avoid leaving trails in the snow. She would figure something out, so she didn't have to do that again. She needed to feel the wind and sun on her face and to breathe fresh air.

Rounding the corner, into the pharmacy's back alley, a gray cat scurried away, trotting down the space between buildings and disappearing through a gap in the fence, a rat dangling from its maw. Robin hoped she was as good a provider as the feral cats that roamed the city, most sleek and healthy, even without owners and dishes of kibble. Most of them had become skittish. She'd love to make friends with a cat, but she and her grandfather couldn't afford another mouth to feed.

She utilized bent wire and her multi-tool to unlock the pharmacy door, snuck inside and relit her candle. The pale glow shouldn't show from the front of the partially boarded-up front of the store, but still she shielded it with her hand while she walked, the gritty floor crunching underneath her boots.

She scooped up a few extra items and stowed them in her backpack, including toothpaste, soap, and an assortment of cough syrups. Even if they just soothed his throat, they'd be worth having. She ran her free hand through her short brown hair, trying to decide if she should ask her grandfather to cut it again. Sometimes she yearned for the shiny, long tresses of her past, but maintaining something like that would be a luxury and a waste of water. On a whim, she packed a mini bottle of fruity shampoo. She missed feeling clean.

Turning to leave, Robin froze, listening. An uneasiness settled in her chest as she waited for the unfamiliar sound outside to become clearer. She donned her still-light pack, checked the laces on her sturdy hiking shoes, and crossed the dirty linoleum to the front of the pharmacy where she listened by the windows. She hadn't imagined it. A faint rumble, then louder as the vibration increased. Then a roar. Motorcycles. Someone must have found a way to make or store fuel. It was a long shot, but she had to know who the riders were.

She pressed her eye to a crack in the metal blinds and watched as a dozen motorcycles with riders clad in black leathers rode up the street, continuing deeper into the once quiet city. She'd run into their kind before, but didn't recognize anyone. Where was their baggage or trailers if they were passing through? Where were the goods they'd collected? Her blood ran cold. Or had they already set up in the city and were here to stay?

She'd have to maintain her watchfulness. These bikers might be part of a larger group. When the roar had faded to a distant nothing, it was time to go. After checking the street, she slipped out the rear door and locked it.

Halfway back to the mall, still listening for the bikes, she ducked down a residential street into the nearby neighborhood, planning to use this outside opportunity to collect food for the next few days. Robin and her grandfather took over several raised vegetable beds that had been left behind and planted a garden behind an empty house with a fenced backyard. They'd grown beans, lettuce, and tomatoes to eat fresh all spring and summer. They had potatoes, squash, and cabbages remaining to harvest through the fall and keep over the winter.

This was the first year since the asteroid that crops had grown properly. Robin had noticed the relief on her grandfather's wrinkled face when their plants sprouted last spring. In the two previous years on the farm, the sparse vegetables had been puny, stunted things that had tasted bitter. The crop had been better than nothing, but not a lot. Too often the last year on the farm, they had gone hungry. Now that they could grow food, maybe they should return there in the spring and try again.

This summer, the ever-present ash-filled clouds had at last relented, at least sometimes. It was a good thing too. Her stock of vitamins wouldn't last forever. She'd been careful to supplement her diet with calcium and magnesium pills, iron, and vitamins C and D—wanting to keep her teeth intact and her bones healthy. No need to get scurvy or suffer from malnutrition.

Planting and caring for the garden, and spending time outside, sunny or not, had also been beneficial for their mental health. Last winter, they'd stayed inside the mall living on scavenged dry rations and slightly expired canned goods. They had limited their outside time to the lowest level of the parkade, near their bunker. They'd been in closer quarters than she ever would have considered in the old days, when even sharing a room with her younger sister had been torture.

She blinked back tears at the thoughts of Shelby stirred up by the bikers, took a deep breath, and shoved the memories of her sister downward. She focused on the idea of fresh veggies and plunged onward. Maybe she would dig up a handful of new potatoes and check for the last round of new green beans for dinner to augment their usual fare of rice and dried beans. Best not to give in to her worries. Food was more important. Besides, perhaps the bikes had been passing through after all.

* * *

Robin didn't linger after harvesting the garden. Slipping through the loose board "gate" on the way out, she checked the street as a nervous reflex and trotted back toward the mall, her pack jiggling with the extra supplies. Despite not seeing anyone, she practiced her silent heel-to-toe steps and maneuvered around the trash and abandoned items. For all her care, she couldn't shake the sensation that she was being watched, and hoped it was just her imagination triggered by the motorbikes and their riders.

She circled the mall, which still appeared undisturbed. No motorcycles in sight. That didn't mean they hadn't stopped somewhere in town, but it was promising that they weren't here. She slipped inside through a service entrance with her key and popped out of the long hall near the Eddie Bauer.

Trying on jackets was the most fun she'd had shopping in some time, forgetting the chaos of the world for a moment. Despite the pleasure of enjoying something as mundane as finding winter clothes, the itch between her shoulders grew. Twice she whirled, expecting to see someone.

Robin was always alone, and she scoffed at her imagination—it must all be in her head. She avoided the flashier colors, like bright red and neon orange in favor of a purplish-gray fleece and a gray, down-filled winter jacket. Looking around, she stuffed another pair of travel pants and a pair of jeans in petite size 2 into her pack. Extra thermal socks followed. Hard to believe owning three pairs of pants now made her feel rich.

She hesitated, burdened by her load, then grabbed a large navy-blue jacket from the men's section for her grandfather. Rather than return another day, she should get everything now. Turning the corner after restocking her supply of waterproof matches, she ran into a slim young man dressed in black leather and dirty jeans. She bounced off him and stumbled to the floor.

Tears pricked her eyes in fear, and she struggled to control her panic. Someone had bypassed the security grates after all. It had remained quiet, so they must have entered the mall while she'd been outside. So much for sneaking. How long had he been here? Had he been watching her?

"Don't go." He extended a hand to help her off the floor, but she ignored it. "I was hoping I could talk to you." The man showed no expression while she scrambled at the floor, backing away before standing, now several yards away.

His presence explained the uneasy sensation she'd had since entering the store. She didn't answer and lurched to her feet, preparing to bolt. From out of nowhere, a second man grabbed her from behind. She panicked and flailed, trying to free herself, but only succeeded in having the gigantic man at her back hold her tighter. She peeked over her shoulder as she lunged, trying to get loose. He was almost a foot and a half taller than her five-foot-three frame—practically a giant. Maybe six-foot-six or seven, and he smelled like campfire and pine trees.

"Chill kid. Where'd you come from?" The voice came from the short man, so she refocused her attention on him, instead of on the massive hands clamping her upper arms together behind her back. When she struggled, shooting pains raced into her shoulders. She stopped struggling, and the pain relented. His grip wasn't cruel, just firm.

The guy in front of her was probably no more than twenty-five. Perhaps younger. He had greasy reddish-brown hair and a hard mouth set in a scowl.

"Well," he said again. "I don't appreciate repeating myself."

She shook her head, having already forgotten his question.

Her confusion must have shown on her face, because he sighed. "Where'd you come from?"

She struggled to keep her voice steady and less feminine. "We live in town."

His eyes narrowed. "Who's we? Are you part of a group?"

"Just me and my grandfather." Robin's whole body trembled. With her words, the grip on her lessened. The truth was probably better. Non-threatening. Making up a fictional group was more likely to cause suspicion or bring trouble.

"I thought it unlikely a kid like you would be on your own," he said with a slow smile that showed his yellowed canines, reminding her of a shark. "Maybe you can show us around town. Me and Kory are part of a club that arrived in town a couple of days ago."

Kory and I. In her head, she corrected his grammar, something her mother might have done. Still, Robin would have felt better if his shallow smile had reached his eyes. As it was, she remained on guard. She would tell him as much as she had to in order to get loose, then hide.

"I heard motorbikes this afternoon," she said, the words reluctant to leave her throat. Her voice sounded raspy and unused. She'd left this morning while her grandfather still slept, and until now, she hadn't spoken today.

"Did you see us?" said the deeper voice behind her. He must be Kory.

She blinked at the rough tone and glanced back, shaking her head. She didn't recognize them.

"He knows nothing. Too stupid to be of use," said Kory.

He? Good. They believed she was a he. A side-benefit to easy-to-care-for short hair and a slight frame. They thought she was a teenage boy. She relaxed a little while, remaining watchful.

"I'm Dillan, by the way." The redhead flashed another false smile.

Who was he kidding? He looked sharp enough to slice anyone who let down their guard. Which she wouldn't.

"What's your name?" He stepped closer.

"Rob." Close enough to her real name that she'd answer or react if it was spoken.

"Mind if we look in your pack?" He nodded his head to the other man.

Her heart sank. She would rather they didn't know there was a drugstore that still had supplies on the shelves and it was important that they didn't realize that she had a garden with food for the winter. That had to remain secret or they would lose everything.

The man holding her arms released her on one side when he hefted her backpack, bouncing it against her back. She couldn't get a read on him, but he didn't seem as scary as his companion, who pretended to be pleasant.

"Not much in it. Mostly clothes. Not worth looking at." His voice was so deep it was almost a growl.

He was lying. Potatoes and bottles of cough syrup weren't that light.

Dillan shrugged. "Where were you scavenging today?" His hand strayed to a sheath on his hip. A blade.

"Houses," she lied. "I found a couple mealy potatoes in an old garden. Some socks and jeans here." Inside, she was quaking. Dillan's flat black eyes and thin lips looked unconvinced. Would he ask where? Force her to show him?

"Time for you to be on your way." The big man released her other arm.

Despite her surprise, without wasting a second, she stooped to collect the new jackets from where they'd scattered on the floor, and dashed for the mall. Her heart hammered against her ribs. That had been too close.

She left the mall at the closest exit, forcing the locked door open with the emergency crash bar. No way was she going to reveal her keys. To get back downstairs, she traveled the long way around, hoping the bikers were alone and didn't follow. When she stopped to catch her breath, the trail behind was silent.

CHAPTER 2: KORY

Kory watched the young woman flee; a fistful of jackets clutched to her side. He hadn't corrected Dillan's assumption that the stranger was a boy. It would be safer for everyone that way. Dillan and the others didn't need to fight over another woman. There were already plenty of other issues that caused tension within their group, like food, fuel, and clean water. Essentials.

Kory pushed her from his thoughts and kept his mind on the mission. They were scouting to find a new location to hunker down for the winter, having left Idaho Falls last week. They'd picked that city clean, and they needed somewhere with untapped stores of food. Their leader had banked on the almost total evacuation of the West after the asteroid strike. Most remaining civilians had already moved east, away from the impact zones, so there wasn't a ton of competition. The Wings planned to push further west next spring, to see what had survived in the worst-hit area along the coast.

The upside of the move was that they wouldn't have to contend with many survivors. If the houses were standing, there should be non-perishable food items. Boise just needed to get them through the winter months.

He examined this section of the mall. It had potential. The ceiling seemed to have remained intact, otherwise there would have been mold and invasive plants already. He scowled. It was just a matter of time. He'd been surprised by how much water and root damage many places had sustained in only three years. He refocused on the inspection. If the

Wings took over several stores, they could have bedrooms instead of thirty smelly bikers crammed together. Plus, they could park the bikes inside the mall and keep them from being damaged or stolen.

The girl might not have seen their motorbikes outside, since they'd hidden them in bushes a block away, but others might. They couldn't afford to lose their wheels.

Kory cracked his knuckles and turned to Dillan. "You satisfied? The kid's not a threat."

Dillan shrugged; his dark eyes guarded as always. That one gave little away unless you looked for subtle clues. He reserved his genuine smiles for things that caused others pain. He wasn't Kory's ideal scouting partner, but with Kory's size, Dillan wouldn't dare pick on him; he preferred weaker prey, like the "kid" who'd just left. If he'd run into her alone, things might have fallen out differently.

Seeing Dillan's speculative gaze still fixed in the direction "Rob" had taken, it might mean the other man was interested, anyway. Prey was prey.

"I think we have what we need," said Kory, aiming to distract his partner.

Dillan turned. "And what is that?"

"We could live in the mall this winter. Rig a stove or two for heat, there's fuel. Park the bikes in the concourse and sleep in stores."

"Can I talk to my uncle about it?" said Dillan, his narrow eyes shifting toward the main section of the mall, as though visualizing Kory's idea.

Kory shrugged. He didn't need credit. Besides, Jake was shrewd, and he'd realize where the idea came from.

The corner of Dillan's mouth curved up, almost a sneer.

Being underestimated might keep Kory alive someday. The Wings could be ruthless in their competitiveness.

Before he left, he checked the back of the outdoor store for better boots than what he wore and claimed a pair, plus an XXL fleece sweater. While some of the stockroom had been picked through, size twelve was uncommon, giving him three choices. He grabbed a waterproof pair to try on and stamped his feet into them. They seemed decent. Bending over to lace them, Kory took a moment to consider his next move. The look in Dillan's eyes had triggered that discomfort he had ignored for too long.

Kory hadn't planned on staying with the Wings for much longer. He would need to decide soon though, because Jake had informed Kory that if he stayed for the winter, he'd need to complete his initiation. He shuddered at the thought. Despite occasional necessity, he preferred non-violence. Once snow settled on the ground, his choice might be made for him and he would do whatever it took to stay.

The last winters had been harsh. They'd spent weeks socked in during blizzards and white-out conditions while several feet of snow accumulated, making roads impassable for months. The cold snaps had also been severe, with temperatures well below zero. As long as he didn't take a bike, the Wings should let him leave—though he didn't plan to ask permission.

Kory wasn't keen to cross the mountains and head back into the coastal zone. That's where he'd lived, on the streets of Seattle. Before that Portland. Unlike most, he'd lived a nomadic life before the asteroid. There'd been rumors that others had gotten out of Portland and Seattle, but he hadn't met anyone once he'd left the refugee center in Spokane four months after the impact. Before the Wings, he'd been alone for years. No clean house or loving wife. In that way, he'd been lucky and had less to miss.

He hadn't stayed at the center long. He could look after himself and had felt guilty taking food rations that others needed more. Not that any of them had much, but kids had been going hungry and there wasn't anything he could do to fix it. He left, leaving one less person to feed, but being on his own was risky. Pockets of armed militias and gangs roamed the countryside, and had claimed most of the bigger cities. Still, better alone than beholden forever to the Wings.

Rumors had made their way west of a thriving walled city in South Dakota. A fortress with underground bunkers where hundreds, maybe thousands, of people had survived. A place like that might be safe and have opportunities. The other option was the Mormons, but he'd never bought into religion and could be unwelcome. He'd looked at the maps and considered trying for the bunker city next year. In his old life, he'd been a bouncer twice and worked a short stint as security. He was strong enough that he would be an asset, even if they only let him in on a trial. As long as the place wasn't just a myth, he could use a home.

* * *

The Wings, fifty members strong, had camped in the Walgreens six blocks north of the mall. The space was adequate with sunny fall weather, but it would be a bitch to heat for the winter. High ceilings, little insulation, and wide open. Therefore, their stay would be temporary. In the two days since they'd arrived, the guys had torn down and moved the empty shelving to build sections for each of the three factions: the old guard, the newbies, and the criminal element.

Jake would have to watch the latter group. There might yet be a power struggle for leadership.

Kory hummed as he walked through the former drugstore, ignoring the other bikers, though a few jumped out of his way as he tromped past in his new boots. Some followed him with their eyes, but he didn't stop to socialize. The only sounds were ordinary, the buzz of voices in the background. He missed music and wished for the thousandth time that he could charge his old phone, which lay dormant at the bottom of his pack. He should have tossed it ages ago, but couldn't part with the possibility of listening to familiar songs.

Though he'd collected a few of his favorite albums as CDs when scavenging, he didn't have space to carry more than half a dozen. He'd also been on the lookout for a portable discman or small CD player. That and a stash of decent batteries—many had expired or only had juice for playing something quick. Perhaps if he settled somewhere on his own, he'd find a place with a source of power, maybe solar or even a generator.

He would give his right arm to blast some Foo Fighters or Rush right now. Something old school with instruments and actual music. None of that boy band crap or noisy, distorted rap. Too bad so many people had gotten rid of their CDs in favor of digital files. They were probably kicking themselves, too. With no internet, electricity, or Wi-Fi, streaming music was a thing of the past. He'd come across some kick-ass stereo equipment, abandoned and useless. What a waste.

He turned toward his new digs in the back left corner, bunked down with the former thieves and drug dealers, near the real bikers, where he felt most at home. Many reminded him of the Seattle homeless. He nodded to Jake on the way past where the leader sat at a table with his inner circle. Four gray-haired, tough-looking road warriors were hard at work, hand-rolling smokes. They must have found a substantial stash of tobacco and paper filters. The heavily tattooed older man who led the Wings used them to incentivize his guys—the smokes were both currency and reward.

A part of Kory itched for one, but he'd quit everything back in the refugee center. He didn't want to kick an addiction again or be beholden to someone for a fix, even nicotine. He threw himself down on his sleeping bag, lit the candle he left by his bedside and, groping under his pillow, removed a tattered paperback. This book was almost done. He'd taken to reading science fiction the last few years, even if real life was as weird as some stories.

Flipping to the dollar bill he used as a bookmark, he angled the page into his pool of light. Who'd have thought he'd be a reader? Maybe only Ms. Wilson, his high school English teacher, who'd encouraged him by loaning him books—even stuff from her personal collection. Leaning against the flimsy wall, he left his new boots on, crossing them at the ankle, and got comfortable, refusing to dwell on the past.

He lost himself in his book until a shadow fell across his page. He glanced up to see Jake and stopped reading. There weren't many people who'd interrupt him. Kory kept to himself and interacted little with most of the men, but Jake was in charge.

"The mall. That your idea or Dillan's?" Jake didn't sound annoyed, more curious.

Kory shrugged.

"It's a good one, but my nephew was thin on the details." Jake raised a bushy gray eyebrow.

"His idea to check it out. Mine to set up there. Pick a store or two to make comfortable and keep heated. There's a central, open area to park the bikes out of the weather. Might be possible to rig something for water from the city pipes. Could be gas stoves in the food court."

Jake pursed his weathered lips and tapped them with a grease and tobacco-stained finger as he nodded. "Thought as much. Anyone occupying it already?"

His question seemed innocent, but Dillan may or may not have mentioned the girl. That could go either way.

Kory would play it safe. "Doesn't look lived in. Lots of stuff still lying around. No garbage, beds, or signs of people."

"You see people?" Jake's steely eyes fixed on Kory.

"Some kid. Maybe sixteen. Dillan's going to chase him down if he can." Kory shrugged—like it didn't matter. Even if she was nothing to him, helping someone, anyone decent, had felt good. Still. He couldn't shake the look he'd seen in her startled blue eyes. She'd been familiar with the store and thought she'd been alone. That one was smart. She hadn't reacted to being referred to as a guy, or given anything away about scavenging or her full pack. Dillan wouldn't find her without a lot of effort.

"Let me know if my nephew gets in over his head," said Jake as he turned to go. He held out a bundle with eight or ten smokes. "I know you don't smoke them, but they might come in handy to trade." He winked. "I hear Bill is smoking a new batch of venison jerky."

Kory took them with a nod. "Thanks." He had a case with a stash he would add them to once he was sure nobody was watching. That was the thing about bunking with thieves. At all times, he kept his valuables on him. His pack doubled as a pillow just to keep everything important safe.

After Jake left, Kory leaned back against the wall, thinking of the young woman from the mall. For all the difference in their sizes, she'd been more scared of Dillan than him. That had surprised him. People were often frightened of Kory simply because of his size. He'd been over six feet by the time he was twelve, so he was used to their reactions. Now he was six-foot-seven, and a hard life had kept him tough and lean. Most folk gave him his space.

There'd been strength in her arms, too. Tough and wiry. She would be a hot number in tight leather on the back of his bike. That fantasy crumbled to dust on the spot. If she was half as smart as he suspected, she would have made herself scarce. If they met again, it would be by chance, not design.

* * *

Jake presented the mall idea to the Wings at dinner and assigned a group to further investigate. The leader selected Kory for the team, but not Dillan. Kory nodded at Jake but otherwise kept his head down as he shoveled in the stew Cook had made.

On his way back from the "bathroom" in the bushes in the dark, Dillan stepped in front of him.

"You fucking told Jake the mall was your idea." He kept his voice to a quiet hiss. "Trying to steal my credit. My uncle has expectations. You're an asshole." Silvery orange firelight reflected gleamed from the blade he tried to hide against his leg.

Dillan might think he was sneaky, but Kory could disarm him faster than the man could strike. Kory kept his eyes up and pretended not to notice the threat.

"Jake asked. I didn't lie." Kory tensed his muscles, ready to grab the knife arm if Dillan struck.

"He pay you?" Dillan's eyes narrowed to slits, almost impossible to see in the dark.

"Nope." A gift wasn't payment. No need to tell this weasel anything.

"Then you're stupid. You should have asked him for a half dozen cigarettes. He was rolling today." Dillan's voice held the sneer that the darkness hid.

"I don't smoke." Kory maintained an even tone.

"What about the kid? You mention him?"

"Ya. Said we saw a teenager who ran off."

"God. You can't keep your mouth shut about anything, can you? I should have been on the mall team since it was my discovery."

Kory didn't correct him. "Volunteer to help then." He kept his eyes trained on Dillan, watching for the slightest twitch from the knife.

"Na. I'm going to see if I can find that kid on my own. Steal their stash or bring them in. Just him and a grandfather. Not much fight in that." He slid his knife back into its sheath as he stepped backward. "I'll have more time this way, even if I'm out the finder's fee." He spat near Kory's boots and stalked away, toward the fire.

Kory went to bed that night, still thinking about the young woman. It had been hard to tell her age, but she might be older than his first impression. It was her petite size that made her seem young. He was twenty-five and she might not be much younger. Plus, with the things they'd all seen the last three years, she wasn't a girl, but a woman.

Maybe he should borrow her idea and search old gardens for leftover vegetables, something he hadn't done since the first year. Some plants self-seeded, like potatoes, which he hadn't considered. Also, he was more likely to run into her scavenging than anything else. The search for food often consumed life.

Laying in his sleeping bag, the stale darkness pressed inward while he listened to the low murmurs of those playing cards, the rustle of others in their sleeping bags, and the usual nighttime grunts, farts, and coughs that came with a group of several dozen men sharing the same space. Sometimes their indoor camps grew pretty ripe. From the back of the room came the whimper of the women. They had three right now, and they got used hard.

Their crying twisted something inside him, but just like the hungry kids at the center, there was nothing he could do for them. But he'd had enough. He couldn't stay with the Wings for the winter.

Kory made up his mind. He would finish this scouting and prep job for Jake because he owed the man that much for taking him in. The leader had also been patient about an answer regarding initiation. Kory would collect a few covert supplies and split in a week or so, which should be before the snow flew. He'd look for somewhere to hole up solo for the winter, then head for that city in South Dakota come spring. The walled city might need some muscle.

CHAPTER 3: ROBIN

"How'd it go today?" Grandpa Clay said, sitting up when Robin returned to their hideaway. He'd probably heard her key in the lock. "You were gone for hours." These days he spent a lot of time sitting on his mattress, which they'd laboriously dragged down from the bedding store so he would be comfortable.

She slipped off her pack and lined up six different cough syrups on the coffee table where they ate, the fronts facing her grandfather. She moved one to correct its position, so they were in height order, from tallest to shortest. That appealed to her sense of rightness.

"Don't think any of those will cure what I've got, Honey." He tugged a handkerchief from his back pocket and blew his nose.

He wasn't fooling her with that move as he dabbed moisture from his azure eyes that matched her own. When she'd arrived on the farm three years ago, her grandfather had been strong and hale. He'd been close to six-two and ran half-marathons. Every widow in his county had asked him out over the last ten years. He'd turned them down, but that hadn't stopped them from coming around. Now, her grandfather was spindle thin, frail, and stooped. He seemed to have aged at least ten years in the last six months. When he coughed, his whole body convulsed. He was dying in front of her and she was at a loss about how to help.

"Not a cure, but something might help you sleep." She was desperate to make a difference.

"I'll sleep when I'm dead." He sounded flippant.

How could he joke about death?

She turned away, a solid lump in her throat. He was all she had left and she couldn't handle it when he spoke like that. Didn't he understand she was terrified of being alone?

"Robin. Look at me." He struggled to his feet beside her.

She angled her head toward him because she couldn't deny his request. She'd do anything for Grandpa Clay. He'd saved her when everyone else was lost and he understood her better than anyone, except maybe her missing younger sister.

"We have to face facts. I'm not improving. We need to make a plan." He rested his hand on her arm, though he seldom touched her, knowing she often found it uncomfortable. "I have to believe you won't stay here on your own. You need a proper home. Somewhere safe and with other people. With family."

She shook her head, hot tears pricking her eyes. She blinked several times, trying to clear them while the tightness in her chest expanded. He needed to be okay.

"Sweetheart," he said, his voice quieter. "Leave. Go look for your Uncle Luke and Aunt Ella. They're out there. If anyone made it, they did."

"I can't leave you. I won't. We're a team." Her chin wobbled.

His voice was gentle, making his words even harder to take. "We've been a great team, but I don't want you stuck here with a dying old man. My Laura's been gone sixteen years. It's time I joined her. She was my one and only true love."

Robin clenched her jaw. She didn't remember her grandmother and didn't have that connection to missing her, but life without her grandfather was unfathomable. "We have no idea if Uncle Luke is even alive." Her tears poured out, and she was helpless to stop them. Dammit. She wasn't a goddamn baby, just terrible at handling her emotions. Despite being an adult, she cried too much—often when angry or frustrated. Or miserable.

She turned back to the table and removed the four large yellow potatoes from her bag and thumped them onto the surface, bouncing two boxes of cough syrup off the edge. They dropped onto the carpet samples that covered the concrete floor.

"I brought dinner." Her voice was too loud for their cramped quarters and held an undertone of lurking anger.

"You're not changing the subject this time. Tell me where Luke and Ella went. I need to know you have every detail filed away in that smart brain of yours." His stare was piercing.

His persistence made her uneasy.

"Vita xTerra." She shifted her gaze while trying to catch her breath before she spiraled out of control. "South Dakota. It's a thousand miles away." It may as well be Europe or the moon. It would be better to stop talking. She clenched her jaw tighter.

"Less than eight hundred," he said with a wracking cough that bent him in half.

She stepped toward him as he wiped his bloody mouth with a cloth, but he held his hand up to stop her. The blood had started last week.

"How am I supposed to get there?" Her voice became heated. "Walk?"

Grandpa Clay remained calm. "If you have to. Or maybe you can scrounge a bicycle and ride to xTerra. Where's the map I gave you?"

She sighed and wiped her stupid tears on her sleeve. "I keep it in my backpack, but I memorized at least half a dozen routes, just in case."

Grandpa passed her a clean handkerchief from the shelf and she blew her nose.

"I'm sorry for crying." Her face burned and her throat thickened.

"Crying is natural," he said. "So's feeling sad, but I need to know you'll try not to be alone forever. I feel in my bones that Luke's family is safe. Like you, they're survivors. You need to join them, and I'm not strong enough to travel with you." Why wouldn't he let her change the subject? They'd been over this months ago, but he held her eyes to make his point.

"Speaking of bikes, there are bikers in town. A sizeable group." Maybe a more immediate threat would distract him.

Her grandfather coughed again, and she grabbed him a mug of boiled water, already cooled to room temperature. He sipped while she shared what she'd seen and about her encounter with Dillan and Kory.

"Dillan's a creep and Kory's the size of a mountain. My best bet was to run."

Her grandfather's creased face looked worried as his mouth turned down. "You should leave now. Before it snows. I don't want to worry about you running into bikers all over town. It won't be safe to go out."

"I'm not talking about this again tonight. Should I cook dinner or not?" She set her jaw. This conversation was over.

He nodded, indicating a truce, and she boiled the potatoes and they dipped into their stash of salt to sprinkle on them as a treat. Fresh food brought so much to their limited diet.

Later that night, trying to sleep, she stared at the dark concrete above while she tossed back and forth. Her grandfather's familiar soft snores filled the room, but she wasn't comforted. The bunker reeked of damp and sickness, with an undertone of the metallic scent she now associated with blood, and Robin cried herself to sleep.

About the Author

Award-winning author Lena Gibson is a storyteller as an elementary school teacher and keeper of the family lore. She holds a First-Class Honors degree in Archaeology, with minors in History, Biology, Geography, and Environmental Education from Simon Fraser University.

A voracious reader from childhood onward, Lena seeks wonderful books in which to escape. Because of her passion for different genres, she combines elements of many in her writing. As an adult newly recognized with autism, she often creates characters that reflect this experience.

When Lena isn't writing, she reads, practices karate, and drinks a ton of tea. She resides in New Westminster, Canada with her family and their fuzzy overlord, Ash, the fluffiest of gray cats.
https://lenagibsonauthor.wordpress.com

TRAIN HOPPERS — ONE
SWITCHING TRACKS
OUT OF THE TRASH
LENA GIBSON

READERS FAVORITE
BOOK AWARD WINNER
THE EDGE
OF LIFE
LOVE AND SURVIVAL DURING THE APOCALYPSE
LENA GIBSON

NOTE FROM LENA GIBSON

Word-of-mouth is crucial for any author to succeed. If you enjoyed *The Long Haul*, please leave a review online—anywhere you are able. Even if it's just a sentence or two. It would make all the difference and would be very much appreciated.

Thanks!
Lena Gibson